Tender

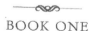

THE TRELAWNEYS OF
WILLIAMSBURG

BOOK ONE

ANNE MEREDITH

ISBN-13: 978-1530853137

Printed in the United States of America

Haunted Oak Publishing

For Meredith Gayle Shuttleworth –
you gave me my name, you gave me love,
and you still give me support.
Thank you for your dear friendship.

With long-overdue gratitude
to Tom Hay, without whom this
book just simply could not have been written

and, as always …
with love …
for Joshua

When we've been there ten thousand years ...
bright shining as the sun
We've no less days to sing God's praise
than when we've just begun.
- John Newton, Amazing Grace

Prologue

Williamsburg, Virginia—1746

At last, God's vengeance had caught up with him.

The thought skittered through Grey's mind as lightning struck an oak a dozen feet ahead. The black stallion cried out and reared, massive hooves pawing the air. Squinting through the storm, he yanked on the reins just as fire exploded in the old oak. With a ponderous groan, a massive branch crashed across the path. It was hopeless; the black was wild with fear, and the reins slipped through his hands. The horse bolted, tumbling him into the lane—leaving him muddied, bruised, but unsmitten.

So, vengeance must wait for another day. In the last seven years, Grey had come to believe God knew precisely what He was about. Waiting for retribution was hell itself.

The torchlight of Rosalie blazed in the distance, a beacon of promised heaven: Emily. It warmed him as he limped through the cold, bitterly black night. She was six years old now—he'd missed the celebration by just a few weeks.

Hellish weeks.

Forty-five had died on the Swallow, and it troubled him for the first time in years. On this last journey, he'd seen his

1

daughter's smile in those of his youngest passengers. Comely faces chosen for the winsome smiles that would serve them well as amusing curiosities for their mistresses. And that last child, in the village south of Sierra Leone …

She'd made the mistake of smiling at him, perhaps seeing him as her rescuer from her pathetic captivity. That spirit had been her destruction; he'd nodded to the agent, who grabbed the girl. Peculiar, how he heard, still, the hysterical screams of the child's mother.

The girl's smile had quickly vanished on board the *Swallow*, along with her spirit. She'd been buried two weeks later in the Gulf of Guinea. He oddly wished he had a name to assign her; they left the naming to the buyers, of course, but she'd had a name, at one time. Did her mother wonder about the life her daughter would lead in an unknown land? Did she dream foolish dreams of someday finding her?

And again he thought of Emily. His wife hadn't blinked when Grey had taken her away. Relieved to be rid of the child, she'd doubtless found comfort in the arms of another lover.

Once he'd thought perhaps he could love Letitia; then he'd taken refuge in hating her; now, he only wished his promise meant as little to him as hers had. Twelve months at sea—three continents, two fierce tempests, a hurricane—and still no woman to warm his bed. And yet the thought of taking a lover repulsed him. He wanted more. He wanted…things he hadn't wanted in years, things he no longer had the right to want. Someone who waited by the fireside on cold, black nights like tonight, laughing with relief when she knew he was safe. Someone who could somehow ease the hunger, the discontent that ate at his very soul. As he reached the house, he mused that perhaps God was merciful after all, for He'd blessed Grey with indifference. No woman had stirred his passion for years.

Rosalie's staunch, steadfast familiarity welcomed him and gave him an odd twinge. How different from the hovel in Liverpool where he'd grown up; lavish and elegant, a tribute to his prosperity. And yet, but for Emily, it held no warmth. He found his way to his bedchamber, glad for the fire burning in the hearth for his return, and changed into a dressing gown. Then he ventured into Emily's room. As he brushed back his sleeping daughter's blonde curls, his heart swelled in contentment and dismay; she'd grown too much.

Restlessly, he went belowstairs, and as he arrived in the library, a crack of thunder ripped through the house. He stopped, hearing a ruckus in the rear entryway, as if someone had taken a tumble. He moved suspiciously through the halls and into the vestibule, then stopped. A woman lay near his feet.

For fully a minute he just stared, fascinated. The most peculiar thing, her lying there as if she'd hurried in from the storm and collapsed, too weary to take another step. Sudden desire surged through him, inevitably. She was quite beautiful, and quite naked.

Abundant, curly black hair wreathed her face; dark eyebrows arched over eyes with long, curling lashes, a straight, slim nose, and dusky rose lips that were parted slightly. Her wet hair spilled over her breasts, and he knelt beside her, his breath shallow as he let one finger draw the hair away. His gaze moved hungrily over her. Skin as white and flawless as fresh cream; full, sweet breasts, with crowns the color of her mouth; long, gracefully curving limbs. He touched her shoulder to rouse her, but the coldness of her skin alarmed him. In a moment, he lifted her in his arms and carried her toward his room.

Then he stopped, for she opened her eyes and spoke. Her voice was husky and soft, but he didn't catch her words—he was captivated by those eyes, as warm and golden as the firelight that shone from his room. And then she touched him—slender, soft hands moving over his chest, resting in the open place against his skin. Her touch was cool—yet it set him afire. The arousal she stirred in him was hotter than anything he'd known in many years.

"I've gotten you wet," she murmured, "and I'm heavy."

He gave her some vague reassurance as he tried to dam his desire. What was it about her that twisted something within him? She seemed like a lost child, hoping for comfort. Yet comforting her was the farthest thing from his mind. His eyes moved ravenously over her until he could look no more. "Who are you?"

She whispered a name and collapsed against his chest wearily. *Rachel.*

In his room, he closed the door behind him. As he lay her within his bed, he thought perhaps he should summon Hastings, or a maid, or—someone. Yet he didn't stir. He only gazed at her. He brushed her hair away from her face, wondering where she'd come from. Who she was. Why he couldn't take his eyes off her.

A shiver wracked her, and like a fool he climbed into bed with her, curling his body around hers. Was she ill, or merely cold? He dwelt on those details, for it gave him something to think of beyond the overpowering temptation of her. He had been too long without a woman, and this one was beyond lovely, her soft curves nestling against him in provocative intimacy.

When her shivering passed and he sought to draw away, she gave a soft cry and turned in his arms, clutching at the robe and then burrowing within, against his bare chest. Her slender hands roved over his chest and his shoulders, and she gave a soft, delighted sigh. And then her limbs intertwined almost innocently with his, and he paused, waiting for her to still. He stroked her hair with faltering resolve, feeling it dry and grow warm. He soothed her, measuring her contented heartbeat with his own racing heart. And when she slept peacefully, he withdrew, pulled his robe around him, and watched her from a chair.

Again it haunted him: Who was she? What was she doing at Rosalie, utterly naked? And why did she stir him so? She had the kind of eyes that made a man yearn for peaceful, firelit evenings. And as Grey nodded off in the chair, a peculiar thought came to him.

God's vengeance perhaps took unusual forms.

Chapter One

On a winding, tree-shaded parkway in the tidewater of Virginia, a sleek silver car turned out of the twenty-first century and into the past.

Two women were inside the car. Rachel Sheppard, the passenger, replayed her boss's briefing in her mind.

No confrontation.

In the world according to Roger, Kingsley's theme park would be the best friend to American history since George Washington.

No competition.

"Kingsley's in the same boat as existing Virginia tourism destinations," Roger had said. "Kingsley's Americana will make the water rise for everyone."

And no conflict with Max Sheppard.

"Whatever you do, don't agree to any photo-op where you're up against your father. You're good at PR," Roger had told her, "but Sheppard's the master. And he knows your weak spots."

Boy did he. She sighed.

Camisha turned down the narrow road. "Looks like they sent the welcome wagon."

Rachel groaned as she spotted the colorful crowd awaiting them. So much for no confrontation.

A sign went past her window. *Kingsley go home.*

Camisha chuckled, pulling down her sunglasses just enough to get a good look, then returning her attention to the road. Amusement flickered in her dark eyes. Tilting faintly at the corners, they always reminded Rachel of autumn—a color somewhere between caramel apples and November pecans. "Could be worse. Least they aren't toting muskets."

Keep Your Theme Parks Off Our Landmarks.

"Nice 'hood rhythm to it," Camisha said.

This poster was shaken at them by a silver-haired woman in an ankle-length homespun dress. A bewigged gentleman resembling a stern Anglican minister hoisted a sign as the car rolled up. More to the point, his sign portrayed a roller coaster inside a red circle, bisected by a red slash.

Rachel felt fire and brimstone in his gaze—as if her soul were going to burn in a special room in hell reserved for defilers of history.

"What have they got against progress and prosperity? Kingsley'll bring so many jobs, and tourist money—"

"Save the pitch for later. If you think you're preaching to the choir, those folks with the signs are singing my *Amazing Grace.*"

"Of all the best friends in all the world, mine has to be a preservationist."

Camisha turned the rental car into the blockaded semicircular drive at the Williamsburg Inn, but the protesters refused to budge. "They ain't goin' anywhere," she murmured, amused.

Rachel pretended ignorance, smiling at the crowd. They were a dignified group, as protesters went. Half looked like bored housewives, for children clung to their skirts. The other half were perhaps retired men and women. It was a little concerning, how many seemed to have closets stocked with waistcoats and petticoats. One man was taping with his smartphone. Another had a minicam with the call letters of a local news station.

"Oh, great. A television crew. Well, just play dumb," she said, rolling down the window. "Is the hotel closed?"

"Only if Kingsley has their way." This woman, with a toddler in tow, also had a sign. *Bull Run Was Not a Roller Coaster.*

Two bellmen rushed past the crowd to the driver's side of the car. "Miss Sheppard?"

Camisha's eyes widened comically as she raised her hands in innocence. "No way."

"I'm Rachel Sheppard. What's the problem?"

"I think your arrival was leaked to the local press. We'll park for you."

When they managed their way out of the car, the reporter surged forward. "Miss Sheppard, isn't it a bit crass to hold your press conference on the date Williamsburg celebrates three hundred years of American history?"

"We're reserving our comments for the press conference day after tomorrow. Thank you for coming out to welcome us with your wonderful Southern hospitality!"

When in doubt, deny.

"It's common knowledge that your own father is leading the nationwide opposition to Kingsley," he went on. "How does it feel, knowing that you've taken on Max Sheppard, one of the most powerful men in corporate America today, as well as a great philanthropist for preservation?"

Just peachy.

Her smile continued as she ignored him, following the white-coated bellman. The elegant Williamsburg Inn was decorated in the sumptuous style of the thirties. But she scarcely noticed its opulent grace as the reporter's question rang in her ears. And then the answer came.

Like watching an oncoming hurricane from a rowboat.

Although there had been rumors for decades, Kingsley's final decision to build a theme park in northern Virginia had first made national headlines six months ago. The call from her father came the same day. Over the next few weeks, he had gone from mild discouragement, to open denouncement of her involvement in the project, to anger when he learned she was traveling to Williamsburg to do spin control.

"You work for a damn cartoon maker. Just stick with promoting the cartoons. I don't like the attention this thing is getting, and I don't like you in the middle of it. You're in over your head. You don't have any business in Virginia."

Stirring up controversy, she thought. Bringing a blot on the spotless name he'd etched in the corporate world. A marketing genius himself, he'd established a computer components empire and made a fortune before he reached forty. Max Sheppard was a man of purpose and control. And he loathed the fact that she'd grown beyond his control.

When she had first taken an interest in the same marketing career that had distinguished him, Max had discouraged her.

Most of his moneyed friends' daughters sought degrees in art history or foreign languages or interior design, knowledge that would serve them well as ornaments to the moneyed men they would inevitably marry.

Not Rachel. She'd followed in her famous father's footsteps, and she was beyond analyzing it. Had she been attempting a long-overdue bonding with the cold, wealthy man who'd adopted her but never found time for her? Seeking his approval?

If so, she'd gone about it the wrong way, finding employment with Kingsley the year before. Her first assignment was the theme park whose controversy would mushroom by the day.

Inside the suite, Camisha asked, "So how *does* it feel?"

"How does it feel having him on your side for a change?"

"If that man gives a damn about history, I'm Mary Todd Lincoln."

"All he's interested in is keeping me from disgracing him."

Camisha stared at her for a long moment. She stared so long that Rachel felt odd—as if her friend's mind were a million miles away. Then she sighed. "Rachel, what do *you* think about this theme park?"

She was giving Rachel the benefit of the doubt, which was a waste of doubt. "I'm paid to influence opinions, not hold them."

Camisha pinned her with a knowing gaze. "One of these days, you're gonna have to stand for something."

"Well, principles aren't on today's itinerary."

"My mama would tan your hide if she heard that trash. She loves Williamsburg."

"Maybe. But she loves me more."

Helen Carlyle's approval had always meant more to Rachel than her own father's, simply because Helen was the one who'd always been there. Max had paid Camisha's mother to lend his home a woman's touch, along with the ironing and mopping, but in the meanwhile, she'd raised Rachel.

They were interrupted by the other bellman's arrival with their luggage, and his gaze lingered appreciatively on Camisha.

When Camisha would have tipped him, he shook his head. "My pleasure. Sorry about the crowd out front; people are pretty ticked off about that. Where're you from?"

"Dallas. But my family's from Virginia."

"Oh? Well, welcome home."

As he reached for the door, Rachel blushed. He acted as if he were about to serve her a home-cooked meal.

"Oh, it's good to be here," she returned, closing the door very slowly, peering at him all the way.

Rachel folded her arms. "Well *that* was pathetic."

Her head lolled, her eyes crossing. "He looked like—"

"It's *Bunker* Hill we're supposed to be thinking about, not Dulé Hill," she said with a grin.

Camisha went sober, that fake anger that always made Rachel laugh. "Bunker Hill's in freakin' Massachusetts," she said with a laugh as she entered the bathroom, "You colossal moron."

Rachel loved that brash, exhilarating laughter, but there was little about Camisha that she didn't love. In some ways, they were quite alike; both twenty-eight, both successful professionals, both raised in Dallas and educated at UT. Yet for all their similarities, they were from different worlds. Helen said that if they'd been old enough to know any better, they never would've even been friends.

"Put on some comfortable shoes," Camisha called. "We're going to be doing a lot of walking. No Manolo."

Rachel followed her, finding her freshening her lipstick in the full-length bathroom mirror. "Walking? Can't we take a cab?"

"Quit whining. Where we're going, they don't have roads."

They exchanged impudent smirks in the mirror. The two women there invited comparison. Both tall and shapely; one with creamy skin, the other, coffee-and-cream; one with long, curly black hair swept up into its usual French twist, the other with shining black hair cropped short, enhancing high cheekbones. Rachel wore a khaki linen Balmain jacket and slacks and cool white shell; Camisha, a frilly, ultra-feminine blouse and jeans.

Camisha found a flaw in the image.

"Girl, *do* something with that hair."

Rachel unwound her French twist, brushed out her hair, then wound it back up again while Camisha stared critically. "Seriously?"

"You want to cornrow it?"

They both giggled at the memory. When they were children, Camisha had played incessantly with Rachel's hair. More than once she'd cornrowed it, and they would pretend she was Camisha's long-lost octoroon cousin.

One summer Max had arrived home from a business trip to find his eight-year-old daughter exploring her assumed black heritage. It was the only time she could remember words ever failing him, and the memory of his apoplectic gape still made her smile.

But that night, Rachel heard Max's angry voice in the kitchen. When she tiptoed halfway downstairs, she heard Helen promising it wouldn't happen again, pleading with him.

"She needs me, Mr. Sheppard. And she needs my little girl."

"What about your girl, Helen? You want her to grow up in the same slums where you did, sirens screaming, bullets flying?"

Helen's protests had fallen silent.

The next morning Camisha and Helen were both gone, and Rachel had awakened to the cold, harsh hands of a strange woman in a starched gray uniform. Mrs. Frost, an austere, parched woman who might never have seen the sun, informed Rachel she was to be her caretaker for the summer—while the maid and her daughter visited relatives.

It was the last time Rachel would ever braid her hair.

But neither Max nor the cold housekeeper could keep her and Camisha from e-mailing and talking on the phone, and they'd even used the childhood alphabet code where every letter was transcribed into a number, where A = 1, B = 2, and so on.

It wasn't hard to crack – as any kid who'd ever passed notes in class well knew—but few who might've intercepted their letters would have had the time to count through the alphabet to decipher the letters.

They'd gotten so used to some of the words that they became shorthand—Rachel had signed her name in notes to Camisha as "18.1.3.8.5.12" for years.

It had been perfect for kids their age that summer, with endless amounts of time. And that summer their friendship grew even deeper. In the end, they'd both graduated from UT—Rachel as the privileged daughter of Texas billionaire Max Sheppard, with a marketing degree. Max had proven mysteriously generous through those years, sending Camisha all the way through law school. It was a mystery Rachel had never solved, considering his bigotry.

Although it was heartwarming to remember when Helen had argued not for herself, but for Rachel, the stubborn memories of Max annoyed her. "Let's get out of here and soak up some of that local color you're so nuts about."

"I'm ready."

As they turned the corner in the lobby and headed toward the door, they were intercepted by an older woman and man she recognized from the crowd. But he smiled as he held out his hand. "I'm Malcolm Henderson, and this is Mary van Kirk."

They exchanged introductions, and Rachel said, "If you'll excuse us, we were about to tour the historic area."

"Yes, we know." A peculiar sort, this man. His hair was an abundant froth of creamy silver-white, but cornflower blue eyes were alert, peering at her over wire-rimmed glasses. "We hoped to escort you."

"Escort us?" Rachel asked. "Are you employees here?"

"Oh, heavens, no." Mary van Kirk was as hard to peg as her companion. Her silver bun and wrinkled skin spoke of her advanced age, but there was a queer energy to her, and lively blue eyes challenged Rachel. "We're caretakers of the past, and all those who hold an affection for it. I'm afraid we have to apologize for the rude welcome you received. As you said, it was unbecoming of Virginia hospitality."

"Don't worry about it," Rachel said. "I understand their resistance completely."

"We insist. You deserve to see Williamsburg through the eyes of those who love her."

"Thank you," Camisha said. "We accept."

And Rachel had no choice but to entertain the enemy.

Chapter Two

A family of wrens were singing their hearts out from an oak tree that grew near the circular drive. It was a spectacular April day—during the past year in Los Angeles, Rachel had forgotten the four seasons.

Malcolm spoke to Camisha as they crossed Francis Street. "Have you been here before?"

"My grandmother first brought me here when I was six— the summer before my mother went to work for Rachel's father in Dallas. But I've visited many times, whenever I come back to visit my grandmother."

They strolled down a path, and a round, squat brick building stood on their left. A man in a dusty tricorn hat, homespun shirt, and short breeches leaned lazily on a long, antique firearm as he glanced at the people filing into the building. They stopped at a wide, dusty boulevard.

The sun was high and bright over the Virginia tidewater. In the distance, a cannon boomed. Nearby, vendors hawked refreshments from rustic stalls. A horse-drawn carriage stood in the shade of an oak tree, attended by a woman in elegant livery, her hair stuffed under her tricorn hat.

A crowd congregated on the steps of another old building. Beyond it lay a green, where half a dozen military tents were populated with colonial types; a woman tending sheep there spoke to a group of schoolchildren. Directly across from them, parents were snapping photographs of their children in the stocks.

But what she noticed most of all was the air; hot, humid, and heady, redolent with myriad smells—pine and pine tar, earth and woodsmoke, and others she couldn't begin to name. Odd, how the strangest, most distinctive aromas somehow seemed the most familiar to her. But it seemed pointless to ask her tour guides to identify an odor, so she asked an easier question instead.

"Where's the gate?"

"What gate?" Camisha asked.

"To get *in*."

Camisha exchanged a look of stunned hilarity with Malcolm and Mary, and the three broke out in laughter. Rachel frowned.

"Honey, we've *been* in for five minutes."

"I don't get it. Isn't there a museum or something?"

Camisha gestured dumbfoundedly. "Look around you, for Pete's sake! It's a whole eighteenth-century town. Nothing within 300 acres isn't colonial. There are hundreds of buildings. Eighty-eight are original, the rest have been restored or recreated the way they were in the 1700s."

"Recreated?" Rachel asked slyly. "Sounds a whole lot like a theme park, without the excitement."

"Oh, you can't begin to compare—" Camisha began.

Mary raised her hand. "The difference, Miss Sheppard, is that these same streets were trod by Thomas Jefferson, George Washington, Patrick Henry, and countless other figures throughout America's history. And Colonial Williamsburg is but one of many such historical sites throughout Virginia."

Camisha smiled. Score one for the preservationists.

"Does everyone wear costumes?" Rachel asked, changing the subject.

She noticed a woman who strolled by wearing a wide-brimmed, beribboned straw sunbonnet. Charcoal-gray skirts, covered with a white apron, brushed the dusty street, and she smiled at them.

"Yes," Malcolm said. "Some are interpreters—they explain colonial life to visitors, while maintaining the persona of someone who lived in the eighteenth century."

"Governor Francis Nicholson designed Duke of Gloucester Street to be one mile long from end to end," Mary went on as they strolled along the dusty, graveled road. "Do you work with Kingsley, Miss Carlyle?"

"Lord, no."

"Oh, no, she's above that," Rachel said. "She's a *lawyer*."

Camisha's mouth quirked. "I'm a junior partner at one of the criminal firms in Dallas, and I do some work as a public defender."

She left out that the PD work was pro bono, and that she also volunteered with a gang rehab program. Rachel had long envied Camisha her sense of purpose in life, but never more so than in the last year, when her own life echoed with emptiness. When her father seemed single-minded in his goal of watching her fail. A sudden suspicion struck her.

"Tell me. Did my father put you up to this?"

Mary and Malcolm exchanged glances. "I can't say that we know your father, dear."

"Oh, really? He's heading your whole group."

"Group?" Malcolm said. "We aren't part of any group."

He seemed just bewildered enough to be believable. These two were on their own peculiar mission.

They arrived at the edge of the green before the governor's palace. Ancient trees lined Palace Green, their leafy boughs stretching far into the cloudless sky.

On either side of the tree-lined mall, a row of impressive colonial homes stood. And a nagging awareness plagued her. She *knew* this place; she *knew* these streets. She recognized the sounds, the sights, the smells. But it was impossible; she'd never set foot in Virginia.

"What kind of trees are these?" Rachel asked.

"My granny called them Indian cigar trees. There were forty-five of them when I was a kid—I counted. Oh, I remember. They're catalpa trees."

And then, the homes that flanked the wide, grassy green seemed to blur as Rachel's gaze was drawn to a house on the right. There was no spectacular grandeur to it; two stories high, built of red brick. Yet she couldn't tear her gaze away.

"Rachel," Camisha asked, "what's the matter?"

"I don't know. It just all seems *familiar*. I must have seen pictures of it somewhere."

While most of the houses were surrounded by tourists snapping photographs or waiting to get in, this house was deserted, forgotten, its windows shuttered from the inside. Its desolation was haunting, the reminder of a forgotten past.

A forgotten past.

And she understood her kinship with the old brick house. The restlessness, the dissatisfaction, the absolute emptiness that had begun to haunt her now solidified within her, and she succumbed to the questions that had no answer.

Who was she? Who were her parents—the man and woman who had given her life, abused her, and abandoned her? She had just one tie to them: the crescent-moon scar at the corner of her eye—carved by her drug-crazed father, Max had told her, when she complained of her hunger. She couldn't remember even that.

But the last of it was the worst. Why, despite the evidence convicting her parents, couldn't she stop wondering about them?

"Thomas Jefferson was educated in that college." Mary gestured toward William & Mary at the west end. Then she pointed due east. "The notion of American history was born in that Capitol, where Patrick Henry delivered to the House of Burgesses the treasonous speeches that inspired a new nation. And here," she said, nodding toward the old church a hundred feet away, "is Bruton Parish Church, built in 1715."

Rachel stifled a yawn.

"In 1926 the rector of that church, W.A.R. Goodwin, persuaded John D. Rockefeller Jr. to save Williamsburg. The rector's vision was brought to life by Mr. Rockefeller's funding. If Dr. Goodwin hadn't found a benefactor in Mr. Rockefeller,

Williamsburg would've been lost in the mists of time, existing only as a dusty college town with asphalt running over its archeological riches.

"The most familiar landmarks remind us that faith in God, education, and government were the cornerstones of eighteenth-century life in the British colony of Virginia. Now, Miss Sheppard, do you begin to see the importance of leaving history in the hands of those who love it?"

She should've been paying closer attention. What was the point Mary thought she'd just made?

"Miss van Kirk, we don't mean to offend the historians. But I personally don't see what all the uproar is about."

"Rachel." Camisha pointed in frustration to an interpreter standing on the corner, drinking from an earthenware tankard. "You see that mug?"

She nodded, suspicious.

"That's the same design popular in Williamsburg in the eighteenth century. Guess how they figured that out?"

"The library?"

Camisha almost choked. "Colonial Williamsburg *is* the damned library! Is Kingsley going to have a staff of archeologists sifting through dirt and broken pottery to get every detail of your theme park accurate to the time?"

"What difference does it make?"

"What difference? You're the one with the soundbites about educating kids." Her voice fell to a near-whisper; her closing arguments voice. She never screamed to make a point; her soft-spoken murmur was far more persuasive.

"Everything you'll see today has a point. If you see a deck of cards on a table in one of these houses, then you can bet it's the kind they used back then. If you see tourist children toting firewood, it's because they want them to know most children had to do it for their families to survive."

Her gaze was sober. "And if you see a black man being taken away from the steps of a tavern where he's just been sold, while his pregnant wife is screaming, it's because in the year 1770, the phrase *politically correct* hadn't been invented."

In that moment, something within Rachel flickered to life. Reverence for this place? No; she saw little good in reminding anyone of the degradation of slavery. Little value in lecturing young children who would never remember it. Perhaps she just envied Camisha her passion for Williamsburg.

"How can you look around at this place and feel any warmth for it? Every house we're looking at was owned by some fine family who enslaved your ancestors."

Camisha's dark gaze lingered at one house after another with brooding wistfulness. "Yes. But that doesn't make my ancestors any less important a part of it than those fine families. There are those who say that slave labor in Virginia was what made the colonies such a commodity that England took notice. Without it, America never would've been worth fighting over. Now tell me where *that* puts my ancestors in American history? I can be angry about that, or I can be proud, but I want you to know this, Rachel. When you see elaborate staircase carvings and intricate carpentry and tapestries today, I'll be reflecting that those carvings and construction and tapestries, many of them, anyway, were done by my ancestors—all artifacts that have lasted for centuries, by the way. And I know that the artisans who created those items did so out of love and pride. Rachel, I choose to be proud of our contribution."

Rachel shouldn't have been amazed, but she still wanted to shout an amen. Camisha neither romanticized nor demonized her roots; she relished them. She herself, on the other hand, had long ago learned that almost everything was illusion. And there was no glamour in the past.

"And that's George Wythe's house," Camisha said. "First law professor in the U.S. – and he taught at William and Mary. *And* he signed the Declaration of Independence."

Camisha gazed fondly at the home. "He hated slavery. He freed all his slaves before he died, and back then, it just about took an act of Parliament to free a slave. His house was occupied by General Rochambeau when French troops were quartered in Williamsburg, after Cornwallis surrendered at Yorktown."

She gestured toward the other end of the green. "Patrick Henry and Thomas Jefferson were both governors of the colony. Soldiers were housed there during the battle of Yorktown."

"I'm afraid I have to ask, Miss Sheppard," Malcolm said. "Why Virginia?"

She brightened at the question. Perhaps he could see reason. "This will be a fabulous benefit for Virginia tourism. The piedmont, where we're building, is within a day's drive of half a dozen major U.S. cities."

"And twice that many historic sites, including the hallowed grounds of battles. Why Virginia?"

"Americana will bring visitors from around the world, Mr. Henderson."

"Colonial Williamsburg, Monticello, Mount Vernon—all of these already do that." He asked for a third time: "Why Virginia?"

He spoke as if Virginia were the luckless target of a blight. Why indeed? Because there's too much money to be made *not* to, she wanted to say. But she had been raised by Max Sheppard, marketing genius of the twenty-first century.

It's all truth versus beauty, Rachel, and nobody gives a damn about the truth. We buy the beauty.

Max's PR motto had served her well.

"The fact is, we have a great appreciation for Virginia's greatest treasure—her scenic beauty, and our environmental policies—"

"Real history, Miss Sheppard, is Virginia's greatest treasure," Malcolm snapped. "Indifference to history isn't just stupid. It's rude."

Camisha gave a crooked smile.

But Rachel was no longer fighting this man. She was fighting a far more arrogant adversary—her racist father, a man whose attitudes would've fit right in with the slave-owners.

"Mr. Henderson, have you even looked at our plans? Americana has been unfairly condemned by a handful of very vocal, manipulative outsiders who happen to own land in Virginia."

Malcolm and Mary hooted. "My dear," he said with a grin, "Kingsley isn't exactly an old Virginia family."

Rachel heard Camisha's contagious laughter, and she sent her a withering glare. "Nevertheless—"

Abruptly, all humor left him. "Now you can stand on a mountain and look out at the land where the most bitter battles of our country were fought. On a cool morning, with the fog rising over the valley, you can almost see the generals calling their troops to arms. If Kingsley has it their way, we'll have the vista of roller coasters, hotel high-rises, and billboards."

"Mr. Henderson—"

"What about twenty years from now?" he pressed. "What if the project goes broke? It wouldn't be the first time. When those wild panoramic vistas are gone…" He focused a sober stare on her. "They're gone forever."

Her eyes flashed. "Many of those battles Virginia reveres were fought to preserve slavery."

Camisha laughed. "Are you joking? You think Johnny Reb was out there shooting squirrels? Sherman isn't remembered for his march through Omaha, Rae. The battles aren't remembered because they were fought to preserve slavery, but because they destroyed it."

The older couple looked at Camisha for a long time. Finally, Mary spoke. "Miss Sheppard, each hand we touch is forever left with the imprint of our own fingertips, each word we speak, forever irretrievable. Your influence will be ever felt if you put an end to this project. You can be that person who changes the face of history, if you choose to."

That was just too much. It was ludicrous to suggest that what she did in her line of work would ever make any difference to *anything*. "Miss van Kirk, people who romanticize the past—"

"Rachel." Malcolm surprised her with the familiarity. His gaze on her was sad. "Tell me, dear—have you no fond memories of a cherished childhood home?"

The question stunned and disarmed her.

"Not one warm image of your grandmother, passing down the lore of your family's past? Have you never wondered if, perhaps, the blood of a patriot flows in your veins? Was there no one to teach you the difference between romanticizing the past and respecting it? We study history not to glorify days gone by, but to understand who we are."

"If you'll excuse me—" She abruptly turned away, shocked at the tears that stung her eyes and closed her throat.

How had this old man—a stranger—unwittingly thrust into the most defenseless wound within her? After all these years of hard work, all the therapists, all the years she'd worked to put it behind her, all the years she'd spent trying to love the man who'd adopted her, trying to forget—

Forget what? How could she forget what she couldn't remember?

Again, the questions haunted her: What had happened during those first six years of her life? Years spent with her own parents, before a man who saw in her a profitable photo-op chose to adopt a disturbed, abused child who couldn't even speak. A child who couldn't remember anything about those first six years. Not even her own name.

Chapter Three

Camisha saw Rachel's eyes focused yearningly on an old home across the way, and compassion welled within her. They'd come a long way since the first night they met, more than twenty years before.

My name's Cammie. I'm the maid's daughter. Who are you?

The gangly girl had only stared gravely at her. Camisha's mother had warned her not to bother the girl, because she was Mr. Sheppard's brand-new adopted daughter.

That child's been through worse things than you can ever imagine, honey. She might have a rich daddy now, but he don't care about her. You let her be.

Camisha, a curious six-year-old, had not let her be. She was a brand new friend, right there in the house! Another month of silence passed while Camisha talked enough for the both of them.

She read *Green Eggs and Ham* to Rachel until the book was falling apart. *Can you say 'That Sam I am?'* she would ask Rachel patiently.

Rachel would only smile hesitantly and point to the book.

When Max was out of town, Camisha was happiest, because she had a friend. When he was home, she steered clear of him; she knew he didn't like his brand-new daughter hanging out with the colored help. He'd proven it often enough.

The girl who once couldn't speak now made her living at it. Even in casual clothes, Rachel was the perfect professional woman.

As Camisha caught up with her, Rachel stared at her with suspicious hazel eyes. Almost flawless pale skin was marred only by a tiny scar at the corner of her eye, in the shape of a crescent moon.

Camisha was heartsick. She knew exactly why Max didn't want Rachel in Virginia—and it was far more sinister than any theme park.

Rachel thought her father was a rich, misguided racist. Of course, that *was* true. But she didn't know the dangerous man Camisha knew. And she had decided that before this day was over, Rachel would know the truth.

When they were children, she had lain awake at night, frightened over how Max might retaliate if she revealed his secret. His threats were effective.

But they were no longer children—and she was past caring what Max might do. In the end, her duplicity had become a self-imposed exile. For so many years, she had dreaded the day Rachel would learn of her deception. Would it mean the end of their friendship? But no matter what happened, that day had arrived.

"When my grandmother brought me here, she showed me William and Mary. 'That's where Thomas Jefferson went to school,' she said. 'And his blood is in your veins.'"

They both smiled. Whether it was myth or truth, Camisha's love for history had been born that day.

"Along with the blood of enslaved men and women," she continued. "But I *remember* that. I *remember* growing up in Virginia. I *remember* Mama tucking me in bed when I was two years old, kissing me good—"

"Stop it."

"All I'm saying is, the past isn't always painful, if you aren't afraid of it. If you know the truth."

"Easy for you to say. Sally Hemings' great-great—however the hell many *greats* apply—granddaughter."

"Uh huh. Even knowing your ancestors were enslaved is better than thinking your own parents—"

"Camisha," she pleaded.

Camisha saw the tears on Rachel's cheeks, and she felt them as if they were her own. She understood her confusion; Rachel hadn't expected to find any interest in this place. She was strictly gathering facts to use against those who loved the old village. But something within it took her back—and Camisha knew why. They walked along in silence.

"Do you remember the first thing you ever said?"

Rachel swallowed, smiling. "Sure. It was the day Dad offered a million dollars to anyone who could prove Oswald didn't act alone."

"And there you stood in that room full of reporters. And when one of them asked you what you thought about your new daddy, you pointed at him and said—"

"That Sam-I-am, that Sam-I-am, I do not like that Sam-I-am," Rachel murmured.

"First time I ever coached a witness."

"It's just that lately, in the last year, since I got the job with Kingsley, I've felt this..." She shrugged, wiping her eyes. "Futility."

She looked at her dearest friend. Camisha's eyes had softened, and she saw in her the spirit of the young girl who'd befriended her when the girls at Hockaday had merely cast knowing glances and whispered.

"This is the kind of place that makes you wonder what you're going to leave behind for your children," Camisha said.

As they rejoined the others, Rachel tried to put herself in the minds of the natives. In the distance, she heard the lively, staccato rhythm of a drum corps. It *was* an amazing illusion. But for the tourists who roamed about, they might have been standing in the eighteenth century. The place was a collection of anachronisms—and yet, none of it was out of place. *They* were the anachronisms.

"Isn't this the coolest place you've ever seen?" Camisha asked.

"It's the oldest," she said with a mischievous smile. "And the dullest. I'm amazed the human race survived, as repressed as they all were."

"Oh, honey, you're mixing up Virginians with Boston's Puritans. William Byrd had a fondness for making love to his wife on his billiard table."

Distracted by the bizarre image of a bewigged gentleman in a passionate embrace on a pool table, she giggled. "Who was he?"

Camisha groaned at her ignorance. "Only the most polished gentleman of eighteenth-century Virginia. Or possibly even all of the time since."

As they headed toward the governor's palace, Rachel's gaze was inevitably riveted to the red brick mansion on the right. Something drew her eye upward; the shutters at a second story window had been folded back, and a young girl appeared at the window, dressed in colonial garb.

She darted an alert glance about the street below, catching Rachel's eye. She was no more than six or seven, tendrils of blonde curling from beneath a dust cap. Lively blue eyes danced with mischief as she blew Rachel a kiss.

Charmed by her ingenuous affection and warmth, Rachel impulsively returned the gesture. She waited hopefully; would the child open the window? Toss off an archaic colloquialism?

"Look at that," Rachel whispered to Camisha, pointing.

"What?"

"That little girl there. They've got her playing dress-up."

The girl looked over her shoulder. She waved once more before she disappeared, and an emptiness stabbed Rachel.

"Ladies," Malcolm urged, "we must be moving along. Hurry!"

"Where?" asked Camisha, still peering at the house.

"Oh, forget it, she's gone now."

The haunting loneliness of the house returned as the shutters closed, matching her own emptiness.

What would it be like to glance at a window of her own home and find her daughter or son waving at her? It didn't

25

seem likely, since having a family of her own was a goal she'd never bothered to set. She thought she saw a flicker at the window—as if someone were watching her.

Abruptly, she hurried after the group entering the governor's palace. A magnificent array of weaponry—hundreds of swords and muskets—gleamed in the entryway, in a beautiful and terrible tribute to power.

Wheelwrights were at work mending wagon wheels behind the palace. Along the brick walls, deep green ivy grew. A pungent aroma pervaded the gardens—not quite offensive, but distinctive. Her reaction to the smells of this place were beginning to annoy her. "What *is* that smell?"

"Boxwood." Camisha gestured toward the tall, sculpted shrubs. "That's the most incredible maze."

"Smells like a cat," she grumbled, unwilling to admit the sensation troubling her. The fragrance reached deep within her, searching elusively for a memory.

"Keep it classy, Rachel." Camisha gave her a wry nod.

"The olfactory nerves are the most emotionally evocative," Mary reflected, watching her closely. "A familiar aroma can instantly bring to mind events of our childhood."

"There are some unique smells here," Camisha said. "And I love every one of them. If you don't like the boxwood, Rachel, it's a good thing you weren't around in the eighteenth century. You'd have smelled a lot worse then."

The group took a break for refreshment in one of the taverns, and she and Camisha sat at a table in the corner drinking root beer. Camisha looked over Rachel's shoulder, examining a portrait on the wall. "Looks like Jefferson and Patrick Henry."

"Who are those guys?" Rachel asked, peering at the portrait.

"I don't know. Some random guys. Would you look at that," she said, a smile lighting her face. "We're sitting in that very corner."

An interpreter stood nearby, and he seemed pleased at her observation. "You've a sharp eye, young lady. No doubt you've noticed that Thomas Jefferson and Patrick Henry sit with the group of men.

"This was the period we call the prelude to independence. The portrait was posed during May of 1776 and was a gift to the owner of the tavern from Jefferson himself."

Rachel turned to peer at the portrait. She recognized Jefferson and Henry at the table. Beside the table, two young men drank from tankards and laughed, the way young men always had and always would.

"Hey, scoot over, scoot over," Camisha said, grabbing her phone.

They struck a pose on either side of the portrait and Camisha fiddled with her phone. "Aw, man! My battery's dead. Give me your phone."

Rachel unlocked it and gave it to her, and they smiled up at the phone, taking a selfie. Camisha then asked the interpreter to take another photo, so the table they were sitting in was included in the photo.

As they left the tavern, two youngsters scampered by, also dressed as colonials. "These children are junior docents," Mary said. "They work with their parents from time to time."

"I saw one in the brick house back down the street."

"The George Wythe house? Near Bruton Parish Church?"

"No. The red brick one across from it."

The woman gazed at Rachel, unblinking. "That can't be."

"I'm sure of it—a charming child. Blonde curls underneath a dust cap, and a pink gown with a white apron. She waved at me. What's wrong?"

Mary looked down, then shook her head. "It's a private home. Clara Trelawney lives there alone, and she's in her seventies." She turned to Malcolm. "I'm sure I would have been told if she had visitors."

"But I'm certain there was someone there. Her granddaughter?"

Rachel saw the dotty old couple exchanging mysterious glances, then finally Malcolm spoke. "Clara Trelawney's only relative in the area lives outside Williamsburg, at Rosalie."

Rosalie. The name conjured an air of romance and intrigue.

"The woman who owns Rosalie, Lottie Chesterfield, is a very dear friend of ours."

"Rachel," Camisha said, with that no-nonsense way of hers, "you imagined that little girl. I didn't see a thing."

Malcolm went on, "She's invited us to her home for supper tonight, and I know she'd love to meet you. Would you join us?"

Once more, Camisha plunged in when Rachel would have declined. "Thank you, Mr. Henderson. We'd be delighted."

Rachel was distracted by the somber, elegant Georgian home. "You go on with the group. I'll catch up."

She crossed the street to the Trelawney home, walked through the white gate and up the walk. She knocked on the door to no avail, and a groundskeeper appeared.

"I'm looking for Clara Trelawney."

"Mrs. Trelawney's out—been gone for hours."

"But..." Rachel gestured toward the windows. "I saw someone, a little girl, in the window—"

He broke into a serene smile. "Blonde curls, pretty as an angel?"

"Yes! Who is she?"

"That's Emily."

She looked like an Emily. "Is she a docent?"

He chuckled fondly. "Oh, no. Wouldn't call her that. Emily's grandfather built this house; they say that's why she comes here now." His voice had fallen to a fond, reverent whisper. "And they say she wears the dust cap so people won't see her halo and be afraid. Course, I haven't ever seen her myself—just know people who have."

"I don't understand. Does she live here, or doesn't she?"

"She lived in Williamsburg at one time." Melancholy mingled with the affection in his eyes. "Emily died in a fire at Rosalie, back in the middle of the eighteenth century."

Chapter Four

"Ghosts! What a gimmick! How can Kingsley compete with three centuries' worth of dead patriots spinning in their graves?"

As they returned to their suite, Camisha smiled at Rachel's cynical complaint. She knew the story about the little girl had disturbed Rachel more than she liked to admit. Hours later, she was still talking about her.

"What's wrong?"

Her innocent question gave Camisha pause. She closed the door behind her, leaning against it, and stared at the floor for a long time before she looked up. "Rachel, we need to talk."

She caught the hesitation in her words. More than once, they'd read each other's minds, and Camisha wished she could do so now. Wished there wasn't the awful telling still ahead.

"You want to order drinks, or something?"

"No." If she didn't get it out now, she knew she might never. And they didn't need any interruptions.

Rachel sat on the couch, but Camisha paced restlessly. "You remember when you first came to live with Max?"

She nodded.

Why couldn't she look her in the eye? She felt Rachel's gaze on her like a steadying hand, but she couldn't bring herself to face her.

At last, she opened her briefcase and withdrew the old, worn manila envelope. She must've opened and closed this envelope five hundred times in the past twenty years.

But never—*never*—in front of Rachel.

The silver chain slid into her hand—cold, lifeless—followed by the heart-shaped locket. She had to reach into the envelope to withdraw the worn section of newspaper.

She placed them on the coffee table in front of Rachel—as if they were in a high-stakes game and she was all in. The envelope dropped to the table beside them.

Rachel stared at the pile, uncomprehending. She glanced up at Camisha. "What is it?"

Just say it. Just get it out.

She'd had a speech all scripted out, but the pretty words of her profession eluded her.

A knock on the door startled them both.

Camisha exhaled.

"I'll get it," Rachel said. "You just relax."

Camisha moved restlessly to the window. The spacious, luxurious room seemed to close about her, and she opened the window, letting in the cool air. She heard the rumble of thunder in the distance. She was beyond annoyed at the interruption; in another minute, it would've been out.

But when the door opened, she knew her time was up.

"Dad," Rachel said, smiling. "What are you doing here?"

"Forget the press conference already?"

At sixty-two, Max Sheppard was still handsome, still fit. Tall, lean, with striking silver hair and wintry blue eyes. Camisha'd always thought he looked like he was made of ice.

He entered the room, noticing her. His smile didn't quite reach his eyes.

"Oh, hello, Camisha. Didn't expect you to be here."

Her heart was pounding—hard. She hated herself for still fearing him. For still admitting that a man like him could hold power over her.

He held a bottle of champagne. "Consider it a peace offering, Rachel. Since you seem hell-bent on this lost cause, I might as well wish you the best. Thought we'd spend some time together while we're both here."

"Thanks. But I thought you weren't coming in till tomorrow."

Those glacial eyes flickered over the room. As he placed the champagne on the table, he hesitated almost imperceptibly. His attention was fastened on the newspaper and silver locket.

Camisha watched in morbid fascination, dreading and anticipating the moment he would turn that gaze on her. Would she face him as the bold, articulate woman she'd become—or the trembling six-year-old he'd controlled for so long?

But he only smiled at Rachel. "Well, life's just full of surprises, isn't it?"

Then Camisha recognized it, as anyone abused by Max Sheppard would—the tightening in his mouth, the white line that encircled his lips as he reined in his temper.

A mass of nerves clenched in her stomach, and she thought that where this man was concerned, she might never be more than that girl he'd terrorized so long ago.

He reached into his pocket and tapped out a cigarette, put it in his mouth, felt around in one pocket, then another.

"Well, Jesus," he said between his teeth. "Forgot my damned lighter." He fished a bill out of his wallet and handed it to Rachel. "Run down to the gift shop and get me one, will you?"

It wasn't a request.

"Dad, you know you can't smoke in here."

"Rachel, I've had a hell of a day. Just go."

She sighed and left. And Camisha understood what he was doing.

His gaze shifted to her. White-hot cold.

After several moments, he shook his head. His breath hissed in through his teeth.

"Funny, how you think you know a person. Give her an easy life, right alongside your own goddamned daughter, spend a quarter-million dollars sending her to school ..."

He reached for the locket and stared at it thoughtfully, then dropped it back onto the table. The newspaper was fragile in his large, strong hands.

For twenty-two years, it had forged a balance of distrust between these two people.

"I take it she hasn't seen this yet," he said. "What fortunate timing."

He slid his hand into his pocket and withdrew a silver lighter. The lid clinked as he flipped it open; the flick of the flint was crisp; the smell of butane, faint.

As he dangled the edge of the parched paper just above the flame, as a wisp of smoke promised fire, rage ignited in Camisha. It was the only link between Rachel and the mysteries of her past.

She snatched it away.

He grabbed her arm, all traces of feigned civility gone. "I swear, if you breathe one word—"

"What?" Her voice trembled with anger and fear. "What'll you do? Hurt my mother? Send me away? Your threats don't scare me anymore. You can't hurt me."

But she backed away, making a lie of her bravado. At last she was against the open window and, with one hard fist, he bashed out the screen.

Camisha's breath caught in her lungs as she felt nothing but the cool evening air behind her. Frantically she grabbed at the window to keep from falling the three floors down.

"Go ahead and push." She taunted him with her final thread of courage. "You know there's only one person who really has any power against you."

"And you've lied to her about it for twenty years."

"Like I'm afraid of what you'll tell her. It's time she knows the truth."

"Like you said. Only one person knows anything."

Camisha shuddered. "You wouldn't hurt Rachel."

"Try me."

Rachel found a lighter in the gift shop, and on her way through the lobby, she saw Malcolm and Mary. They were ready and waiting to escort her and Camisha to dinner at the old plantation. She would've preferred a good night's sleep, but if dinner at a creepy mansion was what Camisha wanted, then that's what she was going to get.

"Just five minutes. We'll be right down."

But when she opened the door to the suite, her mind wouldn't quite process what she saw. Camisha was falling out the window—and Max was catching her.

No—Max was *pushing* her.

"Dad!"

When he turned, Rachel stopped short. His hair was disheveled, his eyes wild with rage. In a moment it struck her. This man was a stranger. She didn't know the first thing about him.

"What are you doing?"

He stared at her, his breath coming hard. "You're coming home with me, Rachel."

She glanced at Camisha, whose eyes glistened with the aftershock of fear. "Don't go with him. Something'll happen to you, Rae. He knows you can—"

"Now."

"Rachel, you want to know why this place looks so familiar to you? Smells so familiar to you?" Camisha's eyes shone with emotion. "Because you were born here. You grew up here. Your parents weren't drug addicts. They didn't abuse you, and they didn't abandon you. They were murdered."

Rachel felt the foundation of her very world shatter.

"The police found you a month after it happened, hiding in an abandoned farmhouse. And Rachel..." Tears ran down her dark face. "There were two other little girls with you. A three-year-old, and a baby. You—you have two sisters, Rae. And you took care of them, all by yourself, for a *month*. When you were just six years old."

This couldn't be happening. It was a horrible dream. It *couldn't be happening*. The man before her had raised her and given her everything any girl ever dreamed of—except a father's love.

Why? Why had he adopted her, in the first place, if he didn't want her? And—even worse—why had he lied to her for twenty years?

For only one reason: Because the truth would destroy him.

"Call the police, Camisha."

Max reached for the phone and held it out. "Go ahead."

A chill stole over Rachel as he spoke, almost pleasantly. "Matter of fact, I phoned an old friend down here before I came. Warned him my daughter had stopped seeing the therapist some time ago...and that the doctor warned me she was suffering from acute delusions."

Defeat closed around Rachel. How well he knew her. The therapist she'd seen since she'd known Max—who'd never taken her an inch closer to recalling her lost memories—held more power over her than anyone, except Max. At least in her mind. When she'd stopped seeing him during her freshman year in college, at the urging of Camisha, she'd felt free.

Freed from Max.

"No call?" Max queried. "Then I have one to make."

He pressed one button.

"Yes, operator. This is Max Sheppard, and I'm in my daughter's room. It seems there's been an unfortunate accident. She hasn't been feeling well lately, and...I'm afraid she's made quite a mess of the place. Of course, I'll be responsible for the damages, long as we can keep things quiet. And I'd appreciate it if you'd get Doctor Patrick Malone on the phone. He's in Dallas ... Yes. I'll wait."

Camisha's pain had given way to anger, and she grabbed her purse. Grabbed the locket off the coffee table. "Let's get the hell out of here."

Max covered the mouthpiece. "I warned you before, and I'm warning you now: There's no place you can hide."

Lazily, Max reached for the bottle of champagne. Rachel flinched as it crashed into the antique mirror above the fireplace.

As the two young women fled the room, Rachel glanced back over her shoulder.

She saw her splintered image reflected in the shattered mirror.

Chapter Five

Rachel was numb.

She sat beside Camisha in the back seat of a perfectly preserved old Buick. Malcolm Henderson was at the wheel.

They'd turned to the old couple because, quite honestly, they'd had nowhere else to turn. Now, they were making their way down a narrow, serpentine road through the woods. She didn't expect to be much of a dinner guest, but neither Mary nor Malcolm cared. Well aware of the threat presented by her father—how she loathed still granting him that tender name— she'd explained it to them, haltingly, uncomfortable at accepting sanctuary from these two she'd belittled. They'd welcomed her without question.

In her palm, she clutched the necklace Camisha had given her. It was a silver, heart-shaped locket, perhaps an inch and a half square. Camisha might have told her it was a photograph of her unknown mother; it was real, and she held it, but it raised no emotion in her. She pressed the tiny clasp and leaned forward, squinting to see in the panel lights.

Where she should have seen two photographs, she saw only the empty shell of the locket: twin silver hearts. She found an engraving on the back: *As time is, so beats our hearts—tender, immortal, forever.*

"Do you remember it?" Camisha's question was quick, urgent.

"No."

"Your daddy was raising holy hell when he couldn't find it the next day. Mama tore that house apart looking for it." Somberly, she went on, "She said you cried so much when you first came to live there that nothing could make you go to sleep. I thought you wanted your locket. I'd sneak into your room and put it in your hands, then sneak in in the next morning and get it again."

Rachel waited, spellbound, remembering those endless nights when nothing would soothe her fearful grief. When she knew she'd lost something—but didn't know what.

"I found the clipping when I found the locket." Camisha gulped. "When I saw your daddy, I told him I saw your picture in the newspaper, and I asked him where your sisters were. When I said that, he grabbed me and told me that if I ever breathed a word of it to anyone..." She hesitated, and her gaze was blank. "He said he'd kill my mother."

"He *what*?"

"I told Mama, but she said it wasn't any of our business. She was afraid she wouldn't be able to find a job if she made him mad. His threats changed over the years, but he knew what he was doing. By the time I was old enough not to be afraid of him, I was ashamed to admit to you that I'd known it for so long."

Rachel stroked her shoulders as she cried. "Oh, Camisha. You know it wouldn't have mattered."

The day had been a nightmare, and she wanted nothing more than sleep—if sleep was to be found. For the moment, she welcomed the refuge of a night in the Virginia countryside. In the morning, maybe things would look clearer.

They turned down a dirt lane, and visibility dropped almost to nothing as a torrent of rain slashed through the night.

Suddenly, black iron gates loomed before them. Thunder rumbled in the distance, and as they drove through the gate, lightning flashed, riveting her gaze on a striking sight no more than a hundred feet from the driveway.

A whispered word sprang reflexively from her heart but remained unspoken; unforgettable silence held the word captive, as if the shrine before her were a castle rather than ruins.

Rosalie.

A mere reminder of what once had been an immense Palladian mansion remained in its place, rain pounding its naked interior. Frightening and majestic, grand and pathetic, menacing and tender. Three massive chimneys stood along the single remaining back wall, which rose three stories from the Virginia soil where it had been built—how long ago?

The hollows of fireplaces—nine of them, she counted in a glance—were arranged on the wall below the three chimneys. For all the flawlessly created beauty of the governor's palace in Williamsburg, it couldn't compare with the emotion that rose up within her as she beheld the remains of what she knew, in the depths of her heart, was once a home that had known love. Though no one had lived here for years—perhaps centuries— the stark, primitive vigor of the home was a palpable thing, rising against the turbulent sky as if in silent praise.

Rosalie.

She recalled the gardener at the old house in town.

Emily died in a fire at Rosalie, back in the middle of the eighteenth century.

"Uh," Camisha said, "looks like no one's home."

Rachel's breath left her in a relieved chuckle.

"Don't be silly," Mary said, unamused. "Lottie's house is up ahead."

They continued down the winding path, arriving at the front of another old house. The Federal style home was inevitably modest by comparison—a two-story home with black shutters flanking the eight windows on its face.

The cold rain pelted them as they hurried to the front door and knocked. A maid admitted them and they were ushered through a high-ceilinged entryway.

The hall was perfectly appointed with period antiques. Ancient portraits lined the long gallery above a wide staircase.

In the drawing room, candles lit a massive chandelier, and an old woman sat beside a crackling fire. She rose with some effort, leaning on a polished hickory walking stick as she hobbled forward. She was small; her dress was pale rose, covered with a white lace shawl. The wig she wore was slightly askew, and compassion stirred in Rachel as the woman focused alert blue eyes on her.

"So. You're here at last." Her voice was a solemn rustle, like a page from an old hymnbook. "Welcome to Rosalie."

Mary and Malcolm joined them in the dining hall, and Rachel was distracted from the nightmare they'd left in Williamsburg, as that nagging familiarity she had come to welcome returned.

The aromas of the food reminded Rachel they hadn't eaten since that morning. Dish after dish was uncovered, an array of the gourmet and the everyday; okra and stewed tomatoes, home-grown string beans, scalloped corn, oyster casserole, baked ham, and a memorable crab soup.

For a moment, Rachel was distracted even from the feast spread before her. Something about the meal roused an uncomfortable awareness in her. A familiarity, as if it were something she'd known long ago. The sensation disturbed her, and she dismissed it with some effort. Afterward, they retired to a drawing room for tea.

Rachel sat on a loveseat beside the fragile old woman who owned Rosalie. She sipped her tea. "Mrs. Chesterfield, we caught a glimpse of some ruins when we came in."

"That's what remains of the original house, built in 1741 by Grey Trelawney. I'm the oldest living Trelawney. My brother's widow lives in Williamsburg."

Her words reminded Rachel of the little girl she'd seen. "I saw the Trelawney home. I saw…"

"You saw Emily. She's Grey's daughter."

Rachel noted her present tense, but she was too charmed by the woman to correct her. Lottie gestured toward the wall. "The gentleman in that portrait is Emily's grandfather. Clara gave it to me some years ago."

Rachel gazed at the life-sized portrait; a perfect eighteenth-century Virginia gentleman. A white wig brushed an elegant black coat. A snowy cravat was knotted at his neck, and in one hand he poised a pearl-handled walking stick. Oyster-colored breeches were buttoned just below the knee, and stockings were stitched with silver threads that matched the shade of his eyes. He was an attractive and arrogant man. And he wasn't very happy.

"That portrait was commissioned around 1760. Thomas Trelawney was a remarkable man. He lived into his eighties, a long life enjoyed by only the wealthy of those days. He was born the son of a barrister, of a fine Welsh family, in 1699, the year Williamsburg became the capital of Virginia. He arrived on the shores of Virginia not yet twenty years old and studied law at William and Mary.

"Over the years he prospered and built the home you saw in town. Later in life he was a successful planter as well as a member of the House of Burgesses.

"Grey, the man who built Rosalie, held a bitter hatred for his father. Both Grey and Emily died in the fire that destroyed Rosalie."

"That's terrible," Camisha said.

"Yes. We believe Emily remains behind at her grandfather's house now because she was never allowed to visit him during her short life."

She felt an odd kinship with the son of the planter who'd lived so long ago; in the portrait of Thomas Trelawney, she saw the arrogance of Max Sheppard.

"I understand you've had an unpleasant afternoon," Lottie said. "I hope you'll stay the night with us. We'd love to have you. Rosalie has a way of making you forget the trivialities and trials of the modern day."

"You're right there, Lottie," Malcolm said. "Sometimes I think I'm allergic to the twenty-first century. Prefer the nineteenth, myself, but the air's clearer in the eighteenth. Go back much farther than that, and things get a little bloody for my taste."

Camisha and Rachel laughed out loud at his dry humor, but he only stared back at them—as if not getting his own joke.

"Thank you, Lottie," Rachel said. "I have to admit, there's something about this place—so remote, so quiet. So peaceful."

"That it is," Camisha said.

Rachel spent most of her life fighting traffic to get here and there, and the rest of it being places she didn't care that much about to begin with.

"We live very simply. It's good for the soul."

"I think I could spend weeks here without missing the outside world," Rachel said.

"What did you put in this tea?" Camisha teased Lottie. "This isn't the Rachel I know."

It was true. Maybe it was the revelation of finding a thread of her own roots. Maybe it was the warm coziness of the house, while the storm raged outside. But for the first time in her life, she felt as if she belonged.

"Do you mean that, Rachel?"

She glanced at Mary. "Yes. It's a wonderful, charming old place."

Camisha said, "You'd be bored in three hours without a to-do list."

"But she would be *safe*. In fact, it's the only place she *can* be safe. The past. Don't you agree, dear?"

"The past," Malcolm repeated thoughtfully. "A place that existed long before you were ever born. Long before the events that are buried within your memory ever took place."

Well, it was a bit of a melodramatic description of the remote old plantation, but Malcolm had shown himself to be a little passionate when he was stirred up.

"You mean, stay here at Rosalie? What about the press conference?"

"The press conference? Let's review the facts, shall we?" Mary set her cup and saucer aside. "Your father is convinced that you pose a threat to him, personally and professionally."

"Miss van Kirk, I can't remember a thing. I have no idea what he's afraid of."

40

"Fact number two. For all these years, he's told you that your parents abandoned you. But he lied, counting on your lost memory and Camisha's compassion to protect him."

Rachel couldn't speak at that reminder.

"Fact number three, he's already brought into question your very sanity. If you insist on returning to Williamsburg, he shall do much worse."

"But—the press conference," Rachel said. "There'll be contacts from every major news agency in the country."

"Oh, of course. That's quite important, and you'll be back in plenty of time, with a much clearer perspective and in a safer, public location."

Malcolm interrupted, his eyebrows drawn together. "You don't know that. You don't know if she'll come back at all—" he began, and Mary shushed him and went on.

"While you're here, Rachel, beginning tonight, you have one task: to remember your past."

"Do you think I haven't tried? I've tried for over two decades, and—nothing. I doubt that in one night—"

"Conventional time is of no consequence to us. And the human mind is a marvelous device, dear. But yours is weary, and it needs rest. Let Rosalie help you heal."

Mary's words moved her. What was it about this place that seemed so ... *therapeutic*?

"Meanwhile, Malcolm and I shall do some poking about, and see what we can find out about Max Sheppard."

"I can't let you do that. He's too dangerous."

"Oh, he doesn't frighten me. Believe me, he won't know a thing."

"You underestimate him, then."

"No, dear. You underestimate us."

Rachel smiled.

"A mystical time for you. A time to look forward, while remembering the past. A time to bring the past into the future—and, perhaps, the future into the past."

"Malcolm, didn't I ask you to be quiet? You'll frighten her with your puzzles."

"To discover what the past means to you." He gave a merry nod toward the oversize portrait on the wall. "And what better place than Rosalie?"

Admittedly, the old estate, tucked away in the countryside outside the town, would be the last place her father would look for her. If she and Camisha stayed there for a day or two, they could plan what to do next.

"We require one promise of you, Rachel. That you make no changes in your surroundings, no matter how dissatisfying it may seem to you. It's different from the world you're accustomed to, but it's as it should be. And you must leave everything—and everyone—as you found it. You are here only to remember."

Mary's warning amused her. Did she look like she was going to trash the joint?

"I promise."

At last, Lottie showed them each to a room for the evening, and Rachel bade Camisha goodnight. Grateful for the solitude, she changed into the nightgown and robe Lottie had loaned her.

Opening a window, she welcomed the fresh, cool air of the storm. A nervous elation was swept away. She had two sisters—and Max Sheppard had known it all along. He had stolen a part of her life forever.

And as she considered confronting him with it, she understood Camisha's silence for the past twenty years. If he had concealed the truth, he was implicated by it.

She listened to the lulling patter of rain against the windowpanes, holding the only thread to her past.

The fragile newsprint was as soft as a chamois. She saw the headline—*Three girls found living in squalor*—but her gaze was riveted to the evocative photograph, printed larger than the story. It brought tears to her eyes, reminding her of photographs of Appalachian children during the Depression, hopeless, hungry gazes staring out of hollow-cheeked faces.

There were three children, two in filthy undershirts and tattered shorts. The oldest girl held an infant, and a toddler huddled against her. Two dirty faces stared at the camera in dazed fear. Haunting recognition stole over Rachel. Each girl—even the infant—bore the mark of a tiny crescent at the corner of her right eye, exactly like Rachel's scar. Her gaze was pinned on the oldest girl.

It was her.

The story was dated the same month her father had adopted her. She stared at the photograph, trying to conjure a single memory of the two sisters she'd once known. They must've played and laughed together, the make-believe games of girls, creating the memories of childhood.

She touched the locket, pressing the catch so it opened to reveal two perfect faceless hearts, shining silver and cold. She closed the locket and fastened the chain around her neck.

Distracted, she listened. Had someone called her name? A thunderclap told her it must have been the whisper of the wind.

"*Rachel.*"

There it was again. She walked to the window, but she heard only the ominous rumble of thunder rolling over the James River, a somber gray line on the horizon. The aroma of rain and earth and pine and river rose in her senses.

Then, she noticed a faint flash of white in the trees below. She focused on the trees, and there it was again. Someone was down there. Why would anyone be out in this mess? The figure was small, and as indistinct as a morning mist. It floated from behind another tree, as if looking for something, and became clearer—dressed in a nightgown, she realized. A child.

Fury flashed in her at the stupidity of parents who let their children wander the woods in a storm. At that moment, the child raced back toward the house, stopping beneath Rachel's window. She looked up, and Rachel's heart seemed to stop.

Cascades of blonde hair hung dripping around the girl's shoulders, and huge blue eyes blinked at Rachel imploringly. She wore a pale pink satin dress, covered with a mud-stained white apron.

"Rachel, help me! I can't find it anywhere!"

Stunned that she knew her name, Rachel called, "Emily?"

She bobbed her head, folding her arms against her body as if to ward off a chill.

"Stay there. I'll be right down. Don't move!"

She hurried through the house to the back door. She still clutched the newspaper, and she stuffed it inside her nightgown.

Emily—if that was her name—darted away from the window as soon as she saw Rachel, urging her on with a frantic wave of her arm. "Hurry! Papa will be so unhappy if he finds I've slipped out of bed again!"

She disappeared into a thicket of trees, and Rachel's heart pounded as she followed, fear over such a young girl being lost in the woods. The underbrush ripped at her legs, but she raced on uncertainly. Whoever the mysterious child was, she was no ghost. She was a disturbed little girl, and she had taken the trouble to find out who Rachel was. How or why she'd followed her to Rosalie was too much to ponder right now.

"Emily!"

"I'm over here! Hurry, we must find it! Oh, they'll be ruined!"

Emily bolted out of the thicket, and Rachel followed her into the clearing. There she was, running toward the archway—

What was she doing in the ruins? That wasn't a safe place for a child to be, with near-gale force winds blustering about. Rain blinded her as she ran toward the ruins.

"I remember now!" Emily emerged from the shadows and smiled through the rain at her. "I left it next to—"

Lightning split the sky, fleetingly illuminating the impossible. The nebulous billowing of the girl's gown melted away in the storm, along with the child. Rachel squinted against the rain that sluiced down her face, and as the lightning faded, Emily appeared again—but in that split second of brightness, clearly and unmistakably, Rachel had seen the back wall of Rosalie behind Emily's shadowy silhouette. She had looked *through* the child.

As she grappled with what she saw—a ghost who happened to know her name?—the girl's form solidified and hurried through the gaping arched entryway of the home that had stood there almost three centuries before. Spurred into action, Rachel dismissed the trick the lightning had played on her eyes.

"Emily, don't! It's dangerous!"

And Rachel had no choice but to follow her over the threshold of Rosalie. She gasped as a fierce, blistering heat covered her—in the midst of the cool storm, it was as if she were walking into an inferno. Abruptly, a blinding pressure seemed to shatter within her. The storm's violent caterwauling was swallowed up in a deafening silence. The rain was gone. The winds, still. And Rachel was engulfed in darkness.

Chapter Six

Rachel wandered in and out of a most peculiar dream. She was cold, bitterly cold, and damp. The chill surrounded her like a shroud, and when she shivered, someone drew her closer into a seductive warmth. Then she opened her eyes, and the dream grew stranger.

A man stared at her, his heavy-lidded gray gaze as turbulent as the storm that had brought her to him. Long, black lashes fringed his eyes, and the faint lines—as well as his tanned skin—told of years in the sun. His mouth was grim, but the lower lip was wide and full. His nose was strong and straight, and glossy black hair was drawn back from his face and fastened with a black ribbon.

"Oh," she murmured. "You work for them."

He held her in his arms, and raising her head from his solid strength was an effort beyond her power. She stretched out her hand over his broad chest, and the sure beat of his heart somehow comforted her. Her wet, disheveled hair dampened his robe.

"Sorry." She felt drugged; her tongue felt thick. "I've gotten you wet—and I'm heavy."

"Nonsense. You're light as a child," he murmured. His voice was deep and soft, yet crisp with an English accent. His gaze moved over her, then his jaw squared as he closed his eyes, almost whispering, "Who are you?"

"My ... my ... Rachel."

Her head lolled against his chest, and she curled into his warmth. He lowered her into a cloud-like softness; it might well be a cloud, and he a dark-haired angel. And a strong hand brushed her hair away from her face, the way a father would his daughter's.

The cold returned, though, and she shivered. A soothing, satisfying warmth surrounded her, and perhaps the angel was holding her again.

It held the finest elements of a dream—a cloud, a handsome angel, the distant crackle of a fire—as well as the colonial influences that reminded her of those unresolved places in her mind that sought peace in dreams.

When he would've left her, she instinctively curled closer to him, exploring the hardened muscles of his chest, his shoulders. As in any dream, she acted with boldness that she lacked in life, and she let her leg slide between his, one hand moving downward curiously. And then the dream was gone, and she only slept.

Rachel opened her eyes. A fat candle burned a foot away in a shallow brass holder. She lay on her side in a very soft bed. A thin little man in an elegant dressing gown and a peculiar nightcap watched her, his hands folded on his lap.

"Who are you?"

"I am Hastings."

She pushed herself up on one elbow, wincing at the pain that went through her temple. Her head felt heavy—was she sick?

"Er ... I was told you may suffer some discomfort for a day or two."

Rachel groaned, remembering the storm.

"Drink this. It will ease the pain. 'Tis an herb potion, brewed by Hattie."

She frowned into the tiny china bowl. Within it was a pale brown, wretched-smelling concoction. Swallowing it in one miserable gulp, she lay still while the taste passed, trying to remember any of these surroundings.

A large brick fireplace. A slant-front desk. A chest of drawers. None of it was familiar.

"What ... where ... how?" she stammered, bewildered.

"The better question might be when."

"What?"

"1746. In the month of April, to be precise."

"I beg your pardon?"

Perhaps in his sixties, he had alert blue eyes, heavy silver brows, a thin mouth, and a slightly hooked nose. Faint disdain was forged upon his face as if by habit. "You're at Rosalie plantation."

"Oh, of course—Mrs. Chesterfield's home. I agreed to stay there, for a day or two."

"That home, I'm told, will be built sometime after the colonials win their independence. Which won't come to pass for another thirty-five years. Again, so I'm told," he sniffed.

She sat up, the pain eclipsed by impatience. She had just about had her fill of colonial phony baloney. "Mr. Hastings, you don't have to put on a show for me. I understand how the interpreters work."

"Interpreter, madam?"

Her attention was captured by what she wore: a frilly, old-fashioned nightgown and robe. "Where did this come from?"

A flush stained Hastings' cheeks as he looked away. "The fact of the matter is, you were—er, disrobed when you arrived. One of the maids was awakened to dress you."

Her fingers fumbled at her neck, locating the locket, and she threw her legs over the side of the bed. "Where's a telephone?"

"All in the twenty-first century, I'm afraid."

"Oh, please. Just tell Camisha—"

"I regret I don't know who you mean," he said, rising. "It's quite late, but if you feel more comfortable moving about, I'll have a maid find you a frock."

"I want my own clothes."

"Gone, too."

"What the hell is going on?"

He wrung impeccably groomed hands. "Miss Sheppard, I fear your language—"

"You're going to fear a lot more than that if you don't explain this charade. Immediately."

"A Mr. Henderson informed me that you'll stay at Rosalie for ... well, a period of time." He paused, then gave a weary shake of his head. "And that I have no choice but to be responsible for your well-being in this time."

Was this a joke? "Do you work for the foundation?"

"I'm engaged by Lord Windmere, the master of this house."

"Who?"

"Of course, he much prefers to forget the title, and you should, too. I speak of Mr. Grey Trelawney, the father of Emily."

"That does it," she muttered, stomping to the door. "The deal's off. Excuse me, Mr. Hastings, but I'll have to be going back to the real world now. I don't care if an axe murderer's after me."

"Mr. Henderson said—"

A hall loomed before her, long and dark and forbidding, illuminated by a candle placed every ten feet or so. She started down the polished hall with Hastings in stubborn pursuit.

The walls shone golden brown as the candle cast eerie shadows as high as the carved crown moldings. The home was ornately beautiful, but not nearly as old as Mrs. Chesterfield's home. The mahogany torchères—George II, if her knowledge of antiques served her—were beautiful and doubtless expensive, but obvious reproductions. The wood shimmered with rich perfection. At the end of the hall, she noticed some stairs.

"No, miss, I beg of you..."

She hurried down steep, narrow stairs—that went nowhere. She stopped short at a dark, stone-walled passageway, trying to find the trail of the stairs. But the passageway was dark, dank, and wind moaned from somewhere farther down.

"Miss Sheppard!"

Relief flooded her at the sound of Hastings' call. "I'm lost," she yelled, following the sound of his voice through the dark corridors. She almost screamed as he appeared square in front of her.

"The candle went out," he said, and relief wracked her at his matter-of-fact complaint.

Then she saw the stairs, and she took them two at a time, anxious to be out of the spooky house.

"How do you get out of here?"

"Where would you like to go?" He retrieved another candle as they arrived back upstairs.

"Out of here," she said, biting out the syllables.

"Let me summon Lord Windmere, he's in the stables—"

But now she could see the entryway, they were just above it, and she hurried down the eight-feet-wide staircase, yanking at the front door.

The driving rain chilled her, a web of chain lightning slashed the night sky, and the wide, gravel drive better resembled a creek.

"May I get you a wrap?" Hastings inquired dryly.

She slammed the door and whirled on him, slinging water over him as she did. "You may get me a cab."

He blinked, wrinkled his nose but slightly, and wiped his eye with calm dignity. "There are none to be had."

"If I have to search every room of this house, I'll find a telephone."

"I give you leave to search, but there are no—er, telephones. Not in the house, not in the capital, not in the entire colony. Not in this century."

"Mr. Hastings, it benefits neither of us for me to be here."

"On that, Miss Sheppard, we heartily agree."

"So you'll help me get home, first thing in the morning?"

"Would that it were in my power."

Her temper went through the twenty-foot ceiling. "*Fine.*" Bracing herself for the wet blast of the tidewater storm, she yanked open the door and started out.

"Miss Sheppard, I implore you. Williamsburg is two leagues off through a dark thicket, and you'll not find——"

His voice faded as she strode into the blinding storm, blinking to see past the sheets of rain that stung her. The drive was lined with gravel, keeping her from sinking knee-deep in the mire. Two leagues in this stuff? And what the hell was a league, anyhow?

Rachel wasn't one to admit defeat, and not so easily. But no more than two hundred feet from the house, she stopped. Could she endure an entire night with that quirky old fellow and his quirkier ramblings?

She looked back. Lightning split the sky, illuminating the brick mansion. For several seconds, she was transfixed. Rising three stories into the sky, three chimneys were placed at the front and three at the rear of the immense Palladian mansion. An electricity went down her spine.

Rosalie.

It couldn't be!

The rain pelted her in cold, stinging sheets that penetrated her denial. The furniture upstairs were neither antiques nor reproductions. They were contemporary, lavish appointments to a house that bristled with newness, from its gleaming interiors to its stalwart fortress exterior. The man had an archaic way about him that defied explanation, but for the one he'd given her.

Your mind is weary, dear, Mary had said.

Acute delusions, Max had said.

Fear caught her breath in her lungs. Mary had intended to comfort her; Max, to control her.

Yet both of them had struck on the truth. The long hours of work in the last year had been devastating to her physically; the revelations of the night before, devastating spiritually.

And what, then, had it all done to her mentally? Somewhere between last night and now, had she teetered over the edge into madness?

But as she squinted through the blinding rain, captured in her terror, she saw a flicker at one of the second-story windows, and her breath caught at the face indistinctly illuminated by a candle. Blonde hair formed a curly halo around the little girl's face. The familiar sight focused her spiraling thoughts. This was the child who had lured her into the storm in the first place, who had taken her on a wild goose chase, and—

She stared as the flame from the girl's candle touched the drapes. Within moments, fire engulfed the drapery. As she stared in terrified fascination, the words of the gardener that day at the Trelawney home came to her.

Emily died in a fire at Rosalie, back in the middle of the eighteenth century.

Adrenaline shot through her as she raced up the pathway, past a soaked and startled Hastings. "Miss?"

"There's a fire—upstairs—" she gasped out, hurrying up the stairs.

She followed the sound of the little girl's soft cries and flung open the door. The fire raged out of control; ravenous, crackling flames had consumed the drapes and now licked at the walls. Acrid smoke flooded the room. If she didn't stop this fire in another minute, the room would be an inferno.

"Emily!"

The child cowered beside the fireplace, her head bowed in prayer. She scrambled toward her, her eyes wild with fear. "Oh, help! I threw some water, but I missed—"

Rachel grabbed her up and thrust her into the hall. "Go downstairs with Hastings. And don't come back up."

The child scampered away, and Rachel fought her panic, fought the smoke that burned her lungs. *Water.* She needed water. A lot of it.

Grabbing the fireplace poker in both hands, she raised it over her head and smashed it against the window. Driving rain slashed through the broken panes—but it wasn't nearly enough. She swung again, wildly, and more glass crashed. But the smoke stung her eyes and scorched her lungs, and the fire now licked at the curtains surrounding the child's bed.

She stripped off her robe and slammed it against the bed curtains. She gasped for breath against the smoke that poured through the room, despite the gaping window and the steady spray of rain.

Suddenly, a great deluge of water crashed over the bedclothes, drenching the remaining flames, drenching her. She coughed against the water and the smoke, gasping, "Hastings—"

Too relieved to be angry, she raised a grateful gaze to him. But it wasn't Hastings who stood there.

It was a man younger than Hastings by thirty years. Taller by half a foot. Eyes as silver as Hastings' brows. Hair as black as the bitter night. That silver gaze, bright with emotion, moved over her; peculiar how it came to her, as she gasped for oxygen, that she stood in a wet, transparent shift before the stranger. But he was no stranger; she knew this man. She had *dreamed* of this man. A paroxysm of coughing nearly overpowered her, and the man removed his coat and wrapped it about her.

"Papa, I'm sorry." Emily's voice came from somewhere beyond the smoke. Rachel was alone with him, enfolded in the surreal fog with the rain pouring in the window, and her head was swirling.

"I'm in your debt, Miss—"

"Sheppard," she gasped out. If she didn't sit down soon, if she didn't get some fresh air—

As if he'd read her mind, he grabbed her and pulled her into the hallway.

"I'm Grey Trelawney." He stroked the hair of the child who tugged at his leg. "And the little girl whose neck you saved tonight is my disobedient daughter, Emily."

Grey Trelawney? And Emily?

As she stared at the pair, the dizziness overcame her at last, and their faces blurred as the world went black. And once again, she landed softly in the embrace of a dark-haired angel.

Chapter Seven

Rachel gazed into her teacup. The quaint cup, painted with white sweet briar, better resembled a bowl. Tea had been delivered an hour ago.

Her aching lungs reminded her this was no dream. The liveliness of her surroundings proved it was no benign hallucination. But the only other solution terrified her.

Her father had had her abducted—and orchestrated the insane scenes of the night before. After all—where was Camisha?

A tap at the door interrupted her gloomy musings, and the door opened, revealing Hastings. "Might I join you?"

"Yes." As he placed an armful of clothing on the chest at the foot of the bed, she gathered her courage. "How much is he paying you?"

"Paying me? Is my salary of concern to you, Miss Sheppard?"

"How much is he paying you to keep me here?" she snapped. "And *where*, by the way, am I?"

After a long moment, he turned and stared out the window. He wore a simple white wig, tied in a queue with a black bow. His coat and waistcoat were black, his shirt white and modestly ruffled. He clasped his hands behind his back.

"Miss, you are at Rosalie Plantation, in James City County, in the colony of Virginia. Today's date is April 22, 1746."

She threw her legs over the side of the bed and rose.

"I beg of you, not again."

"If you're asking me to buy for a second—"

"Madam, I don't care what you *purchase*." He turned, his expression bland. "Mr. Henderson warned me you might be … ah, fractious. And that I should remind you this place will provide sanctuary. I've been charged with your care, and because I've a duty, I shall do it. But if you doubt, I offer a simple remedy."

She waited silently, stunned. Could it be?

A place that existed long before you were ever born. Long before the events that are buried within your memory took place.

"Lord Windmere requests your attendance in the gardens. The child whose life you saved last night is with him. Speak with Emily. Question her at length about her life, about her father, and learn the truth. Children, Miss Sheppard, do not lie."

He gestured toward the nightstand. "I found … a paper, near the entry where you were found."

"Paper?"

"It appears to be a newspaper from your time. Take care to conceal it, dear. No one must know of your true past."

"Did you read it?"

A long silence passed before he said, "I saw only the title of a story. It is not within my realm of interest. I should also mention that while you are here, you will pose as my kinswoman."

"Kinswoman?"

"A relation. A distant one, I hope," he added, those pale brows arching. "Else there may be unpleasing murmurings for your purpose at Rosalie. Shall I send a maid to attend you?"

"Attend me?"

"To help you dress."

"Don't be silly," she muttered.

"Do you know … er—what goes where?"

She stared ruefully at the array of garments. "Is this all one outfit?"

He gestured to a linen shift. "This goes first. Then this."

"What do I need with a back brace?"

"Rather the opposite, miss. Stays." He went on gesturing at this and that. "Underpetticoats. Two. Then pockets. Fasten them around you with this string. Then this petticoat, then the gown. And stockings and slippers. Are you quite certain you need no assistance?"

She sent him a dry smile. "In the twenty-first century, Mr. Hastings, we dress ourselves."

He turned to go.

"Wait. This gown has a big gaping split down the front."

"Yes. Hence the provision of the petticoats."

She grimaced. "Well, yippee."

"When shall I tell Lord Windmere you'll be down?"

She dismally considered the pile. "Fifteen minutes?"

He gave a dignified half-bow, then inhaled and exhaled slowly. "Well, yippee." And he closed the door when he left.

How could it be?

She moved to the window. The land was rich, green, and pristine; in the distance she saw the woods and a faint ribbon of the river beyond. Near that, row upon row of workers tended plants. But something about the scene was wrong.

Every worker in the field was black. Young children worked alongside older men and women. Each of them wore colonial dress. A white man walked between the rows, peering back and forth. And tucked in the waistband of his trousers was a whip.

The realization struck her, hard. As she sank to the foot of the bed, she knew that what she had seen outside her window was no colonial show. It was, firsthand, slavery. And it was all true.

A mystical time for you ... a time to look forward, while remembering the past ... to find out what the past means to you.

And what better place than Rosalie?

As questions tumbled through her mind, she found a pitcher of water, poured it into the basin, and washed. She then dressed—no small task—but skipped the ghastly stays.

When she left her room, she noticed the mansion had lost its eerie shadows, and the faintly sweet aroma of beeswax permeated the hall, along with off-key humming. A maid polished candlesticks. "Is this the way to the gardens, Miss..."

"I'm Bess, mum. Go down the stairs, then make a left and a right and another quick right and you'll find it straightaway."

As she observed the rich furnishings of the home, the house staff at work, she knew Grey must be a wealthy planter. The floors gleamed, the tastefully exotic rugs in the main entryway were impeccable, and fresh flowers splashed color throughout the hall leading to the gardens.

A raw excitement surged through her. It was as if she'd stepped into a storybook land—a world full of quaint people, where she could become anyone she chose. Here, no Kingsley existed, no Max Sheppard, only a woman without a past, on a sabbatical in time.

The back door stood open to let in the sunshine. Never had she smelled such pristine air; it was as if a layer of grime had been removed, and the land bristled with freshness. She heard noisy laughter and peeked outside.

Grey Trelawney's smoky blue brocaded waistcoat had been slung over a chair. Remaining was a linen shirt, blue breeches, pale blue stockings embroidered with navy and silver, and black shoes. He was on all fours in the lush green grass.

Emily perched on his back in a yellow gown, gleefully kicking tiny slippered feet against his thighs as she flicked a fistful of weeds against one broad shoulder. He neighed in protest against her mistreatment.

"Go, Princess, go!" Emily sang out her command.

He exploded in distinctly unequine laughter. "*Princess??* At least provide a fitting name for this faithful steed."

"All right, all right. Go, Bag of Bones, go!"

He twisted around, capturing his laughing daughter in his arms as he collapsed in the thick, blue-green grass.

Rachel laughed softly, shocked that the sight pleased her. She knew neither the man nor the child. Yet their childish play held simple joy.

Her laughter went undetected as she soaked up the almost painful view of the love they shared. Her fingers tightened on the door frame, anxiety gnawing at her as she drew a deep breath. Had she ever seen a man so in love with his child? *Yes.*

"Bag of Bones indeed," he scoffed, hugging Emily close. "I shall beat you, child."

"Oh, Papa, you wouldn't! I'm a big girl. You haven't beaten me in the longest time. Since I was—well, a *babe.*"

"I haven't needed to. You've grown into an angel. And when I did, it was out of my great love for you. Else you'd become one of those indolent little simpletons famous in the county."

Rachel gripped the wood. Something flashed through her mind, disorienting and frightening and strange.

And disturbingly familiar.

Blood pounded in her ears, and a faint thump echoed through her head, along with a memory. It was the sound of a man's voice, and a fleeting glimpse of his face.

I love you, sweetheart. And I spanked you because I want you to grow up to be a decent young woman.

The words were distinct, as if it were a . . .

A lesson she'd learned at her father's knee.

But his face was gone before she could capture his features, and she mourned the loss. Could it be—the fragment of a time with her own forgotten father? Had the voice been that of a man who would cut his daughter's face for complaining about her hunger? No, his words were meant to soothe her bruised feelings.

She relished the near-memory, trying to grasp more. Nearby, a morning picnic had been arranged on a blanket. Had she ever played so, with her family?

"Are you certain, poppet?"

"Quite. Take them off, Papa. Ponies never wear shoes."

"I, my dear, am no pony. I am a stallion, full-grown. A—"

He stopped, noticing Rachel. His silver stare jolted through her, as if seeking something he knew intimately. What was it about this man, whose casual glance seemed to stroke the surface of her skin?

She'd never given much thought to people of the past. When she did, they were the flat, Puritanical icons of history books, people whose chief interests were wars and philosophy.

But Grey Trelawney radiated blatant sexuality. From his tousled black hair to his muscular chest, trim hips, and long, powerful thighs, he seemed a virile, intelligent animal, poised to strike.

His eyes expectantly met hers. Then he came to his feet, swinging Emily onto his shoulders.

The child giggled, fluttering her fingertips into his hair and loosening the black ribbon there. "Why don't you wear wigs, like other gentlemen?"

"Because they itch, dearest. Why don't you wear wigs, like other children?"

"Because my hair is so very lovely."

"Ah, that it is." He caught her in an impulsive hug, lowering her to the ground.

A half-grin lit his face as his gaze rested on Rachel, and his voice was deep and soft. "Good morning. Will you join us?"

Emily gestured expansively. "There's bacon. There's scones. There's apple butter," she finished, with enamored emphasis.

She'd rumpled her father's softly curling black hair. His dark cheeks were flushed with excitement above a white shirt with lacy ruffles at the throat and wrists, and loose, flowing sleeves that played over the hard muscles beneath. He rested his hands on lean hips, smiling at his daughter. "Earlier, you had no appetite."

"Oh, I'm quite hungry now. Do come and eat with us—oh, dear. Whoever are you?"

"My name is Rachel Sheppard." She smiled.

The child executed a dainty curtsy. "I am Emily Trelawney. It is my great pleasure to make your acquaintance, mistress."

He drew near, and as his hand closed around hers, she tilted her head up. He was tall, his shoulders broad, and his dark hair gleamed in the morning sun. Pale gray eyes were startling against the dark complexion, and faint lines crinkled the corners of his eyes.

"How do you fare this morning?"

His words were almost seductive, and his hand lingered on hers. His involvement in Rosalie was etched in his toughened palm, and it intrigued her; no idle hands here. His deep voice made the query almost seductive—as if he'd made love to her the night before. Or considered doing so now.

"What?"

"Last night, the smoke overcame you. I trust you're better?"

"Oh! Yes." She withdrew her hand from his—and as quickly missed his touch.

"Come and share the meal." In a quick gesture that felt oddly intimate to watch, he neatly tied his hair in the ribbon. "There are things I would discuss."

She joined Emily on the blanket, and he sank to the ground across from them. He rested on one elbow, stretching out his long legs as he withdrew another plate from the basket.

"You must have lots of Hattie's apple butter." Emily's small hands carefully cupped the china bowl, setting it beside Rachel's plate. "It will make you so happy."

She smiled, accepting the child's offering.

"My daughter finds delight in sweets." A smile played about his lips as he watched Emily. "Shall we pray, Emily?"

"Let me, Papa." Emily squinted, bobbed her head, and folded her hands in her lap. She then peered at Rachel with one eye. "You're peeking."

Rachel fought down laughter and bowed her head.

"Thank you, God, for bringing Papa home safe. And thank you for the apple butter and the pretty lady. Amen."

Grey caught Rachel's eye. "Apple butter and pretty ladies. Blessings indeed."

What about Emily's mother? Neither of them noted her absence; indeed, despite Rosalie's sumptuous décor, it held the Spartan grace of a womanless household. The fragrance of the cut flowers in the hallway had been placed there by a servant, not a helpmate. How had the child's mother died—and how long ago?

"Hastings tells me you're a kinswoman of his, visiting the colony."

She sipped her tea, nodding.

"You're not from England?"

"No."

"And are you—do you have a husband?"

"No."

The corners of his mouth flickered. Uninterested in the food on his plate, he thoughtfully brushed a long, brown finger against his lips as he lounged lazily, watching her. The sudden memory of her prescient, almost erotic, dream brought a blush to her cheeks.

"Can I begin to try to tell you how grateful I am to you?"

"For what?"

Bemusement settled in his eyes. "For preserving my only joy in life."

The depth of his love for his daughter moved Rachel.

"Papa, if she hadn't been there, I wouldn't have peeked—"

Emily went silent, wariness stealing over her features, a spoonful of apple butter hovering halfway to her mouth as she saw her father's dismay. "Young lady, you had no business with a lighted candle in your bedchamber."

Her round, blue eyes moved from her father to Rachel. She silently popped the spoon into her mouth, still eyeing them suspiciously. Then she swallowed. "The storm frightened me."

He softened, tracing a dark finger down the blonde curls. "I've told you before, darling. A host of angels are sent down through the tempest, just to guard your bed. If you listen very closely, you'll hear their great wings beating in the thunder."

Fascinated at his softly murmured fable, she saw the quiet adoration in his eyes. All at once, the memory of the meal she'd shared with Lottie came to her.

Both Grey and Emily died in the fire that destroyed Rosalie.

She stared at the winsome child, her unruly curls ruffled from playing with her father, her eyes bright with expectation over her scolding, or perhaps the memory of the storm. A dab of apple butter smudged her pink bow of a mouth. Rachel's heart unexpectedly swelled at the irresistible sight: a child, too busy with the things of life to marvel over the fleeting fragility of it. And blessedly unaware that her life was supposed to have ended the night before.

A charged excitement melded with humility; she'd put out the fire that was to have killed this child—and this man. She'd never known this feeling—of making a lasting difference. How would the world be changed, with Emily and Grey a part of it?

"Yes, I heard the angels' wings. But I didn't know if the angels could find you. The storms only frighten me when you're at sea."

With a fond smile, he brushed a knuckle against Emily's delicate chin. "You've no need to fear, poppet. Angels even watch over my ship."

How did the man find time to sail, running a plantation? Then again, how else could people get around in the eighteenth century? The James River was in their backyard, and they weren't far from the Chesapeake Bay. And, no doubt he used the ship to sell his tobacco.

"Miss Sheppard, my home is yours, as long as you wish it." His eyes, still warm with love for his daughter, met Rachel's. "I owe a debt to you that I can never repay. But if you'll stay with my daughter and me, I hope you'll find some measure of happiness."

How could such an innocent invitation hold such sensual undercurrents? Emily scrambled down from her chair suddenly, darting to throw her arms around her father's neck. "Oh, I hope she'll stay forever, Papa. She's lovely!"

He laughed and hauled her across his lap. "Perhaps she shall, dearest. Now it's our task to make sure that if she leaves us, she'll take only happy memories with her."

The child's laughter played in her head as she watched them—wishing with all her heart that she could find even one memory as sweet as those Grey had created for Emily in this hour.

Chapter Eight

"Please, Hastings," Emily cajoled.

"No."

"But—"

"No. It's a barbarous sport."

"The stable boys speak of them—"

His disapproving gaze settled on her. "I suspect they do."

"Rachel," Emily implored.

With some effort, Rachel pulled her attention away from the colorful crowd that milled about Duke of Gloucester Street. "What, dear?"

"I want to see the cockfights."

"Cockfights?"

"Oh, yes!" Emily cast a peevish glance in Hastings' direction. "My father would let me."

"More's the pity," Hastings remarked.

"Look, Emily." She pointed to a woman nearby who'd set up a cart. "That lady's selling little—pastries, or something."

She peered at the cart. "It's ginger cakes. Why don't we buy some and take them to the cockfights?"

Hastings raised his eyebrows at her. *Your turn.*

"Emily, do you have any idea what happens at cockfights?"

"No. Do you?"

She looked at Hastings. "Perhaps the best cure would be to show her."

"Even were I so dubiously inspired, we're due to meet the master. The auctions should be concluded by now."

"Auctions?"

"Yes. Just across the square."

"What are all these people doing here?" she asked, noticing the tents set up on Market Square.

"It's Publick Times, dear. The taverns have men sleeping three to a bed, and many plantations are housing guests as well. The courts convene, and burgesses from throughout the colony descend on the capital, bringing all manner of peddler, merchant, and trader to sell their wares."

They crossed the square, passing farmers haggling over the price of a pig or a sheep, and merchants hawking everything from fresh fish to hats straight from Paris. "Those might be from Papa's ship," Emily said, pointing at the frilly bonnets.

Hastings was busy scanning the crowd. "No. A merchant ship from Europe would have brought those. Your father comes from the West Indies, then travels to England with tobacco."

Now his travels made sense; he was simply selling his tobacco.

"Ah, there he is now."

She stopped short, her lips parting in dismay. Half a dozen men and women were being led away. In chains. The midday sun shone down on their black faces, illuminating hopelessness, fear, and desperation. One woman hesitated, her eyes wide with fright as they darted about the square. A sheen of sweat covered her face, and she looked ill. Chained in pairs, they shuffled along in the muddy street.

"Go on, now!" snarled a tall, thin man. He snapped a whip, and the woman cried out as she fell to her knees.

Revulsion roiled within her as she witnessed a transaction whose final accounting would be costly. She grabbed Emily, burying the child's face against her breast.

Sudden hope rose when she saw Grey. He caught the man's wrist. "Your cruelty is needless, Mr. Black."

The man sneered at him. "And what business is it of yours?"

"Their value to you drops with each stroke of the whip." She thought she heard irony in his voice.

"Mind your own affairs, Trelawney."

The two men faced each other for a charged moment, and Grey flung the man away from him in disgust. The woman who'd fallen staggered to her feet and stumbled after them.

"Two more were lost," Grey said quietly to Hastings. His mouth was set in grim lines, his eyes cool in the noon heat.

"Well. The nature of the trade, I suppose."

"Can't you stop him?" she asked.

"No. He's their overseer."

"But—"

He pinned her with a silencing glance. "'Tis not my business to *stop* the selling of bondsmen."

As he swept his daughter into his arms, abruptly dismissing the incident, she was given pause. He turned a blind eye to the slave-trading; yet something stopped her from condemning him. In her own world, did she stop to correct each injustice she witnessed? In her own world, injustices were given polite names that made their dismissal as easy as Grey's.

And why did she now justify his behavior? She'd seen Camisha suffer a similarly callous treatment more than once, most notably by Rachel's father. But in the end, this man's conscience was no business of hers. Even if it were, could she begin to arouse it?

Emily was laughing with Grey, bringing Rachel out of her reverie. "But the stable boys say they're such fun!"

"Stable boys are filthy ragamuffins amused by the ungodly. I have in mind a much loftier sport."

"Tell me it isn't chasing a pig with a soaped tail," Hastings remarked.

"Would you care to see the pig-chases, Miss Sheppard?"

She smiled at the mischievous gleam in Grey's eyes.

"Oh, Papa, look! It's my grandfather!"

His gaze went cold as it flicked reflexively toward the house on the corner. "No, Emily."

Ignoring him, she darted into the street, followed by Grey. Rachel asked Hastings, "Whose house is that?"

"Peyton Randolph's. He's the King's attorney. An ironic liaison for the Trelawney men, considering that Mr. Randolph works with the elder Mr. Trelawney, and counts Lord Windmere as a close friend. Yet the Trelawney men never speak to one another. The man with Mr. Trelawney now is Mr. Randolph's brother, John."

"Why did Grey react that way?"

Grey caught Emily, steering her back toward Market Square. "He despises Thomas Trelawney."

"Why?"

"That, I'm afraid, you'll have to ask him."

Her gaze slid to the two men standing under the elm tree in front of the home. Both wore the signs of wealthy men: powdered wigs, elegant suits, and a dignified bearing. Both stared after Grey with unrevealed emotions. The younger man— he couldn't be older than twenty-five—glanced at his companion, whom she recognized. Though Thomas Trelawney was younger than the man who'd sneered down on Lottie Chesterfield's dining table, he was unmistakably the same man. Grey strikingly resembled him.

Grey and Emily returned, and he knelt before her, his eyes blazing. "Don't *ever* do such a thing again. You could've been trampled by a horse."

"But Papa, his birthday is soon. And he's my—"

"Who's been spreading such lies?"

She looked at her slippered toes, peeking from beneath her yellow gown. "Just one of the servants."

"And do you believe a...scullery maid over your father?"

"But why do we have the same name?"

He exhaled slowly, then touched his daughter's chin. "How would you like to see the horse races?"

All was forgiven. "Oh, yes!"

As they walked to the carriage, Rachel glanced at the Randolph home. Thomas's gaze grimly followed his son. Horses clopped along the busy street, throwing clods of drying mud;

peddlers hawked their wares; nearby, a man was claiming he'd been cheated; the gay noise added to the festivity of the morning. Yet in the gray eyes that remained locked on the pair beside her, she saw the man's grieving frustration. Grey's irrational behavior troubled her; what right had he to deny his daughter a relationship with her grandfather, a man who clearly yearned to love her?

She climbed into the carriage after Emily, settling herself across from Grey. As Emily bounced upon the seat and played with the shade of the window, Rachel saw him watching his daughter. Now, he seemed older, his face clouded by a storm of emotions. Though it wasn't easy to discern the tumultuous mixture of passions stamped on his face, she understood one indisputable truth: Grey may find some grim satisfaction in denying his daughter a knowledge of her grandfather, but he found no joy in it.

The racetrack lay on a sprawling meadow outside Williamsburg. Men in wigs and silk brocaded coats and waistcoats milled about the circular track, accompanied by ladies in rustling silk taffeta and frilly hats. Their usual parasols were unnecessary, since their hats seemed at least as large as a parasol. Grooms tended the magnificent horses whose coats shone in the perfect afternoon. Even the horses exuded an elegance.

"Perhaps Miss Sheppard and I should remain in the carriage."

"Don't be a dolt, Hastings." He handed Emily and Rachel down from the carriage.

"My lord, the young lady is unescorted," Hastings pressed.

He gave an impatient frown. "So she is."

Exchanging a glance with her, Hastings went on, "So it must be explained that her chaperon is—er, indisposed. And replacing her is a task we consider to be of great immediacy."

A slow smile went over Grey's face. "Hastings, you've a hidden talent for rising to the occasion when it comes to lies." He extended his arm. "I'm afraid you'll have to accept my escort, Miss Sheppard. Else I'll never have any rest from the host of rakes here."

She smiled. "Are none of them gentlemen?"

Amusement played about his generous mouth, reminding her that a gentleman in 1746 need not be a *gentleman*. "All are. The finest in the colony. But that shouldn't stop them."

He pressed her fingers with a warm, fleeting caress before placing it on his arm. Unnerved by the commonplace touch—perhaps an unseemly one, in this era—she felt the raw strength of him in the callused palm and in the solid, muscular arm. She felt the gentleness of him in the delicate reassurance of his touch. And she felt, beyond it all, the depth of passion in him, in the gaze that moved over her as he rested his hand over hers a moment too long.

Then, as if she'd imagined it all, he turned and escorted her after his daughter, who'd easily found her place in the crowd. Hastings followed, and they arrived to find Emily entertaining an elderly man who watched her in animated pleasure.

"Colonel Byrd," Grey said as they approached the man. "I see Emily's handily employed in boring you senseless."

The other man spoke in soft, cultured tones. "Grey, your daughter is precocious and beautiful, but never boring. And I see you've brought a full-grown charmer as comely as Emily."

"Miss Rachel Sheppard," Grey began, his hand brushing hers with an odd intimacy, "may I present to you the honorable Colonel William Byrd of Westover."

The man gave a dignified bow over her hand as his familiar name darted through her mind, searching for a home. In another second it was found—on a billiard table, in an inventive position.

"Does the heat vex you, too, my dear?" Byrd asked. "Your handsome complexion seems flushed."

She swallowed. "Oh. Well. No, I'm—" The picture of this elegant gentleman, wig askew as he found his pleasure on a pool table, was almost too much. She fought the wild laughter yearning for release, and she caught Hastings' eye. His apprehensive blue gaze, focused on her as if waiting for a bomb to explode, made it unbearable. "I'm—"

The battle was lost. *Darn that Camisha.*

Byrd cast a smiling glance in the direction of Grey, who stared at her with expectant, bemused humor. Her laughter bubbled over into a helpless gale of giggles.

Byrd laughed. "I've been admired for my wit, but never with so little effort."

She managed to contain her fit of giggles, and she shook her head. "I'm sorry, Mr. Byrd. It's a great pleasure to meet you."

"Evidently." Byrd sent Grey a smile of approval.

Her unexpected delight at meeting Byrd gave her an equally surprising melancholy.

What Camisha would give to be in her shoes right now!

The thought of Camisha missing this unique slice of history dampened her enjoyment of the afternoon. She'd be able to appreciate this minute more than Rachel ever could.

"Is Traveller racing today?" Grey asked.

"Racing may be a poor choice of word. I lost twenty shillings yesterday."

"To whom?"

"Donovan Stuart's Selena."

Grey chuckled. "Dear God, has the rogue named a horse for Selina Eggleston?"

"At first I thought he'd fallen drunk and entered his mistress in the race. Oh, dear. Hello, Donovan."

The man materialized out of nowhere; strange, considering his size. Unlike the other men, he wore a frilly white blouse, butternut trousers, and shiny black boots. A riding crop was thrust into one boot, and his blue eyes were lively with energy.

"Mr. Byrd, you wound me. I honored the lady for her more noble traits. A sleek, playful thing, and a pleasure to—"

"Lord Dunraven," Grey interrupted, "may I present to you Miss Rachel Sheppard? Miss Sheppard, this is Donovan Stuart, the marquis of Dunraven."

What a bunch of names to keep up with! Donovan turned, resting a startled blue gaze on her. Sun-streaked blond hair was tied in a queue. "My humblest apologies. I had no idea I was in the presence of such a beautiful young lady."

"Remove the thought from your lecherous mind at this moment." Grey's smile glittered with underlying threat.

Donovan bowed over her hand. "I've been struck incapable of thought, Grey. The young lady now holds my power of reason, as well as my heart, in the palm of her dainty hand."

"I see your flirtations have lost nothing in the way of subtlety," Grey said.

"It's a pleasure to meet you, Lord Dunraven."

Then he knelt beside Emily. "Did you bring me a present from Philadelphia?" she asked, her eyes wide with delight.

He smiled and withdrew a pink ribbon from his pocket, placing it in her greedy hands. "Will you grow up quickly, darling, so I might have the most beautiful bride in the colony?"

"I shall have to discuss it with my papa first." Emily gravely patted his cheek.

Donovan lay a hand over his heart. "Then all is lost."

Grey smirked. "Is there no female safe from you?"

Smiling, Donovan rose. "Mr. Byrd, bets are being taken. Shall you persist in your losing streak, or bet on Selina?"

"My faculties may be dwindling, but I suspect I've better judgment than your animal's poor namesake."

Donovan winced, then turned to her. "And you, dear lady? Will you offer a shilling in faith for my bay mare?"

She looked up at Grey, finding his gaze expectant on her. She shyly tucked her hand over his arm, smiling. "Will you place a bet on Traveller?"

"Mr. Byrd," he said, brushing his lips against her fingertips, "I believe your luck is about to change."

Grey disappeared long enough to place her bet. When he returned, they joined the boisterous group of men who lined the track, several of whom greeted Grey and Emily. Most of the ladies clustered together to the side, chatting and complaining about the heat. More than a few cast suspicious glances Rachel's way.

"Grey, you've not introduced us to the young lady." The man had what she was coming to recognize as a typical colonial portliness, as well as the ornate dress and wig.

"My apologies. Miss Rachel Sheppard, this impatient wretch is Peyton Randolph, our newly appointed attorney general."

She smiled. "Sworn to uphold justice at the track?"

"Miss Sheppard, you wound me. I'm here to make certain our office-holders don't lose their silk shirts." He glanced around. "Governor Gooch is apparently absent today."

"Resting for the night's festivities, no doubt," another man remarked. He bowed to her. "Carter Burwell, at your service. And this young man beside me is George Wythe."

His companion bowed silently, and her head was spinning. Each of these names meant something, but she couldn't remember what.

"It's a pleasure to meet you. Are you kin to Lord Windmere?"

Wythe lacked the British accent of the other men, but that detail was forgotten as he turned a disapproving glance on Grey.

"Miss Sheppard is a friend of mine," Grey supplied, ready to answer the younger man's subtle challenge. "And we've come to enjoy the horse races, Mr. Wythe. Surely we can set aside our differences and enjoy a lovely Virginia afternoon?"

Wythe's gaze was ironic. "If so, we do it at the expense of enslaved men and women."

"Oh, do shut up, George," Donovan rejoined. "Now, I'll make my farewells. And when I see you again, Mr. Byrd, I'll be the richer man, and you the poorer."

"Just see that you keep that ill-behaved nag away from my Traveller."

Donovan jumped the split rail fence separating them from the mile-long circular track. He loped off toward the half-dozen horses assembled there.

Grey braced one foot on the fence and perched Emily on his knee, and Rachel stood beside them. "Which one is Traveller?"

He pointed toward a shaggy-looking animal with a thick, short neck and long, muscular legs. Having spent many of her childhood summers at Max's ranch in the hill country near Austin, she recognized the power in those legs though she didn't know the strange colonial breed. Certainly, he lacked the sleek, clean lines of the English horse Donovan mounted. Traveller pawed the ground in unenthusiastic nervousness, as if reluctant to race.

"He's shy, isn't he, Papa?"

He laughed. "Traveller? He's afraid of Dunraven and that devil mare of his."

"Why?" Rachel asked.

He nodded toward the track. The starter raised a pistol over his head and fired. The horses lunged forward, plowing up clods of damp earth as they charged.

She was dumbfounded at the ensuing spectacle. The riders prodded their mounts mercilessly—snapping whips and kicking the animals' flanks—and antagonized their rivals with reckless abandon. Some horses were ridden by black jockeys, but most by their owners. She focused in stunned dismay on Donovan Stuart, who leaned precariously out of his saddle and thrust his riding crop into Traveller's churning limbs. Byrd's horse ignored the distraction, and the jockey flicked his crop at Donovan as if he were a noisome insect.

She gasped. "Donovan's cheating."

"Cheating?" Grey said wryly. "He's merely playing. The man courts danger."

"But—"

"Have you never seen a horse race?"

"Not like this one."

Selina and Traveller were neck-in-neck a few hundred feet short of the finish line, and Donovan guided his horse impetuously near the other. A collective gasp arose from the crowd as he attempted to trip the horse. As they stared in horror, Selina lost her footing. She stumbled and went down, unseating her rider, and Rachel cried out as Donovan was thrown to the ground a dozen feet away. He narrowly missed being trampled by another horse.

Selina tried to stand, but her foreleg was broken, and Rachel recoiled at the sight. Grey swiftly placed Emily on the ground. "Oh, Papa, is Lord Dunraven...*dead?*"

"I sincerely hope not, darling."

As he hurried to Donovan, Hastings reached Emily. "Let's return to town, dear. You've had enough diversion for one day."

"No!" she cried, her shimmering blue eyes focused on Donovan. "I must know Lord Dunraven's all right."

Donovan pulled himself off the ground, gasping for breath. He appeared bruised and scratched, but otherwise unhurt.

"There now. He only had the breath knocked from him."

His horse, however, was another matter. Rachel recognized only too well the unnatural angle of Selena's leg, and she knew what the broken foreleg meant. Dusting himself off, Donovan limped toward his horse. As he knelt beside her, she raised her head weakly, and he gently stroked her throat.

Someone handed him a pistol, and he stared at it in distaste. He shook his head, passed the pistol to Grey, and turned away, lacking the courage to do what he knew must be done.

Hastings ignored Emily's complaining as he led her away.

Grey gave Donovan a somber stare, then knelt beside the horse. She knew the respect Virginia gentlemen held for their horses. As he stroked her handsome forelock, she saw his aversion to the unavoidable task, and an odd sensation flashed through her—just as it had that first morning she'd seen him playing with Emily on the lawn at Rosalie. Although she'd heard of the horrible chore of having to euthanize a horse, she'd never witnessed it. How, then, to explain her reaction to Grey's dismay?

He raised his head, glancing at her, and across the distance, their eyes met. His gray gaze held regret and matter-of-fact acceptance that rang painfully familiar in her heart.

Rachel, I'm so sorry. But she's in pain.

The voice in her memory wasn't Grey's—nor that of the man who'd raised her. Yet it was as familiar to her as her own.

Grey waited until Donovan turned away. Then in one smooth motion he placed the pistol against the horse's temple, turned his head, and fired the shot that ended her suffering.

In a moment she remembered the dog she'd grown up with, a collie who'd chased the chickens for sport and slept on her bed at night. She remembered the lovingly trusting gaze the old dog had given her that morning Daddy had taken the dog to the vet. And she waited with anxious expectancy, trying to remember more.

But that was all. She couldn't see the face of the man who'd spoken those grim, reassuring words.

She turned away in dazed confusion, following Hastings and Emily to the carriage. Emotions clamored within her, and she tried to shut them out as Grey arrived at the carriage only a few moments later. His hand closed over hers, and her fingers were cold against the warmth of his.

"She was suffering."

Unexpected tears blurred her eyes over the death of her dog from more than 20 years ago now. She bit her lip against the sudden emotion welling within her. His roughened fingertips brushed her cheek with tender care, filling her with an elemental yearning.

"I know."

At last, he climbed into the carriage and gathered Emily in his arms. He comforted his daughter and assured her that Donovan would be well enough to marry her by the time she grew up, if he could reform by then.

She felt Hastings' gaze on her, but she merely looked out the window as the colonial racetrack faded into the distance.

Who were Malcolm Henderson and Mary van Kirk? And why had they sent her to this time, where only bits of a forgotten past, with no order or thread of connection, were revealed to her?

To find out what the past means to you ... and what better place than Rosalie?

As she turned to glimpse Grey stroking his exhausted daughter's blonde curls, the ache thrummed against her heart.

Chapter Nine

The governor's palace was teeming with a gay throng when the Trelawneys of Rosalie arrived just after sunset. A lively violin concerto flowed out of the great entryway, where Rachel again noticed the somberly impressive array of swords and muskets. Men and women of the gentry crowded the palace from the entryway through the ballroom, where the musicians played. Countless candles and lamps lit the palace.

Footmen, dressed in bright red and blue, held the doors open for the guests who moved from room to room, and Emily smiled at one, who gave the child a grave nod.

"Isn't it wonderful for Governor Gooch to host a ball for us?"

Grey stroked her hair absently, scanning the crowd. "He's a kind man, Em."

Was he looking for Thomas Trelawney? She wondered.

The ballroom was a colorful swirl of silks and satins, linen and broadcloth. Few heads appeared without wigs; Grey's was one of them. His black hair shone in the candles' light, and he glanced at her, catching her admiring eye and smiling.

"Would you care for refreshment?" he asked.

"Yes. Thank you."

"You can watch the dancing in the ballroom, if you like, and we'll join you there."

He and Emily disappeared into another room, and as she waited with Hastings, William Byrd arrived. "Good evening to you, Miss Sheppard. Mr. Hastings. Are you enjoying the festivities?"

She nodded. "We were just about to watch the dancers in the ballroom."

He chuckled and held out his arm, which she accepted. "My dear, there's no joy in watching life. One must partake."

"Would you like to dance?" she asked impulsively, thinking she might be willing to give it a try.

"Oh, heavens no. I'm too old. Once I would've beat you to the asking, but tonight, there are many able men willing to take my place."

"Hastings?" she asked.

He offered her a courtly smile. "Thank you, no. As a matter of fact, I see someone I need to have a word with. If you'll excuse me?"

As she and Byrd watched the smiling dancers, their faces illuminated by candlelight, he spoke. "Grey mentioned you're a kinswoman of Hastings. Is that true?"

His blunt question, asked without malice, startled her. "No. But I doubt you'd believe the truth."

"I may be more gullible than you suspect."

She only smiled.

"I come from the twenty-first century."

Byrd blinked, then cast her an indulgent smile. "You're testing my sense of humor."

"No, it's the truth."

"Oh," he said, as if the thought of a woman from the twenty-first century landing in his drawing room was commonplace. Perhaps he thought it was a new parlor game. "Tell me. In two hundred years, will the mother country continue to treat the colonies as if we were the stupidest of her children?"

Rachel hesitated, suddenly aware that she might be dabbling in a dangerous area. She didn't want to wind up in an eighteenth-century asylum.

"Tell me," he said, still smiling.

"In your grandchildren's lifetime, the colonies will fight and win her independence from England. A war will be fought to erase the idea of elitism—and a new country will be founded on the notion that all men are created equal."

"Elitism," Byrd said with a laugh. "One doesn't need to travel to the future to be told that. You'd hear as much from the drunken rumblings of some of our own. What's your purpose in this time, dear?"

She hesitated. Dear God, the *frivolity* of it. "The company I work for is building a theme park in Virginia, and—"

"Forgive me for interrupting, but precisely what is that?"

"Well, my employer is an entertainment company."

He squinted. "You make a business out of—diversions? Amusements, as it were?"

Only then did Rachel see how strange this livelihood—and the very idea of her *having* a livelihood—might seem to a man like Byrd. She smiled, and out of habit spoke a language he would understand. "We make a very successful business out of it. Kingsley is one of the most powerful corporations in America."

"Twenty-first century Americans must have a great deal of time on their hands. Do the bondsmen do all the work?"

"There are no enslaved men or women in my time. At least, not in America."

He didn't miss the censure in her tone. "No? Who does the physical labor in this park of yours?"

"Paid employees of Kingsley and our partners."

"Does it provide them a good livelihood?"

She was given pause. "They make an honest wage, and they're free to leave whenever they want."

He pondered this. "Making a business of diversions. How intriguing."

"Natives of Virginia are fighting the project very strongly."

"Oh, you would find me a supporter of it. How very delightful, to think play will be as important as work! Do all Americans visit your diversions?"

"Of course."

"Imagine that. Creating entertainment that even the common man can afford."

"Well ... it isn't inexpensive," she admitted. "Some families visit several times a year. Others save years to visit just once."

And for many children, a vacation at a Kingsley park would never be more than a dream. That, he could surmise on his own.

"Do Kingsley's workers enjoy the parks?"

"As employees, they can visit anytime they like."

"So I gather they're paid a wage that wouldn't otherwise allow them to visit."

She went silent.

Byrd smiled at her. "That sounds rather elitist."

She felt vaguely like a sturgeon flopping in Byrd's skillfully maneuvered net.

He clapped his hands together, laughing. "I win!" he exclaimed. "Now then, I'll start the next one. I come from the twelfth century."

"I see," she said, relieved that he'd written the whole thing off as a game. "What is the medicine like in your time?"

A voice spoke from over her shoulder. "Oh, heavens. Is it politics or alchemy we're discussing?"

Donovan Stuart had arrived, looking none the worse for his accident this afternoon.

"Stuart, you owe me a great deal of money."

Donovan grinned at her. "Isn't he without decency? I lost my dear Selina this afternoon, and—"

"And that doubtless grieves you more than the loss of Miss Eggleston."

"The horse was kinder to my purse."

"Would you care to join us in a game of I Come From the Twenty-First Century?" Byrd asked. "It's quite invigorating to the imagination."

"That's a new game you've invented, sir? I had more physical pursuits in mind. Miss Sheppard, would you join me in the next dance? They're lining up now."

"Stuart, you have a dreadful limp. Dancing might prove fatal."

The soft voice held ironic threat. Donovan frowned and turned. "Must you forever be sneaking up on me?"

Grey smiled and held out his hand to Rachel. "Miss Sheppard is my guest, Donovan. Can I trust you with my daughter?"

"Of course, papa. He's my fiancé, you know."

As Grey led Rachel to the floor, he smiled. "Forgive me for taking so long. I didn't mean to leave you defenseless."

"Mr. Byrd entertained me."

"Are you familiar with the reels?"

She shook her head. "No, but I think I can follow along."

The music began, once more a spirited tune. She was able to follow the dance without any trouble, and when she once more met her partner, he murmured, "I thought you didn't know the dance."

Then he was gone again, and Rachel was left to smile breathlessly after him. How *did* she know it?

The dance continued on into the next song, and as Grey grasped her hand and twirled her underneath his arm, he laughed. "At this rate..."

You'll be the finest dancer in the Shenandoah Valley.

Suddenly it was no longer Grey's hand brushing hers, but a man whose voice was beginning to haunt her. It was no candlelit royal governor's mansion, but a bright sunny afternoon, on a soft grassy lawn. Another child's laughter rang in her ears. *Now me, Daddy! Now me!*

Rachel blinked, suddenly jarred from the fleeting memory as someone bumped her, then stopped. "Oh, forgive me," the man said.

Caught up in her memory, she had stopped dancing in the middle of the reel and now gazed at the dancers who, one by one, also stopped.

Dear God, what was happening to her?

Chapter Ten

Rachel felt Grey's hand on hers, gently drawing her away. "Are you all right?"

She couldn't speak. Her breath came in shallow gasps, and he escorted her through the doors at the back of the ballroom. A footman stood near the door, and he stepped aside, bowing.

The stately courtyard of the palace spread out before them, cool and dark and green. Grey led her down a path. They walked in easy companionship toward the canal that ran alongside the gardens. The evening was cool and they were sheltered within the immaculately sculpted boxwoods.

When they arrived at the edge of the water, he gestured to a bench. She sat there, still wrestling with the snippets of memory she'd glimpsed. She closed her eyes, relishing it. A man's face—indistinct, but very much beloved.

"What's wrong?"

His voice was soft, and she looked up at him. In the moonlight, his eyes seemed brighter against his tan face; lines were etched at the corners of his mouth.

She hesitated, her mouth opening and closing indecisively.

He gently covered her hand with his. "Am I not your friend?"

"Yes," she whispered. "You are."

"Then tell me."

She was suddenly aware of the warmth of him next to her, of the soft curve of his lower lip as he frowned, of the uniquely male strength of him. She rose from the bench, and she felt his gaze intent on her.

"My parents died when I was six years old," she began quietly. "I've never been able to remember anything about the time I had with them. Not what they looked like, not what their names were. Nothing."

He waited silently.

"But since—since I've known you, fragments of memories come to me. Watching you with Emily, seeing how you love her—"

She stopped, unable to speak for the unbearable melancholy.

He rose from the bench, reaching her in a moment. Silently he drew her into his arms, and something inside her unraveled. Cupping the nape of her neck, he let his fingers loosely slide into her upswept hair, gently pressing her face to the solid strength of him. Tears fell to the white silk stock at his throat, and he stroked her back. "It's all right."

Swept with sudden awareness of him, she awkwardly pulled away.

"Do you want to go back inside?"

"No—not just yet." She heard the huskiness in her voice. "Can we—walk a while?"

He nodded. They strolled aimlessly, and she inhaled the distinctive aroma of the palace gardens, thinking of Camisha.

"These are boxwoods, aren't they?"

He nodded. "They don't have them where you're from?"

"No."

He chuckled softly, turning to stroll between the shrubs that grew higher than a man's head. The quiet serenade of crickets soothed Rachel. "Nor where I'm from. It's a unique aroma, but one I very much love. The aroma of Williamsburg."

"Where are you from?"

"Liverpool."

"Oh?"

He nodded and she followed him curiously. "What is this place?"

"It's a maze. Tonight, very much like Minotaur's."

"Who?"

"Confined to a labyrinth by Daedalus, and given innocent maidens to feast upon from time to time."

"Where did you learn that?"

"My mother taught me."

"Oh? Is she in Liverpool?"

The complacent pleasure left his face. "She died in my sixteenth year."

"I'm so sorry."

They fell silent, both lost in the past. Hers, forgotten; his, unable to blot from memory.

"Who raised you?" he asked suddenly.

"A man named Max Sheppard."

"Then you must love him very much."

"I owe him a great deal and am grateful for him, but there's only one person in this world I love very much."

Several seconds passed, then he asked, "Who is he?"

"No, it's my best friend. Her name is Camisha. She is as fond of Williamsburg as you are. Her family's from nearby."

"Oh." Then, he pressed, "But you don't love ... this Sheppard man."

After a moment, she said, "I think my parents were murdered. And he may have had something to do with covering it up."

He stopped, his face in shadow. "Covering it up?"

"I have two sisters he never told me about. Camisha found out, and he threatened—"

She choked on the bitter memory, and he again pulled her close. She felt his breath at her temple, and her uncertain fingers closed over the softness of his shirt. Vaguely, she heard what sounded like the boom of a cannon, and she flinched. "What was that?"

He brushed her chin with his fingertips, lifting her face. "Look."

In the night sky, a brilliant display of fireworks exploded. A starburst of orange-red showered over them, followed by blues and deep yellow. She stared, helpless as another memory went spiraling through her. This time, a woman's voice. *Rachel, my love, this is what history is all about. Freedom.*

And as quickly as she'd come, her mother was gone, lost in a forgotten Fourth of July celebration, leaving her with nothing but the knowledge that she would never know her—nor even the memories of her.

She buried her face against his throat, clutching him.

"Dear woman," he whispered. "How I wish I could remove the bitter memories from your heart, and place there only sweet ones instead."

She raised her face. The wild flash of the fire in the sky illuminated the grim lines of his face, and his silver eyes nearly closed as he cupped her face. "Sweet savior of children, no more than a frightened child yourself—darling Rachel—"

His lips brushed hers, hesitatingly, fleetingly. Then returning again, tasting more deeply, drawing back with indecision. At last settling with hungry need over hers, as his fingers stole over her cheek with restless wonder. His hand drifted to her throat, tilting her head back, and he gave a shuddering sigh as her mouth opened under his.

Her hands slid into the soft, dark hair gathered at his neck, effortlessly pushing away the ribbon until his hair slid like gossamer through her fingers. Still he brought her closer, tasting freely of her mouth, his arm supporting her when she grew weak with arousal, his roughened fingertips exploring more than any gentleman dared and not half what he yearned to. She felt the muscled strength of him in the arm that held her, in the hard male body pressed against her, and in the restraint that she knew held his desire in check.

He slowly raised his head, and she saw indecision in the bright emotion reflected in his eyes, now stormy gray.

"I've a swift slap coming," he murmured shakily.

She smiled, her fingers sifting through his hair. "Your hair is softer than any man's ought to be."

A muscle went tight at his jaw. "I want more than anything to unbound your hair, let it fall about your lovely shoulders. To feel it sliding against my skin."

His images aroused her, and she stared up at him. "I suppose my reputation's already ruined?"

"Dismally." Reluctantly, he released her and turned toward the entrance of the maze. "And I think Minotaur had the better end of the bargain."

"How so?"

"I could live a contented life, were I confined here with only this innocent maiden to give me sustenance." He took her hand in easy companionship, and he lifted it to his mouth, pressing his lips against her palm. "Forgive me, Rachel. I had no right—no right even to use your name—"

"Stop," she said, her palm curving around his jaw. "And thank you."

"For what?"

"For putting sweet memories in my heart."

They sat on the steps outside the palace, watching the fireworks, and he tied his hair at his neck once more. Just beyond the edge of the gardens lay a deep, high meadow covered with lush, green grass. Couples strolled there in the cool shadows, and lingered nearby, occasionally stealing a discreet embrace.

"Grey," she said, emboldened by the intimacy they shared, "is Thomas Trelawney your father?"

Abruptly roused, he let a silence stretch between them as he leaned back on a step beside her. "What is it that makes a father?" he asked, surveying the kaleidoscope in the night sky. "And if he is, what then?"

"Why don't you want Emily to know him?"

He gave a mirthless chuckle. "What's to be gained from it?"

"Gained? It isn't as if it's a profit-and-loss arrangement."

"My dear, life is a profit-and-loss arrangement."

"But if he's her grandfather—"

"He's no more grandfather to Emily than he was father to me."

She didn't know what had caused his bitterness, but it was in the past. "You're a grown man," she went on with stubborn certainty. "She's just a child who wants to know her—"

He rose to his full height. "I shall be indebted to you if you'll confine your interest in my life to those things that concern you, Miss Sheppard."

Glancing now toward the doors, he held out a hand to her in cool disinterest, and she put her hand in his, rising.

With the discussion quite ended, she had no other choice than to follow him inside the palace. While the gaiety of the celebration immediately enveloped them once more, she was left to muse on his sudden mood change. And by the time they returned to Rosalie that night, a plan had begun to form in her mind.

Chapter Eleven

Grey stared out a window in Hastings' modest chambers, watching the housemaids stirring cauldrons outside the laundry. Dissatisfied, he poured a glass of sherry, wishing it were rum. But sherry was all Hastings stocked, so sherry it was.

"The child is glad to see you home, my lord."

"Hastings—" he began with a sigh. They'd long ago struck a compromise that satisfied them both; Hastings could my-lord him all he liked in the presence of witnesses. In private, Grey had insisted, they would forget their differences.

"I concede, sir."

"Thank you. And I'm glad to be home. Adrift for a year in a ship full of fetid tars and sick passengers, the memory of Emily grows all the sweeter."

But this afternoon, his interest lay elsewhere.

"Who is she?" Resting his hips on a table, he scrutinized Hastings. The man who ran his plantation wasn't given to lies, so he wondered why he avoided his gaze.

"I've told you, sir. A kinswoman of mine."

"Yes, yes, visiting and all that." He stretched long, lean legs before him. "But what do you know of her?"

He set his ledger aside, and Grey almost smiled. The poor man never had rest. When Grey was gone, his hands were full running the tobacco plantation. When Grey was home, his hands were busy untangling the knots Grey inevitably tied in his life.

"Why, sir?"

Only Hastings could turn such an innocent query into an accusation. He waved a hand distractedly. "Well, she's splendid, of course!"

"Might I remind you that you have a wife?"

His gaze narrowed coldly. "Letitia is no more wife to me than she is mother to Emily. Nor has she been, for these past seven years."

Seven years it had been.

Seven years since he'd first met Thomas Trelawney, the haughty, self-righteous planter who'd deserted Grey's mother on their wedding night; seven years since he'd rejected Grey's claim as his son. Seven years since finding his father and, in that dubious discovery, honoring his mother's dying wish.

The sudden memory gave him pause. On her deathbed, knowing the life that awaited her son, she'd at last whispered a secret she'd guarded for sixteen years. She had been born Lucy Huntington, the daughter of the earl of Windmere. When she fell in love with a young Welshman who'd come to London seeking adventure, her father forbade their marriage. She'd eloped with the young man, who wasn't much older than her own fourteen years. The morning after their hasty wedding, Lucy woke up in their rented room to find a stack of bills, as if she were a harlot, and a note on the nightstand.

I regret any pain I've caused you, Thomas had written. *Your priest can likely annul the marriage. There's enough for passage back to London.*

She'd been robbed on her way to meet the coach, and all that was left was fare to Liverpool, where she wrote her mother in desperation. Even had Lucy been the Catholic that Thomas was, there was little chance of an annulment, for Lucy soon learned she was pregnant.

Her father, disgraced by her elopement, ignored her mother's pleading and refused to accept his prodigal daughter, instead disinheriting her. Lucy was left to raise her son alone.

She found a meager sustenance in Liverpool as a seamstress, and she'd never told Grey any of it until the day she died, forcing his promise to find his father. It took him eight years and countless unexpected twists of fate before he'd kept it.

His beginnings had been humble, but his mother had risen to the fate she'd chosen with a courage uncharacteristic of the gentry he'd known. In retrospection, his admiration of her had deepened and melded with humility. The young, pampered girl, rejected by her wealthy family and deserted by her husband, had found happiness and purpose in her son. The sacrifices she'd made for him were myriad and a matter of course. When she came home weary at night, she taught him everything she knew in their small room by the light of a single tallow candle. She died when she was his age now, and her remarkable, stubborn love for him came to be revealed as the years passed.

As a boy, he could never have understood the feat she'd accomplished. As a man, he slowly and painfully came to appreciate it. In the years that had taken him from boyhood to manhood—and an ultimately bitter journey to find the man she'd spoken of so glowingly—he had learned the things of sailing, had been press-ganged into service with the Royal Navy, and had learned the trade of slavery. At last he'd arrived in Williamsburg to fulfill his mother's wish. Instead of finding the father he'd hoped to be reconciled to, he'd found only rejection.

Enraged and embittered, he had returned to the only home he'd really known as an adult: the sea. He found solace in the grim rhythm of the triangle trade. Liverpool, West Africa, America, Liverpool, West Africa … And he found irony in the realization, when he was ready to build a home, that of all the places he'd visited, he liked Virginia the best.

So he returned to Williamsburg richer than he'd ever desired. Part of his wealth was the vast acreage he had been deeded along the James River for a tobacco plantation.

On a stop in Norfolk, he'd met Godfrey Hastings, who'd accepted his offer to manage the tobacco plantation he planned to establish. By then, his bitterness over Thomas's rejection had been replaced by a more pleasing goal: that of ultimately making Thomas Trelawney suffer as bitterly as his mother had.

He knew well enough by now that one foolish ambition drove his father: acceptance as an equal by his betters. In everything he did, his pompous self-righteousness and arrogance rang true. He liked to think himself one of the gentry. It was an ironic twist of fate that the son he'd rejected would soon have the distinction Thomas had craved his entire life.

And once while in London, he'd impulsively decided to visit his grandmother. Lord Windmere, it seemed, had died five years before, leaving his widow vast holdings along with the title of countess of Windmere. Philippa Huntington then began the search for her daughter and grandson, which ended in the unhappy news that Lucy had died many years before, and the boy had gone to sea.

When her grandson walked in as if by magic one day, she vetted him for several hours, listening to his stories of his upbringing, his mother's recollections of her childhood, and weeping much of the time as she heard her daughter's and grandson's dismal life.

At the end of their interview, she offered him his full inheritance, with the title that followed him as the only surviving heir, with one requirement. Marrying Peyton Randolph's distant cousin was a price he little minded paying, for at last he would fulfill the bitter dream that had driven him since his mother's death.

And so it had been seven years since Grey had agreed to the marriage that his grandmother had lured him into, with the promise of her title. Seven years of hell with the knowledge that he was bound for all time to a monster masquerading as a beautiful woman. The marriage was almost beside the point, and it would be bitterly too late that he would learn the vicious truth about his bride.

All for a title. Small wonder he forbade Hastings' mylording.

Hastings jarred him from the bitter feast of memory.

"Nevertheless you are bound, and thus unable to ply your affections to another lady."

A slow smile curved Grey's mouth.

"No." Hastings recognized the predatory gleam in his master's eye. "*That* you cannot do."

"Pray tell me why not."

"The matter is none of my concern and, begging your forgiveness, none of yours."

"'Tis a simple enough request. She abides at Rosalie—sharing my food, sharing my drink. I only ask why she should not share my bed as well."

Hastings' thin lips pursed, and he exhaled slowly. "The young lady is ... suffering."

"Suffering? Is she ill?"

"Physically she is whole." He hesitated, staring at his ledger. "Sir, have you not noticed her distress at times? The racetrack? The governor's ball?"

Indeed he had. It was the chief reason he'd sought Hastings' counsel, else he'd be concentrating more on the seduction at hand. But he suspected it required a measure of delicacy. What demon lurked within her, flashing through her eyes from time to time? He had not missed the yearning in her—nor had he failed to notice its appearance when she looked into his eyes, like some lost waif.

In truth, he'd felt an odd protectiveness toward her that first night he found her, and the memory pulsed through his body. A full-grown foundling, one arm raised over her face as if to ward off a blow; black hair tumbling over full, lovely breasts in careless abandon; one long, slim leg bent over the other. The sight of her, lying there naked as if it were her first day on this earth, had riveted him to the spot.

Still he had no answer to that puzzle, but with no servants nearby, he'd risen ably to the task before him. As he'd lifted her in his arms, he thought he'd never touched creamier skin—nor colder.

That was the damned annoying part of it; he'd been so worried about her taking the ague that he could scarcely remember what otherwise would've been impossible to forget. And when she opened her eyes and looked at him—with those alluring eyes, not quite green and not quite brown—he had seen a childlike trust in her.

His conscience had pricked him—then, as it did now. It had been years since he'd sought a mistress, but he preferred them to rouse his flesh rather than his dubious principles. A divine penance, her arrival? Perhaps. Despite the faint taste of guilt, a far stronger passion now claimed him. What he would give to have her in his arms again—and warm! Undoubtedly, the willowy, golden-eyed beauty roused his flesh.

God, he must have her—no matter the cost.

Even now, just the memory of her hand roving curiously over his chest, the faint, womanly aroma of her, surged through his senses; there was an uncanny sensuousness to her. And the likely answer to her suffering finally came to him.

"So she pines for a lover."

"No."

"There's something you're not saying, Hastings."

The man rose agitatedly, thrusting knotty hands into his pockets as he grappled with a decision. Grey stared, fascinated; it was more emotion than he'd seen this man display in six years. At last, he exhaled in defeat. "She was mistreated."

"Mistreated?"

"Abused, sir, as a young child."

His explanation disturbed Grey. It was beyond the cold-water disappointment over the ridiculous notion of not having her. The image of Emily came to him, weeping over an inconsequential injustice, not enough apple butter or somesuch—and then, a picture in his imagination of a slender child with riotous black curls and laughing eyes, suffering at the hands of a merciless man.

Rage twisted at him.

"In what way?" he asked, with deceptive calmness.

"Sir?"

"Was she beaten? Or—" He swallowed his disgust. "Or worse?"

"I do not know, sir. But she is here to heal—not suffer further. You will not hurt her."

Grey's breath left him in a frustrated whoosh. *Damn.*

"Precisely how are you related to this young lady?"

"Consider my vigilance that of a disapproving father."

Grey gave an unexpected grin. "You must've been a splendid father. So I warn you: your diligence shall be tested."

Hastings' face was serene once more, as he ignored the taunt. It was Hastings' misfortune—and his own, Grey thought—that he believed him to be joking.

Chapter Twelve

As the days passed, Rachel fell into the comfortable rhythm of Rosalie. It was no life of idleness, as she'd thought at one time in her life. Grey and Hastings were involved in the business of the plantation by the time she and Emily rose. Grey returned to the house for breakfast, then rode out again when it was finished. She began to notice that he carved out several short periods every day of perhaps an hour each with Emily to conduct lessons. After lunch, the pair had more focused sessions in the library. He left the door ajar, and Rachel could hear snippets of knowledge being passed on, from French language lessons to numbers and reading.

He home-schooled the child! She marveled at the realization.

And she grew fond of Emily. Though she'd known few children, she found in the child a quick and precocious wit, a lively appreciation of life, and a canny wisdom. Simply put, she let nothing get by her—not even the rift between her father and grandfather.

Supper was a leisurely affair, the table laden with fare both exotic and familiar. She grew more aware of Grey each day, and she caught him watching her at odd times, when she and Emily were reading in the gardens, or when a seamstress came to fit Rachel for a suitable wardrobe, at his insistence. His wasn't a peaceful scrutiny. She saw a disturbing mixture of emotions in his eyes, but the most discernible of them was resentment.

What crime must Thomas Trelawney have committed to breed such unnatural hatred in his son? In the palace gardens, Grey's tenderness had swiftly transformed into cold indifference about Thomas's interest in Emily.

The strife between father and son had become an obsession for her. She reminded herself to no avail that the turmoil was no business of hers. She tried to capture Grey in any number of unflattering lights, also with little success.

But when she saw his stolen glimpses of her, she saw a deep, brooding passion—one she'd never known in a man. When he spoke to a servant, she noticed only his gentle concern. When he laughed with her over the supper table, with the candlelight playing softly in his black hair, sparkling in his gray eyes, she saw his appreciation of her intelligence and humor. When she glimpsed him in Emily's room at bedtime, saying a prayer with her, she saw a man with a fiercely protective love for his daughter.

One evening at supper, he announced he was going to Norfolk, over Emily's protest.

"I'll only be gone two days."

"But, Papa, can't your men attend the *Swallow*?"

"As her captain, it's my responsibility."

Rachel decided the time was right. So the next morning after breakfast, she put her plan into action. Grey had left before daybreak, and she and Emily breakfasted with Hastings.

"I'd like to take Emily into town. Who can take us?"

"I'm afraid business keeps me here."

Rachel frowned. "What is it you do here, anyway, Hastings?"

"I tend to the plantation when Lord Windmere is afield."

"Oh. Well, you don't have to go with us. We're just going into town."

Hastings considered this. "As you wish. A groom shall accompany you."

94

A half hour later, Emily and Rachel were on their way into Williamsburg. The coachman stopped at the end of Duke of Gloucester Street, not far from the Capitol. A boy hawked buns on the busy street corner. Men in wigs and elegant suits were engrossed in conversation as they made their way to the Capitol. A pair of women emerged from the apothecary, and as they passed Rachel and Emily, Rachel tried to read their speculative glances.

"Good morning to you, Mrs. Edwards," Emily sang sweetly.

"Hello, Emily," the elder woman remarked.

Rachel didn't like the disapproving stare focused on Emily.

"How does your father, Emily?" This came from the younger woman, who was fashionably dressed and keenly interested in the topic.

"He's in Norfolk, Miss Halliday. I've come to town with Miss Sheppard. She's my new friend."

Mrs. Edwards gave Rachel something close to a smile. "Yes. We saw her at the governor's ball."

"Hello," Rachel said, trying to ignore the woman talking *at* her rather than to her.

"Good day," Emily said with a curtsy. As they continued down the street, Rachel felt twin stares of reproach boring into her back. Unable to understand their censure, she instead dismissed it, savoring the morning with Emily.

They stopped at the milliner's, where Emily selected a yellow ribbon. They sampled a meat pie from a corner vendor, and they watched a harpsichord lesson in progress through a shop window. They stopped at the silversmith's, where they saw an array of silver mugs, spoons, and plates.

"Oh, Rachel, look!"

Emily's blue eyes were round with delight as she stared at a delicate locket.

"Let's go have a better look."

When the silversmith told Rachel the price of the locket, she hesitated. Hastings had given her a generous stack of notes before they left, but this covered only half of it.

"'Twas fashioned in London, ma'am," the silversmith said.

Emily's dreamy smile made the decision for Rachel. "It's very beautiful, but I don't have enough for it."

Outside on the steps, she knelt beside the child. "That was a lovely necklace, wasn't it?"

She sighed. "Yes, but Papa says I'm not big enough for ladies' trinkets yet."

"Well, I have a special trinket that's made just for little girls." She pulled the chain around her neck over her head.

"Oh, Rachel. Not your very own locket!"

The silver heart was heavy in her palm. If she herself couldn't find the memory of who had given it to her, perhaps at least Emily would someday treasure this memory.

"You see. Now you can choose pictures of the two people you love best. Or perhaps one of you and one of your father."

"Why don't you have pictures there, Rachel?"

She settled the locket around Emily's neck. "Because I was saving it for you."

Emily was lighthearted as they strolled down the street, and they stopped to buy a silk flower from an old woman peddling on the corner. Rachel selected a deep blue iris, and while she paid the woman, she realized Emily had vanished.

She quickly scanned the street, amazed at what she saw. The child raced along the path to the Trelawney home, her skirts gathered in one hand.

"Emily!" She glanced at the old woman. "Please excuse me."

By the time she reached the corner of the yard, Emily was running back to her, exhilarated. "I did it! I did it!" She ran into Rachel's embrace, giggling as she wrapped her arms around her.

"Did what?" Rachel asked, laughing, absorbing the child's nervous joy.

"I left Grandfather a present! There, on his steps! Nobody stopped me!"

Rachel spotted the forlorn bouquet Emily had hastily fashioned with wildflowers and the yellow silk ribbon. "Oh, darling," she whispered, stroking the child's soft hair.

Emily's head jerked up, her chin trembling uncertainly. "Do you think he'll not fancy them?"

"He'll love them." She kissed her head and gave her the iris. "But we have to make sure he knows who they're from."

She led Emily straight back to the house, ignoring the girl's stunned awe. Retrieving the hastily assembled bouquet, she tied the ribbon into a bow and passed it to Emily. Darting her a quick, mischievous smile, she knocked on the door.

A servant opened the door, a handsome older woman with vivid red hair heavily laced with gray. "Good morning."

"Hello. We're here to see Mr. Trelawney," Rachel said. The child clung closer to her as the woman examined them.

"May I tell him who's calling?" She spoke with a lilting Irish accent, and she beamed at them.

"Certainly. Rachel Sheppard. And Miss Emily Trelawney."

The woman's eyes widened on Emily as if she were a mythical creature she'd heard of. "You're—" Her mouth snapped shut. "Please, come in. I'll announce you."

They were shown into a parlor, and Emily's small, sweaty hand gripped hers. She pried open the child's nervously clinging fingers. "It's all right, honey. There's nothing to be afraid of."

"Papa—Papa said he's an *odor*."

As if on cue, an impatient voice arose in the hallway. "I'm late to court as it is, Aileen. I've no time for callers."

"But, sir—it's—it's the young miss. Miss Emily."

The hall went silent, and perhaps five seconds passed. The sudden brisk tap of heels in the hallway alerted her, and she rose from her chair, suddenly afraid that she might have been wrong, coming here.

But her heart was broken at the expression on Thomas Trelawney's face as he entered, his eyes immediately seeking Emily. A wig concealed his hair, but in him she saw Grey's eyes, his nose, his supple, well-shaped mouth. This man's mouth trembled almost imperceptibly as he gazed at Emily, and his gray eyes glistened.

Pity swelled within Rachel as Emily hesitantly stepped forward and curtsied. She gulped nervously then held out her bouquet. "God's blessings to you on your birthday, Grandfather."

He burst out in choked laughter as he fell to his knees, gathering the child to his breast. "Dear, dear child," he murmured brokenly, tears in his eyes. "I think I've never seen a lovelier flower than you, my darling. Nor a lovelier bouquet."

He dabbed surreptitiously at his eyes as he rose, lifting Emily into his arms. At last he turned to Rachel, grinning broadly. "I apologize, Miss—"

"Rachel Sheppard, sir. I'm a friend of Mr. Hastings, your son's—er, associate."

"I can't tell you how pleased I am to meet you, and under such happy circumstances. I've imagined this moment many times."

"Then I'm glad. Happy birthday, Mr. Trelawney."

He chuckled. "The finest gift I ever could've hoped for."

A young woman appeared behind him, smiling expectantly from Rachel to Emily. She looked about half his age—and was heavy with child.

"Thomas?"

He turned slightly, putting his free arm around her shoulders. "Jennie, this is Rachel Sheppard, a friend of Grey's."

"Good afternoon." They smiled and shook hands.

"And this," he said with a sigh of pleasure, "is Emily."

"Why, Emily, I feel as if I know you. Did you know your grandfather has a portrait of you in our bedchamber?"

"I had heard Grey commissioned a portrait," he explained, "and I asked the artist to paint another for me."

Just an inkling came to her of the misunderstandings that must have passed between this man and his son. Today she saw firsthand evidence of his suffering. Last night, she'd seen Grey's bitter resentment. But how to breach the chasm between them?

"Will you stay a while?" Jennie invited.

"Oh, we couldn't. I know Mr. Trelawney was on his way out—"

"My dear Miss Sheppard, his Royal Highness the King himself couldn't drag me from this house for this hour."

Rachel offered her help in preparing tea, and Jennie accepted. Thomas and Emily remained in the parlor chatting as the women went to the kitchen. Aileen popped her head through the doorway. "Can I help you with anything, dear?"

Jennie shook her head with a smile. "Thank you, Aileen. I can manage."

"Well, just call if you need me."

"I'll do that." She bobbed her head and left the room.

"She seems to dote on you," Rachel said, looking after the woman.

"She was my nurse when I was a child, and she loves me like the best of mothers."

"I can imagine she'll be a comfort to you in the coming weeks."

"Yes, I'm very happy she's here." Then, without preamble, she asked, "How long have you known Grey?"

"Not long. I'm visiting for ... for a brief time."

"Well, I must thank you for what you've done today. You've taken quite a risk, bringing Emily here. But you've made my husband a happy man."

"What do you mean, taken a risk?"

Jennie wiped her hands on her apron. "Thomas is happy indeed. But Grey may well kill you."

"Why does he hate his father so?"

"In a word?" Jennie gave a wry smile. "Thomas deserted Grey's mother after their marriage."

"But that must have been long ago."

"Perhaps Grey is the only one who knows the entire story. I know only Thomas's side. He was fifteen when he fell in love with Lucy Huntington, Grey's mother. He was of a fine Welsh family, but not the kind of husband a peer of the realm would choose for his daughter. When Lord Windmere—Grey's grandfather—forbade his daughter from accepting Thomas's courtship, she eloped with him. Her father disowned her. The next morning, Thomas was remorseful over how he'd destroyed her life. And he left her.

"By Thomas's calculations, Grey would've been twenty-four when he arrived here, claiming to be Thomas's son. Unfortunately, he sent him on his way. So much time had passed, and he'd never considered that their brief union might have produced a child. But anyone can see the resemblance between them. By the time he found the tavern where Grey had been staying during his visit, he was gone. He had no idea where to find him, and he later learned Grey had returned to sea.

"Two years later, Grey returned with Emily. Since then, he's refused Thomas's attempts to make amends, clinging to his hatred. Although we might say time heals all wounds, in his case he'd grown even more bitter. He was a deeply unhappy man when he returned to Williamsburg—I think for reasons that had nothing to do with Thomas. But keeping Thomas away from Emily seems to be Grey's chief joy."

An uncomfortable awareness settled over Rachel as she realized the awful magnitude of what she'd done.

"But now you came and changed all that," Jennie said, as if reading her mind. Then, she grew uneasy, and she avoided meeting her eyes. "And I can't tell you how glad I am that you're at Rosalie. Emily needs a woman's influence, and it's certain she's not going to get that from her—"

The door burst open, and Thomas had to duck low to enter. Emily rode majestically on his shoulders. Her wildflowers had been fashioned into a daisy-chain crown, with the ribbon threaded through them.

"Look, Rachel, I'm a princess."

He approached the table, and Emily regally held out her hand. "You may kiss my ring."

Rachel dropped a kiss on the small knuckles, loving this child. They had tea in the parlor, and a few minutes later a loud knock at the door interrupted them. The maid peeked into the room. "Lord Dunraven is here to see you, sir."

"Tell him—"

"Oh, stop it, Thomas," Donovan interrupted, barging into the room. "Gooch is ready to call an election for a vacant seat—"

He stopped short, peering blankly from Rachel to Emily.

"Oh, Grandfather, it's Lord Dunraven," Emily chirped, scrambling off Thomas's lap and into Donovan's arms.

"What a marvelous surprise, Emily. And Miss Sheppard. You're the last two I would've ever counted on to be holding up the King's business."

"I regret it, but duty calls me away," Thomas said, and Emily immediately protested. "Perhaps you can return tomorrow."

Rachel nodded. "Perhaps."

"And we'll bring Papa soon, I promise."

"I'll count the hours till then."

"May I escort you home?" Donovan asked.

"Aren't you tied up with the King's business?" Rachel smiled.

"Oh, heavens no," he said as they strolled out into the yard. "I'm merely a poor ill-reputed lawyer, charged as an errand boy to fetch the occasional errant burgess."

Donovan traveled back to Rosalie with them, and Emily fell asleep against the handsome lawyer. He smiled at Rachel. "I'm afraid I can't resist asking. Does Grey know where you spent the morning?"

She gave a slow shake of her head.

"Ah. I thought not."

"How did you know the state of affairs between Grey and Thomas?"

"I live in Williamsburg," he replied, and she remembered the gaping stare of the maid who'd answered Thomas's door.

"Oh, dear."

"Oh, yes."

"Jennie thinks he's going to kill me."

Donovan laughed, stroking Emily's tousled curls. "That, my dear, is a matter of course. The only questions are when and how."

Chapter Thirteen

Rachel had just put Emily to bed the next night when Grey returned. Just outside her room, she caught him staring at her from the end of the hall, and her heart swelled. His damp hair gleamed in the candlelight; he was clean-shaven. But he looked careworn.

A somber smile moved over her face as she approached him. "You look extremely clean for a man who's spent the day traveling."

The lines around his mouth seemed deeper; the shadows in his eyes, darker. "I stopped in town for a bath. The *Swallow*—" he shook his head. "A messy business, mucking out a snow after such a journey. It was harsher than most."

"I'm sorry."

His gaze moved over her with restrained yearning. "I—I apologize for my rudeness with you the night of the governor's ball. I was ... abrupt, without cause. I ask your forgiveness."

She hesitated, trying to find the words to confess what she'd done. But he lifted a hand to brush a curling tendril of dark hair away from her temple. "You have no way of knowing all that's passed between that man and me."

His impulsive, oddly intimate caress moved her. "Grey, if you would just give him the chance—"

He brushed his thumb over her lips, stilling them. Then, startled at the touch, he stopped, his silver eyes playing over her. "Is Emily asleep?"

Say yes! For God's sake, at least save yourself till the morning.

"I don't think so. I just tucked her in."

"All right. I'll look in on her first. Perhaps in the morning we'll go for a ride."

"Grey ..."

"Yes?"

After a moment, she shook her head. "Good night."

Then she was inside her room and he was gone, leaving her to her dread. But she was right, she reminded herself. It was best for everyone, Grey included. As she slipped out of her robe and into the cool sheets, she repeated it again.

As the minutes passed, she slowly relaxed. She had done the right thing, she was sure of it. Both Emily and Thomas were happy now.

Her door abruptly swung open, and dread returned as he entered. Fierce anger flashed in his eyes, in the unforgiving set of his jaw, in his leashed strength as he quietly closed the door behind him.

"*Why?*" His voice shook with rage.

"Grey—"

"Why?" he rasped. "What would possess you to commit such a crime?"

She was silent.

He laughed sardonically. "Did you think she'd not mention it to me? That she could conceal what she believes to be the greatest joy of her life?"

"Why would you consider her greatest joy a crime?"

He moved to the window, bracing his hands against the frame as he stared out into the night. "You don't know the first thing about it."

"I know more than you think."

"True enough," he snapped, whirling abruptly. "You've consorted with the scoundrel."

"Consorted? I'm on your side!"

"I'll not have Emily hurt," he whispered. "And with that man in her life, pain is inevitable."

"For her, or for you?"

Resentment flashed in his eyes as he turned away from her. He sighed abruptly, and she saw the weary slump of his shoulders.

"He regrets the pain he caused you. He didn't know—"

"Didn't know? I informed him in rather plain terms."

"By the time he considered that you might be telling the truth, you were gone."

"More of his lies. Spoken to convince the foolish of his spotless character, to further his own political ambitions."

"Neither Jennie nor I can vote."

"He desired something in Jennie that had nothing to do with politics. Something that his money could buy."

"Grey, aren't you tired? It's so much wasted energy, wasted life. All spent creating cause to hate a man who loves you."

He swung around, and his raw, frightened pain pierced her. He grabbed her arms, shaking her with scarcely constrained rage. "How can you say such a thing? You know *nothing* about him."

"Nothin', you hear me? You didn't see nothin', you don't know nothin', and you damn sure better not say nothin'."

Beefy hands clutched at her shoulders, shaking her. And suddenly it was no longer Grey's face that she saw, nor a candlelit eighteenth-century bedroom that surrounded her. The man was bearded, and sweat streamed down his ruddy face. A foul odor arose from him. He wore a filthy t-shirt, and she glimpsed a tattoo on his cheekbone, in the shape of a crescent moon. The air surrounding her was still and hot.

"You keep quiet and you'll do just fine. You hear me? Open your damned trap and you'll all end up just like them two."

What two? She tried to see, but everything was a vague, indistinct shadow. A little girl cowered behind her, her arms banded tight around Rachel's waist in a vise-like grip. She was softly sobbing Rachel's name, alternately with two other words.

Mommy. Daddy.

She held a doll in her arms—no, a *baby*. She buried her face against the pink blanket, hanging on to her as the man shook

Rachel. *Hold her head, sweetheart.* Rachel tightened her arm around the baby's head. The baby was screaming, and Mama said when she cried, she needed a bottle. Rachel stared at the man, silent tears streaming down her cheeks. Those empty, painful sobs ripped at her breast until she couldn't breathe.

And then, they were walking. Endless walking, until she no longer felt the pain in her feet. Walking through thick brambles, through dry creek beds. Night came, and they picked wild berries and ate them, the way they used to with Mama. They all cried for mama. The baby wasn't old enough to know that Mama was what she was crying for, but she was, all the same. But she knew they wouldn't ever see Mama again.

Why?

Then came endlessly patient hands. The soft white hands that reached for Julie.

No!

Those patient hands calmly patted her shoulders, assuring her that everything would be fine. Once more the hands tried to insinuate themselves between Rachel and the baby. Mama was gone. Daddy was gone. Now, they were trying to take her sisters.

The hands became beefy fists that grasped something she couldn't quite see. She screamed endlessly. And once more the fists transformed themselves into soft, patient hands that effortlessly removed Julie from Rachel's arms.

Noooooo!!

The word burned in her throat, but she couldn't say it. If she spoke, those hands would do something terrible to her sisters. And so her lungs contained the word, her voice swallowed it, and she withdrew into a peaceful place of silence.

"Rachel!"

Grey's face focused in her eyes, and she gasped for breath. Her face was wet with tears at what she'd seen, and in fear of what she hadn't seen.

His eyes softened with concern to a deep, dark gray, and his hand was gentle on her cheek. He lifted her in his arms and sat in an upholstered rocker, cradling her in his lap. "Hush now."

She wept softly, whispering, "Please don't leave me."

"No."

He tucked her face against his throat, and she smelled the sweet, fresh scent of him. She heard the quiet, even breaths he drew, felt the comforting strength of him as he stroked her. His hands were gentle and steady, moving over her with calm reassurance. "Rachel, forgive me."

She felt suddenly shy, aware of his warmth and hardness, his soothing gentleness as he held her. "I'll never forgive myself—"

"No," she gulped. "It isn't you. I—did I say anything, just then?"

He looked at her with a tender sadness. "You tried to speak. You only stared at me in terror, as if I were a demon. You didn't hear me trying to wake you. You began to weep— making no noise whatsoever—and then you screamed."

The awful image of the strange man flashed again in her memory.

"What was it? What did you remember?"

"A man—shaking me. Threatening me."

His jaw was taut with rage. "What did he do to you, Rachel?"

She shook her head. "I don't know. I was holding a baby— my sister. All I could think was, don't drop the baby."

He cradled her against him, setting the rocker into a calming cadence. And as her fear slowly passed, she grew aware of the blatant sexual strength of him, beyond his gentle comfort.

"Forgive me, dearest. I'll never lift an angry hand against you."

"It was wrong of me to take Emily to meet him without you."

He awkwardly wiped at the tears on her cheek. "It's wrong of me to keep her away from him. She shouldn't pay for his sins. He should, if he were aware of any."

"Grey, he knows his sins. And he's trying to make them right."

"He can't replace with Emily what we lost, he and I." His voice was quiet.

"Don't you see? Emily is the only way he can capture what he has left with you." She touched his grim jaw. "I can't heal the hurt he's caused you. I can't ask your forgiveness for him. Only he can do those things. If I was wrong in taking her there, it was only because ... I see you're in pain. And because ..." She hesitated, then finished helplessly, "your happiness is important to me."

He gazed quizzically at her. His hand cupped her chin, lifting it slightly. "Are you an angel from heaven, delivered as my salvation?"

She smiled wryly. "I'm no angel."

"Yet you rescued a lonely little girl, giving her the mother's love she'd always craved. And you would rescue me ... from myself."

"I—"

How can I rescue anyone ... when I don't know the first thing about myself?

Her hand trembled as she touched his hand, lifting it to her lips. For Rachel—who had never let anyone past the barricade she'd erected twenty years before—the chaste kiss was an act of daring and nearly impossible trust. Only then did she become aware that she lay in Grey's arms wearing only a gossamer-thin shift. He'd thought only to comfort her, but now sudden arousal grew within her at the sensation of his warmth against her. She wished she knew anything at all about how a woman went about seducing a man.

Trembling fingers grazed his cheekbone, and she saw the grim seriousness in his gaze as it moved over her face. His fingers lightly skimmed her lips, and she opened her mouth, tasting the clean sweetness of his skin, feeling the crisscross scars of honest work on his fingertips. Her teeth gently closed over the pad of his finger, and her tongue lingered.

"Rachel. How can I make you understand how little I can offer you—" His troubled eyes moved over her as his strong, lean fingers slowly curved along her throat, and his deep voice had fallen to a plea. "And how much I want of you?"

He lowered his lips to hers, and she tasted his indecision. Boldly, she opened her mouth to his, and he pulled her closer as his kiss grew urgent. He drew her in with the arm underneath her head, his other hand gliding to her hips and clutching them against his hardness.

Something within her crumbled at the alluring seduction of his tongue against hers, the undeniable intimacy of their embrace. He held her so close as he kissed her she felt his heartbeat pounding heavily, his hard arousal rising against her soft curves, his hands seemingly desperate to draw her into him. She'd never known anything like this, spiritual and sexual at once. Whoever they had been before melted as he claimed her, made her his, gave himself to her. His soft, dark hair was still faintly damp from his bath, and she effortlessly pushed away the ribbon, enjoying the feel of his hair between her fingers.

Suddenly he pulled his mouth away from hers, and he sat still for several seconds. When he spoke, his voice was hoarse. "Will you be all right now?"

She inhaled deeply, desire still pulsing within her. She was shaken by the line they'd crossed tonight, by the truth she'd learned about herself—not only from the terrible memories of her childhood, but about the woman she had become. No longer was she sequestered in this time for her own safety, watching him from a safe distance. No longer was he merely a gentle man whose love for his daughter inspired Rachel's finest memories. His eyes were heavy-lidded, and the corners of his mouth curved slightly in a smile that was sensual and oddly innocent.

"But—" she began, lifting her hand once more to touch his parted lips.

He caught her hand and gave it a chaste kiss, a fatherly smile. Then he lifted her in his arms, carrying her to the bed.

"Do you know," she murmured, and she heard the huskiness of her voice, "I dreamed of you the first night I was here—before I even met you. It was like this. You held me... comforting me, and you carried me to a bed ..." Embarrassed by her confession—directly after his rejection of her awkward seduction—she trailed away, omitting the worst of it. She could never tell him that in her dream, she'd been naked.

His smile was mysterious as he lay her in the bed, lowering himself beside her. "If you'd like to ride with Emily in the morning, we usually get an early start."

"Thank you."

He loosened her hands from around his neck, dropping a warm kiss on her knuckles before releasing them. His hand grazed her throat, then trailed to her shoulder, and his eyes met hers as he slowly pulled the loose neckline of the shift aside, baring her shoulder and the rise of her breasts. His sleepy gaze rested on her breasts, and he noticed the tightening of her nipples against the thin shift. She ached at his leisured perusal, and a thrill shot through her as he lowered his mouth to the curve of her shoulder, tasting her skin.

All at once, he gripped her shoulders and drew back, as if he feared he couldn't do so in another minute. But his gaze was smiling as he kissed her forehead. "My troubled temptress ... if I must be tormented with the memory that makes me lie awake, remembering each supple curve of the most intimate secrets of your body, it's only fair that you are, too. I should tell you..."

He rose, and her gaze moved down the magnificent length of him, ending at the hard, unmistakable thrust jutting against his breeches. She knew he saw her fascination—or perhaps he heard her soft sigh—for his gaze on her was turbulent, and the corner of his mouth quirked.

"The night you speak of, when I held you, comforted you, carried you to my bed to warm you, felt the instinctive hunger of you as you shivered against my own naked flesh, as you reached for me, moved against me in trusting need—"

She gasped as he described the details of her dream.

His voice fell to a soft murmur as he opened the door. "Rachel, it was no dream."

As he closed the door behind him, her cheeks burned. Only much later, after he was gone and she lay awake remembering, did she understand how close she and Grey had been, from the first moment. He had held her gently, warming her against the cold. He had been given full access to her, yet he had merely cared for her, offering his body only to warm hers. The memory of her own awareness of his nakedness in the dream blended with the bold yearning in his touch just moments ago—the incomprehensible knowledge that he'd held her naked that first night, that the erotic images had really happened—all of it helped her understand the tenderness that had grown within her for this man.

She no longer cared about how she had come to this place, and this time. She had now become inextricably intertwined with it, for she was in love with a man who existed in no other.

Chapter Fourteen

They rode out into a morning crisp and sweet with the aromas of the wild woods surrounding Rosalie. A blue tendril of hickory smoke escaped the smokehouse, and a young boy—no older than Emily—trudged out of the dairy lugging a full pail.

"You ride well. Who taught you?"

Grey's question startled Rachel, and she noticed his scrutiny. He had taken only mild notice that she'd insisted on a standard saddle, rejecting the sidesaddle. "Max Sheppard."

"Papa," Emily interrupted from her place across his lap. "Let's call on Grandfather. He isn't an odor at all."

His lips tightened. "No, Emily. And the word is ogre."

"But I promised him I would bring you." Her small hands toyed with the ruffles at his throat. "And he is your father."

After a charged moment, he sighed. "That he is."

"Then he *is* my grandfather!" She patted his chest gleefully and went on in maddening logic. "And Jennie is my grandmother."

Rachel's smile broadened at Grey's scowl. Enough years had passed to soften his bitterness over the circumstance that he could at least admit wry humor. The child's grandmother was younger than her father.

"Papa, may Rachel stay, and be my mother?"

Rachel's face warmed at the lopsided grin he gave his daughter. "You'd like that, wouldn't you?" he chuckled, pleased.

Again she wondered what had happened to Emily's mother. The child didn't seem troubled by her memory—she'd never mentioned her—so she had assumed the woman died long ago, perhaps in childbirth. That happened frequently, Camisha had told her.

"Yes," Emily said with a decisive nod. "I think you should marry her—after all, she's very pretty."

"That she is." He spoke lightly, avoiding Rachel's gaze.

"Can a man *have* two wives at once?" Emily asked.

The words echoed in Rachel's ears. Surely she'd misunderstood the child. Emily had said, *Can a man have two wives, or just one?*

She looked at him, frantic to hear him explain to Emily that her mother was dead, that he had no wife.

"No, darling." His stricken gaze on Rachel was dark with the impossible news. "And I'm afraid I already have one."

The nervous knot in Rachel's stomach dissolved into nausea as she looked away, understanding his slow answer. He'd thought she knew. Her shock and disappointment must have shown in her face.

"Oh, dear," Emily said sorrowfully. "You like my papa."

Dear God! If the child saw through her so easily, Grey surely had. She remembered his restraint the night before, when—for the first time in her life—she'd actually wanted a man, and her humiliation was complete—and unbearable.

But for Emily who waited, concerned that she'd hurt her—Rachel, whom she'd just said she preferred over her own mother—she smiled brightly.

What must things have been like in this poor child's life, for her to matter-of-fact acknowledge that while her father was married, she herself needed a mother? The thought broke her heart for the bright little girl.

"Of course I like your father, darling," She smiled brightly, her words buzzing in her own ears.

She felt his gaze on her, and she forced herself to focus on the narrow path they traveled through the thicket.

"But Lady Windmere lives in London," he went on, "and Rachel is here with us. And you're as fond of her as I am, and I am very fond indeed."

His patronizing reassurance meant nothing. Their conversation went on, but Rachel heard nothing. The crisp spring morning had grown warm, but she was deadened to sensation.

"In truth," Grey said softly, apparently answering a question that Emily had posed, "I don't know what lure London could hold for anyone, and certainly not you. Rosalie is here. Hastings is here. Miss Sheppard is here," he finished softly.

"Oh, yes! If Rachel is here, I should never wish to leave."

Angry at Grey for bringing her into this tangled mix, Rachel strove to keep her voice steady. "I don't know, Emily." The words fell to a bleak whisper as appalling tears stung her throat. "I won't be here forever, I'm afraid."

And that was the grim reality. Her purpose here was not to fall in love with the child whose imploring blue gaze beseeched her to stay forever. Nor had she meant to fall in love with Emily's father. Yet fallen she had, on both counts.

"But you're here now." Stubbornly, he reined his horse alongside hers. "Look at me, Rachel."

She blinked and swallowed, then lifted cool hazel eyes, refusing him the glimpse he craved of her heart.

"None of us knows the future. Life is a fragile and tenuous creature."

But indeed she knew the future; it was her home. Not this—this quaint time when children frolicked with fathers on sweet spring mornings, unburdened by haunting memories of days that were lost. A time when a determined young man made his fortune off the land and then sought a well-born English lady for his bride. A time that wasn't hers, no matter how she was coming to love it—or those who belonged in it.

No longer able to fight the tears, she abruptly pressed her heel into the horse's side, spurring him into motion.

Given his rein, the animal leapt forward. Down the path he raced, stretching out his legs in easy familiarity. He knew the land and loved it, and she bent low over his neck, ignoring Grey's calls for her to stop. The tears blinded her and the wind whipped at her as she urged the horse on, and she was soon lost. She slowed the horse to a gallop as he emerged into a wide clearing. She wiped her eyes, nonplussed at the scene before her.

Row upon row of tobacco plants crossed the countryside. At each mound knelt a man, woman, or child, tending the plants.

"Stand there, Rufus. Bind him to the pole, McGee."

A huge man on a chestnut mare barked the gruff command, and a tall, lean black man stood with silent pride. Another man grabbed his shirt in one fist and ripped it from shoulder to waist. Wounds not quite yet healed crisscrossed his back in a macabre tapestry.

The overseer climbed down from his horse and pulled a whip from his waistband. A leather thong secured his black hair, and a beard covered a tanned, cruelly handsome face. With almost sensual relish, he let the cat-o'-nine-tails fly, as if testing its supple strength. The corded muscles in the black man's neck hardened; he refused to flinch against the overseer's torture.

She dismounted and raced toward them. "No! Stop!"

The overseer ignored her, letting the first blow fly. The man named Rufus bore it in stoic silence, and a bland smile hooked the overseer's mouth as he raised the whip again.

"Stop it!" she screamed, grabbing his arm.

"Begone!" he snarled, slinging her aside with startling ease. She fell to the ground and scrambled to her feet again.

"Manning." Grey's voice was a quiet rumble of thunder. He drew his galloping steed to a shuddering stop just short of the overseer, leaning to wrest the whip from him.

Manning's gaze glittered. "How am I to get 'em to work?"

"Not with the lash."

She spotted Emily at the end of the path, and she gathered the child in her arms, burying her head against her breast.

"No bondsman is disciplined without an inquiry and Mr. Hastings' consent, as you're well aware." Grey's eyes were cold.

"Hastings knows Rufus is a troublemaker."

"What's his crime?"

"He raped a wench."

"Is this true?" Grey asked Rufus.

The man stared at rich, tilled earth. "No, *sir*," he spat.

"I saw it with my own eyes," Manning growled.

"Rufus?"

The man remained silent.

"If it's rape we're talking about, he's due far worse than a flogging," Grey said.

Rufus's head shot up. Eyes a startling shade of hazel— nearly green—burned with pride and sullen anger. High cheekbones held subtly carved, princely elegance and bronze skin bore the evidence of a white ancestor. He raised his chin and met Grey's eyes.

"There was a rape that occurred. And Mr. Manning was there. But I wasn't doing the raping."

"Why, you lying nigger!" Manning exploded, lunging at him.

The cat-o'-nine-tails hissed near Manning's ear. A strip of leather snapped against his black hair. He went still with fear. Grey's deft expertise with the whip stunned her.

"Touch him and you'll taste the lash yourself."

Manning's face reddened with rage and humiliation, and his eyes flashed pure hatred.

"Return to your work, Rufus," Grey said, his gaze locked on the overseer.

Rufus squared his shoulders and walked silently between the rows of tobacco plants. A trail of blood streaked his tattered shirt.

With deliberate slowness, Grey wound the whip. "Since arriving home, I've heard nothing but tales of your cruelty. I won't suffer the mistreatment of my bondsmen, Manning. Heed my counsel: abuse another, and you'll be prosecuted."

"M'lord, you hired me to drive your slaves."

"Mr. Hastings hired you. And that's a decision I'll discuss at length with him."

"Rufus thinks he's smart, fills the other blacks with crazy notions. And that last one you brought back, that Sassy, she's the devil's own hell. Where's she from?"

"That's none of your concern." Grey settled the coiled whip over his saddlehorn. "But as it happens, this cargo was from Jamaica. And it was a bad journey. Of 184 bondsmen, including those from Sierra Leone, 47 died on the trip. There was illness aboard the *Swallow*."

Dread crept over Rachel, along with memories. She remembered Grey's unnerving ability to wield the whip; she remembered the morning on Market Square, when he'd refused to interfere with the selling of the slaves. She listened once more in her memory to the indisputable facts he'd tonelessly recited moments ago, along with details she'd ignored until it was too late.

This cargo was from Jamaica ... including those from Sierra Leone ... 47 died on the trip ...

The *Swallow* was no tobacco merchant vessel, simply carrying the exotic plant to foreign shores. It was the ship of a man who dealt in human flesh, and it belonged to the man she had come to love.

A slave trader.

Chapter Fifteen

The trio started back to Rosalie in a pensive silence.

"Why did you run away?" Emily asked at last.

"I ... simply wanted to give the horse a good ride."

The scene in the tobacco fields had seemingly little effect on the child. What must she have seen in her young lifetime? Rachel couldn't bring herself to look at Grey.

How kind he had seemed. How tender with his daughter, and with Rachel; how ruthless a beast, to enslave men and women and children no older than his own daughter. She didn't know which was worse: that she had fallen in love with a married man, or that she had fallen in love with a slave trader.

They rode back to the house and dismounted, and she passed her reins into the waiting hands of the groom.

"Will you be wantin' to ride tomorrow, ma'am?"

She met the eyes of the boy; about seventeen, he seemed to want to smile but knew better.

Will you be wanting to ride tomorrow?

The simplest question, a matter of choice.

Suddenly, each black face she saw reminded her of her folly. In the nervous eyes of the boy who took her horse she saw a teenager who didn't know how to read, and never would; who didn't own the clothes on his back, and never would; who hadn't the freedom to walk to town of his own free will. And he never would.

Will you be wanting to ride tomorrow?

Did he even know what freedom was?

The thought chilled her. Of all the people she'd ever known and all those she had yet to know, none could hold more precious nor understand more profoundly the idea of freedom, than this boy.

"I don't know. Thank you." Turning away, she summoned a smile for Emily. "I enjoyed riding with you today."

"Won't you join us in the gardens for a while?" Grey asked. "I thought we could do our lessons outside today, it's such a lovely day."

She saw his surprise at her anger—he truly didn't know what upset her. Even now, the boy was leading the horses away, and her gaze settled on his dusty, bare feet.

"No." Wearily, she headed toward the house. In the dining hall, she found a servant polishing silver.

"Bess, can you tell me where Mr. Hastings is?"

"Abovestairs in his office, ma'am."

She took the stairs to his office and entered without knocking, closing the door behind her.

Hastings glanced at her. "The civilized occasionally knock."

"But we aren't exactly civilized here, are we?"

He leaned back in his chair calmly. "Is something amiss?"

"Grey Trelawney is a slave trader."

Unperturbed, he nodded. "Yes."

Rachel's jaw dropped. "You have no qualms at all about it?"

"Qualms?"

"A slave trader! Why didn't you tell me?"

He hesitated, as if attempting to understand her. "Lord Windmere's profession is entirely legal, and I fail to see why it concerns you."

Why indeed. Because she'd recognized in him a gentleness that she'd never known in another man? Because she'd believed him to be a man of conviction? Because these traits, and countless other noble qualities in him couldn't blot out the deplorable part that committed such atrocities? *Forty-seven had died on the trip.* Forty-seven human beings, taken from their homeland, had then perished at sea. Husband torn from wife, daughter from father, sister from sister.

"What happens to these people if they die on a voyage?"

"They're buried at sea."

"Are they given ... Christian burials?"

"They are not Christian," he replied, confused.

Rachel thought of Camisha's mother, Helen Carlyle, who'd spirited her away to church when Max Sheppard wasn't looking. Any faith Rachel had was to be credited to Helen.

She shuddered. Forty seven, thrown overboard like so much rubbish, their bodies left for the scavengers of the sea. She knew despondent rage for the unmourned, their souls no more than a number signifying lost profits. For the luckless survivors who were forced to begin their lives anew—No. Who were forced to accept that their lives were over, their days to be spent toiling to line the pockets of the wealthy. Like Grey Trelawney.

Her rage mellowed into an impotent despair. Who was this man—this monster who routinely committed the unconscionable; could any love live within the heart of such a man?

"Miss Sheppard ... Rachel."

"How can you tolerate this? You're the most principled man I know, and it's ... abominable."

For the first time she could remember, Hastings' face reflected discomfort. He rose, gently touching her arm. "So there are no bondsmen in your time?"

"No! But we still feel the anger and pain of their children."

His lips tightened as the agony of it pierced her. He awkwardly gathered her into his arms, patting her. She no longer knew what brought her pain. The plight of those lost and damaged lives blanketing these colonies? Or her own loss?

"It cannot improve your opinion greatly, but his trade is completely respected in this time. Only to a handful is the negro as valuable as we are."

Anne Meredith

"And you, Hastings?"

"I am not paid for my opinions, dear."

She raised her head at the familiar phrase. Once, she had been the one with no opinion.

"Is there anything I can do for you?"

"Find Malcolm Henderson. I want to go home."

Her chin trembled, and his eyes were kind as he examined her. He nodded at last. "As you wish."

She turned away.

"Rachel?"

"Yes?"

"You've become quite dear to me, child. It pains me to see you suffering."

She glanced back at him, blinking the tears away. "Then ... let me go home."

In her room, she was drawn to the window, which stood open to let a breeze through. The sound of laughter wafted up from the gardens below, where Emily daintily rolled a small ball toward a cluster of wooden pins. One or two pins fell over, and she scampered toward those left standing, hastily kicking them over.

Her lips curved slightly.

He shouted a protest against Emily's cheating, and he quickly snatched her up. "I shall toss you in the river!"

Emily giggled gleefully. "I love you, Papa."

And I love you, my sweetest darling daughter.

The words echoed within her memory, and her heart swelled almost painfully. She squeezed her eyes shut, forcing the memory to last.

And as the tears came, she saw him at last—her father.

He was young—not much older than she was now. Hair as black and softly curling as her own. Kind, brown eyes that crinkled when he laughed. A generous mouth that loved to laugh, and that pressed a warm kiss on her forehead. His words—words Max Sheppard had never said—played on her mind with quiet sweetness, and she cherished the memory, hers for all time. His eyes smiled at her from behind bookish glasses that only made him more handsome. Mama said all his female students were in love with him. He was a teacher.

The rush of details that had washed over her abruptly stopped. Melancholy, she dried her tears and watched Grey settle his daughter into her lessons. How many men in this era were the kind of father he was? For that matter, how many in her own time?

Once, he glanced up and caught her watching them. He gave her a quizzical half-smile and lifted his hand, and she turned away.

Damn him for awakening in her a wealth of sweeter memories she'd never thought to know, for creating a myriad collection of new memories, then staining all of that with pain, making it impossible to love him for any of it. After a time, the chatter on the lawn faded, and the gardens were silent.

Where the hell was Henderson?

She left her room to find Hastings. Emily entertained a parlor maid in the hall.

"Papa says you aren't feeling well, Rachel. What's wrong?"

Emily was the first child she'd ever known well, and she loved her. A pang went through her; she would miss this child who'd shown ingenuous affection since the first moment she'd ever seen her, waving at her from another home in another time.

And one person was responsible for having created this happy, inquisitive, intelligent child. How could a man who had raised a child like Emily be beyond redemption?

"I'm fine. Where is Mr. Hastings?"

"I saw him go out past the stables a while ago."

"Thank you."

She left the house. As she passed the stables, she heard Grey's voice and saw him inside, crooning to his horse as he groomed the animal. His gentleness irked her, and she entered.

His eyes rested on her in quiet scrutiny. "Hello."

"You treat your horse with a great deal of respect."

"I'm rather fond of the animal. He serves me well."

"Yet human beings aren't worthy of that same respect."

His long, luxurious strokes stopped. "What do you mean?"

"You enslave men and women."

"I hold a number of bondsmen, yes." He placed the brush aside and led the horse into the stall. "What of it?"

"And you trade in these human beings as a commodity."

She realized that until she asked the question, she hadn't accepted Hastings' confirmation. A part of her adamantly denied the possibility of his involvement in such a heinous endeavor.

He gave a slow sigh and left the stall. "Yes."

She turned away. Instantly he was at her side, resting his hands on her shoulders. His palms were warm and soothing, his fingertips urgent. "Rachel—"

She angrily shrugged off his touch—his comfort belonged to another woman. "Don't touch me."

"What's the matter with you?"

"Me? How can you—how can you sleep at night? When you trap and abduct innocent people from their homes and sell them in a strange land?"

"I *abduct* no one. I pay a fair—even generous—price for the bondsmen, from men of their own kind who hold them for that purpose."

"And without you, do you think they'd capture their own?"

His mouth went taut. "Dear God, you're one of those."

"One of who?"

"This land is breeding men who are free and strong enough to do as they choose, unencumbered by the harping of those who would force their opinion on others."

"Force my opinion! I'm speaking for those who have no voice. For a group who loudly rails about freedom, you're selective in choosing who gets the freedom and who has somebody else's choice inflicted on him."

His eyes searched hers with a mixture of anger, wariness, and yearning. "If you believe I'm taking them from a life of ease, you're mistaken. They are better off here."

"It's a lucrative business, your mission of mercy."

He raised his hand to her face, his fingers slowly extending, tracing her cheekbone. "If I thought less of you I would take you along on my next journey, to see the lives of these people. They're scarcely civilized—"

"If you thought anything of me, you'd never have lied to me. You let me believe—let me hope—"

She stopped, appalled. Abruptly she turned, but he caught her and forced her to meet his gaze, his eyes searching hers with regret and yearning. "Is that what this is about? That I deceived you? That I let my own desire for you—"

"No," she whispered, afraid to let him finish.

"You cared little about my slave-owning last night."

His gentle reminder was damning. And it was true.

She angrily lifted her chin, and his hands fell away. "Let me go. I've had quite enough of your quaint theories about what defines a human being, what defines a life, and who deserves freedom. Your grandchildren will know the lesson. All men are conceived in liberty. As for me, I've had enough of this place."

A grim line formed between his eyes. "You're leaving?"

"Yes."

He hesitated. "And ...what of Emily?"

The memory of the winsome child jarred her with its intensity. "I love her, and I'll never forget her."

"And—what of me?" His voice was soft, but his frown gave nothing away. "Will you forget me?"

She steeled herself against his vulnerable persuasiveness, against the place in her heart that whispered, *It's just one part of a man you care deeply about.*

"I doubt it. And each time I'm reminded of you, I'll see the faces of those you force into service against their will."

He looked at her impassively. He raised his hand, hesitated, and the tip of one finger traced her face from her cheekbone to her lips. His jaw tightened, and he turned away.

She stared after him as he strode down the path past the carriage house and blacksmith and across the lawn toward the smokehouse. Reluctant pity rose within her for the man who silently bore her contempt, who stoically absorbed her abrupt farewell. Yet when he'd touched her, it was with all the uncertainty of a boy. His gaze had flickered with misgiving.

It's your imagination, she told herself. The proud, stiff thrust of his shoulders as he disappeared between the trees belied his indecision.

He's a human being, she argued. *Human beings can change.*

Sudden decision swept her; could she ever live with herself, returning to her old life without the knowledge that she'd tried to change his heart?

She left the stables. "Grey!"

He was gone, however, disappeared into the woods that flanked the front lawn of Rosalie. She gathered her skirts in her hands and raced after him, but by the time she emerged into a clearing, she saw only the smokehouse, and a row of cabins alongside it.

As she studied the cabins, she saw him disappear inside one. A black woman followed him, and Rachel hesitated only a moment before following.

The door of the pathetic cabin stood open. A single layer of logs comprised the walls of the meager dwelling. Those logs were sealed with plaster, rather than mud—or, worse, nothing, as she'd heard most slave cabins were—yet the best of them offered little protection against Virginia's cold winters. Now, however, muggy warmth made the cabin stuffy and pungent.

She heard the voice of a woman as she approached. "She's sick, m' lord."

She peered into the dark, cheerless room. The cabin—no larger than ten feet by twelve feet—had a dirt floor, a wooden fireplace, and a single pot over the cold hearth. A woman lay on a straw pallet in the corner on her stomach. A sheet was draped over her back. Her feet were chained together.

Grey knelt beside the woman, gently glancing underneath the sheet. His face contorted in dismay. "Her wounds haven't been treated, Hattie. Why?"

The woman who'd brought him here stood nervously behind him. A brown bandana was tied around her head, and Rachel saw streaks of gray in the strands that escaped. "Mr. Manning wouldn't let nobody."

"And I assume Manning had her chained?"

Hattie's slender hands were folded as if in supplication, and she nodded. "But it don't look to me like she be going nowhere. She don't have none of the spirit she had when she came. I think she done give up."

"Hattie, get hot water and mix your herbs."

"I got 'em all ready, sir."

He leaned forward on one knee, his large hand resting lightly on the ill woman's shoulder. "Sassy?" he whispered. "Can you hear me?"

She didn't respond.

"Dear God," he said, as he saw the woman's face. He gingerly touched the bandana at her temple then removed it. The woman's hair was short and filthy, and he hesitated, his eyes scanning her face.

Confusion rose within Rachel as she saw the revulsion in his face. How could the beating of one slave move him so profoundly, while he dismissed the deaths of forty-seven?

"I don't remember the face of this woman," he said.

"Mr. Manning, he beat her bad," said Hattie. "Came right close to killing her."

"But—I don't recall her on the *Swallow* at all," he insisted.

Hattie asked slowly, "You remember their faces?"

The question held no contempt, only mild curiosity.

"Yes. I always remember." His palm rested over her forehead. "She has a fever, Hattie."

"I tell you, she be sick."

"Send a boy for Hastings," he ordered tersely. "And for the blacksmith, to remove these chains."

Hattie turned, surprised to find her standing there. Rachel moved aside, and the older woman hurried past her.

He looked over his shoulder and saw Rachel. A charged glance passed between them.

"What can I do?" she asked softly, kneeling beside him.

"I don't know. She's very ill. If her fever doesn't break—"

She leaned forward to see the woman's face, and she gasped. Her face bore the evidence of a harsh beating. A fine, coffee-and-cream complexion was mottled with bruises; her cheeks and jaws bloated with swelling; her lip split in several places. Her slim throat held long, purple bruises, as if the man had attempted to choke her. With grim purpose, Rachel pulled the sheet away, and nausea churned in her stomach. Long, thin wounds crossed her back, and the pale brown skin puckered around the lacerations. A stench rose from the woman's flesh; the open wounds, clearly infected, oozed green and brown liquid.

Rachel swallowed down her nausea, bending low over the woman. "Can you hear me?" she asked, refusing to call the woman by the slave name given her. "What's your name?"

The woman seemed to rouse. Delicately arched eyebrows drew together over eyes that tilted faintly at the corners. This woman's fine, exotic features had been battered until they were unrecognizable. She groaned softly, with desperate urgency, and with supreme effort she raised her head weakly. Her eyelids flickered as she turned toward Rachel's voice.

She opened her eyes faintly for the most fleeting of seconds and looked into Rachel's soul. The eyes gazing at her in imploring hopelessness reminded her of autumn—a color somewhere between caramel apples and November pecans. A stunned cry rose up and was trapped in Rachel's throat.

Camisha.

Chapter Sixteen

The comfortable laughter of the men and women fell silent with their master's arrival. They nervously watched the man who stood between the rows of cabins.

Grey's eyes roved over the men around the campfire. He'd come upon such a scene only once before, on his last trip home. They'd been unaware of his presence, as he watched them in silent bewilderment. He'd left the house that night seeking contentment. Walking along the James River, he'd arrived just behind their cabins and had to pass by to get home.

Laughter and mournful song had enlivened the peaceful summer evening, and the depth of passion these people found in their existence had astounded him. On that night, he'd witnessed one of their weddings, and the desperate joy of it would never leave him.

Now, his eyes met the eldest man. "Samuel, can you tell me where Rufus is?"

"He sleeps in the woods, sir." Samuel gestured toward the thicket. "Don' likes the cabins."

He moved behind the cabins, grim with purpose. Was it true, what he'd heard on his arrival in Norfolk? A free black from Boston had been traveling through the tidewater on his way to meet his brother in Norfolk. He'd never arrived, and his brother feared he was being held on one of the plantations against his will. The authorities feared a more dire reason for his detention. This Adams family of Boston was well known for their rumored ties to risings in the South. They moved throughout the land by darkness and spread discontent where they went.

Could the man he'd met in the tobacco fields this afternoon be called Ashanti Adams? No African bondsman could have answered him with the speech of the man they called Rufus.

"Best be watching out for him, Trelawney," an acquaintance had told Grey in Norfolk. "He'll have your negroes in a lathered frenzy and leave Rosalie in ruins."

He stepped into a clearing and saw the man, staring out at the river. "Good evening, massa," the man said without looking at him.

Grey let a long moment pass between them. "Who are you?"

"I's jes a lowly niggah, restin' for the moanin's work." His voice dripped with sarcasm.

Grey walked forward until he stood between the river and the man, who gave him a level stare with glittering hazel eyes. "I've no record of your purchase."

"You nigger mongers best clean up your bookkeeping."

"Are you Ashanti Adams?"

The man smiled at Grey—a slow, bitterly ironic smile. "Is there a reward you're wanting to claim?"

"What is your business on Rosalie? Do you have people here?"

"You might say that."

"Your brother is concerned over your welfare. I'll accompany you to Norfolk in the morning."

"These people need me."

"We'll leave in the morning," Grey repeated.

The man's eyes glinted. "That's mighty generous, considering I was taken captive and flogged just for crossing your land."

"Manning has been warned against his misdeeds."

"I'm staying nonetheless."

"I'll not have you filling their heads with rebellion. I treat my bondsmen well and they have a modicum of freedom here as well as a life that they could never afford on their own, and certainly never have had in the place they came from. I keep families together, they learn to read and write, and they would not leave if given the choice."

The man laughed and pointed a sly index finger at Grey. "But that's a theory you're not willing to test out, isn't it?"

"Make no mistake. If you stay, you'll work like the rest."

"If you discharge Manning, I'll leave tonight."

"Manning is no threat to you. I vow on my honor."

Adams raked Grey with a disdainful gaze. "Forgive me, sir, if I find your honor lacking in substance."

Fresh on the heels of Rachel's disgust, this man's contempt irritated Grey. Adams met him not as an equal, but as a moral superior—a man who fought for his people, matched against the man who enslaved them.

"If you're planning an insurrection, mark my words—"

"I'm not."

"Why do you persist in remaining?"

"Why do you allow the savage beating of a free woman?"

"I don't know what you speak of."

Adams rose to his full height with all the righteous anger of an avenging angel. "The woman you call Sassy is no servant. She's a free woman who's been beaten without cause and imprisoned without proper care for her wounds."

"She's in my home at this moment, being personally tended to by a friend of the family," he said, a blank gaze concealing his confusion.

What connection did this man have to the woman Sassy— for whom Rachel had displayed such concern?

Adams didn't trust him, that much he could see. Grey turned to go, then stopped. "Know this. You trespass on my land and have refused to leave when I offered to escort you to safety. If any trouble arises at Rosalie, I will find you and you'll be punished to the law's full contract. And if you cause discontent in the hearts of my bondsmen and women, you'll regret it."

"Oh, I wouldn't dream of upsettin' your happy darkies, massa." Again he adopted that affected tone. "Soon's me an' my woman can get off'n dis lan', we be gone."

Irritated by his arrogance, Grey shot Adams a harsh glance. "The woman you speak of is beloved by a woman dear to me. Were that not the case, you would be gone this moment."

Adams's gaze was shuttered once more, and Grey turned away. He returned to the house, passing Rachel's room. Inside, she tended her friend, and he was sick at heart. Only twenty-four hours ago he'd held her, knowing she had grown dearer to him than he liked to admit. Whatever tenuous bond had been forged last night in her arms had been severed today.

In his room, he undressed and lay sleepless, staring at the ceiling. How, he wondered, had he gotten the notion that Rachel knew of Letitia? Odd, how the topic of a wife never came up over supper with a beautiful woman.

That only added to his miserable disgust for himself. He'd thought—he'd thought the ridiculous: that she simply didn't care.

He knew little of her precarious circumstances in life, but the more he learned, the deeper his concern for her grew. Her parents had been killed; she had been abused by a vicious man, as a child no older than Emily. His hands fisted in the darkness. He'd heard of those demonic men who—he couldn't finish the thought; it sickened him.

And it convicted him. He'd ignored Hastings' concern for her, determined to lose himself in the excruciating ecstasy her body promised. Even now, the memory of her soft skin that first night, the rounded heaviness of her breast brushing his arm as he lifted her in his arms, fired his desire.

From the first, he'd intended her as his mistress. Over the past few days, as he saw her affection for him shining in her eyes, as he watched her spirit begin to heal and bloom, it had gone beyond that. Now, he wanted more—and he had no right to it.

A bizarre thought darted through his mind, and he almost smiled. What if Letitia had died recently, and the news simply hadn't made its way to him yet?

He recognized it as a sign of desperation, but it was a pleasant diversion, imagining himself no longer saddled with her. He'd neither seen nor corresponded with her in four years, not since those miserable few months she'd spent at Rosalie just after it was built. She'd heard of her husband's sprawling plantation and thought she might find excitement here—a funny thought indeed.

But her time at Rosalie wasn't amusing, at least for the inmates of Rosalie. When she'd failed to stir her husband's enthusiasm for her grotesque sexual games, she'd been forced to look elsewhere for her pleasure.

Letitia's perversions were beyond debauchery. In his youth, he'd discovered his own sprightly aptitude for depravity. The sophisticated mistresses he'd taken had been hard-pressed to keep up with his penchant for novelty.

It was a dubious sport, drawing a line between invention and aberration. But Letitia had defined it for him on their wedding night: pain. More than once that night, he'd had the frantic thought: *This isn't fun anymore.*

When Hastings had informed Grey that his bondsmen were in a state of near-revolt over their new mistress's abuse, he'd learned the full extent of her proclivities. He'd set her on a ship back to London.

The memory of the near uprising brought him back to the memory of today. Fool that he was, he'd also thought Rachel knew of his trading.

And how could he ever have guessed that the woman they called Sassy could be the same woman, Camisha, that Rachel had spoken of so fondly and so often, someone Rachel loved? And love her she did, for she'd instantly demanded that Grey carry the beaten woman to her room. Her eyes had flashed at his hesitation, imagining he resented the chore.

Truth to tell, he'd feared she carried one of the diseases that had been aboard the *Swallow*. But—he cringed at his ignorance—he'd known the woman had never been aboard his ship. Who was she?

The memory of her brutal beating still angered him. It reminded him too much of that dark place in his heart—the indistinct shadow separating mere greed from abomination. It was difficult, drawing a line between the two. And the thought troubled Grey.

He threw off the covers and grabbed a robe. He was tired of pondering a wife he had never loved, and a livelihood he had never liked and could no longer tolerate.

Chapter Seventeen

Rachel smoothed her palm over Camisha's filthy hair. She had yet to rouse from the fog of her illness, and Rachel was worried. White linen bandages covered the grim web of suffering etched across her back; she couldn't count the number of times the lash had fallen. Twenty? Thirty?

This afternoon, as she'd bathed the wounds, the mystery plagued her. Why had Camisha been brought back in time with her? What had she endured during the time Rachel had spent entertaining the man responsible for this brutality?

And, above it all, where was Malcolm Henderson? His absence frightened her; had she and Camisha been abandoned in the wrong time? Yesterday, she'd recognized the love that had grown within her for this place—for Grey. But yesterday, she'd believed a lie.

A soft tap sounded at the door. "It's Hastings, miss."

She invited him in.

Twilight shadows played about the room, and Rachel swatted at a stray mosquito that had wafted in through the open windows and buzzed about Camisha. She hastily closed the windows.

Hastings closed the door behind him and sat in the chair near the bed. He crossed his legs and gazed grimly at Camisha.

"She's very sick, Rachel."

Her eyes met his in silent accusation.

"Who is she?"

"She's my dearest friend. And if anything happens to her..."

Hastings exhaled wearily. "It would appear something rather dire already has."

"How did she arrive here?"

"You ask me as if you believe I know."

"Where is Henderson?"

"My dear, I am at a loss. He gave me instructions on how I might maintain contact with him. But he failed to arrive at the arranged place."

"She has no business being here, Hastings. Look at her!"

"The responsibility, I am afraid, lies with me. I hired Mr. Manning only a month ago."

"And have you fired him?"

"He's been censured. He had no knowledge she was a free woman."

"What?"

"And I believe it's in your best interest—and certainly hers—to allow him to remain in ignorance."

"How can you say that? *Look at her!*"

"It's deplorable."

"Why didn't Grey dismiss him?"

"Lord Windmere would've preferred to—ah, I believe his words were, 'hang the miscreant from the yardarm.' I persuaded him such emotionalism would encourage a rising."

"God forbid a human being should get a crazy notion like freedom in his head. Better they shuffle through life letting people beat them within an inch of their lives."

"We do not allow our bondservants to be mistreated. If Manning raises a hand against another without cause, he'll be dismissed and prosecuted. But if news travels that we're keeping a free black, it may cause trouble. Proof may be demanded—and that, my dear, would serve no one."

She sighed. "Camisha isn't the most soft-spoken woman I know. How am I to keep her out of harm's way?"

"Lord Windmere suggested she be your personal attendant."

Oh, wouldn't Camisha just love that.

"He thinks she's merely another slave, doesn't he?"

"He's in fact quite confused, because he doesn't recognize her."

"All right."

"Shall I send up a supper tray for you and—er, what was her name?"

"Camisha. Camisha Carlyle."

"Miss Carlyle, then."

Another hour passed with little change. Everyone was abed by now, and the house was still. Her gaze fell on the tray a kitchen maid had delivered earlier in the evening. She'd managed to dribble a little herb tea down Camisha's throat, but the tray remained untouched. A scrap of paper lay where she'd left it, and she read it again.

Rachel—Emily missed you this afternoon and begs you to reconsider your decision. Ask whatever you need for the young lady, and it's yours. As I am ... Grey.

Her mouth twisted in frustration, pain, and foolish hope. She tossed the paper back on the tray.

Camisha's forehead was still warm, and she smoothed back her hair in grim affection. "Child, you'd have a fit if you could see this hair."

Wearily, she dressed for bed and sat in the soft rocker near the bed, reading *Pamela*. Presently the plot lost her attention, and the book fell unheeded from her lap. She turned in the chair, found a more comfortable position, and slept.

Sometime later she awoke. The candle had burned low, its flame flickering brightly over Camisha's face, which was bathed with sweat and contorted in pain. Rachel hastily bent over her.

"Camisha," she said, grasping her shoulders. "It's Rachel."

She pressed her hand against Camisha's forehead and gasped. Dear God, how hot! Dipping the washcloth into the bowl of water, she bathed her forehead, then repeated it. And again. Still her fever raged. Fear battered Rachel, and she grabbed the cup, dribbling more of the tea between Camisha's cracked lips. Her hand flailed out.

"No!" She cried out in childlike tones, "don't hit me! I won't tell, Mr. Sheppard. I promise."

Tears welled in Rachel as she stroked her hand. "It's all right, Cammie. I swear he'll never hurt you again, if I have to kill him with my bare hands."

Camisha quietened, her head tossing restlessly against a foe she couldn't escape: memory. For all these years, she had silently borne bitter memories Rachel had been spared. Now, as she fought her most desperate battle, those unspeakable acts returned to torment her anew. What had Max put her through?

Her dry fever terrified Rachel, and she stubbornly cupped her face once more, forcing the liquid down her throat as she fought tears.

The comfrey was working, but it needed time; for no more than want of an aspirin, Camisha could die here while she watched. The tears rolled down her cheeks.

"Damn it, Camisha," she cried angrily, her hand curving around her jaw, "you can't do this to me. I need you too much."

Her tears fell on Camisha's cheeks, and as she dipped the cloth into the water and rinsed it, she silently prayed. Presently Camisha went limp, and her head lolled to the side.

Consumed with her tears, Rachel didn't hear the door open. She didn't know Grey was there until he knelt beside her, resting his hand on Camisha's forehead. Then he straightened, gripping Rachel's shoulders. He softly murmured her name, drawing her to her feet, and she sank into his strength in weary grief. His arms supported her, holding her close. "Come with me."

"I have to stay with her. She needs me."

"The fever broke. She'll be all right."

Her tears caught, and she looked at Camisha. She still lay on her side, and her chest rose and fell in deep, heavy breaths.

"She needs no more than time to rest, and heal. As you do."

He wore a robe of charcoal silk. His hair was loose and rumpled, his eyes fraught with concern. Framing her face in large, gentle hands, he traced her eyes with his thumbs, wiping away the lingering tears. His eyes flickered in earnest indecision over her face, and he gave a deep sigh, dropping a kiss on one eyelid, then the other. Inexplicably moved, she slid her arms around his neck, pressing her face against his throat.

His voice caught in a wordless sound as he scooped her into his arms and carried her down the hall. His room was twice as large as hers, bathed in the soft glow of a dozen or so candles. An oriental rug of charcoal and dove-gray, interwoven with black and crimson, ran the length of the room. Pale, ethereal moonlight spilled in through the window, and a candle burned on a stand near the bed.

But all was dominated by the bed, framed with deep burgundy curtains. A second layer of sheer white was drawn and hastily flung back, as if he had bolted out of bed.

He nudged the door closed and crossed the room, laying with her within the rumpled bedclothes. She moved over, seeing the hesitation in him; at last he climbed into the bed, drawing the sheer drapes closed. Bathed by the candle's flame beyond, their sanctuary was infused with a golden luster. His hair was silhouetted with fiery tones, and gray eyes gleamed silver. "Lie there and relax."

She lay her head on the soft, down-filled pillows. He leaned on one elbow, his scrutiny troubled. "Who is that woman?"

Her gaze fell away as Camisha came between them.

"Rachel," he said, lifting her chin. "Please don't draw away from me. I'm only a man, and—my mistakes are many."

She saw the place within him that he'd opened for her, and she sighed. His hand rested on her throat, hesitantly stroking with one long finger.

"Do you remember the night of the governor's ball?"

His eyes kindled. "I'll never forget it."

The memory swept her: fiery blues, reds, and yellows exploding overhead while he held her. She remembered the moment's sweetness—before she had known he could never be hers.

"You mentioned a friend that night. You said she was the only person you loved in this world."

"Yes. That's her—her name is Camisha Carlyle."

He smoothed a stray strand of hair away from her face, and his hand lingered in her dark curls. "She'll be fine. Put that out of your mind."

He dropped a kiss on her forehead. "Get some sleep. I suspect Miss Carlyle will keep you busy in the morning."

Flinging the drape aside, he threw his long legs over the side of the bed and rose. The yellow glow in the room slowly went dark as he snuffed the candles one by one, and the moon's brightness suffused the room with a pale blue light that glimmered in his eyes as he slipped into bed. Spreading the sheet over her, he stretched out and shoved a pillow beneath his head. "Sweet dreams," he murmured.

"Sweet dreams?"

"It's what I tell Emily. If I forget, she reminds me."

"My father used to say that to me." She stopped. How did she know that? She couldn't remember—and yet, it was true. Was there nothing about her that wouldn't be revealed in this man?

He watched her, but his eyes were in shadow. She saw only the grim lines at his mouth. Silently she examined him.

Tender restorer of time-ravaged treasures, and conscienceless creator of unimaginable atrocities. All in one enigmatic man. Beside her lay the man who was responsible for the cruelty that had delivered Camisha to death's door; what kind of a woman was she, to welcome his comfort—to exonerate him of his crimes because of the sweet pleasure he gave her?

Was her hunger for her lost family so great that she would accept him at the expense of her dearest friend? So great that she could forget he belonged to another woman? She'd learned too late; now she could not envision him loving another woman—but he did.

She abruptly thrust him away, scrambling over him in her haste to get out of his bed.

He caught her shoulders, pinning her in place above him. She fought it all—the hard, comforting length of his body underneath hers, the slow slide of his bare thigh against hers, the stubborn, impassioned gaze that sought hers.

"Rachel—"

"Let me go."

"I won't. Not before you give me a fair hearing."

"Fair hearing! You don't deserve a—"

"No. I don't."

She stared impassively at the curtains. He caught her chin, forcing her to meet his eyes. For a suspended moment, she let herself fall into the hypnotic force of that gaze—sweet, tender, and pained.

"How can I make you see—"

She closed her eyes, but the pain in his voice swept her.

"I'd give all I own to undo the pain I've caused your friend. And you. Don't you understand how it hurts me, to see you grieve so?"

Her eyes opened, meeting a gaze that was clear and earnest.

"You've brought me nothing but happiness. My daughter lives for the tread of your foot on the stair; she wishes you were her mother, rather than the vicious monster who is. Do you think I would knowingly bring such pain on you? Rachel, my fondest wish would be for the freedom to offer my heart honorably to you."

His fingers traced her cheek, then encircled her neck with quiet compassion. Stroking her throat with his thumb, he coaxed her down until her mouth settled over his. His lips parted slightly, enticingly; he hesitated, allowing her to lead the way. When he felt her soften against him, long, strong fingers intertwined in her hair as he gave a soft sigh, his tongue dipping into her mouth with carefully leashed passion. She felt the heat of him beneath her, the hard, hair-roughened strength of his thighs naked against her own, the smooth, male texture of him as she curved her hands around his neck.

Gasping, she pulled her mouth away from his. Her heart pounded in wild fear and nauseating betrayal. What had possessed her, to melt in his arms as if he were the man she'd once believed him to be?

Her voice trembled with rage as she spoke. "When Thomas Trelawney sees you on the streets of Williamsburg, does it give his heart pride to say, 'There goes my son, who deals in human flesh'?"

Her blade thrust deep. In a moment, his eyes went from the color of soft, crushed cinders to that of polished steel. He pushed her away and rose from the bed, and the slamming door reverberated down the hall as he left.

Chapter Eighteen

Rachel awoke with a stiff neck. She'd spent the night on the floor beside the bed where Camisha slept, but she rose swiftly, eager to check on her.

She still lay on her side, but one hand was tucked under her face. She touched her forehead lightly. It was cool.

Camisha opened her eyes, staring at her in disoriented surprise, with slow suspicion, for several moments.

Rachel gave a grim smile. "You look like hell."

"Come to Williamsburg, you said. It'll be *fun*, you said."

"What happened to you?"

"What happened to me? You mean before or after I was mistaken for a runaway slave?"

"Do you feel like talking about it?"

"I'm thirsty," she whispered. "Is there any water? I dreamed somebody kept trying to make me drink swamp water."

Rachel stifled her laughter and reached for the tea the kitchen maid had left earlier. "There's tea. When you feel better, I want you to tell me everything that happened."

Camisha started to turn over, then moaned in agony. Rachel set the tea aside and helped her into the only comfortable position—on her stomach. Rachel rested on the side of the bed, supporting Camisha while she sipped her tea.

"I'll get you some of Hattie's tea for the pain. Also known as swamp water."

"How—how did I get here?"

"I had Grey carry you up here."

"Grey?" Camisha frowned, then a small smile hooked the corner of her mouth. "Ah, that'd be massa."

"Well, *that* isn't helpful."

Camisha shook her head, her pale smile fading. "Guess not. Tell me where you've been."

Rachel explained the story, and she nodded. "So you get to hang out with some Jeeves dude, and I get thirty-nine lashes."

"My God, Camisha. Did you?"

"Can I have another sip?"

Rachel helped her drink, then set the cup aside.

"Look, honey, I'm not feeling so good right now. Do you think—"

"Sure." Rachel started to rise from the bed, then hesitated. "Camisha, last night—you thought—did my father… did Max Sheppard ever hit you?"

Her soft, dark eyes held the blank outline of distant memory for several seconds. At last, she looked at her. "It was a long time ago, Rae."

She squeezed her fingers. "I'm so sorry."

"Hey. I did what I had to do. Anyone would've done the same thing."

"*No one* would've done the same thing."

"Only cared about two people … and that man had the power to hurt them both."

Rachel's admiration and respect for her deepened. She rested her palm lightly on her friend's swollen, discolored cheek. "I love you."

Camisha's slender brown fingers grasped hers weakly. "Love you, too. But I'm gonna kill me an overseer." Her eyes closed. "I can't talk anymore, Rachel."

Rachel gently stroked her high, noble forehead and rose. She removed clothes from the wardrobe and walked to the door, glancing back; she was already asleep. *I'm gonna kill me an overseer.*

Grim resolution rose up within her.

Not if I get ahold of him first.

Emily was playing quietly on the floor in her room. When she saw Rachel, she leapt to her feet. "Oh, Rachel! I'm so happy you're awake. How's the wench?"

"Camisha is no wench, Emily. She's my dearest friend."

"A negro?" she asked, stunned.

"Yes."

Emily considered this. "She's not very pretty."

"She's beautiful, darling."

"I peeked in this morning, when you were asleep. She looks like a monster."

"She's been beaten badly."

"Then she must have behaved badly. There's nothing worse than a negro who doesn't know his place."

"Emily! What a horrible thing to say."

She gazed at Rachel in shock, her chin trembling. "It's what Bess says," she whispered. "It's what everybody says."

Dear God, her mind was well on its way to being poisoned.

She knelt beside Emily, hugging her. "I'm sorry I was sharp with you, sweetheart," she murmured. "I wouldn't hurt your feelings for the world."

The child quivered. "I didn't mean to be horrible."

"I know. When you get to know Camisha—"

"I thought her name was Sassy."

"No."

"Camisha's a pretty name," Emily said, recovering from her chagrin.

"And do you know what? She absolutely adores children."

"Truly?"

She nodded, and Emily smiled hopefully. "Then I shall help her get well. Does this mean you'll stay with us?"

"Perhaps."

"Oh! That makes me very happy!" Abruptly, her gaze grew critical. "You're still in your shift."

"So I am. I thought you might let me dress in here. Camisha's sleeping in my room."

"Oh, I forgot. Papa wants to see you."

She summoned a servant, ordering one of Hattie's herb potions for Camisha. The girl bobbed and hurried away. Rachel noticed Emily, too, had vanished. She mused over what Grey might want of her as she dressed, then returned to her room, surprised to find the door ajar. But what she saw inside gave her pause.

Emily sat cross-legged on an empty spot in the bed, her skirts spread in a dainty circle. She stared at the sleeping woman in silent curiosity. Rising to her knees, she stretched out her fingers and cautiously touched Camisha's hair. A frown of concentration crossed her face and she jerked her hand away, then returned and lingered, patting gently. Her blonde head cocked as she leaned closer, her palm hovering over Camisha's head as lightly as a butterfly. The delicate line between her pale eyebrows deepened as she trailed her fingertips along her cheek, tracing the dark, purplish-blue marks. At last, her palm rested quietly over her swollen face, and her fingers patted softly.

Camisha stirred, and Emily jerked away. But she stopped short, as if paralyzed. Camisha's eyes opened, and she stared at Emily for only a moment before smiling weakly. "Hello."

Emily stared, stricken, her arm still outstretched.

"What's wrong?"

The child gulped and slowly lowered her arm, folding her hands before her. "I only—I wondered …"

Still smiling, she said, "My name's Camisha. Who are you?"

"Emily Trelawney, miss." She dropped to the floor for a curtsy.

"How long have you been there, watching me?"

Emily frowned, kneeling beside the bed. She hesitated, then once more touched Camisha's bruised face. "Do they hurt you, too?"

Camisha watched her for a long moment. "Yes. They hurt me, too."

Rachel cleared her throat and pushed the door open, and Emily swung around, her eyes bright. "Oh, Rachel!" She sighed in relief.

Had she feared Grey finding her here, speaking with a negro?

"I see you've met Emily. How are you feeling?"

"About the same."

They chatted until Hattie arrived with the herb tea. Rachel helped Camisha sip the tea, glancing at Hattie. "Should we change her dressings?"

"No, ma'am. Best leave 'em be so's they can heal."

"Rachel says you're her friend," Emily said as Hattie left.

"Since we were about your size."

"Where did you meet?"

"My mother worked for her father."

"Was she a slave?"

Camisha's head lifted as she raised a delicate eyebrow, the corner of her mouth turning up in a wry grin for Rachel. "I think Mama sometimes thought so. But no, my mother wasn't a slave."

"You don't speak like other negroes," Emily observed.

"I have a good education."

"You know how to read?" Emily asked, awed.

Camisha's eyes widened in emphasis. "I even know how to write my name."

"Oh, pish," Emily said in outright rejection. "No negro can do more than make a mark."

Camisha sent Rachel a meaningful glance. "Who's this child been hanging out with?"

"I think she may have inherited it."

"Uh-huh. Honey, we're going to straighten you out."

Emily looked over her starched frock and apron. "Am I crooked?"

"No," Rachel said with a laugh. "But for now, Camisha and I need to talk. Can we be alone for a few minutes?"

"But Rachel—"

"If you're a good girl, you can come back and visit later."

"Oh, may I?"

Camisha reached out to pat Emily's arm. "Sure enough. You've got pretty eyes."

Laughing, Emily jumped to her feet. "Thank you. So do you. They look like…"

"Like what?"

Emily hesitated, then laughed gleefully. "Like apple butter!"

Camisha chuckled, and the sound cheered Rachel. It wasn't quite her familiar, hearty laughter, but it was close. "Apple butter, huh? You're a charmer, child. Now go on."

Emily scampered away, and Rachel saw Camisha's eyes follow her.

"She's something. She's his daughter, isn't she?"

Rachel nodded. She rose and closed the door, then sat in the chair beside the bed. "So, what happened?"

"You remember that first night?"

"Sure."

"After I went to bed, I thought I heard you yelling down in the gardens. So I ran downstairs and went out the front door. Then I didn't hear you anymore. When I looked around … well, the house was *gone*. I saw a—a man in the distance so I ran to him." She fell silent for a moment, and her gaze was unfocused.

"Was it Manning?"

"No. It was Ashanti. You may know him as Rufus."

Rachel remembered the proud, silent man she'd seen in the tobacco fields.

"He said he was going home, and asked me if I wanted to go with him."

"Home … to where? Africa?"

Camisha snorted. "No. Boston."

"Africa was a perfectly logical assumption. How many—"

"Does he *sound* like he's from Ghana?"

"Okay, maybe it was a stupid question."

"Anyway, he isn't supposed to be here. He's a fourth-generation freeman."

"Really? How did that happen?"

"Girl, you are so dumb sometimes. You think blacks were always second-class citizens? The first ones that were brought over came as indentured servants, just like whites. But not long after that, people figured out they could just conveniently forget to release them when their time was up. And a peculiar institution was born. Ashanti's great-grandparents were lucky. They got their freedom after fourteen years."

"How did he end up as a slave, then?"

"He isn't a slave!" Camisha said, exasperated. "Manning took him when he found him on Rosalie one night a few weeks ago."

"Took him? Why didn't he just tell him he was free?"

Camisha laughed. "Please."

Blushing, Rachel said, "But I knew the first moment he opened his mouth he was no ordinary slave."

"You know, I don't get it. He's a smart man; he could walk right off this place if he wanted. The night I met him, I was terrified. I didn't know how it had happened, but I knew I'd gone back in time. I didn't know you were here, so I agreed to go with him. We were almost off the land when we heard a scream in the woods." Her face bore faint disgust. "Manning was raping one of the girls. It was the most horrible thing I've ever seen. When Ashanti tried to stop him, Manning overpowered him. We were both chained and flogged. Thirty-eight lashes between the two of us."

Rachel shook her head. "I'm so sorry, Camisha."

"You and your damned theme park!"

"You know that if I'd ever imagined—"

"Oh, I know. I was the fool who thought it'd be cool to get a good look at history."

"Remember when we were kids?" Rachel asked. "You used to wake up saying you dreamed you went back in time."

"Uh huh. And we'd play make-believe all day, pretending we were ladies-in-waiting."

A soft tap came at the door. "Miss Sheppard?"

"Yes?"

Hastings appeared in the doorway. "You've a visitor."

"Who?"

He raised his eyebrows, then stepped aside.

Malcolm.

Chapter Nineteen

"Well, it's about time." Rachel folded her arms across her chest.

"I beg your pardon?" Malcolm wasn't any happier at being summoned than she was at his tardiness.

"We'd like to go home. Now."

"Home," he repeated, as if she spoke an unknown language.

"Yes, please."

"Why?"

"Will you *look* at her?" Rachel shrieked. "Look what's happened—she nearly died!"

He gazed at Camisha with compassion in his eyes. He quietly closed the door behind him, then knelt beside her. He gently touched her hand. "Isn't quite the picture postcard you imagined, is it?"

She only gazed back at him evenly.

"You said this would be a haven," Rachel reminded him.

"From your father. A man who knows you have the power to destroy him—and his family."

"And we all know I *don't!* I don't *remember* ..."

He watched her shrewdly, his gaze rich with otherworldly wisdom. "Don't you?"

Her lips compressed into an angry line. "All right. I am remembering things, I'll admit that much. But to tell you the

truth, I really don't care, if it means Camisha being treated like
… an animal, or—or worse."

"As I understand, that's been remedied."

"You've been wrong before."

He rubbed his jaw. "So you would go back to face your
father, without the means to defend yourself—or Camisha—
against him."

"Take us back, right now, and put us inside a police station
in Dallas. Camisha knows people in the legal system there,
and—"

"And what's to be done to warrant an arrest in Dallas? Idle
threats he can easily deny? What proof do you have? Do the
police in Dallas have jurisdiction over a 20-year-old murder in
Richmond, Virginia? And assuming he were arrested for
anything—which is a wild assumption at this point—he would
be out on bail within hours."

"I want to go home."

"No." Camisha's voice was soft but resolute.

Rachel's mouth fell open. "What are you doing?"

Her gaze on the old man was reflective and troubled. "Why
am I here, Malcolm?"

"That's a question you have to answer yourself."

She gave him an empty smile. "Sent along to keep the
boss's daughter company?"

"Camisha!" Rachel was stung at her retort.

"Oh, hell, Rae. You ever see a woman raped?"

The question sent a harrowing awareness through Rachel.
The sensation reminded her of those eerie glimpses of her
forgotten past—but no memory came. Only an answer, from
deep within: *Yes.*

"I'm not going anywhere, long as that Manning's around."

"Camisha, listen to me. This is the eighteenth century. It
isn't famous for its fair and equitable treatment of blacks."

"No, but even these folks have laws to protect the slaves."

"And you think you're going to come in and fix it all? Play
some sort of Moses, freeing your people? You can't change
history."

"I suspect she knows that, Rachel," Malcolm put in.

"No, I can't," Camisha agreed. "But I sure as hell can't walk away, leaving that bastard here to persecute those women. That blue-eyed slave trader of yours might put up with it, but I'm not going to."

Discord jangled in Rachel's brain with a riot of emotions. Guilt, for her own ill-begotten love for Grey Trelawney. Admiration for Camisha's integrity. Remorse, for her failure to understand that determination. And, worst of all, unfounded resentment of Camisha for condemning Grey. She didn't understand, Rachel thought—he had as little regard for Manning as Camisha did.

"So, ladies, what shall it be?"

Rachel sighed, then shot him a murderous glance. "What do you think?"

He smiled. "I knew it. And I must remind you, while Mary and I are about our work, you have just the one purpose. To find what the past means to you."

There it was again—that phrase that had come to haunt her.

"I would add one point. Do you recollect when Mary told you to make no changes to the world around you?"

Rachel remembered—when she'd thought the old woman was warning her to be a neat houseguest. She nodded.

"Well, forget it."

"Forget it?" she asked.

"Mary tends to be a practical sort, bless her heart. She scoffs at my romanticism. If she asks, I did not tell you this. But two and a half centuries stand between now and the time where you once lived. Much will—or won't—happen in that time."

"What do you mean?"

"Dear, you're an intelligent girl. You'll come to understand."

She sighed. Malcolm and his riddles.

"You said you and Mary were at work. Doing what?"

"Finding out about your father."

"What have you found out? What happened at the press conference? Did he—"

"Oh, dear, you still don't understand windows in time. Well, I'm afraid I don't have time to explain it all. Mary's expecting me. But this much I can tell you: he is a man whose power is far-reaching. If you go back to your time without the certain knowledge of what happened to you, you'll be at his mercy."

His gaze was grave. And within another minute, he was gone and they were alone.

Rachel sank to the floor beside the bed. "So I guess I've got some remembering to do."

Camisha scrutinized her.

"What is it?"

Her brown eyes were shrewd. "I've been thinking. What have you been doing, up here in the big house with that blue-eyed slave-trader?"

Rachel gave her a churlish smile. "His eyes are gray."

"I knew it!"

The lively expression in Camisha's eyes was half shock, half pleasure.

"Knew what?"

"Girl, you are gone."

Rachel didn't bother denying it. Camisha knew her too well.

"You know he's married, don't you?"

"I found out yesterday."

"Hm. So tell me about this slave trader of yours."

Camisha's matter-of-fact support soothed her. "Why do you keep calling him that?"

"Because you didn't like it when I called him massa. Are you forgetting who you're talking to? I'm the one who was there all those nights you spent studying instead of going out, because the guys you knew bored you silly. There's something going on here. What do you see in him?"

"He's not what you think. He's the most passionate, tender man I've ever known. And he's gentle with Emily, and with me—"

"Lord have mercy, it's worse than I thought. You're in love with that guy."

"I don't know. How can I love a man who—who—" She shook her head, gesturing helplessly at Camisha's bandages. "Camisha, he gives me something I never hoped to find. The memories of my family. I ... remember things when I'm with him—things I thought I'd forgotten. I remember things about my sisters, and my mother. I remember what my father looked like—and how much he loved me. And then again, I remember other things ... horrible things."

Camisha's lips parted. "Then—it's true!"

"What?"

"Malcolm just said it! Rachel, you're here to—"

"Remember my past. I know."

"No! Not just that. Didn't you hear all that doublespeak? He said something about changing things, about things that had or hadn't taken place yet. All your life, you've wondered about your parents. Rachel, they won't be born for two hundred years. Maybe you can ... keep them from getting killed."

A chill stole over Rachel, and immediately logic took over. "Camisha, two centuries? What could possibly happen now that would have to do with my parents' deaths?"

"Hell, I don't know. But ... maybe you do."

"But what if it meant ... I never met Max Sheppard. Then, you and I never would have met."

The two women turned that over.

"But we're in a timeline that can't be changed by that. This timeline is influencing that timeline."

She could only hope that somewhere within her lost memories was lodged the answer.

Later she left Camisha to rest. And because she knew she could put it off no longer, she looked for Grey and found him in his study. Aside from the library, this was one of her favorite rooms at Rosalie, although she was rarely inside it. The walls held scrollwork from a master craftsman, including a mural of a harbor filled with tall ships. The room was situated on a corner, with a large window on each adjoining wall, and plush window seats with drapes and pillows, the sort of place one could happily pass a rainy afternoon.

Grey stood at one of those windows, grimly staring out over the tobacco fields. He wore dove-gray breeches and a white silk shirt and black boots. He glanced at her. "Good morning."

His stiff reserve reminded Rachel of her last words to him, and she grew remorseful. Why? She had every right to hate him. He was engaged in an immoral livelihood that had put Camisha in peril; he indulged a monster like Manning to fatten his coffers further; and worst of all ...

Had he been right yesterday? Were he the kindly widower she'd thought him to be, would she still find him to be so abhorrent?

"Will you close the door?"

She obeyed. He gestured at a nearby chair, then resumed staring out the window. What did he see there, in those fields?

He turned at last, resting an impassive gaze on her. "I wish to know if you're still leaving Rosalie."

"Do you want me to?"

Folding his arms across his chest in presumed disinterest, he rested against the wall, bending one leg and propping his boot there. Something flickered through his eyes. He was a poor liar, and the knowledge stung. How much easier it would have been to think of him as utterly amoral.

"What I want no longer matters," he said quietly, his gaze falling to the carpet. "But I would have you know the truth about my marriage."

Without ever raising his eyes, he began speaking. "Whatever intimacy might once have been possible between me and the lady I wed ended on our wedding night."

Immediately he stopped, as if regretting his decision. He moved to the desk, lounging on its edge as he chose his words. "By intimacy, I mean spiritual. Why I married her is beside the point, but ... I did hope to love her."

She looked away, unable to bear the depth of his loneliness.

"I learned that night that my hopes were in vain. There is no human love in her." He raised his head, and their eyes met. "After that, I never sought her bed again—and I denied her mine. A year later, she gave birth to Emily."

Her lips parted in dismay. "A year?"

He looked away. "I do not seek your pity, Rachel. Emily is a blessing in my life."

"But she isn't your daughter?"

"She is more my daughter than Letitia's," he retorted. She'd touched a nerve. "Lying with a woman may make a child, but it does not make a father. A father is made one moment after another, over a lifetime, not of blood, but of more solid stuff. Morning laughter. Bedtime prayers. Midnight soothings. Do you think I love Emily less because of something beyond her control? A deed that God used to bless me?"

In this description, he had been judging—harshly—his own father, but now it was she who could no longer bear it. She rose awkwardly, turning away as tears stood in her eyes. He'd just spoken phrases she'd once imagined Max Sheppard speaking to her.

What is it that makes a father? He'd asked her, that night in the palace gardens. Now she began to get an inkling of how much he had once, as a small boy, yearned for his own father.

"Rachel."

She turned. He clenched the edge of the desk, as if letting go would send him into her arms. "I'm sorry. I had forgotten your own childhood."

"What was your mother like?"

Her whisper bemused him, and he almost smiled. "Why?"

"She taught you how to love."

Grey's eyes moved over her with distant yearning. "Have you any tender feelings for Emily?"

His question caught her unawares. "You know I love her."

"Then I ask you to reconsider and stay with us. To serve as the mother Emily will otherwise never have." He gave up his struggle, dropping to one knee before her. "My daughter loves you. She needs you. And I ..." He hesitated, then abruptly stood. Grasping a pink blush rose from a vase, he murmured, "I see the benefits of a woman's influence in her life."

His dispassionate remark distanced her, perhaps his intention. "I should also warn you that if you stay, many will assume the worst of your presence here. You will have a comfortable home for as long as you like, as will your friend, and you will have the love of my daughter. But make no mistake—you'll have few friends outside Rosalie." He paused, then continued in a rush. "Will you agree? I cannot afford for you to grow dearer still to her, then leave."

"Why did you marry if you didn't love her?"

"It's of no interest to you."

She smiled bitterly; how little he knew of her heart. "Nevertheless, I want your answer before I give mine."

He tossed the rose on the desk. "My grandmother arranged the match. In exchange, I was named her heir—the earl of Windmere."

He hadn't mentioned the wealth of the Huntington family. "All this—for a *title*?"

"You speak as if they were smiles passed out by a flirtatious woman."

She studied him, trying to understand. He was a man for whom others' opinions were insignificant. Yet he'd married a woman he didn't love for a meaningless stamp of approval. An approval refused by Lord Windmere, who had heartlessly turned his back on Grey's mother—all because his daughter had dared to love a man without proper pedigree.

Understanding struck her. With it came reluctant compassion. True, Grey cared little for the opinions of any man—except one: the man who'd not been quite good enough for the Huntingtons. His motive in marrying had been no more than to torment Thomas Trelawney.

But the fact was, why he'd married Letitia made no difference in Rachel's decision; she had no choice. She believed what Camisha had said: that there were untold mysteries in her memories that might be revealed, but only in this time.

And only with this man.

She thought of Emily. He was beyond reforming, but his daughter's mind was young and pliable and yet not wholly spoiled by the indifference that would give birth to a legacy of mutual hatred and discord.

And what about Grey—this enigmatic man she loved? She could no more leave him than she could leave Camisha.

"Let me understand this. If I agree, Emily will ... be my daughter, so to speak."

He nodded. "Yes."

"We'll spend all our time together."

"Yes."

"And you'll raise no protest if she spends time with Camisha?"

He gazed at her blankly. "Of course not. The woman is your friend. You'd not let harm come to Emily."

She was given pause at his matter-of-fact faith. Perhaps for the first time, the significance of his entrusting Emily to her care sank in.

He waited, his expression still carefully guarded. But when she looked at his hands, crossed over his lap, she saw the whitened knuckles of one hand, unconsciously fisted.

"I don't have any children," she said, and her next words—the truth—chilled her. "And I—don't expect to ever have any. But if I were to have a daughter, I would want her to be just like Emily."

His eyes were clouded, and he remained silent.

"Yes," she whispered. "I'll stay."

Chapter Twenty

Grey adjusted his silk stock, studying the trio in the gardens. He admired Camisha Carlyle, though her contempt for him equaled Rachel's. All things considered, he couldn't fault her. She had healed well in the past fortnight and now, dressed in Rachel's clothes, she bore little evidence of the brutal abuse she'd endured. While Rachel spent the time nursing Camisha, he scrutinized Manning's every move. And Manning knew it.

Rachel held Emily's hands as they danced, and his heart swelled unexpectedly at the sight. A woman who loved his daughter, playing with her. Until now, Emily had never known the tender touch of a woman. Rachel's generous affection reminded him of the memories of her touch on him, and his blood suddenly ran hot.

He hated the arrangement they'd struck; now, he wanted her more than he had before. But she'd spared him little notice, and he feared her affections were beyond reviving. Fear? The realization startled him. When he'd watched his mother's health fail, he'd known fear; when death freed her from pain, he was freed as well. Never again had he allowed anyone—except Emily—to grow dear enough to him to provoke the helplessness that had eaten at him the year he watched his mother die. He'd guarded Emily so closely that there was no room for fear.

But now, he knew fear.

Rachel had stolen into his heart without his own knowledge, until now his every thought dwelled on her. He was lost, unutterably lost. His days were made up of excuses to be near her; lingering at home when he should be tending his estate, dawdling over breakfast when he had no appetite, secretly watching her in the gardens, as he did now.

Emily's laughter captured his attention, and he smiled. Oddly, Letitia crossed his mind. The child looked nothing like her mother; she was the graven image of her aristocratic father. But her joy was exclusively her own. He was suddenly captured by the memory of the tiny, squalling infant he'd first met at Letitia's London townhouse, when he visited her home to view the infant who was to be his heir. A girl, he learned upon arriving.

"Donovan Stuart is the father," Letitia had told him that night, with blasé indifference. *"He sired her in our box at the opera, while the hall emptied."*

That would have been a tamer sort of dalliance for Letitia.

The confession he'd demanded of her had bemused Grey. Not that she would betray him; by then he knew her lascivious spirit. But—Dunraven hated the opera.

As he left her chambers on that long-ago day, the babe's wrenching cries pierced his fog of apathy. He hesitated at the nursery, with no intention to enter; the nurse paced the room, jostling the child over her shoulder, and the sight fascinated him.

Her howling took on a pathetic plea, as if she were crying out to him alone. The sound reached deep within him, finding a place he hadn't known existed.

"Let me hold her," he'd said.

The nurse cast him an inscrutable glance, no doubt fearing he might do the babe harm. But she passed the fragile bundle into his waiting arms. The surprising lightness of her, the frustrated wiggling of the creature, had captivated him. He stroked her tightly balled abdomen, marveling as she strained from the tips of her tiny toes to the crown of her head, dusted with soft fuzz.

He was overcome with the mysteries of life as he cradled the babe against his shoulder, humming tunelessly, murmuring reassurances as best he knew how. Though time would soften his bitterness, his first—and strangest—impulse had been to chase down Dunraven and throttle him. What was it that made a man lie with a woman and then desert her the next morning without thought for the child left behind?

His second thought had been much like the beggar finding a diamond unwittingly cast into the gutter. Mentally, he looked around to see if anyone noticed the moment.

This beautiful little girl was his own daughter.

"What's her name?" he had asked the nurse.

"She's not got one, my lord."

That pricked him. And as he held her and she quietened, listening for the sound of his voice, a magical thing happened. One end of a nebulous cord was sewn deep within his heart; the other end sprang from the heart of the babe he held, the child she became. His daughter.

"Oh, Papa!"

Emily's cry startled him from his reverie, and a surge of warmth rushed over him. "It's time to leave for Westover."

As his eyes met Rachel's, he had an unexpected glimpse of someone he'd seen little of late: a woman who enjoyed the sight of him. Then it was gone, shuttered by blank unconcern.

"Why can't Camisha go, Papa?"

The negro woman raised her chin as a smile lifted just one corner of her mouth in clearly amused curiosity.

"Miss Carlyle was invited, and Miss Sheppard declined on her behalf."

"As I told Mr. Hastings, I have little need of someone to wait on me at a party."

"Lord Windmere, more than anyone I can appreciate your gesture. But as it happens, I have plans."

Rachel giggled indelicately at the lady's gracious rejection.

Camisha looked from Rachel to him, wagging a finger at him. "Now I'm not sure who that giggle was intended for, but I'd say you're the odds-on favorite."

Grey laughed. The affront he might've felt was lost in his amusement—and amazement. Her English equaled that of any well-born gentlewoman and her wit exceeded it. He'd avoided her, for she was a reminder of all that stood between him and Rachel. Now, fashionably dressed, she was a comely woman of surprising refinement, education, and confidence. Yet he refused to accept her barb without returning to her an equal measure of her own sharp tongue.

"I humbly accept your regrets, Miss Carlyle. And I hope you'll include us in your social calendar in the future."

Her mouth tightened at the corners, but she remained silent.

"Emily, darling, go with your father," Rachel said. "I'll be along soon."

Though her words were soft, her hazel eyes glinted with fire as she looked at him. Concealing his surprise, he took his daughter's hand. If the woman felt confident enough to taunt him, certainly she could rise to her own sport. In his own way, he thought it quite obvious he was treating her as his equal, sparring with her.

Rachel saw the puzzlement as they left. Had he really thought such a gibe necessary?

"Yassuh," Camisha murmured with a flip salute. "I's gwine make sho you get a invite t' the nex' corn-shuckin'."

"If you don't want to go, I won't go."

"Don't be an idiot. That poor child would be left to her own devices. And the truth is, he was just teasing—just a battle of wits—which would be fine, you know, if not for that whole slave-trader thing ... And besides, it's true. I do have plans tonight."

"What?"

"There's going to be dancing, down at the cabins. And there's a Yankee boy I have my eye on."

"You are hopeless."

"He *is* fine." Camisha threw her a challenging glance.

"Yeah. Much hotter than Dulé Hill."

Camisha's slow, hearty laughter soothed her. In the past few days, she had watched the woman she loved more than a sister be restored to her, as her spirit slowly returned and her beauty emerged. She'd seen Grey's admiring glance on Camisha, and were he a different man, Rachel might've worried for her. He wasn't the kind of man to force himself on any woman.

"So you just go and have yourself a good time, Cinderella. The fairy godmother'll stay behind and tend to the cottage."

The Trelawney carriage arrived at Westover just before sundown. Splashes of color brightened the green lawn, the silken gowns of ladies arriving on the arms of men dressed with equal elegance. As the footman handed Rachel down from the carriage, she heard a lively violin and cello concerto flowing through the august plantation house. Vivaldi, perhaps; after all, Mozart had yet to be born.

A sporadic burst of laughter peppered the conversation of guests in the banquet hall. The essence of freshly slain flowers blended with that of powdered wigs and wood oil and Virginia ham and Chesapeake oysters to create a feast for the senses.

She sat in a chair, watching the handsomely dressed couples go through the gay motions of the dance. Emily stood beside her, silent. The gregarious child knew that in the Byrd home, with countless guests fluttering, chattering, and minueting about her, she was to be seen but unheard.

"That's a lovely gown, isn't it, darling?" Rachel said.

"Oh, yes. The color of a robin's breast." She leaned close. "Rachel, I'm very thirsty."

She glanced about for Grey, but he was immersed in conversation with another man. "Well, we'll just help ourselves."

She led her to the heavily laden table in the next room, and Emily accepted cider. "May I go say hello to Lord Dunraven?"

"Certainly. Remember your manners."

As Emily passed the immense, tiered crystal dessert centerpiece on the groaning board, her eyes lit up. With some effort, she moved on toward Donovan.

"Miss Sheppard. How good to see you again."

Bright, sherry-colored eyes that matched his waistcoat were alert on her. A hint of a smile hovered over his dimpled chin.

"Mr. Byrd, what a wonderful party! Thank you for inviting me."

"It's my pleasure, dear." He smiled at her, then: "Thomas mentioned yesterday that you had brought Emily to visit him. 'Tis a good beginning."

"Do you know of the rift between Grey and his father?"

"Few who know either man don't."

"I can't understand what makes a man behave this way."

"Strange," he mused. "Men spend many a sleepless night concerned with things that are of no consequence—a pointless ambition, a perceived slight by someone unaware of their actions—yet pay little heed to matters that will haunt them in their old age."

She watched him silently.

He went on. "All my life, my heart was set on one task. To improve myself. Now, as president of the Council, my authority in the colony is second only to that of the governor. And yet, I can think of naught else but..."

His gaze played over Emily. "How she reminds me of my daughter Evelyn. She entertained the noblemen at court just as Emily now charms Dunraven. King George told me, 'I am not surprised why our young men are going to Virginia if there are so many pretty Byrds there.'"

Rachel laughed. "I'd love to meet her."

After a long moment, he said, "Evelyn passed from this world some years ago."

"Oh, I'm sorry."

"She loved a young Catholic man. I ... thought him to be unsuitable, and I forbade her from marrying him. Her spirit left her, and in the end she perished of a broken heart. At times I still imagine her heels tapping in the hall, but it's only my own broken heart."

Empathy filled her for this man, questioning the decisions of his past. Camisha's revelation returned with surprising sadness; how different he must have once been, a younger man impatiently passionate for his wife.

He nodded toward Grey, in the adjacent room. "Now, I see that young man, and I know he feels a grievous pain for his father's error. And I wonder whether too much time has passed to mend it."

"I believe some things are beyond time."

"'Tis true. But the paradox is, timelessness and time ever collide."

"What do you mean?"

"My feeble motions have been made by men before, and will be made by men in other times. The same halting steps of improvement, the same foolish mistakes. Here, time collides with timelessness. Each breath you take, each tear you shed, will be breathed and shed by women long after you're gone. And yet, never will they be duplicated. Upon each hand you touch is left a tender impression that will never be rubbed out."

His words rang with familiarity; it was almost exactly what Mary van Kirk had said, that first day. Rachel didn't like the reminder of the world that was hers, a time she'd toiled in blind futility over affairs as shifting and immaterial as shadows.

"Rachel, in this world that will never make sense, one thing matters. We are all different, you and I and each soul yet to be born—but we are ever intertwined. And we share an urgent need to remain mindful of this: our time here is not long."

From surveying the lively party before him, he turned to look at her. "Would that it were in my power to place forgiveness in Grey Trelawney's wounded heart. But perhaps that task is better left to someone he holds dear." His smile was gently knowing. "Now, much as I prefer your company, I've other guests whose enjoyment I must see to."

With that, he was gone. Grey and Emily arrived from different directions, and she showed her father an elaborate pastry. "Isn't it lovely?"

"What have you there, poppet?"

"Why, I don't know. Lord Dunraven fetched it for me. May I eat it?"

He laughed. "Certainly."

She perched herself on a chair nearby, nibbling the treat.

He stood beside Rachel, and his gaze was grim. "Have you yet forgiven me for my misdeeds?"

She fought the slow fire he kindled within her, despite her resentment. "Have you yet repented?"

He gave a surprised chuckle. "What am I to do with you?"

He introduced her to a passing gentleman with a stunning beauty on his arm. As they moved on, Grey's mouth curved. "An acquaintance of mine had a passion for Mrs. Derham in his youth. She little resembles a professor's wife, do you not think?"

His idle gossip was meant to distract her, and it did—but not as he'd intended. The words raised an odd suspicion in her.

"She's very beautiful."

"Neddy said he'd gladly trade all he had to have been of an age to court her."

The jest worsened it; she'd heard that people who were prone to seizures grew to recognize their onset. For her, these moments of disorienting awareness had become a harbinger of her lost memories.

Sheppard's an annoying pain in the ass, a distraction to the class.

Oh, Rob, Jack's but a lovesick lad.

I swear, I'll have him expelled if he writes you again.

"Darling?"

She gasped at her numbing grip on Grey's arm. She released him, shaking her head.

"What is it? What did you remember?" His words were urgent.

As she told him, she tried to make sense of it.

"Jack Sheppard? Is he a kinsman of yours?"

"The name is familiar, but ... I don't know why. Max doesn't have any family at all. That I know of, anyway."

She hung onto the memories of the voices. Her father's. And the laughing, crisp diction of her mother. No wonder Grey's British tongue raised so many memories in her; her mother was English. Even the half-dozen words she'd spoken held archaic grace. And they'd spoken as a loving couple; her father seemed jealous, but her mother gently chided him, dismissing his suspicion. What could it mean? Who was Jack Sheppard?

"I find myself murderous with the thought of anyone hurting you. Think, my love. Can you remember nothing else?"

She shook her head. "It's gone."

"Papa, who's that pretty lady?" Whipped cream wreathed Emily's delicately pursed mouth.

"Emily," he murmured, "don't speak with food in your—"

Then he fell silent; his tan paled. Rachel stared at the woman in the doorway. Dressed in an exquisite, emerald green silk, she'd forgone the convention of a wig. Red hair had been powdered and artfully arranged, and the eyes that scanned the room were as green as her dress and highlighted with makeup. Her skin was pale and translucent, her lips complacent. She knew all eyes were focused on her, and she commanded their reaction to her bold, classic beauty. Beside her stood a vaguely familiar man, and Rachel placed him after a moment as the man to whom Grey had introduced her at the racetrack: Peyton Randolph.

"Dear God," he whispered. "It's Letitia."

But she had known. She'd seen it in his stricken expression.

"Have the carriage summoned. And take Emily home." Without further explanation he left them.

She gave Emily a vague answer to whatever she'd asked, watching Grey approach his wife. He bent low over her hand, and Rachel saw anticipation in her eyes. She stretched her fingertips along his arm in a sensuous, possessive gesture as Grey escorted her into another room.

Resentment knotted in Rachel, and it had nothing to do with Grey's careless dismissal of his daughter and her. The fiery spirit in the green eyes of his wife, the slow curve of her mouth as Grey approached her, were the features of a woman who appreciated the pure male appeal of her husband—and who fully planned to enjoy it.

Chapter Twenty-One

Grey silently bore the thundering in his head. Over the past hour, his wife's perfume had battered his senses until he no longer smelled it. And that was the most tolerable part of her.

Her cat's eyes glittered as she flirted outrageously with him. As they danced, she removed a glove and let her bare hand drift over his knuckles in blatant temptation. As he introduced her to others, she stroked his arm with knowing possessiveness that truth to tell frightened him a bit.

Rachel smelled of lilacs, the aroma of the French soap she liked. When she looked at him, it was with veiled yearning, and she touched him as if he were a gift she savored unwrapping.

Yes, Letitia suffered by comparison.

What in hell was she doing here? The acrid memory of hastily sending Rachel away shamed him. Her regard for him had been bruised mightily enough already; this was atrocious, and she would assume the worst.

Then, as if conjured from Grey's deepest childhood wish, another guest arrived to soothe his chagrin. He found the task he'd once anticipated had lost much of its appeal in the past seven years. Nonetheless, he welcomed the distraction of introducing his wife to her father-in-law.

Thomas bowed over her hand. "A pleasure to know you at last, Letitia. I understand you're Peyton's cousin. How did you ever win such a comely young bride, Grey?"

A flat smile hooked the corners of Grey's mouth. "Our marriage was arranged by a woman I met only as an adult. Perhaps you remember Philippa Huntington?"

Thomas's genial gaze narrowed. "Yes. Your grandmother."

Grey patted Letitia's arm. "He forgets because it's been so long since he gave much thought to the Huntingtons. You see, he was separated rather abruptly from my mother, many years ago."

"Yes, Grey," Thomas said evenly. "It was many years ago."

"Of course, Mother passed away. And he's since remarried."

Did you even think of Lucy Trelawney before you made your vows to Jennie Dandridge? Did you consider you might still be a married man, or did you know—did you care—that my mother lay in a pauper's grave?

But such sentiments were unseemly at such a gay party as the Byrds', and he confined them to his own heart.

"I was but a lad when your mother and I married, Grey."

Rage burned in Grey's gut. Damn the man! To take his mother from a life of ease to a miserable existence that would kill her, then dismiss his deeds as too frivolous to recall. But then, had he expected anything else? So many years later, Thomas still didn't care; and so many years later, that still enraged Grey.

He had heard of forgiveness and mercy, and had given it many times in his life, to those deserving of it, those who had asked for it. He had yet to learn the paradox that forgiveness releases the giver from the wrong, enlarges his heart, lightens his step—even when the forgiven is unaware of their sin.

"Dear husband, you're quite mauling me!"

He hadn't noticed how tightly his hand gripped Letitia's forearm, and he hastily loosed her. When he met her gaze in startled apology, he felt only annoyance at the sudden desire that flashed in the light green eyes. His shoulders slumped.

"My apologies. Sir, we'll leave you to your diversions."

As they moved away, her hand smoothed possessively over his forearm. "Your strength quite bewitches me, my lord."

Revulsion swept him as he examined a vase of flowers on a table. "I assure you, it was not meant to."

And she insipidly ignored him. After another hour, she pleaded a headache, and he felt one coming on as well. They made their farewells and left Westover in her cousin's carriage, since Grey had conveniently dispatched his own to sequester Rachel and Emily.

"Why are you here, Letitia?" His mouth was unsmiling as he stared out the window. "You have free command of my purse, so it cannot be money."

She smiled, removing her gloves. "Money, my dearest? Is that what you think I want?"

"It cannot be excitement. You'll find none at Rosalie." It was a warning, not a commentary on the countryside.

"You wound me. I am not the thoughtless girl I once was. I am a gentlewoman who missed her husband."

Even watching her was a purposeful, self-inflicted injury. The mind said *Look away!* while the eyes remained transfixed. Why again had he married this woman?

Her talons moved over his chest. He did not miss her attempt at subtlety, and he couldn't help comparing her touch with Rachel's ingenuous explorations. "Surely you've missed me, Grey."

And been a happier man for it, he thought. "What are you about, with this?"

"I mean to prove my love for you."

He resisted the urge to laugh. "And your daughter?"

A pause. "I ... shall learn to be a proper mother for the child."

So Emily had slipped her mind. Did she remember her name?

"There's no need. I'll escort you to Norfolk tomorrow. A ship should be bound for London within a few days, and you can entertain the Royal Navy in the meantime."

She ceded the argument. "My headache is truly shattering. Perhaps I can persuade you of my devotion in the morning."

As they approached the plantation, Rachel's face floated in his memory. Dear God, what must she be thinking by now? He handed Letitia down from the coach and escorted her inside, noticing the pall that had fallen over the servants with her return.

When she was settled, he retired to his room, relieved to be rid of her. Stripping off his clothes, he poured water into the basin and washed, trying to scrub away the smell of her. He splashed water over his head, and that helped a little. Rubbing his head with a towel, he drew back the bed curtains and climbed into the bed—and the thought of Rachel. He propped a pillow beneath his head, closing his eyes and savoring the memory. What an array of lovely memories he had of her in relation to the short time he'd known her. He succumbed to the seductive innocence of the images; her mouth upon his, her hands lightly exploring him—and his body hardened.

His door silently opened and closed. He sat upright in bed, wary. *Why didn't I lock the door?* he thought.

Letitia's hair hung loose and unbrushed, and he noticed the dull mess of it, guessing she hadn't washed it in many days. Once, such a thing wouldn't have bothered him, but he'd grown spoiled by Rachel's finicky cleanliness. Her insistence on daily baths was famous at Rosalie for its peculiarity. Unwillingly, he forced his attention back to Letitia.

She wore only a lacy night shift which displayed the angular, muscular body. Her small breasts were visible through the scanty nightgown, and Grey's gaze narrowed in dismay. Her ruse of reform had been a flimsy one.

She moved to the bed with a complacent, satisfied smirk. "I could not sleep either," she murmured. Her hands moved over his bare chest as she rested beside him, scoring him with her nails.

"I am tired and not in the mood."

"Not in the mood?" Her gaze darted down the sheet draped over him. "On the contrary. You've been thinking of me, haven't you?" Her hand dropped with knowing ease to his groin. "*Yes.*"

He grabbed her wrist. She raised an eyebrow, her breath shallow. She wrenched her arm out of his grasp, straddling his thighs. "Think, dearest. Just remember how very good it was."

It was *never* good.

Slowly, deliberately, she removed her lace belt. Separating it into two long scarves, she let one fall to his bare chest. The other, she tied at a bedpost.

Out of patience, he flung her hands away from him. "Remove yourself from this bed this instant, or I'll—"

"You'll what?"

His eyes were cold. "I'll petition Parliament for the divorce I am due."

At last the insipid flirtation in her face was replaced by frosty indifference. "Is it true what they say, my lord? That you prefer men?"

An assortment of retorts crossed his mind, but he let them go. "Good night."

Her eyes skimmed over him, and she slowly shook her head. "You'll change your mind, dearest. I shall see to that."

When she was gone, he rose from the bed, feeling the need for a bath. The lace scarf was still dangling from his bedpost, and he ripped it off, flinging it aside. What the hell was her purpose here? He pulled on a dressing gown and started down the hall, intent on the liquor cabinet in his study. As he passed Rachel's room, he hesitated. The hallway was dark on either end.

He only wanted to check on her, he told himself, to make sure she was safe. Succumbing to his worst impulses, he opened the door, slipped inside, and closed it silently behind him. The sight of her instantly soothed him, and he knew he'd ventured into her room for one reason: to remove the lewd memory of his wife. Just standing in the same room with Rachel imbued him with peace.

Now leave.

Ignoring himself, he moved forward to stand beside her bed.

She lay curled in the bed, her hand tucked under her cheek, her face illuminated softly by a candle she'd left burning. He approached the bed and leaned against a post at the foot of the bed, captivated. The light played over her face with golden tones, glistening in the curls that spilled about her pillows like a halo. How could one woman have come to mean the world to him so quickly?

He lowered himself to the edge of the bed, letting his knuckle brush her cheek. An almost imperceptible smile curved her lips, and he wondered who she dreamt of.

Let it be this poor fool of a man.

He leaned over intending to snuff out the candle, but his gaze caught on something on the nightstand; a gazette of some sort. He grasped it, curious about what interested her.

What on earth?

He blinked at the remarkable realism in the sketch of the three children. Unlike the paintings and drawings he had seen in his lifetime, where children seemed to be miniature adults, these children were bafflingly realistic, perfectly proportioned. And the shadows and nuances of the world around them were captured in its minutiae. The oldest child regarded him with fearful bravery, holding the newborn tightly to her, bending her head over the head of the middle sister as if to protect her.

Presently his attention was distracted by something familiar in the eyes of the eldest child—and the locket that hung around her neck, the same locket Rachel had given Emily. Then he read the report accompanying the drawing. Pathos and anger melded within his heart—Rachel's parents? Who would do such a crime?

She stirred, and he hastily put the newspaper aside, troubled. He toyed with a strand of hair that had fallen over her face and brushed his lips against her cheek, intoxicated by the aroma of her. "Sweet dreams, my darling."

Then he snuffed the candle and rose from the bed. As his hand rested over the doorknob, Rachel's sleep grew fitful. She gave an unintelligible, frightened murmur, and Grey returned to the bed, touching her shoulders. "Rachel."

"No," she whispered.

"Dear heart. Rachel."

"Daddy, I can't see you!"

He fetched a candle from the hall and placed it on the night stand. "Rachel. Wake up."

When she opened her eyes and recognized him, her arms banded about his neck. Pulling him close, she buried her face against his throat. He shifted in the bed, cradling her in his arms, soothing her quietly. Her hands loosened on him, trailing down to his chest.

"I'm sorry. I didn't know you feared the dark."

"It isn't me. It's ..."

"What?"

"My sister. My sister was afraid of the dark."

As awakening slowly came to Rachel, she grew aware of his solid warmth underneath her hands. Her fingers moved curiously over his chest, feeling the sweetly coarse silk, and she let one hand curve around the nape of his neck. "Grey—"

His eyes were the color of summer rain, and they were troubled as they traveled over her. "Imagine the paradox. A man at odds with honor. Confronted with one he is obligated to—" She pushed at his shoulders, but he held her fast. "And offered hope and new life in a woman like none he's ever known. A woman whose injured heart he wishes to heal—not break."

"Grey—"

"The paradox of knowing that this woman rouses within me things I once saw as foolish dreaming. That happiness lies within a fingertip's grasp—and to reach out for that hand that offers it, I must dishonor her. And then what? Can there be happiness for us, Rachel? Can there be happiness indeed, without honor?

"For my part, there can be no happiness in my life, without you. And dishonor is all I'll ever have to offer you. You, who would open your heart to a child who's never known a woman's love. While the woman who bore her has forgotten her existence."

She was stung by the reminder of his wife, and though his melancholy pierced her, she turned away. "Leave me alone."

"I will not. I saw something in your eyes just then. What was it?"

"Nothing. I'm tired."

He lifted her chin, forcing her to meet his gaze. His frown blurred as she stared, and then his expression softened. He traced her trembling lip, then the corner of her eye, where the tear fell. "Do you have tender feelings for me?"

"Why should I care for a man—who has so little respect for humanity?" Her voice caught with the pain of it. "And who belongs to another woman."

"Because he's only a man, with a man's failings."

It was true. She loved him despite it.

"And if I put away that sin you despise, Rachel—were my heart and hand free to give you—would you love me then?"

His plea fell on a soft place in Rachel's heart.

I love you now.

She looked into his eyes, releasing the bitterness that clouded her gaze, giving him that love the only way she knew how.

His mouth settled over hers, delving within her in gentle question, in knowing answer. She tasted his soft sigh as his fingers threaded into her hair, as his lips parted and his tongue found hers. Her hands slid upward underneath the silk robe, grazing the hard chest, the corded muscles at his neck, the taut strength of his shoulders.

He pulled gently at the sheet covering her, and his breath left him in a sudden rush. "Sweet Christ."

His shock blazed into desire as he realized she was naked beneath the sheet. Darkened gray eyes moved over her bare breasts, and his appreciative scrutiny enflamed her. No man had ever seen her so—and she was glad.

A seductive murmur of pleasure came from him as he cupped her breast, and his palm skimmed over the blushing nipple that rose to welcome his touch. Her fingers threaded through the softness of his hair, instinctively urging him to—what?

His thumb rotated her nipple, and she saw the desire in his silver eyes just before he lowered his head. Closing his eyes, he let his lips part and took her nipple into his mouth, his tongue stroking with enticing seduction, rocking her with pleasure. Gentle, roughened fingers shaped her other breast, and then his mouth explored there, too. His teeth nibbled with playful abandon, and her fingers threaded through his hair, boldly pulling him closer. Her encouragement enflamed him, and his soft murmur of satisfaction hummed against her nipple.

Rachel pushed hastily at his robe, and it fell about him as her hands smoothed over the nape of his neck. Her gaze traveled the breadth of his chest, a thing of beauty—as if each hair had been placed by a divine artist. When he raised his head, kissing her in hungry need, her hands roamed over his back, anticipating the smooth warmth of him. She stopped, distracted by the faint ridges across his back. Her mouth stilled under his, and he raised his head slightly. "What's wrong, my darling?"

"What—what is this?"

"Nothing."

His head lowered once more, but she hesitated. Her gaze moved over him with shy appreciation of his male beauty; the robe was loosened and hung about his shoulders. The hard strength of his body was only haphazardly veiled from her seeking gaze, and she wanted to see every last bit of it. But her concentration was broken, now focused on what she'd touched.

"They're scars," she said, her voice breaking. "The scars of a whip."

His face went taut as he awkwardly withdrew. "Yes," he muttered, sitting on the edge of the bed. Long, muscular thighs, sprinkled with black hair, were revealed for only a moment before he straightened the robe. "They're scars."

"Grey!" she cried, surprised at his withdrawal. "Just stop and talk to me."

"Hush. You'll awaken Letitia."

Her passion chilled, and she gave a soft laugh. "It's unimaginable, but I'd simply forgotten that tiny detail."

His clouded gaze was tinged with resentment and anger—and what else? Fear?

"Rachel."

She turned away from him, ignoring his quiet plea. Was his wife waiting in his bed for his return? The image appeared in her imagination and sickened her.

He left the room as quietly as he'd come, and silent tears of hopelessness streaked her cheeks in the darkness.

Chapter Twenty-Two

In the clearance between two rows of cabins, a bonfire blazed in the mild, early summer evening. The fertile scent of the river wafted over the still night, along with the sounds of lively music and reckless laughter.

Camisha's pulse raced as she watched the scene; the *ban-jar* and the drum reached deep inside her and found a place of abandoned joy. She sat beneath a tree, clapping and keeping time to the ancient rhythm. Beside her sat Hattie and Ruth, the house servants she'd grown close to. Through them, she'd learned that the two hundred people held by Grey Trelawney were more tightly bound than those on the handful of tidewater plantations that held as many workers. In the five years since Rosalie had been built, none had been sold, and few had died. Many had been born, and their family only grew. Trelawney treated his workers well, and Godfrey Hastings ran the tobacco plantation fairly and shrewdly. Three years before, Grey had established a small school for the children, despite the protests of other plantation owners in the region who seemed to think nothing was more dangerous than an educated black person.

Until James Manning came on the scene, floggings were few and runaways rare. Simply put, they couldn't imagine a better lot in life. Of course they couldn't; they'd never known anything different.

Hattie passed Camisha a mug, and she gave it a quick sniff before passing it on to Ruth.

"Try some," Hattie said. "It be *good.*"

Camisha laughed. "I imagine so. It smells like two hundred proof."

"You let that boy be, Sukey," Ruth said, swatting her daughter's bottom.

The five-year-old laughed and continued to pick at her brother's head. Dan, the three year old, howled and ducked, waving his hand in distracted fury.

"What it be like, being a freewoman?" Ruth asked.

Ruth, no more than twenty, had four children. The others were asleep in a cabin that Ruth shared with her husband, Daniel, and another family. Camisha found the cabins in good repair, as far as slave cabins went. Dirt floors, true, that would freeze in the winter. But the log walls were insulated with clay plaster, unlike most plantation cabins, where bitter cold easily swept through.

She smiled at Ruth, carefully choosing her response. The girl would likely never know herself the answer to her question. What benefit could come from such secondhand knowledge?

"You decide what you want in life. And you work hard to get it."

Ruth's perplexed gaze met Hattie's. "How?"

"You just do it," she said with a shrug. How could she explain the countless steps of revelation, the empowerment and autonomy and civic responsibility, that separated slavery from freedom?

"What you want to get in life that I don't already got? I got a husband, my chil'rens, food, my home. I have friends. What else is there?"

"What's it like, being a sl—a bonded servant, on Rosalie?" Camisha asked instead.

Sukey plucked at her mother's apron, and Ruth accepted the sleepy child in her arms, cradling her head against her breast. "You gets up at daybreak and you tends yore chil'rens. Then you all goes in the fields and tends yore plants."

"Who tends the children while you work?"

"Tends the children?" Ruth and Hattie exchanged a look of stunned hilarity, then broke out in laughter. "They works, too! Sukey, she feeds the chickens an' gathers the eggs and pulls weeds in the garden. Little Dan, he picks worms off the tobacco. They learns to work early, they does, and they learns to work late. We works till candlelight. Then, we *sleeps*. We sleeps good," she finished with a cheerful smile.

Camisha frowned. She'd known all this. She'd just never imagined that a woman could find contentment in such an existence. Immediately, the thought rang untrue.

The memories of her own time haunted her. In her work, she routinely witnessed unimaginable existences. Babies born with heroin in their blood. Five year olds stealing for older boys. Twelve year olds delivering drugs and finding affirmation in gangs that presented themselves as a ready substitute in the absence of fathers. She thought of the hollow eyes of people who felt powerless to find their way out of a maze of poverty. Could that be called contentment? By comparison, Ruth seemed to live a wholesome, satisfying life.

Aside from the notable absence of freedom.

None of it cheered her. She disliked the reminders of two mere clichés of her history that were only a shard of a broken whole. Her volunteer work amplified that bleaker side, a people who were trapped in as nightmarish an existence as that of slavery, but Camisha had been raised in one of those black families no one ever heard about. A strong, loving family. Her father, a police officer in Richmond, had been killed when Camisha was just a small child. Not long after, her mother moved to Dallas, where her sister lived, and went to work for Max Sheppard. And although—with the exception of Sheppard himself—her memories of her childhood were sweet and life rewarding, she was forced to recognize one undeniable fact. Within the black community in America, just as in Ruth, lived the stubborn, stoic ability to find some semblance of contentment in their lot in life. A disturbing aptitude that was born the first day an African male was captured and torn from those he loved.

"If it ain't the missus's wench." The soft, cultured voice held an ironic, affected drawl.

"Rufus, you let us be." Hattie's lip curled in disdain.

"Now, Miss Hattie, I's jes' bein' kindly to the house n—"

"Stop it!" Camisha jumped to her feet. Her lips went tight as she faced him. She cocked her head to the side, pointing a flattened hand at it. "We get it! You think anyone who doesn't drop what they're doing to start burning down plantations doesn't give a damn about their people. You think you're better than we are, smarter than we are. Having opportunities in this life and mocking those who don't *doesn't* make you better. In fact, it makes you one sorry excuse for a human being."

The music stopped. Along with every other person within earshot, Ashanti stared at her. With the firelight playing over his face, he seemed carved from an ancient mahogany. Ashanti Adams was the proudest man she'd ever known. His eyes were deeply golden, almost green—the eyes of his white grandmother. His nose was straight and strong, his mouth uncompromising.

Hattie burst out laughing. "You be a troublemaker, boy. You's getting' us all in a heap o' mess, an' I don't want no part of you. What you doin' out here, anyway?"

Ashanti laughed, and Camisha tried to ignore the stirrings that begin deep within her. Long on common sense and short with those who lacked it, she cared deeply about this man who routinely dismissed good sense when his principles were violated. Since the night she met him, he'd been given few opportunities for flight. And then, like now, he failed to take advantage of it. The thought puzzled her.

"Did you want something?" she asked.

"To talk to you." He folded his arms across his chest.

"So talk."

He pressed his lips together, then silently held out an upturned hand to her. After a moment, she put her hand there, feeling the hard strength of him. He was unlike any man she'd ever known, intelligent and contrary, hard-working and fiercely independent, proud and—

Kind. She remembered the first night she'd ever seen him, soothing a young boy whose father had died of a fever. The boy had decided to run away, until Ashanti intervened, changed the boy's mind, and walked him back to his mother's cabin. Since then, Ashanti had guarded the boy's steps with a watchful eye.

He took her hand as he looked at her with that intensity so unique to him; he was as full-strength as a fine Italian espresso. Then, he silently led her away from the group at the fire, and the music slowly faded behind them. The woods were cool as they walked along the river's edge, and he released her hand. They sat on the stumps of two trees that had been cleared to build the dock where tobacco was loaded before it made its way down the James. The river was quiet tonight, and its soothing cadence melded with the faraway music.

"How are you, Camisha?" He spoke her name with a lyrical rhythm she'd grown fond of, and his gaze on her was serious.

"I'm fine."

"Your wounds?"

"Almost healed. Why?"

His gaze rose to the stars that blinked in the black sky, and he smiled. "So these are stars that you'll see someday, when you return to your old life."

She'd told him the truth the first night she met him, and together they'd wondered why she'd been brought to this time, and into his life; she, who loved history and loved to help people, returned to the age that was cruelest to her people. He, who had grown despondent in the knowledge that more than a century would pass before blacks were given the freedom that was theirs by right. And yet another hundred years before they found equality. Now, the reminder of the time that stood between them filled her with melancholy.

"Well, of course, now we're looking at stars that also burned hundreds—or even thousands—of years ago."

"So another three hundred years from now, they still won't catch up?"

"I hope they do, someday," she said, sobering.

Their eyes met for a long moment, and he rose abruptly, thrusting his hands into his pockets as he stared out over the river. "I've come to say goodbye."

The words buzzed in her ears. "Goodbye?"

"I'm leaving tonight."

"Where—where are you going?"

"Home."

The silence enveloped them, and she gave a grim sigh. Then, she burst, "*Damn!*"

Ashanti turned, his eyes wide. "What?"

She sprang to her feet, facing him with righteous rage. "I've been sitting over there by that fire, wondering how these people can just accept whatever's thrown in their faces without even complaining. And you sashay in here and expect me to wave bye-bye when you tell me you're *leaving*? After—after—good Lord, man, I thought—" She exhaled impatiently, turning to leave. "Fine. *Go.* See ya 'round. Don't let the door hit ya—"

"You thought what?" he asked, catching her in his arms. His eyes were soft brown now, as his roughened palm skimmed over her face.

"I thought you cared about something besides yourself."

His long fingers curved around her throat, and she saw the poignant yearning in his gaze, blended with passion. "I lie awake thinking of you, wanting you with me. Thinking any overseer's lash is worth bearing, if you're beside me at night. Thinking I'll die if I don't know you'll always be there. Thinking I'll kill the bastard if he ever lays a finger on you again. And then what'll happen to you?" His mouth tightened bitterly, and his eyes blazed as they searched hers. His palm curved against her jaw, and his voice was a harsh whisper. "Camisha, I love you more than I ever wanted to love a woman."

His lips settled softly over hers, and she clung to him. She, who'd ever thought of herself as too strong for any man, reveled in her womanhood as he kissed her with the claim of a man who—

Who *loved her*! The euphoria of it rose within her until she forgot to breathe, and the laughter spilled out of her. He raised his head, and though he smiled, she saw the unhappiness in his eyes. "Just the sound of your laughter is enough to send me flying. And I don't even have the right to ask you to marry me in this godforsaken place. But Camisha—"

His awkward hesitation was startling, and she lifted her hand to his cheek—lean and strong and warm and reassuring.

"Do you love me?" he asked.

"With all my heart."

"Then come with me. There's a boat, waiting half a mile downstream."

His words broke her heart, and she knew he felt her hesitation.

"Are you worried about me providing for you?"

"No," she said quickly, hugging him. "It isn't that."

At last he sighed. Then he released her. "It's *her*, isn't it? That goddamned white woman."

"Rachel is my closest friend."

He nodded, and bitter lines formed around his mouth. "And it sure don't hurt that she's bedding down with massa, does it?"

She slapped him.

His mouth fell open in stunned disbelief. Immediately, she encircled his neck with her arms. "Forgive me," she whispered.

He was stiff for only a moment before he yielded and drew her into his arms.

"You don't know Rachel," she went on. "The truth is, I think I'm here more for her than for me. My mama and me were dirt poor—but I always knew she loved me. Rachel never had that. And now, I can't stop wondering. What happened to her, that she can't remember? And what connection could it have to the past? It's like she said. Nearly three hundred years have passed."

He stroked her quietly. For a man with a lethal tongue, he knew how to listen. "I thought I was an enlightened man, and it's hard for me to believe," he murmured. "If evil men could journey in time, imagine the havoc they could wreak."

"Yeah, I suppose that's true."

"Well, you think man is essentially good. I know us for the greedy cowards we are." For some minutes they sat in silence, neither wanting to end the embrace that would be their last.

"This must have been here when the first slave ships came over." Camisha traced one of the countless rings on the stump.

He glanced at a sapling near the stump. "And yet in its shadow grows another. This tree will see the dawning of enlightenment in men's souls." His eyes on her were grave. "Camisha, you ask me why you're here, in my time. I ask you: why can't you see? You came out of the twenty-first century and into my arms. Me, a free man in a time when only a handful of black men on this continent know freedom. You, with a strength of character surely known by few women of any time. Think of what you can do—in this time, with what you know."

She stroked his cheek. "Then—can you wait? Another day, or two? While I try to see what I'm supposed to do? And I'm told Manning's hours here are numbered. I'd like to see him gone before I am."

"All right. But our time is limited, my love."

As they neared the group around the bonfire, he squeezed her hand. "If you love me, choose swiftly."

She nodded silently and he was gone. The celebration went on into the night, and Camisha left with a heavy burden.

This tree will see the dawning of enlightenment in men's souls ...

That night, as she fell asleep, she prayed for the wisdom to make the right decision.

Just before dawn, she awakened with a jolt, disturbed. The house was silent, but Ashanti's words echoed in her mind with an urgent, diabolical warning.

If evil men could travel in time, what havoc they could wreak.

Chapter Twenty-Three

"Did you ever hear my father talk about anybody named Jack?" Rachel asked Camisha as they strolled the narrow dirt path behind the cabins. The warm evening was cooled by a light breeze.

"That name is so familiar."

"I know. But I was told my father has no relatives."

"What did you remember?"

"Some conversation I overheard between my parents. My father was mad about a letter Jack Sheppard had written my mother. And he said if he wrote her again, he was going to get him expelled."

"He must have been a teacher of some sort—well, a professor, he wouldn't have been so angry about a kid with a crush, I'm sure. And this student of his had a thing for your mom."

"My mother said—" Her lips curved. "She said he was only a 'lovesick lad.' She was English."

"Ashanti said something that I can't stop thinking about. I don't know why it's bothering me so. He said, what if evil men could travel in time? They could cause a lot of trouble."

"But what does it have to do with anything?"

"I don't know. Maybe nothing. It's just a gut feeling."

"Ahem."

Hastings had materialized between two cabins, and he now awaited Rachel. Last night, Letitia had announced an impromptu supper party for tonight, and the servants had been in a tizzy of preparation since then. Apparently, Rachel's absence had been noticed.

"Do I have to?" she whined.

"Lord Windmere is rather unswerving on the point."

She glumly followed him into the house, where dozens of guests had arrived. Rachel had avoided meeting Grey's wife since her arrival, and she didn't look forward to it now. Hastings escorted her to the drawing room, where she observed the scene from a spot near the fireplace. Hastings was idly chronicling the guests. Conspicuously absent was Thomas Trelawney.

"That's Peyton Randolph. You've met him, as I recall. Along with Dunraven and George Wythe. Ah—the gentleman there is Colonel William Fairfax, and beside him is his son-in-law, Lawrence Washington. I believe the boy is Mr. Washington's brother. I believe the other man with Fairfax is his cousin Thomas, Lord of Fairfax. Remember: address the one as 'Colonel Fairfax,' and the other as 'Lord Fairfax.'" He gestured toward another part of the crowd. "Charles Carter is there, with Mr. Randolph's younger brother, John."

Rachel dismissed the names he recited. "Where is *she?*"

"The mistress of Rosalie, I presume you mean, is in the next room with Lord Windmere. Remember as the wife of an earl, she is afforded the title of countess. So when you're presented to her—"

"Yes, I know, I know." She adopted a fawning blue-blood sneer. "It is indeed an honor to make your acquaintance, Lady Doodyhead."

Hastings lifted his head. "She'll be suitably impressed."

"You people have a lot of parties."

"You've come at a busy time. I assure you, you would find it rather dreary most of the year. Lady Windmere certainly does."

"Hastings, what do you know about Grey's past?"

"Not as much as you'd like, I'm rather certain."

Rachel hesitated. "Was he ever in prison?"

"Prison?" he said, aghast. "Good heavens, no."

After a moment, she said bluntly, "He has whip marks on his back. And he's rather sensitive about them."

Hastings hummed thoughtfully. "That might not be the sort of thing you'll want to mention when you meet Lady Windmere."

She exhaled impatiently, "Oh, don't be a boob. Why would he resent me knowing about them?"

"A matter of pride, of course. Such marks are the brand of disobedience. Of—servitude. No gentleman bears such marks."

"But—"

But I'm not the gentry, to look down on him for such a thing.

"A man with the humble beginnings of Lord Windmere presumably dislikes being reminded of it."

Curiosity distracted her, not for the first time. What kind of life had Grey Trelawney lived? He was clearly well-educated, and not without conscience; a man who doted on his daughter as few colonial gentlemen apparently did; yet he'd married a woman who hated children and one he did not love—for a title that he prized little in other men. What sort of life made such a man?

"Oh, here comes Lord Dunraven. Pray be wary of the man. He has an eye on you."

Rachel smirked at Hastings, then turned her attention to the blond who appeared at her side. "Miss Sheppard, I've scarcely seen you in—well, quite some time, isn't it? Will you indulge my company at supper?"

"Would it be terrible for you to call me Rachel?"

"Scandalous. How wonderful!"

She laughed at his adventure.

"Hastings, old boy, will you excuse us?"

Hastings' eyes gleamed with warning. "Have I a choice?"

Donovan clapped him on the back, then offered her his arm. "So. Shall we begin?"

"How does one create a scandal?"

"Dance twice with me. Three times would be better, but I hate to waste a good scandal on a mere dance."

She let Donovan lead her into the ballroom, where a minuet was going on. Rachel frowned. "I think I'll sit this one out."

"The next reel, then. How do you like Grey's wife?"

"I haven't met her. Have you?"

"Letitia and I have known each other for many years."

"She's very beautiful."

"That she is. But I much prefer the quiet, natural charm and grace I'm gazing on now to her bold comeliness."

"You're quite the talker, aren't you, Lord Dunraven?"

He gave a grin and almost blushed. "Shall we ever make a scandal if you 'my lord' me to death? My name is Donovan."

She conceded, and he glanced toward the dining hall. "Drat; they're seating for supper. The dancing shall have to wait."

"You're not a very patient man, are you?"

"You should know by now I'm not."

At last she saw the couple. Letitia stood by Grey's side at the head of the table, wearing a rich teal silk, trimmed with ecru lace. A white wig had been dusted with green powder. Grey's dark good looks were enhanced by a black suit; frothy lace at his throat and cuffs softened the severity of the black.

At the end of the table near Letitia, Lord Fairfax waited to sit. Peyton Randolph stood nearby. Across from them, two empty spots stood, where Donovan escorted Rachel. Letitia's gaze grew guarded as they approached, but she smiled genially. "Lord Dunraven, I haven't the pleasure of knowing your guest."

"Well, I urge you to look around more, dear lady. Miss Sheppard is a house-guest at Rosalie."

One auburn eyebrow raised. "Oh?"

Grey stepped forward, and Rachel steeled herself. Even now, with two dozen genteel guests—including his wife—awaiting supper, with an astonishingly handsome man at her side, Rachel felt as if she were alone with Grey as he gazed at her.

"Lady Windmere," he said, his eyes never leaving Rachel, "may I present to you Miss Rachel Sheppard, a kinswoman of Godfrey Hastings. Miss Sheppard, this is …my wife."

Had she imagined his hesitation as he spoke those words? She could almost read the lady's mind as a condescending gaze swept her. The relative of a man who was little more than a servant, at her supper table?

"Of course. This is Hastings' impoverished … whatnot. I welcome you, dear lady."

Rachel saw the muscle in Grey's cheek harden as Letitia spoke, and she wondered if all the gentry were so ill-bred.

"It's a pleasure to meet you, Lady Trelawney," Rachel said with a smile. No, she thought absently—that wasn't quite right. Donovan laughed under his breath. "Windmere, dear."

She gaped inelegantly at Donovan, who lifted his eyebrows in startled amusement. His twinkling eyes seemed to say, *Our scandal's off to a jolly good start.*

Lord Fairfax hovered uncertainly, and Rachel fumed. How was she supposed to keep track of all these people with all these names, Lord This and Colonel That and Lady the Other Thing? At last, Grey ended their misery by seating the lady, and the fun began.

"It's my understanding you lost a horse at the track recently, Dunraven," Fairfax said.

Rachel missed his reply, as her gaze went past him to find Grey watching her. Subtly, his attention shifted to Donovan. She saw the golden candlelight catch in his eyes, and he gave in and returned his attention to her, holding her gaze. She remembered last night, his reaction to her discovery of the scars.

What can be so dreadful that you can't trust me with it? She silently asked him.

His eyelids lowered, and he frowned into his wine.

"I'm partial to a good horse race," Fairfax went on. "I hope to attend during this session. Do you use a jockey?"

"Heavens, no," Donovan said. "That takes the fun out of it."

"And the risk," said the man at Fairfax's side.

"Better indeed, to leave the risk to the negro."

The young man who spoke sat a few places down, and she vaguely remembered him from the racetrack. George Wythe. A stilted silence passed for several seconds, and Rachel glanced at Grey, who ignored his crab bisque. His eyes were intent on Wythe.

"Are you saying the blacks in the tobacco fields have a better lot?" Donovan asked lightly.

"I'm saying no black has a worse lot than those in the southern colonies." His contemptuous gaze focused on Grey. "I've heard a free black man is enslaved on one of our plantations."

"Nonsense," Fairfax said. "Such a thing is impossible. His papers would guarantee his safe passage."

"Do you jest? He has no papers with him," Wythe said. "He was visiting a friend in Henrico, and he never arrived in Norfolk, where his brother awaited him."

"Where did you hear of this?" Randolph asked.

"His younger brother is a friend of mine. Jeremiah Adams. Peyton, you know Jeremiah. What do you propose can be done to help him?"

"It's an unfortunate matter, but you must realize a dreadful fate may have befallen him. What makes you think he's being held against his will?"

"Jeremiah believes Ashanti lives. And that he may be—" Wythe cut himself off.

"The man's staging a rising. Why else would a free man travel through plantations unless he wanted to be detained?" Fairfax said, in slow, angry realization. "The Adamses are free men of several generations, and are infamous for their lawlessness."

"Lord Fairfax," Wythe said, "they only believe—"

"Do you condone the violence they spread, in the name of their beliefs? Mr. Wythe, the law is on the side of the proprietor."

"I condone no violence. Neither do I condone the enslaving of human beings."

"Yet your family owns them, well enough." Donovan flicked at a piece of lint on his sleeve.

Wythe sighed. "The Assembly's made it impossible to free them, without a writ from Parliament."

"Just what we need in the colony," Donovan said, raising an amused gaze to Fairfax. "Another *attorney.*"

The man beside Fairfax laughed. "Donovan, you speak for the worst of them."

"Lawrence, you're a sailor. You've no right to dispute my ill-gotten gains in the Court, busy as you are ill-getting gains at sea."

Relieved laughter spilled from those near Rachel at Donovan's levity.

"What about you, George?" Donovan asked. "Are you going to follow in your brother's footsteps and go to sea?"

"I wish it, sir," said a grave young man who sat beside Lawrence. "But my mother—"

Lawrence *Washington.* Rachel was stunned, and without thinking, she raised her arm and pointed. "You're George Washington!"

A half-dozen pairs of eyes focused on Rachel at her astonishment over the obvious, including those of the startled adolescent. "Why—why, yes."

Though she wanted to scream in delight, she merely gave a light, nervous laugh. "Imagine that."

Letitia's green gaze settled on her in unsmiling censure. Then, she looked at the boy. "You'll have to have a word with Lord Windmere. He's captained his own ship for many years."

"Have you? Is it a large ship? A merchant ship?"

"The *Swallow* is a snow. Three masts, eight guns," Grey said quietly. "And a slaver."

"A slaver?" Fairfax repeated. "I didn't realize you had ventures outside Virginia."

Grey signaled the girl who hovered near his shoulder. It was Ruth. Rachel caught her eye and smiled as the girl removed Grey's untouched soup. Ruth gave Rachel a quick half-smile as she reached for Letitia's empty bowl.

"You stupid, clumsy fool!" Letitia jerked away from Ruth, who'd spilled a dollop of bisque on the lady's shoulder. The girl stared in paralyzed horror at the ruined silk.

"Idiot! Don't stand there gawking like the oaf you are! Fetch a cloth and remove this stain."

"'Tis only a spot, my lady," Grey said with even, meaningful emphasis, handing her his napkin.

Unperturbed at throwing a fit in the presence of guests, Letitia glowered at Grey. Twin spots of rage glowed on her fine cheekbones. "Are all the kitchen wenches so clumsy?"

"It's my fault," Rachel said. "I caught her eye, and she was distracted. I apologize, Countess Windmere."

Donovan chuckled. "*Lady* Windmere."

Ruth returned with a towel, which she dabbed awkwardly against Letitia's sleeve, all the while attempting not to actually *touch* the woman and risk further offense. "I'm so sorry, ma'am. I din' mean—"

"Shut up! The gown is ruined, and you'll be punished for this."

Donovan caught Rachel's arm as she half-rose in her chair, and his glance silenced her. "Lady Windmere," he said, "'tis only a gown, one of many I'm sure you have. And one, I might add, that can do your loveliness little justice."

Rachel saw the look Letitia gave the marquis, and it startled her. Something passed between them that spoke of more in their past than meetings over the supper table.

The fury in her gaze softened into appreciation as her eyes moved over Donovan. "Thank you, Lord Dunraven."

"I remember fondly a gown you wore in London, several seasons past. I believe it was at the opera."

"Yes. A most memorable night."

Although Grey sat squarely between the two, he seemed unaware of their flirtation. His gaze was focused on Lawrence Washington, who spoke with his brother.

The meal went on interminably, as course after course of this shellfish and that soufflé made its way onto the china.

Letitia had recovered from her pique and now resumed flirting with Grey, despite his distraction. Ruth had been removed from service, and Rachel was glad when the miserable meal came to an end.

In the drawing room, she found Hastings observing four gentlemen engaged in a game of loo. She debated telling him what she'd heard about Ashanti. She'd almost approached him before, but Camisha had forbidden her. Now, she considered Fairfax's accusation. What if Ashanti *were* planning an uprising? What if—

This is Ashanti's business, Camisha had said. *He'll handle it the way he sees fit.*

What if Camisha knew? It was well within the realm of possibility for the woman she knew to risk her life for others' freedom.

"How may I be of service?" Hastings asked her.

"Have you seen George Wythe?"

"He left just after the crab bisque incident."

Sighing, she shook her head. "Thank you."

Rachel succeeded in avoiding the reunited husband and wife for another hour, until she passed the ballroom and caught sight of them in the merry steps of a reel. Her heart swelled with the pain of the memories. Grey's eyes sparkling silver with excitement, the night they'd danced at the governor's ball. Grey's concern when he drew her outside to reckon with forgotten memories. Grey's tenderness as he held her while fireworks exploded overhead, whispering words she could never forget.

I wish I could remove the bitter memories from your heart, and place only sweet ones there instead.

And he had—memories so sweet that their unexpected reminder pierced her. She turned abruptly away from the scene, her tears blinding her.

Chapter Twenty-Four

The pale fragrance of agapanthus and nerines, transplanted from their native Africa, welcomed Rachel to the gardens. She strolled past, drawn by the aroma of the river, and sat on a white iron love seat concealed in a circle of ancient oaks, watching the moon overhead. The man's face shone tonight, and his somber, hollow stare intensified her sorrow. In her time, all would be the same; the river, the oaks, the moon. Yet all she loved would be gone. Her old life was now meaningless; the events of her tattered memory held no connection, the man who'd raised her had become her enemy.

Now, all she loved was in this time. The family she'd once loved, who'd once loved her, were gone—lost for all time, just as their memories were. But here, in another past, in a world that had never held interest for her, there lived a child she loved. There lived her truest, dearest friend. There lived the man she loved.

And his wife.

The cry of a bird echoed over the river. Despite his unconscionable failings, she saw only the devotion of a man loving a baby who otherwise would've known a more bitter rejection than the one he'd known. And within Emily he'd nurtured the memories of a father who loved her.

"You left my table without my leave."

She closed her eyes against the soft persuasiveness in the unexpected voice behind her. "I apologize."

Grey walked silently around the love seat and leaned against a tree, toying with his pocket watch. A brooding discontent blanketed his face as he remarked, "I find that dissatisfies me. Is it not customary to offer something more between friends?"

Emptily, she asked, "For instance?"

She tried to ignore the excited thrum of her heart as he came closer, then dropped to one knee beside her. He knelt so near she saw the moon's glow in his clear eyes and on his smileless lips. "A kiss."

"No."

"'Tis the custom ... in farewells. Or a handshake."

"Fine."

Grey covered her hand with his. "You're cold."

She tried to pull away, but he held her fast. Slowly, inexorably, he guided her hand up to rest against his cheek, and she feared he saw the unhappiness in her eyes. He pressed his lips into the softness of her palm, inhaling contentedly. Raising his head, he gave her a look of regret and longing.

"And—a soft kiss on the cheek?"

Though she tried not to, Rachel heard the soft huskiness of his voice, caught the faint masculine scent of him as he leaned near. He was married to another woman; morally destitute; reprehensibly manipulative. And he loved his daughter. Could that love cover his multitude of sins?

Dark, gentle fingers brushed her chin, and the moonlight filtered through the leaves of the oak and glinted in his black hair as his lips grazed her cheekbone. Then she saw the desire in his gaze, in his expectantly parted lips. He was going to kiss her, and the thought raised excitement in her—and fear.

"What—do you want of me, Grey?"

A contented breath escaped him as his eyes, glittering and troubled, searched hers. "To always hear my name on your lips as softly. To always feel you trembling under my touch. To know— to know you'll never leave me."

She laughed wryly. "Is this a proposal?"

"Rachel—"

"She's come back for some reason, Grey. Perhaps she's changed. What if—what if you fall in love with her?"

His eyes were soft and dark and unreadable as they moved over her. "What if she falls in love with me?"

She avoided the enigmatic persuasion in his questioning gaze.

"For her to have loved me, she would first require a heart. Rachel, if I had never met you, it would be no different. I've told you. She'll never share my bed, nor my heart. I swear you'll be the only woman who ever knows my loving."

For a moment sweet joy swelled up within her until she understood. What he meant was sex. And the joy was replaced by the copper taste of revulsion. He was indeed proposing to her: a future as his mistress.

"If you'll only let me, I'll be ever faithful to you, and a loving father to our children. Letitia will go as soon as I can arrange it. And I'll never leave Rosalie again. I'm making arrangements to dissolve my trading ventures. I'll fit the Swallow as a merchant ship, or dismantle her, but I'm not selling her. She'll never carry another human being against their will. I cannot undo what is done, Rachel. But I control what has not yet come to pass."

Bittersweet longing pervaded her at his offering. He spoke as an ardent young suitor, offering all a woman could hope for. With one niggling detail; she would never know the right to his name.

Her lips curved in a joyless smile. "I'm glad—so glad—that you'll stop the trading. But I can never love the husband of another woman."

"Rachel—"

She touched his mouth, silencing him. But as she felt the soft warmth of his lips under her fingertips, her eyes met his. She thought she would never see as imploring a gaze. The temptation was too great, and she slowly curved her hand around his cheek, settling her lips over his.

Startled by her kiss, Grey was immobile for a moment, adrift in sensation. Odd, how he'd never noticed the shy, virginal catch in her breath just as her lips touched his; the lightness of her fingers on his throat; the enflaming, instinctive lift of her breasts against his chest, an innocent, involuntary invitation. And remarkable that she could perceive this as a farewell kiss; it fired his desire, reminding him of all he was losing if he lost her.

Rachel felt the exact moment when an almost desperate hunger seized him, when her kiss became his. He pulled her close, his fingers sliding into her hair, his body half rising, curving over hers, his mouth exploring hers in a plea and a demand. He drew her tongue still deeper into his mouth as his hand traveled from her hair to the slim column of her throat, as he strove to dam the desire that raged through him. Lean, strong fingers brushed the pale, malleable curve of her breasts with delicate longing.

"Please," she gasped, tearing her lips from his.

"Please what, darling? My only love—"

She wrenched herself out of his grasp, rising unsteadily, and her voice shook. "Please don't ask me to do this."

"Rachel!"

She hurried down the path away from him, and in another minute knew he hadn't followed. As she stood alongside the edge of the river, she gazed out over the water. The moon over the horizon was reflected in the wide, gently rolling river, and she raised her gaze to the skies. Never had she seen as many stars in a night sky; and as she stared, those long-dead bits of long ago blurred into blinding starbursts.

By the time she started up the path toward Rosalie, the moon had risen high in the sky. As she neared the house, she heard the soft, subdued laughter of a woman and a man. Embarrassed to have happened on a lover's tryst, Rachel stepped into the shadows.

"God above, how do you stand it?"

"I don't miss London." The man was Donavan; the woman, none other than Grey's wife. "What was it you wanted, Letitia?"

Her laughter was that of contrived seduction. "Donovan, you were once attuned to my every whim. Whatever happened?"

"I'm growing older," he chuckled. "My reflexes are slowing."

They were standing farther up the same path Rachel had trod, and in another minute would have run square into her. Letitia turned to him, laying a hand on his chest. She raised her face to his, and in profile, only a few inches separated their lips.

"Yet you've the same reckless enticement you had that night in my box at the opera."

"Grey's box. The memory brings me little pleasure."

"And it brought me little more than a thickened waistline."

"And a lovely child," he murmured grimly. "Emily."

Rachel's mouth dropped. Donovan Stuart had fathered Emily? It struck her as remarkable that Grey could behave without rancor toward this man, who he knew had betrayed him.

"Enough of her," Letitia said. "Do you not remember our time fondly, Donovan? It certainly seemed otherwise at supper."

"'Twas to distract you from persecuting the servant. You were making a dreadful scene."

"Donovan, make love to me. Here. Now."

Letitia's impulsive demand surprised Rachel, and she gasped, clapping her hand over her mouth—but the noise went unnoticed.

"For the love of St. Michael, Letitia—let me go! I refuse to make a cuckold of Grey thrice in this lifetime. Faith, in his gardens! That's quite funny!"

Letitia stiffened into a ramrod-straight line. "You dare deny me? Over something as trivial as consideration for a rival?"

"It would seem so." He sighed. "As I said, I'm getting older. Now, if you'll excuse me, dear?"

Letitia abruptly swept up the overgrown path, and Donovan laughed, watching her go. Then he turned, his amused gaze resting squarely on Rachel. "So you know my tawdry little secret."

Rachel gulped, embarrassed. "I—I—how did you know?"

"Gasping gives the game away." His blue eyes gently mocked her. "Although perhaps even I would've been breathless at the prospect of such perverse entertainment."

"It wasn't that!"

"I know. I stayed behind to warn you, Rachel. The lady suspects something between you and Grey."

She sighed. "What kind of woman is he married to?"

"An exceedingly lusty and cruel wench," he said, with a philosophic twitch of his head. "Which is why I warn you. Nothing—and I mean *nothing*—is beyond her deviant appetite." Now, his gaze was hard. "Beware of her."

The moon was high when Camisha arrived at the meeting place. As she saw Ashanti, she thought: *So this is how it feels, to know the man you love, loves you.*

He enfolded her in his arms, reassured by the sound of his heartbeat. "Have you decided?"

"I want to marry you, Ashanti."

"Thank God. We'll leave in an hour."

"No. I want to marry you here. I want Daniel to marry us."

"Daniel? But he's not a ..." Slow understanding came, and he muttered, "You mean a *slave* wedding."

"The vows these people take mean more to them than the vows people take before a priest in the twenty-first century."

"These people don't *have* anything else," he said bitterly. "You and I do. I want to be married in front of our families and our friends—"

"What do we have? We don't even have tomorrow. Listen to yourself—our families and friends? My family and most of my friends are in another time. I don't know what I'm doing here, and I don't know how long I'll be here. But it won't be forever."

"Why?"

"This isn't where I belong. For whatever reason, God put me in another time."

"Perhaps to be given an understanding of why the time you would someday live in must be changed."

"You *can't* change the past. None of us can."

"But for you, this is the present! The future isn't etched in marble. Those little children trapped in that concrete jungle you told me about, never taught the pleasure of accomplishment, just to be taught how to settle for whatever's given them—they don't have to be born that way. They can be educated and stop the cycle."

"For a few brief hours, you and I are together. We can't guess when it will end. And I want to know that when I go back to the life I was given, I'll know that once, I gave myself to the man whose love I was meant to know. And when I say the words that seal this wedding, I'll thank God He gave me a man who deserved the vow."

Her voice caught. All those years, how many friends had she heard speak those words—till death do us part—without considering the grim origin of the vow?

He brushed at the tears that streaked her face, and she swallowed and continued.

"Just as the auction block can't sever the vows Ruth made to Daniel, time will be powerless to destroy my promise to you. I'll honor my vows until I draw my last breath."

Ashanti lowered his lips to hers, tasting her love for him, her uncommon fire and strength. At last he spoke. "As will I. And when the last breath leaves my body, it will be your name."

The night was cool and quiet when they started back toward Rosalie. The sudden sound of laughter rose up, only twenty feet away. Instinctively he pulled her into the shadows of the trees, and they waited silently.

The figure of a man emerged, wearing only breeches. A knot formed in her stomach as she recognized him: Manning.

At his side was a woman she didn't recognize, dressed in a sheer lace nightgown. The woman gave a low, throaty laugh as she stripped the shift over her head and jumped into the river. Manning followed her, fumbling with the buttons on his buckskins. She was shocked at the sight of the overseer, cavorting with the unknown woman where anyone could see. Ashanti swiftly pulled her away. "That must be the basest man ever to walk the earth," he muttered.

When they found Ruth and Daniel sitting outside their cabin, they stopped to tell them of their plans.

"You gone jump the broom?" Ruth asked.

"Yes," Camisha said with a smile.

Daniel retrieved a jug and a mug from the cabin, and they passed the wine, celebrating their good fortune and laughing into the night. At last Ashanti walked her back to the house.

She climbed the servants' stairs to the second floor, and she'd almost made it to her room when she heard a noise on the stairs below. She recognized the woman who'd romped naked with Manning on the riverbank. Sneaking up the back stairs!

"Can I *help* you?" Camisha asked with a frown.

The woman's hair hung in dank strings, and her shift was damp, but pale green eyes glittered imperiously as she arrived at the top of the stairs. "I dislike your tone, wench. And yes. You may help me undress."

Camisha snorted. "I don't think so."

The woman slapped her. The act was swift and stunning, and Camisha had to stop herself from slugging her.

"You're speaking to your mistress," the woman lashed.

I'm speaking to a slut of the first order, Camisha said to herself in dismay. *This* mess was Letitia Trelawney? Ruth had cried for hours over her abuse and still feared a flogging.

Did the woman know Camisha had seen her at the river? Of course not. She made a hasty decision and bit her tongue. She bowed to the woman. "I beg your forgiveness, madam. I regret I'm not trained to assist such a fine lady as yourself, but I'll find someone who is."

Letitia was mollified at this, and Camisha descended the stairs and roused a chambermaid to tend to the lady. All the while her mind quickly assembled facts. Above all else, one fact shone clear.

The gray-eyed slave trader was about to receive his due.

Chapter Twenty-Five

Rachel squinted against the sun's first rays the next morning. Camisha was humming as she dressed.

"You're pretty darn chipper this morning," Rachel mumbled.

"It's my wedding day, honey." Camisha laughed softly.

"Shut your mouth, Rae. I can see all your fillings."

"Your *what*?"

"You heard me. Me an' my man, we's jumpin' the broom." She frowned. "We drank some blackberry wine last night, and I have a screaming headache. Got any aspirin?"

"Very funny." Rachel threw her legs out of the bed. "You're marrying Ashanti? And what's this about ... jumping the broom?"

"Just get dressed. We need to get Emily up before all the blue-bloods start rousing."

They found Emily in her room, and as they dressed her, a maid arrived with a tray for her breakfast. The dish of apple butter brightened her mood. While she ate, Rachel and Camisha gathered the things Camisha had wanted for her wedding, simple gifts from Rachel. A bottle of perfumed oil, a bar of soap, a silken nightgown. They giggled over it, then returned to fetch Emily. She wasn't in her room, and they began a swift search. "I hear her," Camisha said, frowning. "Damn it, she's in that woman's room."

That woman who happened to have given birth to her.

An irritable mutter came from the room they approached. "Stop plaguing me, brat. Your prattle is making my head throb."

"But if you just taste it, you'll see it's so very—"

They arrived just in time to see Letitia whirl on her daughter. She grabbed Emily and shook her until the small china bowl fell from her trembling fingers and shattered. Apple butter splattered across the rug, and the lady's nightgown.

"Now see what you've done!"

Letitia raised her arm to strike Emily, and Camisha stepped forward, grabbing her wrist, her voice a harsh grate. "Pick on somebody who's big enough to pick back, lady."

Letitia's eyes glinted with green fire. "Take your hands off me." The words dripped from her tongue like slow drops of poison.

Emily was stunned, and her eyes shimmered with tears. Rachel pulled her into her arms, pressing her face against her apron.

"You'll be flogged for this."

Camisha's voice shook with rage. "I've just about had it, watching you pick on every helpless creature who happens to cross your unholy path. You touch this child again, and you'll get worse than a flogging."

With that, they carried Emily outside. As they soothed her in the gardens, Rachel remembered Grey's words the day after Camisha was found, when he'd spoken of his wife.

There is no human love in her.

She remembered everything else she'd learned of Letitia Trelawney; how had he promised his life to such a person? Worse, how could he subject his daughter to her? It was unthinkable.

By early afternoon, they joined the women out in the kitchen preparing the wedding meal as well as the evening meal for the Trelawney guests. Emily played outside with Sukey and

Little Dan; they, along with Ruth, had been relieved from their chores to help Camisha with her wedding. Camisha snatched a small cake, biting into it. "Oh! Just like my grandmother used to make!"

Breaking it in two, she shared it with Rachel. "What is it?"

"The most heavenly crab cake you'll ever taste." Camisha moaned, her mouth full.

"Now you stop that, or there be none left for supper," Hattie said, shooing at her.

Crestfallen, Camisha asked, "Oh, they're for the visitors?"

Hattie grinned, her face shiny with sweat. "No, they're for you. Ashanti, he bought them crabs in town. Now go on."

"Let's get you ready," Ruth said. "You got a man waitin'."

In Ruth's cabin, she gave Camisha a shy smile. Fine, delicate features were alight with a mixture of pride and humility as she struggled with her words. "Camisha, I knows you be a fine lady, an' used to fine things. But ... it would do me ... *honor* if you'd wear what I wore when me and Daniel jumped the broom."

"Oh, Ruth, I'd be proud to."

"I took good care of it. You get on out of that fancy dress, and we'll make you right pretty."

Camisha undressed down to her shift and stays. Ruth pulled a petticoat over her head, then another. "You be a free woman, but you seen what can happen when white men's around, and I reckon they's always gone be around. My mama, she be a dower negro down in Caroline, and when Heartbreak Day come, and we knowed I be sold, she told me that a day come when I be wanting babies of my own. Now, I's gone tell you, just like Mama told me."

The younger woman spoke to her with a maternal, no-nonsense plainness that spoke of experience. Camisha understood what seemed to be a ritual, and although some of the girl's facts might be skewed, the truth of it all in this age was unarguable, and she listened intently.

"It all be on you to keep the family together. Your Ashanti, he might get sold away tomorrow. And if'n that happens, the children you got by him stays with you, if you be lucky. And they be yours long after they be gone."

"How do you live that way, Ruth?"

"You just *does*." She patted Camisha, then reached for the frock. Though it was a simple walnut-dyed cotton, its deep mahogany color gave it a subtle richness. She dropped it over Camisha's head and began to hook the dress.

"Some say it be better not to have little ones. You just breedin' more souls for the white man to work to death. I say, they's my children, and they always be, wherever we goes, wherever they goes. Just like my Daniel—he be my husband, no matter what. An' the Lord, He watch over you, child, just like he watch over Joseph when his brothers sold him away."

Ruth reached for one last item on the chair—a worn but brightly colored scarf. Her eyes were grave. "My mama wore this in her hair when she was taken from the motherland," she said, draping the cloth around Camisha's shoulders. "She say it stands for the day we all be back together with our loved ones in Glory, when he wipe every tear from our eyes, and there be no more mourning, no more crying, no more pain.

"Now don't do that," she scolded, brushing at Camisha's tears. "That Ashanti, he gots the big mouth, but he be a good man. And he take care of you, best he can."

Her philosophical reassurance moved Rachel. How demoralizing it must be for a man whose most fundamental instinct was routinely denied him; men whose very instinct had become escape.

"And he be mighty pleasing to the eye," Ruth added, smiling.

Camisha burst out in hearty laughter, wiping at her eyes.

"Now, I'm gone go get my Daniel and tell him you be ready."

With that, Ruth left them alone.

"You look beautiful," Rachel said, hugging her.

"Bet you never figured my wedding dress would look like this, did you?"

Smiling, she gently brushed her finger against the soft scarf. "Camisha, have you ever wondered …"

"What?"

"What the world would've been like, if there hadn't been slavery."

"Have I ever wondered?" Camisha burst out laughing. "Lord have mercy. Honey, this is just one tragic act in an epic drama."

"But if the Africans had been left alone, to live their lives the way they wanted, maybe America wouldn't have so much strife now."

"No kidding. But if you're imagining some white utopia—"

"You know I didn't mean that. I was honestly thinking about modern-day Africa."

"People of all color play that game all the time. What if Lincoln had had his way and shipped everyone back to the motherland? Never mind how he would've sorted out who went where. Honey, you know they're still selling human beings in Africa, don't you? In Pakistan? In freaking Haiti, 800 miles from Florida? We don't like to talk about that, do we? Maybe that's the dark continent's payback for their enabling slavery; a continent made up of third-world countries. And imagine America without any black faces. No open heart surgery. No traffic lights. No jazz. My God, Rachel, imagine America without Elvis Presley!"

"Elvis Presley?" Rachel asked. "He was white."

"Yeah, but his music was about as black as it comes," Camisha smiled knowingly. "Girl, for somebody who's so smart, who knows me so well, you sure can be dumb sometimes. How many times have we had this talk? I am not defined by my skin color any more than you are. Slavery *happened*. But it doesn't make me think I'm any less of an American. Either way, it's only one little part of our history, an even smaller part of mine, and it doesn't define who I am. It'll take another hundred years or so—and I mean from our time—before the world catches up with us. But girl, it's catching up." She put her arm around Rachel's shoulders. "Now, I got me a man a-waitin'."

They laughed.

When Rachel opened the door, they both fell silent.

The sun was sinking into the trees, and a crowd of hundreds—men, women, and children, all strangely solemn and jubilant—waited in the clearing. Some from other plantations had been allowed to attend. A bonfire blazed brightly, casting earthy shadows across the expectant faces. The soft beat of a drum provided a peaceful, lulling beat, and a man sang softly.

Just outside the door, Ruth waited with several other women, watching Camisha. Feeling suddenly out of place, Rachel started to step away, but Camisha caught her arm and smiled. Camisha followed behind the women who led them to the clearing, and only when she saw Ashanti did she step away from Rachel, moving to stand beside Hattie.

Ruth's husband stood before the crowd. Daniel was at least ten years older than Ruth, and he stood as tall as Ashanti. Rachel knew little about him except he had been educated, and that he served as a preacher for the Trelawney community of enslaved workers. He moved with calm deliberation, and his normally somber bearing was even graver tonight. He waited until the singer finished and the drum stilled before he spoke.

"Brothers and sisters, we stand in the presence of the Lord tonight to witness a promise to Him. Many of you don't know Ashanti Adams as I now do. Although he is a free man, he has lived among us, as one of us. He is a man who prays for the day when all black men can know the freedom he knows. And he knows, as we do, that this day may not happen in our lifetime. But it will come to pass, in the Lord's perfect will."

His words pierced Rachel. How mysterious, faith; how miraculous, hope.

A quiet murmur of affirmation circled around the crowd, and the sound reassured her. They were the same *amens* Rachel had heard on Sundays when Max was out of town and she'd gotten to sneak away to church with Camisha and her mother and aunt.

"Camisha Carlyle, too, is a free woman. She has agreed to become Ashanti's wife, and to please God, she wants to pledge her life to Ashanti.

"Most of us can appreciate why they come before us today—each day God gives us a gift of life, to be given back to Him. He will watch over them in the journey they begin today."

Two brooms were placed parallel on the ground between Ashanti and Camisha, and they stood facing each other. They seemed little aware of the crowd as Daniel spoke. "The straw of the broom means life. May the life you share be long and healthy, and may the children you're given be many."

Rachel felt a sudden warmth near her, and she glanced over her shoulder. Grey stood there, and when his gaze dipped to hers, she abruptly turned back to the wedding.

Daniel accepted the jug passed to him. "The libation means happiness," he went on, pouring a stream of the spirit between the brooms. "May your days be filled with joy, and guided by the Holy Spirit."

He placed the jug aside and said, "Now, Ashanti and Camisha would like to say a few words."

Ashanti's dark eyes moved over Camisha's face, and at last he spoke. "Camisha, my life began the first moment I saw you. In you I have found happiness no man has the right to expect. Once I prized freedom above my very breath—but freedom without your love has become true bondage. Today I pledge to you my heart, my body, my life. No matter where life takes us, I vow to God I'll cherish and protect you. Till death do us part."

A few nearby murmured, and only later would Rachel learn that the vow enslaved men and women traditionally made was *till death or distance do part us.*

"Ashanti," Camisha said, and her voice was soft as she looked at him. The crowd leaned in to hear. "I've never known another man like you. With you I know I am loved for the better part of me—and without you I cannot see the better part of me. Today I thank God that He led me to you. And today I give you my love, my respect, and my devotion—for all times. Till death do us part."

As she spoke the words, her gaze intent on Ashanti, tears clouded Rachel's eyes. Common sense said this was only a temporary marriage—lasting just until they returned to the twenty-first century. But somehow she knew that today she was losing a part of Camisha that would never return. The many moments they'd shared together flitted through Rachel's memory as she futilely wiped at the tears streaking her cheeks.

My name's Cammie. I'm the maid's daughter. Who are you?

The six-year-old Camisha who had rescued Rachel from a hopeless grief.

Don't let that boy treat you that way, Rae. Want me to beat him up?

A nineteen-year-old Camisha who had reassured Rachel that nothing was wrong with her, just because she had no desire to sleep with a college boyfriend.

I did what I had to do. Only cared about two people, and that man had the power to hurt both of them.

And a twenty-eight-year-old Camisha who had for all those years suffered to spare Rachel pain.

Now, that Camisha was gone—the devotion that had sustained Rachel in her darkest hours, rightly pledged to the man she loved. Rachel was happy for her. But somehow—she knew the vows spoken here today had changed their lives forever.

Grey's hand brushed her shoulder, and she accepted the elegant handkerchief he handed her. His gaze was reassuring yet troubled.

Daniel stepped between Camisha and Ashanti, joining their hands under his. "On this joyous day and in all the trials and joys ahead, I wish you God's richest blessings. May He chart your days and make warm your nights. And what God has joined together, let no man put asunder."

He stepped back, releasing their hands as they leapt over both broomsticks.

A gasp arose from the crowd, followed by stunned silence. Camisha, too, stared in dismay at her broom. As she'd jumped, her foot had grazed it, and it now lay awkwardly across Ashanti's.

Puzzled at the anxious glances the women nearby exchanged, Rachel looked at Grey for answers. He shook his head.

Daniel took the couple's hands in his and bowed his head, offering an earnest prayer for the couple. When he ended the prayer, the assembly enthusiastically *amen*ed. Then Ashanti bent to gather Camisha in his arms and strode toward a row of cabins. There, a new cabin had been built last night, raised by Ashanti and a few other men working after dark. Within its new walls, Ashanti disappeared with Camisha. A cheer of joy rang in the gathering, and the drummer began pounding out an exotic rhythm, lively with sensual joy. Two other sounds joined in from several men and women; one was that of a strangely shaped instrument, the other the pulsing hiss of gourds containing beans.

Some men and women joined in the ancient dance near the bonfire; others joined in the feast. Rachel's awkwardness returned. No matter how close she and Camisha had ever been, this was a part of her friend that she had never been able to claim as her own. Now, she grew painfully aware of Grey standing quietly at her side, watching the proceedings.

"Look at Emily," he remarked, chuckling.

She played with the other children in the dirt near one of the cabins, her blonde curls tied up in a bandana as she indelicately leapfrogged over Sukey's back. The commonplace sight troubled Rachel. Children had to be taught hatred. In another time, their friendship could blossom. In this time, one would remain in servitude to the other.

"Massa, here be some of that bumbo you sent."

Grey turned and accepted the mug from a young girl. "Thank you, Lydia."

He tasted the drink then passed the wooden mug to Rachel. "Shall we drink to the happiness of the newly wed couple?"

She tasted the drink. Sweetened, spiced rum. "To Camisha and Ashanti," she said, and they drank again.

"It was a stirring ceremony."

"I don't understand—there at the end, why was everyone upset?"

"She tripped on the broom—a bad omen. It means that trouble lies between them in the future."

"So it's just some silly superstition?"

He almost smiled. "Young lady, you are speaking to a ship's captain. Superstitions are not foolish."

She tried to understand, as she had all day long, what was in Camisha's heart. She knew she had fallen in love with the proud Yankee freeman the first moment she heard her say his name. Now, she suspected she wanted to carry with her back to her time the memory of a love that defied time. Camisha held deep Christian principles, but she'd agreed to a marriage that held no legal significance.

"Do you trust in God, Rachel?"

She slowly turned and peered up at Grey. It was absolutely the last question she would ever have expected of him. "Yes."

"And do you believe He blesses the vows we just witnessed?"

She saw the solemn expectation in his heavy-lidded gaze, as if he himself hadn't quite made up his mind on it. "Yes. I do."

"Then I would ask you to share the same vows with me. Rachel, you must know I—"

"Neither of them are married to another, Grey," she said, astonished. Peculiar, that he might see the romance of a ceremony created by the lowly. But that he could suggest a similarity between the love Ashanti held for Camisha—the man literally risked his life to remain in Virginia—and the lust Grey felt for her cheapened the transcendent beauty they'd just witnessed. The boisterous laughter and joy suddenly bathed her in a profound loneliness, and she silently left him.

Camisha had come to this time to find a man who cherished her more than the sweet breath of freedom, of life. Rachel found only memories of a family that was gone forever; and the instinct that she once had a mother and a father who had loved each other deeply made even more bitter the knowledge that her love for Grey Trelawney was utterly foolish.

She had come to accept that Camisha had not traveled here to accompany her. She herself had traveled here to accompany Camisha. Their entire journey to the eighteenth century had not been for Rachel, but for Camisha.

Chapter Twenty-Six

By the next morning, Rosalie was quiet once more, her guests returned to their homes. Only a single guest remained at the plantation, and that was her unwelcome mistress. That lady had now taken an interest in decorating the place, and her settling-in didn't surprise Rachel. The woman was too hot-blooded to marry a man like Grey without enjoying him.

Hastings had made himself scarce, for which Rachel didn't blame him a bit. She missed his dry wit, but he and the lady—like most feeling human beings she was forced on—didn't get along. This morning, he'd left for Norfolk.

Rachel, Camisha, and Emily were enjoying the sunshine weeding the gardens behind the cabins when a young boy arrived, excitedly babbling. "Miss Sheppard, Miss Sheppard! You be wanted in town!"

"In town? By whom?"

"Lady named Jennie. She said you know why. She sent a footman over, an' he be waitin' to carry you there."

"The baby," Rachel said, glancing at Camisha. "Can you watch Emily while I'm gone?"

"You know I will. You just go on. We'll be fine."

She quickly washed and changed, then set out in the carriage. An hour later, they pulled in front of the Trelawney home, and Rachel hurried up the walk to the front door, knocking.

The servant opened the door and showed Rachel inside. As the girl closed the door behind her, she asked, "How is Mrs. Trelawney?"

"She's in her bedchamber," the maid said. "She said for me to take you up, soon as you got here."

She followed the maid upstairs, fearful of what she might find. Inside the elegant bedroom, she saw Jennie sitting at the window, clutching the armrests of her rocker.

When the maid opened the door wider, she turned. Her face was swollen from weeping, but she smiled.

The maid closed the door, and Rachel crossed the room. "What's wrong, Jennie?"

"Thank you for coming," she said, catching her hand in hers.

"Has your labor begun?"

"No. But it will soon—" She dabbed at her eyes.

Rachel sat on the footstool beside her. She lay a reassuring hand on Jennie's arm. "What happened?"

"Oh, I've done something dreadful, and I know my child will pay the price."

"Tell me all about it."

The young woman clutched a handkerchief, and she twisted it in her hands. "I've visited a seer."

"Like a psychic?"

"I'm sorry, I don't know that word. A *seer*," she repeated. "A woman who sees the future."

"Why?"

"I've had this overwhelming sense of doom recently, and I'm not sure why. Well, she told me why."

Rachel waited, watching the macabre parade of emotions across her face; fear, worry, and—strangely, for a woman who'd struck her as stubbornly optimistic—hopelessness.

"She told me my child will die before his time."

Rachel exhaled in quiet rage. She stopped herself, though, not wishing to castigate Jennie for an act she'd no doubt been raised to see as heresy.

"She said things—incredible things about me that no one could know. But how could *she* know?"

"Who is she, anyway?"

"That doesn't matter." Then she gave Rachel a meaningful look. "One of Rosalie's servants."

"Have you told Thomas?"

"Good heavens, no." She dabbed her eyes with a crumpled handkerchief. "He has no patience for superstitious things. He says only the ignorant African or Irish believe in them. I haven't slept in days."

"What do you think has caused this anxiety? Perhaps you're worried about something else, and it's manifesting itself in concern for the baby?" She didn't know how useful psychobabble from the twenty-first century might be, but she gave it a try.

Jennie surprised her by abruptly becoming evasive. "I don't know that anything *caused* it. Does it matter? I'm worried about my baby!"

"Have you called the doctor? This worry can't be good for you or the baby."

She snorted. "Oh, Dr. McKenzie will tell me to stop borrowing trouble."

"There is something to it being no more than superstition. Plain and simply, the future hasn't taken place yet. Anything could happen."

"A seer doesn't *make* events happen," Jennie argued. "She simply *knows* they will occur."

Rachel fell silent. As she pondered, she noticed the portrait that stood on the opposite wall: Emily, no more than four years old. Ironic, she thought, that Thomas had denied Grey as his son, and yet now doted on Emily as his granddaughter—a child without a drop of Trelawney blood flowing in her veins. She turned to Jennie and tried again.

"We cannot change forces of history that are driven my many people, like the explorers forging new nations abroad. The events of one life, however, I ... yes, I do believe we can change. Otherwise, there would be no hope in some lives. There would be no reason to live our lives with autonomy and purpose."

"The past is written, in other words," Jennie said. "But my child's future is not."

"Exactly."

Jennie sighed, comforted somewhat. "Thank you. If you don't mind, I think I'll lie down a while. Thank you so much for coming into town, Rachel. You've helped a great deal."

Rachel helped her into the bed, knowing her time was very near. "Where's Thomas?"

"In the capitol. Court's still in session. I hear Grey's wife is back."

"Yes. She had a big party last night."

Jennie nodded. "We received an invitation."

"I'm glad. Why didn't you come?"

"The invitation was hardly out of respect for his father. He merely wants to antagonize Thomas. I declined without mentioning it to him. The woman disgusts me, and I can't watch how Grey treats him, while Thomas continues to try to bridge the gap. He says that perhaps it will help Grey come to terms with the mistakes Thomas has made and that, in time, it might help him win Grey's forgiveness. And that he might perhaps feel more favorably about letting Thomas know Emily."

Rachel's gaze rose to the portrait of the child, wondering how Thomas would feel if he knew the truth.

"But what about you, Rachel? Will you stay at Rosalie?"

Rachel met her gaze, seeing the kindness there. Yet the sight gave her an awkward discomfort; she didn't need to know the situation Grey had suggested, so she merely smiled. "I don't know how much longer I'll be here. It's become quite uncomfortable with his wife there. She's just not a very nice lady."

Jennie touched her hand. "Then will you consider—staying with us for a few days?"

"Jennie—"

"'Tis selfish of me, I know, to prevail upon your goodness for my frail cowardice. But it would be best for you, Rachel. People—not many, mind you, just one or two—whisper about your—" Clearing her throat, she whispered, "your purpose at Rosalie."

Rachel paled.

"But I admit I would feel comforted with you here. I know not why, but fate has bound us together, dear. You must know that as well as I. Please, will you consider it? I would love to have you here with me."

She remembered Grey's passionate plea for her to swear an illicit vow of faithfulness to him, and resolution stiffened her will.

"All right. I'll bring Emily in the morning."

Jennie heard the unhappiness in her voice, and she patted Rachel's arm. "Thank you. And don't worry, dear. The Lord knows what's best."

Her eyes closed, and Rachel turned away, wishing she had the benefit of divine wisdom.

Chapter Twenty-Seven

Later, long after Rosalie slept, Rachel dressed and left the house. She strolled aimlessly, hearing the sounds of celebrating in the slave quarters. The night was hot and still and muggy. Was he with her? She doubted it. And somehow, the knowledge of his loneliness intensified her own. In another time, perhaps they could've found a way. But it wasn't meant to be. Her reason for being in this time was half-done.

And the mystery grew deeper. Who was Jack Sheppard? What had happened that night she'd remembered in Grey's arms? What was the connection between that, and all else she'd learned? She and Camisha had endlessly tried to piece it together, to no avail.

As she turned toward the house, she saw Grey. She watched him move toward the stables with that easy gait. When he was out of sight, she moved on, troubled by the memory of his proposition. It couldn't be considered a proposal. Before, his offering had enraged her; now, it moved her. He had offered her what little he had.

When she approached the house, she heard a woman's scream and froze, her attention riveted on a small door she'd never noticed in a recess of the house. The scream had come from somewhere beyond that door. Should she run to get Grey?

Instead, she wrenched open the door and saw nothing but darkness below. Propping the door ajar with a large stone, she hurried down the narrow, winding stone steps. The air was dank and it closed about her the farther down she went. The moaning grew louder as she heard a hissing strike of leather. She reached the bottom, turned the corner—and she tried to make sense of what she saw.

She stood in a wretched room—a dungeon. Letitia Trelawney lay on a bed, her wrists and ankles secured in irons. The overseer Manning stood over her. Stripped to the waist, he wielded a delicate riding crop.

Rachel gasped, and Manning's head jerked up. Before she could do more than turn to the stairs, he grabbed her. "If it ain't Lord Windmere's whore. Look, Letty, I believe we've a playmate."

Manning's arm strapped across Rachel's chest, cutting off air. His beefy strength held her powerless, and her pulse was pounding in her ears. He pressed a latch, freeing Letitia.

"My dear," Letitia said, "you were quite rude to me this morning. I suppose you know punishment is in order."

Rachel jabbed at Manning's ribs, screaming Grey's name long and loud, for all she was worth.

Manning slapped her.

And the coolness of the macabre dungeon suddenly became the stifling heat of a summer evening in her childhood. It was coming back, and she fought it. This time, she feared, it would be too much. Too real.

He threw her to the bed, pinning himself over her as he grabbed one wrist and then the other, shackling her. Sweat dripped from his ruddy, bearded face as he loomed over her. But it was no longer Manning, only a man who looked strikingly like him. *That* man, with the crescent moon on his cheekbone, and she smelled the overwhelming stench of him.

"A mark to remember," he whispered. "Forever her mark will be upon you, as it is upon me."

She fought the memory; she knew what lay there, didn't want to see it again, couldn't bear to face the unthinkable fear, confusion, and heartbreak. Now an adult, she could place names to the awful acts her child's brain had been unable to process. And she wasn't ready; she would never be ready. She rejected the memory.

She felt the blow fall, slicing through her thin gown, a hot sting between her breasts. And even as she heard a familiar voice—Grey's voice, forcing her still deeper into the memory—she slid away into a chasm of darkness as she gave up her fight.

She saw the glint of a silver knife the man wielded, and a scream burst within her as she felt its tip enter her face. He slung her away, and Rachel covered her face in her hands, screaming at the pain as tears mingled with her blood. She heard a piercing cry and her pain was forgotten; he'd cut her sister's face, too. Rachel stumbled to her cowering sister, but the man was already lumbering toward the cradle, where the baby lay peacefully sleeping, spared the horror. Rachel began shouting. *No! No! No!*

The baby's screams, sudden shuddering shrieks that came from her tiny abdomen, horrified Rachel, and she rushed to the cradle. Blood trickled from her tiny face, where the man had left his gruesome mark.

"They're here," the woman said from the window. "Where's the babysitter?"

"Gone."

Rachel tried to calm her sisters, and then her heart raced with a sudden idea. They would hide in the closet while the man and woman were arguing, and when Mama and Daddy came home they would come in and find them. Mama would take them to the doctor, and he would bandage up their cuts, and everything would be just fine.

"Everything will be fine," she assured them, drawing the baby out of her cradle.

Hold Julie's head, sweetheart. Mama's instructions returned to Rachel as she carefully gathered the bundle in her arms. The baby's name was Juliana.

"Come with me, Merri."

Merrilea. They called her Merri.

She grabbed Julie's bottle from the cradle and the girls peered at the man and woman as they stole down the hall toward Mama and Daddy's bedroom. They crept into the closet and Merri tiptoed to reach the closet light.

"No!" Rachel whispered. "He'll find us."

She whimpered when Rachel turned off the light, and they burrowed behind the racks of clothes. She placed the nipple of the bottle into Julie's howling mouth. She choked, sputtered, and gulped, then finally her tears stopped as she pulled on the nipple. Time passed as the hot stillness of the closet began to close around them. As they waited silently, fear rose up within her. It had been too long, Mama and Daddy had had time to come home. Where were they?

"Here, you hold Julie. I'll see what's wrong."

"No, Rachel. I'm scared of holding her. And it's dark."

Rachel knew she was going to have to take the baby with her. She stroked Merri's cheek, feeling the dried blood. "It's all right, honey," she soothed her, just the way Mama always had. "I'm just going to go find Mama and Daddy."

She silently crept into the hall. She heard a strange grunting noise coming from the living room, and she heard a woman weeping, and then her pleading voice. A voice that rang with the trills and bells of a church hymn. *Mama's voice.*

"Please, John. Please let me go. My girls need me. I'm all they have left—"

Mama knew this bad man? Her voice broke off abruptly, and Rachel waited fearfully for her to speak again. At last, Rachel rushed into the living room. The lights had been turned off.

"Mama? Daddy? Daddy, I can't see you!"

Rachel's arms were full, holding Julie, but she leaned against the wall for support, tiptoed to reach the light switch and pushed it on, then quickly grabbed for Julie again, facing the room once more.

She stared, uncomprehending, at the grisly scene before her. There was Daddy, on the floor near the door. The bad man was bent over him, and he abruptly rose. His knife was stained red.

Rachel knew her father was sick. He lay very still, and she rushed forward, kneeling beside him, laying Merri on the floor for just a moment. "Daddy?" she whispered, shaking his shoulder. "Daddy, wake up!"

She shook harder, and his head lolled to one side. Rachel tried to scream, but couldn't. Why was there blood all over him?

She carefully pulled Julie into her arms again and scrambled unsteadily to her feet.

A hand grabbed her shoulder, jerking her away from her father. She swung around, seeing her mother, then, lying not far away. Her dress—one Rachel loved, because it was covered with yellow daisies—was bunched up around her waist. Mama stared at her, and she cried, "Mama!"

Mama didn't answer. She just kept staring at Rachel without moving. Without blinking. "Mama! Mama, say something! This man cut us, and we're scared—"

"Shut up!"

She flinched at the man's shout, but she forced herself to say, "You hurt my daddy. And you hurt my mama."

"You didn't see nothin', kid."

"Call the doctor, mister," she pleaded. "Please hurry. My mommy and daddy are hurt, and I saw you hurt them! I'll—"

"Nothin', you hear me? You didn't see nothin', you don't know nothin', and you damn sure better not say nothin'!" He shook her and she buried her face against Julie, holding tight.

"Jack, I don't feel good."

Rachel looked up at the woman. She huddled on the couch, her arms wrapped around her waist, shivering.

"We gotta get rid of these damned kids, too."

"Jesus, Jack, they're just kids! They ain't gonna know what to tell anyone."

"They're *his* kids, damn it. I told her I'd do it if she didn't come with me. I don't care what Max says—it happened, just like I said. He knows—"

"Your brother thinks you're crazy, Jack, and if he finds out about—"

"I'm getting rid of the kids," he repeated bitterly.

"Then let's come back for them," the girl said, and her whisper was raw. "I gotta have something."

"Mister—" Rachel began again.

He grabbed her shoulders, and she flinched, hugging Julie tightly.

"You keep quiet and you'll do just fine. You hear me? Open your mouth and you'll all end up just like them two. I swear, we're coming back for you."

"Come on, Jack."

"We'll be back in a while, kid. You better not move."

The door slammed, and Rachel stared from her father to her mother. Dazed, she walked to the phone and dialed the number Mama had taught her and Merri long ago. As she dialed, she tried to blot out the horrible images etched indelibly on her memory.

"Richmond Police Department," a woman said. "What's your emergency?"

Rachel focused on her mother's unseeing gaze, and she worked to get the words out.

My mommy's hurt. My daddy's hurt.

"Hello? Can you speak?" And then, in the background, the woman spoke some numbers. "Wellness check, 14 Harriman Road. I can hear what sounds like a little girl, crying." Then she spoke again to Rachel. "We'll have someone there soon, honey. Can you tell me your name?"

My name is Rachel Louise Miller.

"That's okay, sweetie. Don't worry, everything will be fine. Do you know your address?"

Help me. Please hurry. My mommy and daddy are hurt badly.

"Rachel?" Merri's soft cry from the bedroom reminded Rachel of her sisters. They could never see Mama and Daddy, hurt this way.

In a rush, she put the phone down on the table and ran back to the closet. They had to hurry and get out of the house, now. The man would be back, and when he came, he would hurt her sisters just as he'd hurt Mama and Daddy. She washed her sisters' faces then tried to remember everything Mama did when they went on a long Sunday afternoon drive.

First, she found their red wagon on the front porch and raced to the kitchen, now in a hurry. Those people would be back soon.

She looked into the fridge and the pantry, dumping in items that she thought they might need. Apples, the gallon of milk, the loaf of bread, the sliced ham left over from yesterday's Sunday dinner, bottles of water. They only needed enough until Mama and Daddy got well enough to find them.

She quickly grabbed all of the cans of condensed milk and reached in the drawer for the can opener. Two of Julie's empty bottles. She returned to the bedroom, bundling Julie in a cotton blanket and stuffing a handful of her cloth diapers into her diaper bag. All things she'd seen her mother do. Then she swaddled Julie into the empty space in the wagon, and they left the house. As they walked, Rachel remembered.

"Rachel."

Tears streamed down Rachel's face in the still summer night as they walked, as she remembered the mother who had loved her and laughed over her and taught her to watch over her sisters. As she remembered the father who had indulged her and treasured her laughter and taught her to always protect herself. She remembered the times they'd all spent at Grandpa's house in Richmond, or in the mountains, or at the beach. She remembered lazy summer afternoons in the backyard when Daddy let them run through the sprinkler after he got off work. He giggled uproariously when they grew bold and grabbed the sprinkler, turning it on him.

Then they'd arrived at the old farm house. Rachel knew that when Mama and Daddy got better, they would come for them. They would find them. And as day after day passed, she waited. And waited.

But they never came.

"Manning!"

Rachel fought the intrusion of Grey's voice, drinking deeply of the life-giving waters of memory. Days with gilt-edged beauty, photographed and locked away in a box that was guarded by a sentinel of unimaginable horror.

The sudden rush of noise jarred her from the past, and she saw Grey as he stormed into the room. In less than a moment he took it all in: Rachel, spread-eagled and shackled to the bed, silent tears streaming down her cheeks; Letitia, without emotion save annoyance, and Manning, half-naked and wielding a riding crop above Rachel, poised to strike again. Grey's eyes were cold, his face a mask of rage. And then his arctic silver gaze settled on Manning.

"You'll die for this."

Before Manning could realize the magnitude of his foolish mistake, Grey was on him. He slammed the larger man to the ground, wresting the riding crop from him and smashing the stock into the overseer's face with merciless wrath. Twice, thrice—then he flung aside the crop and used his fists. The huge overseer's brawn was powerless against Grey's violent rage.

And only one thing was able to pierce his blinding fog of rage: the sound of Rachel's voice, calling his name urgently.

His anger frightened her; she feared he meant to kill Manning, and she begged him to stop. At last, Grey straightened, jerking Manning from the ground. "You'll be off Rosalie in five minutes, if you hold your life dear."

"My lord," Letitia interrupted. "The number of whores you bed makes no difference to me. But I'll not tolerate your interference in my private affairs."

Grey whirled on her, and he grabbed her arm, their eyes clashing. Revulsion contorted his face as he released her, and his voice was deadly calm. "Madam, as a solemn vow, if you ever show your face on Rosalie again, I shall kill you where you stand."

Chapter Twenty-Eight

When Letitia and the overseer were gone, Grey rushed to the bed and released Rachel. He gathered her close, stroking her hair. "Are you all right?"

She nodded. "Manning only struck me ... once, I think. I don't know."

"Don't know?" He raised his head suspiciously. "Did you remember something?"

Her arms went around his neck, gripping tightly.

"What?" he asked, brushing her hair back tenderly.

"I remembered it all. I remembered my parents, and—" She stopped, revulsion wracking her at the freshness of the memory. Unremembered for more than two decades, it was as if it had happened yesterday. "I saw them murdered."

For some minutes, he comforted her. Then he swept her up in his arms and made his way through the labyrinth. Taking the stairs nimbly, he stopped at his room, carrying her inside. The door slammed behind him as he gently deposited her on the bed.

"Tell me what you remembered."

"I understand it all now. Well, most of it. The man who killed my parents was Max Sheppard's brother, and he had a woman with him. But I don't think she had anything to do

with it. And then we hid in the closet, and when I came out ...
my parents were dead. He raped my mother as she lay dying.
She called him John, the woman with him had called him
Jack."

His mouth was grim. "Did you remember anything else?"

"Yes." The memories soothed her as she sifted through her
childhood, choosing the brightest and most beautiful to show
him. "My father was a history professor. And Grey—my
mother was English! She had this wonderful accent, and this
cultured, old-fashioned way about her. She stayed home with
us while my father worked. And we were at a house my
grandfather owned, when it happened. It was this big stone
house outside Richmond."

"A stone house, you say?"

Rachel nodded. "Why?"

He shook his head. "What else?"

"Mama had a beauty mark on her cheekbone," she
murmured, "in the shape of a crescent moon. I guess that must
be why he cut us. He had a tattoo like that, also." She was
silent for several moments, then at last went on. "And the
locket—my sister, Merrilea, gave it to me for my sixth birthday.
Merri didn't have anything to give me, and the poor little thing
was just three. She took it from our mother's jewelry box.
Mama didn't have the heart to ruin Merri's surprise, even
though she was a thief."

"Oh, Rachel, Emily can't keep it, then."

"I want her to have it. Daddy had given it to Mama for
Christmas, before Julie was born. At one time there were
two—um, portraits, in it. One of me, and one of—of Merri—"

She was overwhelmed by fresh grief as she felt anew the
loss she'd blotted out for more than twenty years. For several
minutes, he held her silently, allowing her to feel the sorrow
that had been locked away too long.

"I remember Mama and Daddy talking about Jack
Sheppard. He was a student in one of Daddy's classes, at
William and Mary. My father was worried about him, but my
mother said he worried too much."

He stroked her hair. "My dearest heart, I'm so sorry."

"My father was a wonderful man, Grey. You've … always reminded me of him, since that first day I saw you and Emily in the gardens, although I didn't know it then. He was gentle and funny and he adored all three of us. I had no idea how much I'd missed him—even without consciously remembering him—until I met you. He was tall, and handsome, and…"

He saw the melancholy spear through her wistful gaze, and he drew her close. "It's all right, darling."

She felt his fingers probing at the tattered silk. "There's no blood. Is it bad?"

"Not very."

Dark, lean fingers brushed her cheekbone. "Forgive me."

"It wasn't your fault."

His eyes searched hers as he spoke. "For not seeing the truth … for hurting you … for waiting until it was almost too late to see that you've become the dearest part of me … for all of these things, I ask your forgiveness."

She traced the faint lines at his eyes, the strong cheekbones, the smooth curve of his cheek.

"You looked within me and found a flawed and damaged heart. And you believed you could make it whole."

She traced her fingertips along the base of his throat, feeling his pulse, slow and heavy.

"You endured undeserved harshness at my hand, in that hope."

Somber wonder shone in his eyes as his voice fell to a desperate whisper. "And you offered, with tender grace, your own heart."

She raised her hand to his face. "Yes."

"Knowing I might never be able to offer you more than my own heart in return."

The bitter reality of his statement pierced her, and his beloved face blurred before her eyes. A silent moment passed, and she saw a muscle move in his lean cheek.

"And you'll never steal that gift away, when I've come to need it most? You'll ever be with me so, with nothing between us but frail mortal frame? You'll abide with me though all else desert me?"

Tears ran into her hair as he softly pleaded her devotion, as he almost begged her to deny it now, if she would deny it at all. As he swore he had nothing to return for it.

She gently framed his face in her hands. "Always."

His eyes closed, and when he opened them again, nothing stood between them. "Then I can offer you no less in return. My heart, so long as it continues to beat."

Her arms circled his neck, but he touched her shoulders, pushing her back. "Give me the faintest of hopes that what I see in your eyes now is what I've yearned for always. Tell me you love me, Rachel, as I love you."

Joy rose, swift and sure, and she lifted her mouth to the warmth of his neck, spreading kisses there, rising to his jaw. "Yes," she whispered. "I do."

He gave a soft murmur of pleasure as he turned his face slightly, capturing her lips with his. Hesitant questioning kisses, fleeting butterfly kisses were a petition for the promise she'd just given. Slowly, they evolved into an exploration of amazement at her own yearning response. His lips brushed hers with the knowledgeable delicacy of an old world artist revealing a beauty he knew lurked within. He tilted her jaw, his fingertips playing through the thickness of her hair, his palm moving with discovery and appreciation over her throat.

A slow warmth spread through her at the unhurried glide of his lips. When he kissed her, it was as if he were trying to learn each nuance of her most intimate secrets.

Sleepy gray eyes smiled as he lifted his head. "It is most pleasurable, tasting you."

Her thumb rested against the shallow indentation in his square chin, and his mouth opened, capturing her thumb between his teeth. He drew it in against his tongue, and her lips parted breathlessly. Drawing her thumb away, she replaced it with her lips. Her tongue flickered out hesitantly and Grey welcomed it, delving inside. She tasted his sigh, felt the hard cords of his neck underneath her fingertips, heard the steady thump of his heart against hers. His hand roved over her hair, and he laughed, raising his head. "I cannot have enough of the touch of your hair," he murmured, watching it sift through his fingers. "As silky and soft as a child's."

His hand drifted to her cheek, and silver eyes held a dark gleam of anticipation as he examined her throat and the froth of ruffles at her breasts. That dark hand dipped to her flat waist, resting just below the generous curves exposed to his gaze, and his eyes met hers as he felt the rapid rise and fall of her sharply drawn breaths. "Tell me it isn't fear I feel here, in your woman's heart."

"No."

"I've yearned to touch you so. You've never known a man, have you?"

A slow stain rose to her cheekbones at the frankness of his question. "No."

His smile was rakish. "There are many ways for a man to give a woman pleasure."

She watched him with breathless anticipation. "Oh?"

He nodded, his fingers nimbly opening the gown's clasp between her breasts then brushing the smooth valley, and she knew he felt her tremble. "And every one of them gives her man pleasure equal or greater."

His fingertips were as delicate as a bird skimming over the surf. A tempest built within her as he traced the cleft between her breasts, noticing the pink welt from the lash. His jaw hardened, and she saw it.

"You were speaking of pleasure," she reminded him, attempting to distract him from his anger.

His gaze kindled, and he impulsively lowered his mouth, tracing with his tongue the path of the mark. Fireworks built within her at the sight of his warm, wet tongue stroking her skin. He loosened the tiny hooks hidden in the ruffles, opening her bodice with dazed expectation. The chemise did little to conceal the lush curves there, and he glanced into Rachel's eyes.

"'Tis far better to show you," he murmured. "Shall I?"

She was afire at the prospect of learning the things of sexual love from Grey, and her voice was a husky whisper. "Yes."

He inhaled deeply, and a dark index finger hooked on the slender lace strap of the chemise. "Here's the irony," he murmured. "The pleasure I can give you is only as great as you allow."

Her smile grew quizzical. "What do you mean?"

"Well," he went on, and his voice was a deep, hypnotic lull. "I cannot know my touch pleases you, unless you tell me."

Through the chemise, he sketched an erotic line from the curve of her breast almost to her nipple, and he watched as the peak stood up in anticipation. "For instance, see how you respond to my touch. My guess is that you enjoy this."

Moving to the other soft mound, he repeated the seductive motion. Again he stopped just short of the peak, which stood out in aching eagerness for his touch. "Shall I continue?"

His thumb sketched invisible circles around her nipple, drawing nearer with each stroke, until it throbbed anxiously.

"Grey—please ..."

"Then, perhaps you'd like this better."

Both palms cupped her breasts, lifting them slightly and pressing them together to deepen the place between them where she felt his warm, moist breath. With two dexterous fingertips, he pulled at the lace. The slow drag against her nipples made her gasp with pleasure.

"Ah," he said, his eyebrows lifting slightly. "That, you liked."

He pulled just slightly on the lace once more, and her nipples emerged, dark rose and erect. Only inches from his mouth. Her fingertips rested against his dark, glossy hair and tightened in shy encouragement, drawing him closer.

His eyes met hers, innocently puzzled.

Her tongue glided over her lower lip, and his pulse leapt at the thought of such a touch against his own skin. He drew his mouth nearer one rosy peak.

"Yes?" A bold, slow, hot whisper that moved across her nipple in a tantalizing caress.

"Yes," she sighed.

"No," he said, smiling, his palms moving against her, drawing the silky lace in a sweet friction downward, revealing more. He teased her other nipple, letting his breath flow there as he spoke. "'Twas a request for further instruction."

"What?" she whimpered distractedly.

He slowly straightened the chemise, then lounged on one elbow beside her, and she gave a soft cry of frustration. As he scrutinized her, one palm stole lightly down her throat, resting over the swell of her breasts. "Distinct displeasure," he murmured, his eyes blazing from her breasts to her face. "How might I make amends?"

Her trembling hands shoved at his shoulders, and he collapsed in surprise against the mound of pillows behind him. He smiled as she rose over him, admiration flashing in his silver eyes. She framed his face and lowered her mouth to his in desperate desire.

She didn't know how to fight this fire he'd kindled, knew only that she wanted something she couldn't begin to define. Her tongue suckled his into her mouth, an invitation and then a demand. She tore her lips from his, gasping. "I ... *ache* for your touch, Grey."

Passion raged in his stormy eyes, and his hands slipped upward from her waist, cupping her breasts. "Better?"

"Oh, yes."

"And this?" He captured her nipples between thumb and forefinger, rotating the hard tips. She gasped, arching helplessly into his touch.

Desire rocked his body as she straddled his hips, straining closer. He felt the warm cradle of her femininity settle instinctively over his hardness, and his breath left him when she restlessly moved against him, her eyes meeting his. His veneer of nonchalance—that façade he'd erected to put her at ease—was gone, and he feared the strength of his passion for her might frighten her. Yet he was powerless to curb it. He grasped her waist, drawing her nearer until his mouth closed over one peak, suckling earnestly, fascinated at the taste and texture of her. He impatiently pulled at the straps of the chemise until her breasts were naked in his hands, and then in his mouth. There were no subtleties to his kiss; his head was swimming with the frank urgency of her desire. She whispered his name, thrust her fingertips through his hair and pulled him close, crying out as he flickered his tongue over her nipple. He thought he'd never heard a more pleasurable sound than her low, appreciative groan as he closed his teeth, and his hands tightened on her waist, arching her still closer into his touch. The soft fullness of her breasts pressed to him, the heady aroma of her, made waiting a nearly impossible feat. Good heavens, if this was only the beginning, what might the end be! Yet this exquisite joy—the sound of her pleasure, the hardness of her nipple within his mouth, the demanding encouragement of her, loving his touch—how could he deny himself?

She felt the tremor of joy as he nibbled her breast, as his tongue played there, as he told her of his own pleasure with muted, wordless sounds. Withdrawing for just a moment, he moved to her other breast, lavishing the same erotic treatment on that throbbing peak. He saw the tight pink crown rise even higher, darkening to a rosy blush in anticipation.

"Christ," he gasped. "I can scarcely breathe at the sight of you so."

His gaze hot on her felt like a caress, before his mouth returned.

"Can we do this all night?" she whispered, her fingers toying with his hair. She went still at the sensations he wrested from her.

He chuckled, his fingers sliding over her voluminous skirts, gathering them in his fists. "Yes, but my heart may well stop."

He felt the smoothness of her legs clad only in silk stockings, and the satiny softness of her thighs above the stockings. His fingers curved around the lean thighs, smoothing upward to her hips, and his breath left him in a hiss. "Nothing underneath except the silk of your skin. Darling, what is it you have against undergarments?"

She heard the bemused wonder in his whisper, and she smiled. "There are just so many of them. How did you know?"

"You never wear stays. I knew it the night at the governor's palace, when I held you. I wanted to have you there in the gardens."

She rose gracefully from the bed, letting the disheveled gown fall to the floor, taking the petticoat with it. As she hesitated, she saw his gaze narrow, heard his sharply indrawn breath. She grew suddenly shy, knowing what he saw. A hastily half-removed chemise caught beneath her breasts. Twin white stockings that rose to her thighs. And nothing else but milky curves. She reached for the petticoat, covering herself awkwardly.

A dry chuckle came from him. "Ah, poppet. And you were doing so well.'

Grasping the petticoat, he let it fall to the floor. He took her hand, his gaze sparkling with anticipation. "Shall we continue learning of pleasure?"

"I don't know if I can stand much more of it."

He leaned forward, touching her chin, pressing his mouth to hers. "You misunderstand whose pleasure I mean." His voice fell to a low flurry of French.

"Oh," she sighed, bewitched by the soft murmur of his voice. "What did you say?"

"In lovemaking, darling, it is infinitely more pleasurable to give than to receive."

Drawing her into the bed, he settled her comfortably astride his thighs, easily removing the chemise and letting it fall to the floor. His eyes never stopped as they moved over her in leisured appreciation. Large, strong hands soon followed, his palms curving around the delicate hollow of her waist, the flare of her hips, the strength of her slim thighs. He peeled off one stocking, and then the other. "You enjoy riding."

Her eyebrow rose suspiciously, and his grin was wicked. "Horses, my darling. You've a prurient mind."

She laughed softly.

"I can see your love for the sport. I feel it in each line of your lovely thighs. As firm as the rest of you."

The warm palms skimmed upward between her thighs, and Rachel's breath grew shallow with timid fascination as his gaze slowly rested on the dark curls there. Reaching out, he settled his palm over the female rise, and her breath caught. Long, strong fingertips were almost unsure as he touched her stomach, and his other hand rose ever higher along her thighs, reaching the juncture. Her eyes closed, and she gave a low sound of pleasure.

Grey's heartbeat doubled. His eyes shot open as he lightly explored the cleft there, exposed to his touch, and he slipped trembling fingertips down just slightly. His breath left him in an abrupt hush at what he found there. Her body yearned for his—she was ready for him, now—and his breath returned slowly as he dipped a finger into the sultry warmth. He heard her gasp, saw her eyes as they sparkled with expectant wonder. More than anything he wanted to taste her—but at the moment, he enjoyed watching her respond to his touch.

Her position gave him intoxicating access to her secret female mysteries, and the wonder blazed in her eyes as he lightly played over the erect rise hidden in her flesh, as his other hand closed over a firm breast, as he leaned forward and captured an aching nipple within his mouth.

Rachel had never known such blinding pleasure. His tongue and teeth incited sparks of yearning that sizzled along the tips of her breasts to the center of her body, where his fingers stroked, cajoled, lured her to a frightening place of abandon that she'd never felt before. His mouth released her wet, distended nipple, and she saw his eyes linger darkly there for a moment before he pressed warm, slow kisses from her breast to her waist. He shifted slightly in the bed, his hands cupping her hips, lifting her even as he raised her thighs over his shoulders.

"Grey!"

But his name dissolved on her tongue as all at once he settled her over his mouth. The intensity of pleasure shocked her as his mouth delved within her, and she instantly tried to draw away. His strong hands clutched at her hips, fixing her in place, and his kiss deepened. First a light, tentative exploration, then a knowing advance and retreat, and at last a seductive assault that sent an explosion of joy surging through her body.

His name was a plea on her lips as he gentled his kiss, lowering her to the pillows and rising over her. She saw the solemn desire in his eyes, and her hands rested on his shoulders in bemusement. His sated smile belied the yearning that raged inside him.

"You're—you're still wearing your tie," she murmured in wonder.

"Easily remedied." A grim smile tilted one corner of his mouth as he rose from the bed.

She curled on one side, watching him undress. The act was intensely sexual. His eyes moved over her face, her breasts, her thighs, in deliberate enjoyment as he quickly unknotted the cravat and tossed it aside. The silk shirt followed, then the breeches and the rest. Rachel's heart thudded heavily at the sight of him naked—powerful and vulnerable, needful and infinitely giving, beautiful and very male. He rested one knee against the bed, his eyes somber.

"Give me your promise that you'll love no other," he said, cupping her chin. "For you have mine."

"I promise." She touched the hard muscles of his arms, then the supple shoulders, pressing her lips there. She felt the scars, but said only, "Grey, I want to give you the pleasure you've given me."

His mouth settled over hers as he molded her breasts. "It would give me pleasure," he whispered, "to feel your female softness—that intoxicating joy I just tasted—surrounding me."

She felt the arrogant male thrust warm on her thigh, and as she touched him, her thighs parted in instinctive need.

He gave a soft groan at her invitation, and as his mouth suckled once more at her nipple, his hand closed around hers, tutoring her in the strokes that pleasured him. Even as he stroked her with his tongue, his hips moved slightly, and he sought shelter within her. One dark hand slid between their bodies, and she went weak as he fondled her, as he began shallow, teasing thrusts, reaching the thin barrier that reminded him no man had ever known the path he traveled tonight.

His fingertips stroked her, kindling a desire that yearned for his full, abandoned thrust. She thought he meant to distract her from pain; she didn't know that watching her orgasm was one of the fiercest sexual pleasures he'd ever known. Her hips arched, and he knowingly increased his beguiling motions until the sensation rocked her, eclipsing all else as he sank within her.

He poised motionless over her, watching her as the excruciating pleasure of it rolled over him. Tight and sleek, she convulsed around him as he relished each secret caress. Her eyes were closed, her eyebrows wrinkled faintly, lips, softly reddened from his kisses, were parted, exposing the tip of her tongue. And her thighs rose instinctively, her legs locking around him. Her name was wrenched from him as he helplessly moved within her, the feeling of her weaving a haze of blinding sensation throughout him.

His lips lowered to her ear. "'Tis too much. I've imagined being inside you too often, and ... still, the reality is far better."

He felt the release building within him, and he shifted her hips slightly, changing their position, the sound of her appreciative cry forcing him to slow. What heaven, to feel her pleasure once more, pulsing around him. He thrust again, riding the sweet folds of her sex. And he raised his head—he had to see her.

Her eyes were open—shimmering gold, lazily watching him, moving over his chest, then meeting his in amazement, and her lips were parted, almost smiling. Her breasts were round and full and slick with his sweat, her nipples rosy from his vigorous laving.

So this is what it's like, to see a woman with love and desire in her eyes, examining you.

Her teeth captured her lower hip as her pleasure rose. "I've imagined this," she gasped.

The knowledge was nearly his undoing, and she caught his face in her hands, pulling him down to settle his open mouth over hers. It was a hot, urgent kiss, and she turned her face aside, finding his ear with her mouth, dipping her tongue inside, whispering the sort of things he'd never dreamed of her saying— yet she did it with innocence and shyness, making it somehow even more potent.

He would never know the rest of her thoughts, for his breath caught on a harsh gasp as his orgasm went through him. The pleasure became almost unbearable at the sudden, intense spasm of her around him. He muffled the sound of her name against her throat as he gave one last thrust.

Rachel was numb with pleasure. Her hands glided over the slick sheen on his shoulders as she felt his heart's beat within her, and he shifted to his side, drawing her with him. They lay in the warm aftermath of passion's storm, finding contentment in their quiet shared heartbeat.

Presently, her palms smoothed over his back, and she kissed his chest. He felt a sleepy contentment move over him, but he had no desire to sleep. He meant to make love to her until dawn.

"Grey, will you tell me—please—where these scars came from?" She felt his hesitation, the slight withdrawal in his touch. She held him closer. "If you love me."

"The story will put you to sleep, my love."

"You don't know how much I love you, then. Please?"

A minute passed, as she began to accept that he would never trust her with the story.

"I left Liverpool the day my mother was buried in a pauper's grave," he said at last. "On her deathbed, she made me promise to go to Williamsburg to find Thomas Trelawney. I found a ship in the harbor whose captain was willing to take on a raw lad, and I took to it readily enough. Truth to tell, ships had always held a fascination for me. The only thing my mother had ever told me about my father—until she knew she was dying—was that he had long ago sailed to the New World. From the time I was a boy, I dreamed of the day that I, too, would make such a splendid journey."

The thought of a boyish Grey, wistfully dreaming of the sea, moved Rachel.

"It troubles me that Lawrence Washington's brother so romanticizes the sea. All boys do, though, and I was no different. At any rate, in the year I was on that ship, it made only one American landing, in Charleston. I returned to

Liverpool a year older and no closer to fulfilling my promise to my mother. I met a man named Percival Snouth, who told me of a ship he owned that was traveling from Liverpool to Africa to Norfolk. In a year, he told me, I would be in Williamsburg. "My mother educated me well, but she'd never told me of the things I would see on that voyage. She never told me about slavery. The ship's captain was a crueler sort, and I had little respect for him. We purchased two hundred along the coast of Sierra Leone, and I managed to swallow my revulsion. It was all worth it, I told myself, if I could only get to Williamsburg."

He paused, and his hand stilled on her hair. "One man— one man had been taken from a wife and five children. That was a matter of course. But...the man he was chained to died, and the corpse remained chained to him for a day before it was finally removed."

She heard the disgust in his voice as he spoke. "The man went slowly mad on the voyage, and attacked the first mate. As a lad in Liverpool, I thought I'd witnessed every atrocity known to man. But none compared to what I saw on that voyage.

"The captain ordered the bondsman flogged for the attack, and I interfered once it began. For my insubordination, I was to receive fifty lashes." He gave a humorless laugh. "I believe I lasted thirty."

Dull horror pervaded her at his matter-of-fact description.

"I was not allowed to leave the ship when we reached Norfolk. Once more in Liverpool, I decided to again try a merchant ship. Unfortunately, the Royal Navy interfered in my plans, and I was press-ganged into service."

"Press-ganged?"

"Impressment. The Navy's method for finding new enlistees," he muttered. "Any able-bodied man can be abducted in an alleyway and taken aboard ship. Once there and out to sea, leaving the ship in another port amounts to desertion.

"I spent the next five years drifting from port to port— none of them near Virginia—which gave me plenty of time to repent of my compassion for the man I couldn't save. My protest had made no difference to his fate. He died despite my intervention. Now the promise to my mother was almost beside the point; Virginia had become a prize I was focused single-mindedly on winning. I once more met Percival Snouth, in port in London. Snouth's a powerful man, and he had fatherly feelings for me. He mentioned one of his slavers was en route to Norfolk, and that the captain of the ship was a more charitable man. And indeed, the ship arrived in Norfolk a little less than a year later.

"By the time I found my father, I'd seen far worse than what I saw on that first voyage. But I simply no longer cared. I was dead to the abomination of it. Once one accepts a wrong against humanity, it's devilish easy to find arguments to justify it, and devilish hard to turn away from it. At any rate, I met Thomas Trelawney, and he—"

He stopped, shaking his head, and a grim smile quirked his mouth. "Well, at least I learned a trade for my trouble. A small price to pay, I suppose—eight years."

The fathomless depth of his determination, his love for the father he'd never known, finally penetrated her. She searched his eyes. "It's all in the past, Grey."

"Is it?"

The dimness of the candle reflected the utter sadness in his eyes at the topic.

"Grey—"

He drew her close once more. "I was a pathetic wretch of a man until you came to me, my darling. You revived my scarred and lifeless heart and breathed love into it. And—" He cradled her head in his hand. "Know this as a solemn vow. If I would spend eight years sailing the seas for a man who dismissed me when I found him, I would move heaven and earth to ever have you by my side. The joy I know, holding you thus, is such that men dream of knowing. You blot out the blackest parts of me, and find worthiness in me where there is none."

She stroked his hand, and the words that stirred within her were words she'd never spoken to another. "I love you, Grey."

His arms tightened around her, and his lips burned a kiss on her shoulder. "As our hearts beat now, so they'll ever beat. Nothing shall ever stand between us. No man. No woman. No law of heaven or earth. I will never let anyone take you from me, nor will anyone ever hurt you, so long as I live. That I swear as a solemn oath to God and to you."

Chapter Twenty-Nine

Grey was awake to see the first gray streaks of dawn filter over Rosalie. Unable to sleep, troubled by the choices he'd made and those yet to be made, he'd spent most of the night watching Rachel sleep. As he watched her, he pondered what he'd done—exactly what he'd yearned to do since the night he first saw her—and found a curious creature abiding in the bed between them: his conscience.

God in heaven, what could be done?

Put away his wife? An unsavory prospect to his pride, to be sure. Divorce was reserved for connubial nightmares even a bishop despaired of, yet he had both cause and desire. And he cared little for the opinions of others—nothing for his wife—but he had never dishonored a promise before.

Or—keep a woman whose taste for cruelty was demonic? Was honor so sterling a trait as to make innocents suffer for it? One fear kept him awake through the night—that of dishonoring the woman who cuddled against him, trusting in his vow.

The depth of her faith pricked him anew. She'd trusted him with her blackest secrets—trusted him so completely that those secrets had been revealed only in his arms. He had thought he would persuade her to stay with him, to build their own haven that none could destroy. Now, he saw that haven only as a prison she would one day despise—and him along with it, for having trapped her there, rather than allowing her to find the love of a man who deserved her, who would honorably offer her his name.

A soft hand moved over his chest, instantly liberating him from the melancholy of despair. He rested his hand over hers, arriving at a solution he liked little.

"I've dreamed of waking up in your arms," she said, her voice slurred with sleep.

And I yours, my love. For the rest of my life.

He tugged back the mosquito netting and threw his legs over the side of the bed. He put on a robe, walked to the window, and stared out. A thin fog had moved in from the river over the tobacco fields, where the bondservants were already at work.

"Grey, what's the matter?"

He looked at her—a mistake. She sat on the bed, the sheet wrapped haphazardly about her. She looked ridiculously young sitting there, her amber eyes large and frightened, her lips soft from his passion—and hers. He remembered the soft warmth of her mouth on his skin, and he abruptly returned his attention to the fields.

"I'm taking you and Emily to Thomas Trelawney's home."

She watched him from the bed, disturbed by the distance he'd placed between them. "Why?"

"Do you think he'll not welcome you?"

"Of course he will ... but last night, I thought ..."

Wounded at the awkward dismay in her voice, he turned. "Do you love me, Rachel?"

"You know I do."

"Then I ask for your trust."

Trust me. Rachel, who before had found only Camisha worthy of her trust, didn't hesitate to give it to the man she loved. "It's yours."

She saw the emotion in his eyes, the grim set of his jaw, and she forced herself to ask the question. "Are you ... are you going to stay married to her?"

His gaze fell to the floor, and she went numb. At last, she began to dress, her fingers trembling on the hooks. By the faint light of dawn, their hastily discarded clothing, littering the floor, the chair, the nightstand, looked tawdry.

"Rachel," he said, touching her shoulders, "does my word mean nothing?"

"Yes. I would expect you to try to make the marriage work."

"Make it *work*?" he said, dumbfounded. "The woman is a— a—she's a succubus! I meant my word to you. But—what right did I have to ask your hand? I've no idea how long it shall take to dissolve the marriage. And that's assuming I'm successful in my petition for divorce."

She struggled against him, but he held her close. "I love you," he whispered. "I'll love you always. I only ask for your patience. I don't trust her, and I don't want you or Emily hurt."

She saw the earnestness of his plea. She slowly raised her hand, tracing his eyebrows, sliding her fingers through the softness of his hair. "Then I'll wait as long as you need me to."

She roused and dressed Emily, and they met Grey on the front walk, where he waited with the carriage.

"Where are we going, Papa?"

"We're going to your grandfather's, Emily. Perhaps you'll stay a few days there."

Emily's drowsiness evaporated. "With Grandfather?"

He nodded. They reached Williamsburg at last, and Grey hesitated at the brick house on the palace green. She saw the somber fascination in his face as he helped them down. He knocked at the door, and presently Thomas answered, dressed in a black nightgown. Without a wig, he looked even more like Grey. He stood aside, welcoming them in.

"Grey? Come in. What's wrong?"

As Thomas closed the door behind them, Grey spoke haltingly. "I ... would ask a favor of you—"

He stopped abruptly, as if biting back a word that wasn't quite appropriate.

"Then it's yours."

Grey cast a quick glance at Emily, who gazed up the stairs. "May Emily and Rachel stay here—just for a few days?"

"Of course. Would you stay as well?"

His father's unconventional blessing should have comforted him. Instead, he only wondered—was he no better than Thomas, to dishonor the vows he'd once made? Oh, they were different, so different, and yet now bound together. "No, sir."

She wondered what Grey was thinking as his gaze narrowed at the invitation. No matter what poor Thomas did, it vexed his son.

"Well, then." Thomas led them upstairs to the end of the hall. Inside the room, he lit another candle, illuminating a spacious, charming room. He looked from Grey to Rachel. "I'll ... see if Jennie is awake. She'll be delighted you're here."

Emily scampered after him, and Rachel watched them go. She touched Grey's arm. "You've got to forgive him, Grey, for Emily's sake and for your own—if for no other reason."

She turned away, swallowing unexpected emotion, and he touched her shoulders. When he drew her into his arms, she spoke softly.

"I would gladly give all I own for the chance to see my father again. Just once. I had so little time with him. Now, I treasure a single memory of him. It's too late for me to know my father. But it isn't too late for you."

He looked down at her silently.

"If you would remember anything of me," she went on, "remember that I want you to be happy. The only way you'll ever find peace is to know that those times are gone. What might have grown between you and your father twenty or thirty years ago—it's gone. All you have is today. For yourself, I beg of you, stop letting yesterday ruin today. Let it go."

He held her close once more. "I wish I could restore your father to you, my darling. But your father and mine are two different men. And..." He stopped, kissing her forehead. "Forgive me, but I've a long, urgent journey to make today, and I should get started now."

"Where are you going?"

"Richmond. I should be back in four or five days."

"Richmond? What for?"

"'Tis nothing to concern yourself over. I'll be back soon."

He descended the narrow stairway and left the house, and Rachel stared after him, wondering if it were possible to bridge so wide a river of bitterness.

Jennie was a patient teacher. She bent over her charges with calm direction, instructing them in the turn of a needle, the selection of floss. Emily held her hand with practiced grace over her hoop, and her stitches were neat, even, and tiny on the cotton apron.

Rachel, on the other hand, had just ripped out her last dismal effort at the gentle art of embroidery.

"I give up."

Jennie smiled. "You'll never make a proper colonial bride, Rachel."

Emily's head swung around. "Are you betrothed?"

"Not that I know of."

"I'm glad. I want you to stay with us forever." She moved away to the window, where she could alternately gaze out over the sunny day and then add a stitch or two to her apron.

Rachel smiled at the girl's easy appreciation of life. She wondered what this child would do in her lifetime—and she knew Emily would be a remarkable woman.

"Rachel, when can we go home? I miss Sukey and Camisha."

The reminder pierced her. Two weeks had passed since Grey had left, and the chasm that began with Camisha's wedding widened each day. Rachel had written her, but her response had been that of an old college chum; friendly but distant. She wrote to Hastings, and he sent a pleasant note reassuring her.

Lord Windmere left instructions that the Adamses are to be accorded the privilege and protection of house-guests at Rosalie. Mr. Adams declined the invitation, content for the time to remain with the bondservants. Have a care, Rachel. Yours is a precarious circumstance.

"Rachel!"

She glanced at Emily. "I'm sorry, darling. I miss her, too."

Jennie's mouth fell open in feigned offense. "Am I not properly entertaining my guests? Well, perhaps it's time we quit this stuffy house." She smiled at Emily. "And you, my dearest child, are desperately in need of a new frock. A pink one, I think, to match that merry apron you're stitching."

"Oh, yes!" Emily cried, hastily putting away her sewing.

They set out for the milliner's, which Rachel had learned was the colonial equivalent of a dressmaker. They spent the morning exploring town, and she observed William & Mary's Wren building, whose halls her father would someday walk as a professor. She knew why this place had raised so many emotions in her, that first day. Her parents had brought her here when she was a child—yet she didn't remember being so disturbingly aware, then, of the Trelawney home. There was a supernatural bond between her and Emily—the child whose ghost would lure her into the past ... to find herself.

When they returned home, Jennie was exhausted. "I think I'll lie down a while."

Rachel helped her into the bed, knowing her time was very near. "Where's Thomas?"

"In the Capitol. Court's still in session."

Rachel moved downstairs restlessly, arriving in the small courtyard out back. Jennie's flowers bloomed there—she'd pointed them all out to Rachel: larkspur and cornflower, Sweet William and primrose, rhododendron and gillyflower, something Rachel had always known as a carnation. The garden held a delicate womanly fragrance. It was Jennie's pride and joy.

She thought of Grey. He loved her, and it gave her a joy she'd never imagined. And yet, how could they find lasting happiness? She'd arrived at a sobering conclusion; for as long as she was in his time, she would love him—no matter what became of his marriage.

Can there be happiness indeed, without honor?

Grey's question returned to haunt her.

Thomas came home for dinner at two, and Rachel marveled at the love he held for his dainty young wife. He laughed over her feeblest joke, he guarded her every step, he watched her with a quiet, discreet yearning. An unfillable hollow settled in the midst of Rachel's chest as she thought of Grey, the man she loved more than life itself.

A peculiar guilt stung her. If he was married, at least she knew it. He had pledged his love to her and demanded as much of her; how, then, could she continue to deceive him about her past? Didn't he deserve to know the truth—that her time here was short? But what if ...

Oh, it was tempting and intoxicating, that hope. What if she were allowed to live out her life here, with Grey? Camisha's last letter had held the subtle message that she meant to spend the rest of her life with Ashanti Adams. Could either Camisha or she herself abide in this time, where men and women were treated as chattel?

They moved into the drawing room after dinner, and Emily left to fetch her sewing. Thomas watched her, smiling. "Rachel, I've never thanked you for bringing Emily into my life. And Grey."

"I'm sorry about Grey, sir. He's still very cautious."

"If it takes the rest of my life, I'll restore what I can of what I foolishly took from him. And me." He sighed, then went on, hesitantly. "I was quite literally a boy when I married Grey's mother. Lucy was little more than a child, and we eloped to Gretna Green. I truly didn't believe the marriage was a legal one, but Lord Windmere disowned her nevertheless. I thought that if I deserted her, Windmere would take her back in, but ... it escaped me what a prideful young girl Lucy was. She said she would rather die than beg her father's forgiveness. Or forgive him." He frowned into his tea. "Grey is quite like her in many ways."

Several moments of silence passed before he went on. "Since Grey appeared on my doorstep seven years ago, it's baffled me why he chose Williamsburg to settle in, or how he even had the means to arrange such an expensive passage."

"Don't you know?" she asked, amazed. "He worked on merchant ships. He was forced into service with the Navy, and spent years at sea without ever approaching Virginia."

"That's ridiculous. Why would anyone do such a foolish—?"

"He was only a boy," Rachel put in. "And he had made a promise to his mother on her deathbed."

Fierce protectiveness for Grey melded with understanding. Despite the bitter lessons he should've learned, Thomas was annoyingly sure of himself.

"Grey started trying to get to Williamsburg when his mother died. When he was sixteen years old. By the time he made it here, he'd worked on merchant ships, on ships of the Royal Navy, and on slavers, where he learned his gruesome trade. He did all that—for eight years—with one goal in mind, Mr. Trelawney." Rachel met his eyes with grim seriousness. "To find you."

His face was ashen as he abruptly rose and left the room. A stilted silence passed as the women exchanged a glance, before Jennie followed her husband. As she heard their muffled exchange in the next room, the terrible sounds of his grief, she realized she'd wounded him with a truth he'd never suspected.

Emily started to rise, and she stopped her. "What's wrong with grandfather?" she asked, woebegone.

She patted the child's hand. "He's all right, darling. He's just missing your father."

"I miss him, too!"

Tears pooled in Emily's eyes with the emotion of it all, and Rachel quickly gathered her up in her arms. "Papa will be home very soon, and in the meantime let's cheer up Grandfather, shall we?"

When Thomas and Jennie rejoined them, his face bore the evidence of weeping. "Were I deserted by my father at birth, I'd never have crossed the street to see him. My son crossed many oceans to do so. And I dismissed him with no more courtesy than I would a stranger. No wonder he despises me."

"He doesn't, sir. He's simply made such a *habit* of bitterness that it's hard to break."

"I'll change that. Somehow." Then he tilted his head in realization. "But what a fine man that young lady Lucy Harrington raised! How grave to him, the matter of honoring his vow to his mother."

The thought gave her pause, and she remembered him on the last morning she'd seen him. *Does my word mean nothing?* That question would return to trouble Rachel in the days to come.

The next afternoon, she and Emily knelt in the front yard, planting a rose bush beside the steps. Emily sat back and lifted her hand theatrically, gazing toward the setting sun. Suddenly, she squealed with delight and without explanation sprang to her feet, hurrying down the stone walk.

Rachel saw Grey, striding along the lane to meet his daughter. He caught her in his arms, swinging her around and hugging her close. Something twisted within her; she'd never thought to love a man or a child as she loved them.

His eyes locked with hers as he perched Emily on one hip and entered the gate. She rose, rubbing her hands against her apron.

"Hello." He looked weary, and his clothes held the dust of a long journey. His eyes roved over her with leisured appreciation, but when he met her eyes, her heart lurched. She couldn't quite define what she saw, but it was disturbing and strange. It was gone as quickly as she noticed it, as if she'd imagined it. But her instinct told her that deception had flashed through his eyes.

"Papa, Jennie took me to the dressmaker's yesterday and ordered a gown for me. And it's in your favorite color!"

"Oh?" he remarked, setting Emily on the ground. "How is Jennie?" His uncharacteristic concern startled her.

"Fine," Emily said. "And where have you been?"

He chuckled at her scolding. "Ah—Richmond, dear."

"Richmond? Whatever for?"

"Nothing that would interest you, dear. No frocks, nor ponies, nor flowers. But I do have a surprise for you."

"Oh!"

He smiled, reaching into his pocket and withdrawing a small velvet pouch. He knelt beside Emily and held in his palm two small heart-shaped objects, and she gasped.

"They're for your locket."

"But who is it, Papa? I didn't get to choose the two people I love best! I don't know this one."

"They're the two people I love best," he explained.

Emily chortled with delight, patting his face coquettishly. "Oh, Papa."

"Yes, poppet, of course this one is you," he began, sliding one portrait into place in the locket. Then he secured the second. "And this is the young lady who, I decided in Richmond, I'm going to ask to be your mother."

Rachel's contented joy vanished. What fresh hell was this?

"Look, Rachel!" Emily held out her hand, where the open locket lay. "I'm getting a new mommy—and she's *little*, like me!"

Cautiously, she inspected the open locket in Emily's small palm. One of Emily, and one of—

The artist had offered a colonial rendering, but the face there was unmistakable, complete with a faint crescent scar.

He gave her a hesitant smile. "I—er, borrowed your newspaper. And read the entire thing. Face to back, advertisements and all. 'Tis a curious place, where you were born."

Emily crowed with joy. "Why it's you, it's you! Do you mean it, Papa? Is Rachel going to be my new mother?"

"If she'll have me," he said quietly. "And if the fates smile on us."

Her eyes met his in sudden realization. He'd read the newspaper; he'd seen the dates there. He *knew*.

Chapter Thirty

Rachel watched from the bedroom door as Grey knelt beside his daughter.

"Why do I have to go to bed?" Emily asked. "It isn't even candlelight."

"Candlelight?" He smiled, raking his fingers through her blonde curls. "Where did you learn that from, as if I didn't know?"

"Sukey," she said. "Camisha says she's my girlfriend."

Rachel laughed.

"I'm having a wonderful time with Grandfather," Emily went on. She suddenly grew somber. "He says he loves you, Papa. He cried when he knew he hurt you."

She watched the scene in silent hope. Perhaps, where she had failed, his daughter could succeed.

"Oh?" he asked.

"Why can't we all just live here? I'll have a new little aunt or uncle soon, and I could play with them all the time."

He smiled, shaking his head at her absurdly logical reasoning. "Emily, I don't know how I ever got by without you these past few days."

She giggled suddenly, placing her small hand against his face. "Why, Papa, you're flattering me."

His laughter was soft and deep, and he brushed his lips against her forehead. "That's what papas are for."

They left the room, and he closed the door behind him. "Will you walk with me?"

She heard the earnestness in his tone, and she nodded. "What's wrong?"

After a long moment, he shook his head. "Nothing. I need to be with you."

They left the house, walking away from Williamsburg, a path unfamiliar to her. A pair of mourning doves cooed in the dusk. She watched him as they walked down the lane. He frowned, staring at the dust beneath their feet.

"What's the matter? You seem different."

He turned to her, and she felt the discouragement in him. He held out his hand, and she placed hers there. He drew her against him, and he hugged her close. "I missed you."

His hand closed around hers as he led her into the woods. She followed, ducking her head and growing increasingly charmed by the mystical woodland noises that encompassed her. The vespers of songbirds, the rustle of water nearby. At last they emerged into a clearing, and she smiled.

A rushing creek cut a swath through the woods. To their right, a small waterfall, perhaps twenty feet high, fed into a pool so clear she could see the smooth stones at the bottom.

"It's lovely." She was once more struck by the difference nearly three centuries could make to the land. The stream's clarity was unspoiled, the air so sweet and crisp it was almost painful to breathe it.

"It's fed by the James."

She remembered Camisha's joking words that very first day, about the smells of the eighteenth century. Peculiar, how little she'd noticed those smells. They were undeniable, when she stood near someone who bathed once a week rather than once or twice a day, but in the end they were no more distracting than the hideous aromas unique to her time. Bus exhaust, polluting industrial plants, all the array of chemical cleaners available in the twenty-first century? She couldn't imagine explaining those smells to Grey—or Byrd, the man she so enjoyed debating. Perhaps those of this time might view her time as unfavorably as she had once viewed theirs. And it occurred to her, at last, that perhaps each time should be judged on its own merit, without millions of second-guessers condemning people who, at worst, were simply trying to live their lives.

Removing his coat, he spread it on the bank. He loosened his pocket watch and lay it alongside his coat. The waistcoat followed, then the boots. He watched her as he unloosened his tie and removed it, then began releasing buttons.

She stared silently, her face growing warm with awareness of their intimacy, his comfort in watching her view his undressing.

"What are you, uh, doing there?" she asked, folding her hands behind her back.

"I told you. I'm having a bath." He pulled his shirt over his head, kicked off his breeches, then almost smiled at her discomfiture. "Will you join me?"

The undeniable intimacy of his invitation surged through her. With a flick of his wrist, he removed the ribbon from his hair then entered the water and gave a soft groan of utter exhaustion. Floating lazily, he opened one eye and peered at her. She sank onto his coat, bending her legs and bracing one elbow on her knee. She rested her chin in her palm, wishing there were a full moon out tonight. Wishing she could watch him so, in the light of day.

"A twilight swim would do you a world of good."

Cheered by the lifting of his weary gloom, she toyed with his pocket watch. He swam a stroke or two, then he stood, and water sluiced over his shoulders and down. She saw the glistening strength of him in the dusky shadows; the water rose as high as the dark hair that arrowed down from his navel. He walked to the bank, holding out his hand. "Will you join me? 'Tis shallow."

She hesitated, glancing at the waterfall's powerful beauty. The steady, unobtrusive *tick* of the watch in her hands sounded faintly above the waterfall, sobering her. She set it aside and rose silently in the twilight.

She loosened the hooks of her dress easily and let the simple frock fall, aware of his gaze on her. When she stood naked on the creek bank, he once more held out his hand, and she moved into the water and into his arms. She felt the steady rhythm of his heart along with the rushing waters nearby, and she turned her face into his embrace, memorizing the feel of him, the gentleness of him.

"I've missed the aroma of you. Lavender tonight, is it?" His palm skimmed over her hair, removing the pins and tossing them vaguely toward their clothes. Her hair fell around her shoulders, sliding against his chest, and he rubbed his cheek against her hair. "I can't abide another night apart from you."

She stroked the supple hardness of his shoulders, the lithe strength of his waist. "Your father would welcome you."

Humor glimmered in his eyes. "So you would have me live there as well, with my new little brother or sister?"

She chuckled softly. Major progress! He was at least laughing at his own grudge.

Sobering, he led her across the rippling water. The energy of the waterfall pervaded her as they reached the other side of the clear, surging creek. An assortment of boulders lay beneath the water. The patient, relentless currents of many ages had smoothed the largest boulder to a surface as glassy as marble.

He lowered himself there and leaned back, resting against another flat rock as he pulled her closer. "Sit here."

She hesitated, enjoying his pose. Long, powerful thighs were parted, with one leg bent, leaving an intimate hollow where she would just fit. Her eyes clashed with his, but she saw only steadfast patience there.

"It's a peaceful way to pass a lovely evening, darling. We can watch the stars together."

She gripped his hand, gliding into his arms, facing away from him. She heard his soft sound of contentment as his arms encircled her—one over her waist, one just under her throat at her collarbone. Rachel lay her head within the space beneath his chin, and he moved his palm against her shoulder. "There now. This isn't so bad, is it?"

His warm breath stirred the hair at her temple, and a cool, lazy current of water swirled around their feet. The aroma of him mixed with the bracing scent of the woods, the wild song of a nightbird rose over the water, and the moonless night enfolded them in a uniquely intimate solitude.

"No." Smiling, she rubbed her cheek against the reassuring warmth of him. "It isn't at all what I'd call bad."

He held her with quiet gentleness, stroking her, his hand gliding in a leisurely path. As his palm rested above the swell of her breast, he paused. "I enjoy the sight of you, Rachel. I can't wait to make love to you on a sunny afternoon."

A tremor went over her at his low murmur against her neck; his voice held a low huskiness as if he were confessing unspeakably carnal thoughts. She noticed the anxious tightening of her nipples, anticipating his touch. "And the sight of me touching you."

Her hand rested over his, boldly drawing it down. The darkness of his hands lent an erotic contrast as they cupped her breasts, his thumbs brushing her nipples as his mouth opened over her shoulder. A soft whisper escaped him, and she laughed breathlessly.

"You laugh?"

"You never speak French unless you're making love to me. And I do so love the sound of you speaking French."

He laughed.

"What did you say—just then?"

He inhaled thoughtfully, his fingertips fondling the rose crests, and his breath was warm against her ear, "Something that doesn't translate, I'm afraid."

"At all?"

"Well," he said, his voice low and soft. His words were teasingly light as he nipped her ear, as his hands closed over her breasts, "dubiously translated from a language of lovers into a language of conquerors, it would mean that this poor mortal wretch holds dreams too bold to find the light of day."

Turning her head slightly, she leaned back, feeling his breath soft and hot against her mouth. "Such as?"

She saw yearning glitter in the fathomless gray, and she lifted her mouth, imploring him for his own mouth on hers.

His gaze dropped to her parted lips, and he ignored her plea, as if savoring the sight of her. "Dreams of awakening within you," he murmured. "Dreams of plucking these luscious fruits from your gown at our supper table, and giving you pleasure there. That is an especially frequent dream in this wicked heart, since we do share a dining table. But most of all, dreams of growing old with you ever at my side, my true and only friend."

His poignant confession moved her, and his lips brushed her forehead. He gently turned her so that she sat across one strong, hard thigh, and he tilted her face up.

"How did you come into my life, Rachel?"

His quiet question, laying open the truth between them, took her by surprise. After a long moment, she lay her palm against his chest, feeling the hair sliding slickly between their skin. "Next time I'll tell you."

A fire lit his eyes. "Next time?"

"This time, I fear I'm distracted."

"Indeed. But why did you never tell me—how short our time was together? I've been so foolish—"

She touched his face. "Some people never find the person they're meant to be with. They never understand the meaning of love. We're lucky. We knew, for a while at least—"

He settled his mouth over hers with urgent need, and he clutched her to him in desperation. "Never say it, Rachel. Say we'll awaken every morning in each other's arms, that you'll never leave me. Say you'll love me for all time."

"That I can promise you," she whispered, her fingers sliding through the damp, dark locks that curled softly against her palms. "I will love you always."

She lifted her mouth to his, drinking from his hope, offering a portion of her own. He gave and took from her, spanning her waist with his hands, settling her over his lap. The searing intimacy sent desire pulsing through her, and her palms skimmed slickly over his broad shoulders. His gaze dipped to her breasts, and he lifted her, fastening a warm, eager mouth around a nipple.

Her fingers threaded through his hair and she rose to her knees, pushing herself closer. She felt his sharp intake of breath against her nipple at her boldness, and his urgency as his hands roved over her, clenching her hips.

"Rachel," he murmured, lowering her until she just felt the heated thrust of him teasing her. "I would have you for my wife."

His soft, husky voice, his quaint proposal, his profoundly sexual gaze on her, heightened her arousal to a dizzying level.

"Grey." She dared not sort through things like a proposal from a married man, especially in this state. She spread her thighs farther, pressing her pelvis down to reach him. He held her in place with strong hands clutching the soft flesh of her upper thighs and hips.

"No," he murmured. "Not without your consent."

Her need for him was desperate. Her hands slipped down between their bodies to clasp him. She gave a soft moan at the hard readiness there; she felt the craving in him, saw it in his anxious gaze, in the taut line of his jaw. His soft, disheveled hair fell over her throat as he leaned to suckle her breasts.

"*Will you.*" His question was a soft entreaty, an ardent demand.

She pressed him close, until she felt the soft warmth of his tongue on her breasts. Rachel arched against him, flexing her thighs. His grip tightened on her, refusing the admittance she sought. Then he lowered her slightly, stroking her in a maddening slide. She ached for him.

"Say it," he demanded.

Her mouth dropped to his shoulder; her lips pressed there, her tongue tasted, her teeth sank gently into the soft flesh. Then, acquiescent and soft, she leaned close, moving her breasts against his chest, letting her mouth fall to his ear. "Yes, my darling, I will never leave you, no matter what."

He thrust within her waiting haven, finding sultry welcome and provocative seduction in the feel of her. An elemental sound escaped him as she arched into his thrust, her eyes closing, her head thrown back, her hair falling down her back. The sight of her abandoned desire captivated him.

A fiery current swept through her at the unleased passion that consumed him. He clutched at her waist, curving her closer until his teeth closed gently around one breast. The new angle sharpened the pleasure within her even as he captured her nipple within his mouth, encircled it with his flickering tongue, mercilessly teasing her.

She felt as if she were one with the waterfall that crashed nearby, the rush of water raging beyond control just as the storm consumed her. She cried out his name and laced her fingers through his hair, drawing him even closer into the whirlpool of pleasure. She felt the resonant cry that rose deep within his throat and moved through her, and he pulled her down to him, burying his face against her throat as he whispered her name. The intensity of his climax rushed through her and intensified her own, until at last they came to rest.

Eventually they realized that night had fallen around them. The quiet song of crickets arose, along with the mournful cry of a woodland animal, and he stroked her hair, leading her from the water. Reluctantly they helped each other dress.

He held her arms, gravely regarding her. "You gave your promise."

She nodded.

"And you swear by it? No matter how long it takes?"

"Yes."

The look he gave her held hope and sadness and question without answer. He linked his arm around her waist and they walked quietly back to town. The silence of the night was broken only by the quiet, occasional conversation of a man and woman who were content in their love.

When they turned the corner near the Trelawney home, he froze. Alarmed at his sudden anxiety, she let her gaze follow his. Three men stood there, one of them watching the couple approach.

"Who is that?"

"Stephen Clancy. The sheriff."

"Oh, dear." Thinking of Jennie near her time, she rushed forward, and he followed close behind. "What's happened?"

The sheriff gave him a grim look. "Lord Windmere, I would have a word with you in private."

She saw Grey's troubled glance. "No. She'll stay."

"Your wife—" The sheriff cast her a quick glance.

"Out with it, man," Grey snapped.

Clancy met his eyes impassively. "I'm here to arrest you, Grey."

Her jaw dropped, and she looked at Grey. All traces of their lingering contentment were gone. What remained was a weary man.

"Lady Windmere's body was found in the James River. And you're charged with her murder."

Chapter Thirty-One

Rachel felt as if she were caught in a bad dream. Unbidden and unwanted, the memories rushed through her mind. Grey's strange distance of the past few hours, as if something weighed heavy on his heart. And then, his impassioned vow, the night they'd first made love.

Nothing shall ever stand between us. No man. No woman. No law of heaven or earth.

Was it possible? No. Immediately, she rejected the thought. No man so devoted to honor would commit such a dishonorable act. He'd traveled for years to keep a promise to his mother.

And on the way learned slave-trading, which he found abhorrent—yet was able to tolerate, to meet his greater goal.

No, she told herself again with insistent resolve.

"You're making a mistake, sir."

"Mind your own business, madam." The sheriff's gaze raked her damp clothes. "Whatever that might be."

"You'll apologize," Grey snapped, anger glittering in his eyes.

The sheriff's gaze was speculative even as he apologized to Rachel. "Come with us, my lord."

"On what grounds do you make these charges?"

"Two witnesses who saw you drown your wife, sir."

She felt fear slowly steal over her.

"Give me but a moment." Grey's eyes moved over her as if memorizing her. "Rachel, look at me."

Please, she thought, trying to blot out the thought of someone having witnessed the crime. *Not just yet.*

She slowly raised her face, and his dark brows wrinkled as he searched her eyes. At last, quiet resignation descended over him.

He turned to the sheriff. "I'm ready."

"No!" She clutched at his sleeve. "You don't understand. I thought—"

Clancy keenly watched her, and she dropped her hand abruptly. This was all going to end up in court, if they deigned to give him a trial. "You're mistaken, Mr. Clancy."

He nodded thoughtfully. "And how are you so certain?"

She hesitated. "Because—"

"Just go inside," Grey rasped. "Please. Emily's watching."

She glanced at the upper floor windows. Emily stood at one, rubbing tiny fists against her eyes. Rachel saw her lips form the word *Papa*. He lifted his hand and blew her a kiss, and she mimicked his gesture in confusion, darting away from the window.

Exactly as she had that morning so long ago, the first moment Rachel ever saw her.

She shivered at the premonition that stole over her. She hesitated, torn between Grey—who even now turned to go with Clancy and the gaolers—and Emily, who any second now would be racing out that door. Knowing his agony, she did what she knew he would have her do. She ran through the gate and to the door to intercept the child. She stopped, turning her head for a last glance at him, but they'd rounded the corner and were gone. She opened the door and heard Emily's excited footsteps on the stairs. "Papa?"

Rachel caught her at the bottom of the stairs. "No, darling. He had to go."

"Go where?"

"Well, he's going home." She stroked Emily's shivering body. "Here, let's close that door. It's cool out."

"But why didn't he wait to kiss me goodbye?"

"He told me to kiss you, and to tell you—" Her voice trembled. "That he loves you very much."

Emily sighed, crestfallen.

"Rachel?"

She heard the gruff voice at the landing. Thomas leaned one hand on the rail, watching her in confusion. She gave him a meaningful look. "Let me put Emily back to bed."

After tucking Emily in, she returned to find Thomas waiting in the hall, his gaze questioning.

"Grey's been arrested."

His face went slack with incredulity. "Why?"

"Letitia's body was found in the river."

Slow recognition traveled over his face as he arranged facts. "Dear God, this looks very bad. I'm his father, and it's bad even to me."

"And," she added blankly, "he thinks I suspect him."

"Oh, certainly not."

"Yes. I don't know whether Jennie has told you or not, but, um, well, Grey and I—"

He raised his hand. "I have eyes to see. But as it happens, she did tell me."

"He'd told me he'd let nothing stand between us. God help him if I'm called to testify against him which, after tonight, I likely will be."

He ran a hand through his hair, shaking his head free of the last remnants of sleep. "I'll go see what I can do."

She was downstairs in the drawing room, staring blankly at the harpsichord, when Thomas hastily descended, pulling on his waistcoat as he came. In one arm he carried his coat.

"I'll be back soon. There's nothing to concern yourself over."

No, nothing at all. The man she loved had been arrested for the murder of his wife. The case against him was grim. Nothing at all to worry about.

Thomas was gone for only a few minutes. When he returned, he seemed even wearier. "They wouldn't even let me see him. He's to have no visitors before the arraignment."

"Thomas?"

The soft, sleepy voice came from the landing above. Jennie stood there, watching in confusion. "Is something amiss?"

"Go back to bed, my dearest. 'Tis something I'd prefer you weren't worried with tonight."

Predictably, Jennie lumbered down the stairs. "What is it?"

"Letitia's body was found in the James River, and Grey's been arrested for her murder."

"Oh, my heavens!"

The three gathered in the kitchen, where Rachel put water on to boil for tea.

"This is ridiculous. Why would Grey *want* to kill her? He had no motive."

"Jealousy."

The women turned to Thomas.

"That's precisely what they'll name as his motive. The woman's lascivious nature was chronicled in the seedier conversations at Raleigh Tavern. In the end, they'll say, he flew into a jealous rage."

"Grey had every reason to want her alive," Rachel argued. "He stood only to lose by killing her."

"Were he not the passionate man he is, such a foolish act would be unbelievable," he agreed. "But the fact is, he is known as a man with a tempestuous nature. And the lady was rumored to have taken up with Donovan Stuart."

"That isn't true, though. I overheard her proposition Donovan—and he rejected her."

Jennie waved her hand impatiently. "The more obvious question is this. If not Grey—and we're agreed it isn't—then who?"

Thomas leaned back in his chair, folding his hands across his abdomen. The corner of his mouth quirked wryly. "You question who detested Letitia Trelawney? Our work might be shortened were we to list those who didn't."

"Well," Jennie said, "perhaps we first consider those who hated her enough to kill her."

"I had no great love for her," Thomas admitted. "She abused my Emily, and knowing that would have been quite enough for me to've throttled the woman."

"Cast out any heroic notions this minute," Jennie said plainly.

Rachel placed three cups on the table, then poured tea. "What about one of her lovers? Did she have any former beaux here? Aside from Donovan?"

Thomas gave an impatient snort. "Again, the list may be long. Truth to tell, I don't know."

"Perhaps," Jennie said, "it's the opposite. Perhaps she found a willing liaison, who grew skittish at discovery. While court is in session, ours is a town full of the gentry, many of them away from their wives. Any number of them would be destroyed were the news of an affair to come to light."

Thomas sighed, rubbing his eyes. "I'll speak to some people in the morning. Peyton Randolph may be helpful."

"The cousin of the deceased?" Jennie asked wryly.

"And the son of Sir John. As well as the King's attorney, and a close friend of Grey's. He'll uphold the truth. At any rate, we've time. The spring session is almost concluded, and they'll likely not hear his case until the winter."

"Winter!" Rachel exclaimed. "But …"

A cry upstairs silenced them, and Rachel skipped up the stairs. She opened Emily's door and heard the child's weary whimpers. "Papa … Papa!"

Rachel rushed to the bed, bending over the child. "Wake up, Emily."

A moment later, her eyes opened. She stared at Rachel in disorientation, and Rachel took her into her arms. "It's all right."

"Oh, Rachel, it was awful! Papa gave me a pony, and we went for a ride, and he raced away from me, and I couldn't catch up to him, no matter how I tried," she wept.

Thomas arrived at the edge of the bed, petting the child. "'Twas only a dream, my own love. Nothing more."

His eyes met Rachel's, and she saw the grim fear in his gaze. "You stay here with Emily. I'll take care of Jennie."

She nodded, wishing she could offer him the same reassurances he gave his granddaughter. They both knew his words were no more than that.

As he rose, he patted her arm awkwardly, and he gave a weary sigh. "This shall be the longest night of our lives."

Chapter Thirty-Two

Just after daybreak the next morning, Rachel strolled down a side street to the gaol with a basket over her arm.

At the front door, a gaoler stopped her. "Trelawney's to have no visitors."

"I have his breakfast." Rachel opened the basket, revealing innocuous contents. "He has a right to eat. If you give me trouble, Mr. Randolph will deal with you."

He relented. "Awright then. 'E's there on the right."

He swung open the massive wooden door, and she was overwhelmed by the stench. She moved toward the dank cell where Grey was locked. Johnny opened the door, then slammed it behind her and locked it once more.

The first rays of the sun slanted in through the small, barred window, and her eyes hungrily sought him. He stood in one corner, a shackle around his wrist chaining him to the wall. A dark growth of beard shadowed his tanned jaw, and Rachel stared. Stripped of his dignity, abused, unshaven, and exhausted, he still raised in her a poignant yearning.

"Why have you come here?"

Refusing to be put off by his male pride, she placed the basket near his feet. "I've brought your breakfast."

His eyes never left her. As she straightened, she saw something move through his eyes so fleetingly she thought she'd imagined it. So, he was going to punish her for her moment of doubt.

"How is Emily?" He spoke with a civil curiosity.

Rachel was certain of his ruse now. He was dying for news of his daughter, yet he spoke as if she were but a casual acquaintance of Rachel's.

"Fine. Except for nightmares of her father deserting her."

He jerked away, staring at the floor. He swore.

"They won't let me stay long. I only came to ask you—"

She saw the weary pain in him when he raised his head and gazed at her.

"Who might have done it?"

He shook his head, and each word was the ponderously spaced expression of a night spent wondering. "I *don't know.*"

Rachel lifted the lid of the basket. "I brought you some cakes, and some—"

"Kiss me, Rachel."

His words were so soft, she nearly missed them. They were a demand and a plea.

She straightened, and his free arm wrapped around her waist, holding her close. With despondent yearning, he searched her face. "I shall always love you," he whispered.

She lifted her lips to his and tasted his despair, and he held her as though it were the last time he would ever do so. And the terrible fear rose in her that quite possibly, it might be.

"I love you," she whispered against his mouth.

Her fingers sifted through the sweet, soft dark locks, curved about the hard jaw, trailed down the rumpled shirt. Her heart ached at the dismal sight of him. It wasn't this place—Grey at his filthiest was more splendid than any other man at his finest.

It was the devastation of his spirit.

"Some good shall come of this. My bondsmen shall be freed even sooner."

The chilling truth sank in; he meant at his death. He believed this was divine retribution for his dealing in human lives.

"Do you want Emily to remember you as a murderer?"

His voice was raw. "How can you even ask that?"

"Leaving her now with neither mother nor father?"

"Stop it," he snapped.

"Then pull yourself together! Tell me who you think might've wanted to kill her. Could it have been a love affair?" He sighed. "Likely more than one. But it could've been something much simpler. You saw her proclivities, Rachel. She may have simply found someone whose appetite for cruelty surpassed her pleasure."

"Have you at least discovered when she was killed?"

"She was found perhaps an hour before I was arrested. The coroner believes she'd been dead less than a day."

"So she was killed the night before."

"'Tis likely."

"Where were you that night?"

"Traveling the countryside."

"Were you with no one?"

"No. I saw the man who painted the portraits, but I don't even know his name, let alone how to find him."

Rachel felt hopelessness threatening, but she ignored it.

"What were you doing?"

"Trying to find out about a man named Robert Miller."

"Miller?" It was a common enough name. It was her father's name.

"Time's up, milady," the gaoler called.

"Just another minute, please." Her eyes searched Grey's face. "My father?"

His gaze met hers impassively. "I looked at the newspaper again when I was almost home. Only then did I understand where you'd come from. Rachel, if you'd only told me—"

The door swung open as the awful truth sank in. Grey had no alibi because he'd been searching for her father's killer—a man who lived in another time.

He straightened. He gave Rachel a long, hungry stare. "Thank you for bringing me sustenance."

"Grey!" she whispered, even as the gaoler escorted her out.

On the steps of the gaol, she stood for only a moment. "I'd like to see Letitia Trelawney's body."

The gaoler's mouth screwed up in distaste. "Why?"

"I'll give you—oh, all the money I have in my purse."

His eyes went round at the exorbitant bribe, and Rachel dipped into her bag, producing a handful of gold coins. "Where has she been taken?"

He jerked his head, hiding the money away. "Out back."

He led her to a small shed a few feet away from the gaol, and inserted a key into the lock. The chain fell away, and he opened the door.

"Griffin's to bury her this morning at Rosalie."

"Griffin? Who's that?"

"Deputy sheriff."

She'd steeled herself for what she might find, to no avail. The foul odor almost drove her away. "Can you—" she began, gesturing toward the body.

"Don't touch no dead folk, 'less I have to."

She forced herself to examine the woman. "Was she found this way?"

"What way?"

"Unclothed."

"The coroner had to disrobe her to get a look at her bruises."

"I thought she was supposed to have been drowned."

"So the coroner says."

She inspected, finding three sets of bruises. One at either wrist. And the clear imprint of human hands around her slender neck.

"Who found her?"

"Griffin."

"Thank you. Can you tell me where Mr. Griffith lives?"

"Down 't the other end of town. 'E runs a ordinary down there. Just look for a shingle with a bird on it."

She walked quickly down the street, not stopping until she found the sign of the phoenix. She rapped at the door persistently until it opened. None other than Jarvis Griffin stood there, wearing hastily donned trousers and shirt.

"What?" he snarled.

"How did you say Letitia Trelawney died?"

"What the—"

"You said she drowned."

"I said I found her body in the river, and that's where it was. The coroner's the one who said her lungs was filled with water."

"She has several unidentified bruises—"

"How would you know that?"

"—around her neck," Rachel went on. "And—"

"I expect Trelawney can strangle good as the next man."

"What of the bruises at her wrists?"

"What bruises?"

"Large, wide bruises on both wrists. The sort of bruise a tight shackle might make."

"Lady Windmere, shackled? That's a right pretty picture."

"What about those bruises?"

"'Twas dark. I didn't see 'em."

Rachel faced him calmly. "How much do you hear about the goings-on of the gentry, Mr. Griffin?"

"I ain't no gossip!" he retorted, his ire rising with each accusation.

"But you've never heard gossip of Lady Windmere? Her fondness for instruments of torture?"

"Hell, you're acting like I'm on trial here. Be gone, or I'll toss ye in the cell next to m'lord's."

And he slammed the door in her face.

Jennie was sitting in the garden when she returned. Rachel saw her unfocused gaze on the carpenter's yard in the distance, and she wished she could ease the concern for her child that weighed upon the young woman's heart.

Jennie noticed her presently, and she broke into a bemused smile. "Oh. Hello."

"I went to the gaol and saw Grey."

"How is he?"

"Discouraged."

"Grey's a respected man. But suspicion has been cast upon him, and Williamsburg deals swiftly with criminals."

"He isn't a criminal! Anyone who knows Grey knows—"

"That he's a man of quick temper, when he's been wronged. Thomas is right."

"Jennie, did you know ... well, of course you couldn't have."

"What?"

"Grey says that Letitia had strange appetites. Sexually."

"She was indiscriminate with her favors. That's common knowledge."

"No. I mean—she enjoyed, well, sick games. Inflicting pain and having it inflicted."

Jennie's mouth fell open. "Rachel!"

"I wonder—Grey suggested that perhaps one of her games got out of control."

She looked ill. "I doubt the court would even discuss such a matter."

"What?"

"We're discussing a dead lady's reputation. And whether she bedded half the colony, that wasn't a reason to kill her. She was still a *lady*."

"See! Now there you have it. The only reason they're so jacked up to pin her death on someone is because she's a member of the gentry."

Jennie's frown went deeper, and Rachel realized how politically incorrect her words were, for these times. But Jennie only asked in confusion, "Jacked up?"

"You don't understand. If she were—"

"No, dear, you don't. A gentleman won't discuss such things."

"When a man's life is at stake?"

"I'm not saying all is lost. I am asking you not to raise your hopes too high. And certainly don't pin them on Letitia's misdeeds. The case against Grey isn't good."

"But..." She grew fearful at the somber warning in Jennie's tone. "Thomas said Peyton Randolph might be helpful?"

"Peyton Randolph," Jennie said quietly, "is the man in charge of prosecuting Grey."

Rachel felt her breath leave her in a moment. "What? Wouldn't he—recuse himself, or something?"

"Why?"

"Well ... he's Grey's friend."

Her blue eyes gazed unblinkingly at Rachel. "And the cousin of the victim, a lady whose reputation you propose to sully in order to free Grey. Friendship means nothing in these matters, Rachel. He'll prosecute this case as impartially as if Grey were a stranger. Peyton Randolph has been charged by King George with executing justice in the largest American colony. A greater honor cannot be bestowed upon a man; nothing is more highly prized than his honor. Mr. Randolph will be fair. But if two credible witnesses are produced, Grey has little hope.

"Where's Thomas?"

"He was gone this morning before I awakened. He left me a note saying he'll be back tomorrow or the next day."

"Where did he go?"

"He didn't say. It has something to do with Grey, but I've no idea what."

If two credible witnesses are produced.

Rachel felt panic and fear, and she did something she didn't often do. She offered a silent prayer for wisdom.

She walked into the front room, gazing out on the street, watching two men in ornate wigs and waistcoats walking along the street as if on their way to court. Her mind raced in endless, insane circles as she sought an answer. Hopeless. It seemed absolutely hopeless.

She sighed. What they could use right now was a good, old-fashioned twenty-first century bulldog of a defense lawyer.

Rachel stopped in her tracks. And she ran through the house, searching for a servant. "Get me a horse—and hurry!"

Jennie stared, bewildered. "Where are you going?"

"To Rosalie."

Chapter Thirty-Three

The modest cabins were quiet when Rachel rode in on horseback. She knocked at the newest of them, and after a moment Camisha opened the door.

Rachel sighed. "I'm so glad you're here. May I come in?"

After only a second, she nodded. Dressed in the simple homespun garments of a slave, she stepped aside for Rachel to enter. She did so, uncomfortable. She was about to ask something of her that, in another time, Camisha would've already offered to begin with. Now, Rachel felt awkward; Camisha had never had reason to hold Grey in high esteem.

"What's up?"

The casual greeting surprised her, but perhaps she hadn't heard the news. Rachel met her gaze, finding only the faintest veneer of interest in her friend's eyes.

Something wasn't quite right.

"Did you know Letitia Trelawney was murdered?"

Camisha blinked, and she slowly nodded. "I'd heard that, yes."

Her prevaricating bothered Rachel. Contempt for Letitia, she understood. But it was unlike her to callously dismiss a woman's murder.

"Doesn't that surprise you?"

She laughed shortly. "Not much surprises me, Rachel."

"Grey's been arrested for her murder."

Looking away, she exhaled. "I'm sorry, Rae. I guess you kind of cared about him."

"Kinda cared about him?" Rachel was wounded that the woman who'd always known her heart before she herself did, could dismiss such a fundamental part of her life. "I love him, Camisha. The way you love Ashanti."

"Big difference. Ashanti doesn't run up and down the coast of England, capturing pasty Trelawneys to sell."

"What the hell? Are you saying that because of his past, Grey deserves to die for a crime he didn't commit? That's nothing like you. You spent your life defending the innocent, *especially* those with murky pasts."

Several moments of silence passed. "Rachel, do you know how many slaves will eventually be brought to America?"

"No."

"Six hundred thousand. And just take a wild guess how many American lives will be lost in the Civil War?"

"What does that have to do with Grey?"

"God has a way of working things out. Maybe he's getting exactly what he deserves."

She voiced the fears Grey had voiced that very morning.

Her indifference transformed Rachel's anger into desperation. She was her only hope. She had every right to her hatred of Grey. But somehow, Rachel knew she needed her help if his innocence were to be proven.

"What did you want, Rachel?"

She wasn't making it any easier. "I've got to figure out who really killed her. I know you don't like Gray, and I frankly don't blame you. But Camisha, he's changed. You showed him, where no one else could, that what he was doing was horrible. Now, maybe you can help ... save his life."

She turned away. "I'm sorry. I don't know anything. And if I did—I just can't help him."

Rachel's throat ached with unshed, frightened tears, and with the pain of her rejection. She moved numbly across the room until she stood just behind her, awkwardly making her listen to what she must say.

"Camisha, you know you're the dearest friend I've ever had. You befriended me when your own mother said you shouldn't. You ... you were put on this earth to help people who'd been deserted by everyone. You started by standing up to Max Sheppard when you were just a little girl, and you never stopped. Wherever you saw injustice, you did your damnedest to make it right.

"You've been there for me through the worst times of my life, even when I didn't deserve it. And now—although I know I don't deserve it, I beg you to help me." Rachel wiped futilely at the tears streaming down her face. "Please, Camisha. You've spent your life fighting for those who were without hope. Now—"

"*I can't help him, Rachel,*" Camisha's voice, thick with tears, was a tense, constrained whisper. "Don't ask me to."

"I'm asking you—I'm begging you—to help me. If you ever loved me, please try to understand. He's everything to me." Rachel bit her lip, resting her hand on Camisha's shuddering back.

"Oh, God, Rachel!" Camisha cried, dissolving in wrenching sobs. Her voice was thin and high when she turned, and her face was contorted with grief. "Don't you *know*? You could always read my mind. Now, you can't even see what's right in front of you. To save the man you love, I'll have to condemn the man I love."

Through her tears, she saw the agony in Camisha's eyes. Sickening realization settled over her. "No. Not Ashanti."

Camisha buried her face in her hands, and Rachel took her in her arms, absorbing the force of her fear. At last, a grim calm came over them, and they moved to sit on the straw pallet. When she finally spoke, it was with the soft-spoken grace Rachel had always loved in her.

"Night before last, I was sent to the house with the news that you were back and calling for me. I didn't feel very good about it, because I knew you wouldn't 'call' for me. Ashanti didn't want me to go. Still I went, because I thought it might be an emergency. The house was empty, and it was almost completely dark. When I got to the second floor, someone hit me over the head. And when I woke up, I was shackled to a bed."

Disgust filled Rachel.

"And that damned Manning was there, with Letitia." Camisha gave her a grave glance. "Then Manning thought he heard gunfire outside, so he went out to investigate. Letitia was standing over me with a riding crop, half naked, laughing this insane laugh as she hit me with it. And the next thing I knew, Ashanti was there, and he had her around the neck, choking her.

She looked numb. She gazed vacantly at the floor, and she slowly shook her head. "He was in a blind rage. I've never seen anyone like that. But I made him stop—and I did not think he killed her. I still think she was just unconscious."

"What happened when Manning came back?"

"Oh, we were long gone by then."

Rachel frowned. "I looked at the corpse. And there were bruises on her wrists."

Camisha pulled back one cuff, then the other. "Like these?"

"Yes." Rachel examined the ugly dark bruises at her wrists.

"That was one sick woman. She had all kinds of devices you could never even imagine. Manning had probably used the same cuffs on her recently."

For several moments, they sat in ponderous silence.

Camisha exhaled. "The thing is, I really don't think he killed her."

"He didn't. The coroner says she drowned."

"Oh, okay, that makes sense. Then she was probably still alive when Manning came back, but he thought she was dead. And he figured he'd be executed for her death, so he threw her in the river.

"Then, when somebody found her ... How much you want to bet that son of a bitch is one of the witnesses they have against Grey?"

Rachel felt sick. "They won't really execute someone just based on the testimony of two people, will they?"

"They will. Perjury's a serious crime, Rachel. At least, back in these days it is. The only reason somebody's going to lie is when the truth is going to get him killed."

"We're going to have to tell someone about this."

"Rachel, do you know what they do to slaves who kill their owners?"

"Ashanti isn't a slave. And she had no right even to be at Rosalie. Grey had sent her away."

"They burn them at the stake," Camisha went on, her voice shallow. "Then they behead them and quarter their bodies. And they place the head on a pole in town, to discourage other transgressors."

"Surely self-defense—"

"Lord above. You've got a hundred-pound white woman, a freaking *countess*, and you think some 200-pound buck's going to be able to convince anyone he was afraid of her?"

"You were chained to the bed, and they were abusing you. Ashanti's your husband—he had to stop it."

"And you think any of those slave owners sitting there on that council are going to care about some black wench—the common law wife of a man whose family is known as instigators—when the cousin of the blasted King's attorney is dead?"

Her mind raced. "What about Hastings? Where was he during all this? He had to have heard something."

"Carter Burwell had some kind of party, and Hastings went in Grey's place. He stayed overnight."

Rachel pressed her face into her hands. "What are we going to do?"

"We need somebody who's respected ... who'd believe—" she gasped, touching Rachel's arm. "Find George Wythe."

Rachel's head jerked up. "He knows Ashanti's been missing. He was speaking of it the night he was here."

For the first time, she felt a bit of hope, and she was suddenly eager to get back to Williamsburg. "All right."

At the door of the cabin, they embraced. "It's going to be all right," Camisha said.

Rachel gave her a wry smile. "Y' still think this is such a great time?"

Camisha's gaze held a somber wisdom. "Yes. The two people I love most are here."

Chapter Thirty-Four

When Rachel returned to Thomas's home, Jennie was waiting fretfully in the parlor. "What now?"

"The sheriff just left, Rachel. The examination court heard testimony of the witnesses today. Mr. Randolph agreed that there's enough evidence to proceed with the trial. The general court is going to hear and decide his case this session. The trial begins tomorrow."

"Tomorrow? But Thomas—there's no time—"

"Thomas may not even be back before it's over."

Snippets of thought floated like confetti in her mind, and she tried to focus on one. "Do you have any idea where he might be?"

"Westover seems likely. Mr. Byrd could perhaps help, at least to provide guidance. I've sent a footman to find him. Did you learn anything at Rosalie?"

"I found out who killed the woman."

"Then our problems are solved!"

"Not exactly. It's hard to explain, but it implicates the husband of a friend of mine."

"But—why did he do it?"

"She was abusing his wife. And he choked her and left her there. We think Grey's former overseer then threw her in the river."

277

"And she drowned."

"Ashanti is a free man, but that will be forgotten in such a trial."

"Your friend is a negro?"

"Yes," she said with an impatient sigh. "At any rate, I need to find George Wythe. If we simply tell the court the truth, the finer details will be lost and Ashanti will be executed."

"And you know Grey's certain to hang otherwise."

"Can't there be some solution?"

"'Tis a miracle we've found an answer for saving Grey, Rachel."

But—at what expense?

She sent a servant to search for Wythe, and they spent the rest of the evening distracting Emily from her father's extended absence. It was late when they heard the crunching gravel of a carriage stopping at the gate, and Rachel flew to the door. Relief flooded her as the carriage lantern illuminated Thomas's silhouette. With him were William Byrd and George Wythe.

"It's Thomas!" she called to Jennie, who clapped her hands in delight. Rachel flung open the front door, and the three men stood on the steps.

"Rachel. How good to see you again." Byrd kissed her hand. "I only wish it could be under happier circumstances."

"So do I, sir. Mr. Wythe, I assume you received my message?"

"Yes, just a few minutes ago at Raleigh Tavern."

"I know you have strong feelings about Grey's past livelihood. For that matter, so do I. But I beg of you to put that aside."

The young man gave her a grim glance. "Injustice of any kind grieves me. I will do what I can to help."

"Did you hear the trial is to begin tomorrow?" Thomas asked.

His eyes met hers, and the soft, familiar gray pierced her. The business that had occupied her all day was gone now, leaving only the memory of Grey.

"Yes. Is there any hope?"

He touched her shoulder, smiling. "For those of us who choose to find it, dear. How is Jennie?"

"She's sleeping now. But I think the baby might be here soon. She's very tired."

Thomas nodded. "Will you join us in the drawing room, Rachel?"

The men had a glass of sherry, but Rachel merely sat on the edge of her chair, explaining what she'd learned.

"I knew he was here," Wythe said. "He's too stubborn for his own good. But why, I wonder, is Jarvis Griffin lying for the overseer? He's the second witness, you know."

"'Tis dangerous, allowing a free black to abide with bondsmen," Byrd said. "It can do neither of them good."

"Mr. Byrd, Grey intends to free all his bondsmen."

His expression was perplexed, and he shook his head wearily. "Then he must have plans to leave the colony."

"Why do you say that?" Rachel asked, startled.

"He cannot make a profit without them," Thomas said. "Hungry farmers throughout the countryside serve as proof of that."

"Then I suppose there are things more important to him than profit."

Odd, how much she'd changed since knowing Grey. It had taken the unprincipled greed of his world for her to see that of her own.

"Can you cite an example?" Byrd said with a smile.

"Passing on a worthy legacy to his daughter. Not a legacy of dishonor. Mr. Byrd, your town has taught me a great deal."

"And what's that, my dear?"

She searched for the words. "Things that were once important to me now seem frivolous. Utterly meaningless. I've learned that the past is a very relevant part of the present. And that our actions today create consequences for our grandchildren and their grandchildren."

Byrd nodded. "What you say is the gravest sort of truth. I wish Virginia would exclude the chattels entirely. Slavery harms not only the bondsmen, but the bondholder as well."

Thomas shot Byrd a glance. "Yet you own them well enough, William. And as reward for his deed, my son now plays scapegoat for the crime of one of these free men."

"Mr. Trelawney," Rachel said, "Ashanti did *not* kill her. What he did do was justified. The woman was abusing his wife in the cruelest sense, one I cannot even describe to gentlemen such as yourselves. But I bribed the gaoler to show me Letitia's body, and the marks at her wrists must have been made by— well, some sort of restraining device. Anyone who knows her also knows how those bruises could have appeared. And anyone who knows her is aware that any number of men could've put them there."

The trio exchanged thoughtful looks.

"Is the lady at Rosalie now?" Wythe asked. "Your friend?"

"Yes. You'll find them in the newest of the servants' cabins."

"Then I shall go there. We have much to do tonight."

Thomas turned to gaze out the window. "Soon, the sun's rays will be filtering through the leaves of that tree," he mused. "'Tis strange, how solemn a simple sunrise can be when their numbers seem to grow short."

And it might well be Grey's last, he implied.

She decided she might be more useful getting out of their way, and she left them to their planning and climbed the stairs to the room she shared with Emily. Changing into a nightdress, she turned down the opposite side of the bed and climbed in. Her heart turned over as she glanced at Emily's face, wreathed in candlelight. Rachel dropped a kiss on her cheek, whispering, "I love you."

Then she settled into the unavoidable memories of Grey. Her glimpse of him that first morning, as he played on the lawn with his daughter. The night in the gardens at Rosalie, when he'd asked her to spend the rest of her life with him. And the night he'd held her and forced her to confront memories too horrible to face. At last, the resigned yearning in his gaze that morning, as he bade her goodbye, perhaps for the last time.

No. *No.*

Her sleep was fitful, and when she awakened early, the men were already gone. Emily was in Jennie's room, softly serenading her. The sight gave Rachel peace. "Rachel! Good morning."

She hugged the child. "Hello, dear. Are you hungry?"

"Oh, famished! Shall we have breakfast here?"

"What do you say, Jennie? Would you prefer to stay in bed?"

"Heavens, no." Jennie awkwardly pushed herself up. "I prefer to have this child out, so I can go about the business of mothering. Darling, I hope this child is even half as sweet and charming as you are."

Emily giggled. "I shall teach her how to be charming."

"What if it's a boy?" Rachel asked.

"A *boy*?" Emily repeated, aghast. "Well, she shan't be. Those shaggy creatures with the nasty fingernails? She'll be beautiful, just like Jennie."

After dressing, they joined Jennie in the breakfast room. She noticed the exhaustion in Jennie's face and the effort it took her just to get around, and it worried her.

After breakfast, Rachel said, "Jennie, I'm going to run down to the Capitol and see what I can learn. Will you be all right for a little while?"

Jennie's smile was patient. "Of course. I understand."

She hurried down Duke of Gloucester Street to the Capitol.

At the entry, she was relieved to find a friendly face: that of Godfrey Hastings.

"I'm so glad you're here," she said to him.

"And I you." After several moments of silence, he said, "If only your friend Malcolm could take *me* back in time to the minute before I hired the blackguard Manning. Not my finest hour."

"We can't know how our choices will turn out—can we?"

His eyes were soft on her, and he held his arm out to her. "Shall we?"

She placed her gloved hand there, and they entered. The room was packed. Hastings hesitated, glancing around, then led her forward through the crowd to where Thomas had held seats for them. The air in the room was still and hot and miserable, and whispers buzzed through the crowd.

"He didn't do it, I tell ye—" a woman said. "A man that fair and handsome, sweet as he is to that little girl of his, couldn't kill a woman. And even if he did, she had it coming."

A hearty chuckle. "True enough, Myrtle. He's too dashing a chap to have his neck stretched. And the world's better off without her, from what I hear."

The courtroom grew somber as a group of men entered. The last to enter was the distinguished gentleman Rachel recognized as William Gooch. Her gaze swept the chamber as she sought a glimpse of Grey. When she saw him, her heart swelled.

He stood in profile near the edge of the gallery where the men stood, with Clancy nearby watching over him. At least they'd allowed him to shave and change his clothes for the trial. His head was bowed, his gaze on the floor, his hands folded in front of him. She thought he very well might be praying.

Standing stalwart at his side was his father. It was grim indeed, what finally brought some families together.

Chapter Thirty-Five

The men took their seats in the council chambers. As president of the council, William Byrd sat apart from them. The court crier tapped a tall staff against the floor. "Silence in this court!" The rabble slowly dwindled.

"Oyez, oyez. Silence is commanded in this general court of the colony of Virginia while his majesty's justices are sitting, upon pain of imprisonment. Let all manners of persons who have anything to do with this court draw near and give your attendance. If you have plaint to enter or suit to prosecute, come forth and you shall be heard. God save the King."

The courtroom repeated, "God save the King."

The clerk faced the governor. "Your excellency, the first item on the docket is the Crown versus Grey Trelawney."

Governor Gooch gave a nod. "Call the case."

The crier tapped his staff once more on the floor. "Mr. Attorney General, call the case."

In his august surroundings, Peyton Randolph, the King's attorney, seemed older than his twenty-five years. "Your excellency, I am ready. Bring the prisoner before this court."

Clancy stepped forward with Grey. Peyton Randolph faced Grey grimly, and Rachel thought of Jennie. *He'll prosecute this case as impartially as if Grey were a stranger.*

"Grey Trelawney, you are brought before this court on charges of murdering your wife, Letitia Trelawney, Lady Windmere. Do you understand this charge?"

Randolph's voice held a solemn hush, and she knew that no matter what honor the King had bestowed on him or how well he performed his duties, this man could never look on Grey as no more than a stranger.

"Yes." Grey's voice was quiet.

"How do you plead?"

"Not guilty."

"Will you be tried by the justices of this court, or by God and by country?"

"By the justices of this court."

He was waiving a jury trial, leaving his fate in the hands of the men who made up the council of Virginia. Among which were William Byrd, but she knew better than to hope for unwarranted leniency. Had he chosen a jury trial, a dozen men would've been plucked this moment from the crowd to form a jury.

"Your excellency," Randolph went on, "I call the honorable Mr. Peter Jones."

A wigged man was sworn in. "Mr. Jones, please state your name."

"I am coroner of James City County, in the colony of Virginia."

"Please read to us your statement," Randolph said.

The coroner read from a sheet of paper. "Letitia Trelawney, countess of Windmere, was found dead in the James River on the morning of the first day of July, 1746. She appeared to have been dead for several hours, but no longer. The lungs were filled with water, and distinctive and hideous bruises were upon the throat and wrists. The cause of death was drowning."

"Please describe for the court the nature of the bruises."

"The bruises at her throat were made by large human hands."

"There were other bruises?"

"Yes, sir, upon her wrists."

"Can you describe those bruises?"

"'Tis harder to say. I doubt they were made by human hands. A hand would've left the impression of the fingers."

"Could they have been left by ropes?"

"I cannot perceive how. Ropes would have made smaller stripes. And a rope tied tightly enough to leave bruises would also have left burns. There were no burns."

"Who found the body, Mr. Jones?"

"I am told it was Mr. Jasper Griffin, the deputy sheriff. I did not see that firsthand."

"Thank you." Randolph glanced at Thomas. "Do you care to question the witness?"

Thomas approached the coroner. "Mr. Jones, about those bruises you saw. Can you theorize when the deceased may have sustained them?"

Jones tilted his head. "They could have been made any time in the last forty-eight hours. They were fresh enough."

"Thank you, sir."

The coroner was dismissed.

Randolph said, "I now call Jarvis Griffin to the stand."

Griffin was sworn in, and Randolph approached him.

"Sir, what is your occupation?"

"I work for Sheriff Clancy. I'm deputy sheriff of James City County."

"And how long have you been so charged?"

"Almost two months, sir."

"Please tell us what you know."

"'Twas last Monday night, sir, around nine o'clock in the evening, that I was out near the James River, when I heard a woman screaming. Begging for mercy."

"How far away from the woman were you?"

"About a hundred yards."

"Are you certain of the distance, sir?" Randolph asked. "That seems quite a distance to be able to hear screams."

"My hearing is quite good."

"Please continue."

"Well, I started toward her, but she stopped screaming all of a sudden. By the time I got to where I could see what was going on, I got scared. I saw him wrapping ropes around the lady's wrists and feet, and throwing her in the river."

"To whom are you referring, Mr. Griffin?"

"Him," he said, pointing at Grey. "Grey Trelawney."

A low murmur moved through the crowd, and the governor tapped his gavel.

"You didn't try to stop him," Randolph asked.

"No, sir. I didn't have a way to protect myself, and it looked like the lady was already dead."

"What were you doing on Trelawney land at nine o'clock in the evening?"

"I was fishing, sir."

"Did you hear Lord Windmere or his wife say anything?"

He thought for a moment. "Yes, sir. He said, 'That's the last time you'll ever make a fool out of me.'"

Again, a stir in the crowd. Again, the governor impatiently tapped his gavel.

Randolph paused. "Do you have any evidence to indicate what he meant by that?"

Griffin considered that for a bit. "No, sir."

"What happened then?"

"I left, sir, and went home."

Randolph took a step back. "You what?"

"I went home, sir. My wife was expecting me."

"Were you able to verify that the victim was dead at that time?"

"No, sir."

"Yet you made no attempt to rescue her?"

Griffin looked at his hands. "No, sir."

"You didn't go to the sheriff?" Randolph asked.

"No, sir."

"Why not? You're a servant of this colony, Mr. Griffin."

Rachel was astounded at what she was seeing. The prosecuting attorney was grilling his own witness. Could it be true, what Jennie had said?

"It made me sick, what I saw."

"How did you come to find the body of the deceased?"

"I went back early the next morning. I couldn't sleep—my conscience bothered me, as I hadn't tried to stop Trelawney. When I got to the spot, she was tangled in some brush near the bank."

Randolph nodded slowly. "Thank you, Mr. Griffin. Sir?" he prompted Thomas.

Thomas stared at Griffin for a moment, then slowly looked over the gallery of justices. "Where is your home, Mr. Griffin?"

"Here in Williamsburg."

"And how far would you say Rosalie is situated from your home?"

"About five or six miles."

"Is the sturgeon especially tasty at Rosalie, sir?"

"I beg your pardon, sir?"

"I assume there was a good reason for you to travel that far to fish, when a number of appropriate places would have crossed your path on the way there?"

"I'd been at my mother's home, over in Surry."

Thomas nodded, hesitating another moment. "When you found Lady Windmere, what was she wearing?"

"A nightgown, sir."

"And what of the ropes at her wrists and ankles?"

Griffin stared at Thomas. "Why, they'd been removed."

"By whom? Perhaps those famed fish of the James River?"

"The ropes was gone," Griffin said flatly.

Nodding, Thomas asked, "Mr. Griffin, you operate an ordinary here in town, don't you?"

"The Phoenix."

"Do men gamble at your tavern?"

"I expect so. 'Tis what men do."

"And are you one of those men?"

His eyes shifted nervously. "Sir?"

"Do you ever join in the gaming at your tavern?"

"Once in a while," Griffin said, shrugging.

"Thank you." Thomas turned to go, then pulled a Columbo. "Mr. Griffin, are you aware of the penalty of perjury?"

"I am."

"I once saw a man who'd perjured himself. His ears were nailed to the pillory, and what was left of them at the end of two hours was cut off. He wasn't especially pretty to begin with, but after ..." He shook his head.

"I'm a deputy sheriff, sir. I've seen it all."

"And yet, when you witnessed the murder of a woman, it so sickened you that you couldn't go to the sheriff with this news, as is your sworn duty?"

Griffin fell silent.

"I've no further questions, Mr. Randolph."

"Your excellency, I call Mr. James Manning to the stand."

Manning was sworn in, and Randolph stared at him thoughtfully. "Sir, what is your occupation?"

"I'm an overseer."

"For whom?"

"Until recently, I worked at Rosalie, the estate of Grey Trelawney."

A sudden commotion arose as two people entered the courtroom and made their way through the crowd to the area where Grey and Thomas waited. Aid had arrived from two unlikely sources: George Wythe, the man who had reviled Grey for his dealing in slaves.

And Camisha.

Manning observed her warily as she and Wythe crowded in beside Grey. But Camisha ignored him and quickly began examining Thomas's notes.

"Please give us the reason for your dismissal, Mr. Manning."

"Mr. Trelawney and I differed on the disciplining of unruly niggers."

"By that, am I to assume you mean bondservants held by Lord Windmere?"

"Yes, sir."

"If you were no longer in Lord Windmere's employ, why were you at Rosalie?"

"I don't want to slander a lady's reputation."

"Pray tell us what you know, sir," Randolph said curtly.

"I was on my way to see Letitia—Lady Windmere. She was unhappy, and she sent one of the niggers to get me."

"What do you mean by unhappy?"

"In her marriage."

"Did she give you an indication why?"

"He's a cad." Manning directed a black gaze toward Grey. "The poor lady came across the ocean, leaving her homeland to be with her husband, and when she got here, he had his mistress living right in the house with him."

The crowd rumbled, and the governor spoke. "If there can be no peace in this court, spectators will be removed."

Rachel was sick hearted. Manning was lacing the story with just enough near-truth to lend it credence.

"Lady Windmere sent for you. Why?"

Manning hesitated. "'Twas precious little happiness, for a woman who had nothing to look forward to but heartbreak. And it only happened the once, between us."

The crowd's restless anxiety grew as Manning went on. "Trelawney's never at home at all, from what I know. When he is, he squanders his days on the affairs of his estate. And I've heard he takes it upon himself to teach his daughter."

Manning spoke the words mockingly, and a few chuckles crossed the room.

"Mr. Manning, the man you describe—from hearsay, I hasten to add—sounds like an industrious citizen and devoted father. That he chose to educate a *female* is hardly a reason to execute a man. Can you explain what this has to do with the murder in question?"

"A devoted father doesn't have a woman living right under his wife's nose. Lady Windmere was an unhappy woman. She turned to me in her unhappiness."

Randolph sighed, as if weary of muddling through the mire. "When you worked for Lord Windmere, did you ever witness anything untoward in his behavior toward his wife?"

"Yes, sir. He quarreled with her the day he dismissed me."

"Please explain what happened."

"Well, like I said. Trelawney likes to go easy on his slaves. When one of them got out of line with Lady Windmere, she had me flog the wench. He stopped the flogging and told his wife he was angry enough to kill her."

Dear God! The man was re-inventing history, yet staying true to the incriminating threat Grey could never deny.

Randolph's voice was quiet when he spoke. "Describe specifically what you saw the night Letitia Trelawney died."

"I was on my way to meet her behind Rosalie. When I came upon them, he was choking her. And then he threw her in the river."

"Did you endeavor to stop him?"

Slowly, Manning said, "I'm not the bravest man, sir."

Randolph's eyes were bright on Manning for a long moment. He then turned to the gallery of justices. "Gentlemen, we have not one but two men who claim to have watched a man strangle his wife to death and neither raised a hand to stop him. We may have corralled the two most cowardly men in all of the colony."

He turned back to the witness, clearly aggrieved. "Thank you, Mr. Manning." He nodded toward Thomas. "Your witness, sir."

But Thomas simply stood by Grey. When Camisha instead approached the witness stand, Manning's outrage exploded. "What the bleeding hell is this nigger wench doing?"

Governor Gooch pounded his gavel against the tumult in the courtroom. "Sir, I remind you that you're in a court of England. You will conduct yourself with the reverence accorded it. Mr. Randolph, pray enlighten us."

"Your excellency, the lady is Miss Camisha Carlyle, a free woman who is educated and qualified to question the witness and who speaks on behalf of the defendant."

"Proceed, then."

Camisha had changed into a somber brown silk of Rachel's, and Rachel watched her in admiration and anticipation. Bearing the stigma of her color, she exuded only calm, shrewd competence.

She stopped before Manning, her gaze expressionless. She waited until each murmur in the courtroom fell silent, each person leaning forward at the curiosity before them. When she spoke, she commanded attention with that soft-spoken murmur; she had perfected a pitch she used in the courtroom that was just loud enough to compel listeners to hang on her every word. "What time was it when you came upon the man you allege to have seen choking Lady Windmere?"

Manning's resentment melded with nervousness as he grappled with whether to answer her at all. Before him he had a human embodiment of the truth of his own deeds. He glared at Randolph, who merely waited. "About nine in the evening," he muttered, looking away from her.

"Please speak up, Mr. Manning. A man's life is at stake."

"Nine in the evening," he said, his voice booming.

"Where were you?"

Manning continued to address the floor as he spoke. "As I said, I was on my way to Rosalie, to meet the lady."

"Specifically, how far were you from Lady Windmere and her killer?"

"P'raps thirty yards."

"Thirty yards. The area where Lady Windmere's body was found is rather densely wooded, would you not agree?"

"Woods surround the James River on Rosalie."

"Where was the killer standing?"

"On the riverbank."

"The riverbank, which is also overgrown with trees."

"Yes."

"When you heard the cry for help, did you recognize Letitia Trelawney's voice?"

He scowled. "I don't recollect saying I heard her cry out."

"Oh, of course. My apologies. That was the testimony of Mr. Griffin. What did you hear that night, sir?"

Another pause, as his eyes shifted. "I heard nothing."

"Your chivalry isn't on trial, Mr. Manning. Just tell us what you heard—was the lady calling for your help? Was it disturbing to hear her cries?"

"I heard *nothing*."

"Is your hearing impaired?"

"What? I can hear fine."

Camisha frowned. "Yet Mr. Griffin, who was three times the distance from the murder scene as you, claimed to hear Lord Windmere say, 'That's the last time you'll ever make a fool out of me.'"

"The wind was strong that night. Griffin may have been in a better position to hear."

"You recall a strong wind that night?"

"Yes."

"Then can you tell me what sort of moon was out?"

"What?"

"The light—was it bright, average, dim? Did clouds obscure the moon?"

Manning hesitated, sensing the snare.

"You were approximately ninety feet from Lord Windmere when you say he choked his wife to death," she pressed. "You were in a densely wooded area. What sort of light did you have to aid in your identification of him?"

His throat bobbed as he swallowed.

"I repeat, Mr. Manning. You stood in a thickly wooded area. Letitia Trelawney's killer also was surrounded by trees. Can you *swear* it was Grey Trelawney you saw that night?"

"I've said it was Trelawney," Manning snapped. "I saw his face as clear as I see yours."

"Sir, you see me in the bright light of day. But on the night Letitia Trelawney was murdered, there was no moon."

Dull hatred flashed in the gaze he focused on her.

"Mr. Manning, do you often gamble?"

"I've been known to play a game of loo," he muttered.

"Loo, yes. And whist, and every card game known to mankind. And dice."

"What of it?"

"How long have you known Jarvis Griffin?"

He met her eyes in challenge. "Mr. Griffin and I barely know each other."

"On the contrary, sir. It's my understanding that you and Mr. Griffin often meet over the tables."

"We may have played a game or two. Grey Trelawney and I may have met over the tables, for that matter."

"Yet Grey Trelawney has not lost Rosalie to you as a result."

"What?"

"Did you not play a high-stakes game with several men just last week at the Phoenix? A game in which Mr. Griffin was a consistent loser?"

"I don't recall the outcome of the game you mention."

"That's peculiar, since Mr. Griffin's bondsman Isaac remembers Mr. Griffin overbidding so recklessly that, in the end, he was obliged to stake the deed of his establishment."

"And?"

"And you held the winning hand."

"Madam, have you proof of this allegation?" Governor Gooch asked.

Camisha walked forward and placed a document before the governor. "I submit to the court for consideration this sworn statement Isaac Goodman gave before the court clerk this morning, your excellency."

"And it proves ...?"

"Jarvis Griffin's liability to James Manning. His motive for offering false witness."

"She's lying!" Manning shouted. His tanned face was ruddy with rage. "No slave can testify against a white man!"

Governor Gooch, busy reviewing the document Camisha had offered, eyed Manning shrewdly. "Mr. Manning, you are not on trial. As of yet," he added curtly. He nodded to Camisha. "I'll accept it."

"Thank you, your excellency. I've no more questions."

Manning walked back to his seat, and Rachel saw the angry glint in his eyes as he passed Camisha.

Chapter Thirty-Six

Randolph rose. "Your excellency, I'll now call Mr. Stephen Clancy." Clancy was sworn in and took the stand. "Mr. Clancy, please tell the court what you know regarding this case."

"As sheriff of James City County, I was summoned to Rosalie on the morning of the first of July to witness the coroner's examination of Letitia Trelawney. When two witnesses swore they saw Grey Trelawney murder the lady, I arrested him."

Randolph nodded. "Please state where he was at the time of the arrest, and with whom."

Rachel's heart sank.

"On Duke of Gloucester Street, approaching the home of Mr. Thomas Trelawney, and he was with a woman."

"Who is the lady?"

"I have only the hearsay that she's his mistress." Clancy gave a slight smirk. "I've seen her in town, bringing Lord Windmere's daughter to town to visit her grandfather."

"I find this unremarkable."

"Peyton, you yourself have said there's never been any love lost between the Trelawney men."

Randolph glanced at Governor Gooch. A peculiar quiet descended the courtroom, and the men under discussion stood stoically, watching Clancy.

"Describe the arrest, if you will."

Governor Gooch stopped him. "Of what interest is the arrest, Mr. Randolph?"

"In the interest of establishing motive, sir."

The governor nodded at the witness. "Go on."

"Well, we'd traveled to Rosalie that evening to locate him, and a chambermaid said Mr. Trelawney—Grey, that is—had just come from a trip, and had left straightaway for his father's house. We had just arrived at Thomas Trelawney's home when we saw Lord Windmere and the lady approaching. It was around ten o'clock in the evening, and they appeared rather—well, intimate."

"Intimate?"

The sheriff looked at Grey. "They were both ... they looked as if they'd recently bathed. Their clothing was wet. And Lord Windmere, well, his arm was about her waist."

A restless, faint murmur passed through the court. The governor ignored it.

"The woman twice told me I was mistaken, and ... Well, sir, I can't say for sure, but I think she was about to provide an alibi for Lord Windmere, without knowing when the crime occurred."

"You have no proof of this allegation?"

"No, sir."

"Then I remind the council to exclude this from their consideration. Thank you, Mr. Clancy. Mr. Trelawney?"

Thomas went forward. "Mr. Clancy, about those bruises. Were there any comments made at the time of the coroner's examination?"

"Yes, sir. 'Twas all conjecture, some of it occurring after the examination ended. Someone said—and I regret I don't remember—'looks like she finally came upon someone who didn't understand the rules of the game.'"

"Game?" Thomas asked, puzzled.

Clancy hesitated. "Games played in the bedroom, sir."

"Sex, you mean."

"Yes, sir."

"Were you surprised by the suggestion?"

"No, sir. There have been rumors about the lady for years. Never paid it no mind, till I saw those marks. They were the marks of shackles."

"How would you know?"

"'Tis my business, the restraint of criminals. But I'm not sure how they left bruises since her wrists were so small. "

"Thank you, Mr. Clancy."

Presently Randolph rose and walked forward. "Governor Gooch, honored justices, I have presented to you the evidence of this case: two witnesses who have sworn that they saw the accused, Grey Trelawney, strangle his wife and leave her body in the James River. I will now ask the defendant to present any witnesses."

Thomas rose. "Your excellency, I call Mr. Godfrey Hastings."

Hastings rose and went forward. The gray queue wig he wore emphasized his somber black waistcoat, and his slender, elegant form was ramrod stiff as he was sworn in.

"Mr. Hastings, in what capacity and for how long have you known Grey Trelawney?"

"I have been engaged as the lieutenant of Lord Windmere's tobacco plantation for five years, sir."

"Is he an honorable man?"

"Scrupulously so, sir."

"Mr. Hastings, please tell the court what your salary is."

Hastings shifted where he stood, frowning sharply at Thomas. "Sir, I fail to see—"

"Do you receive a salary?"

Hastings glanced at Grey. "No, sir. Lord Windmere evenly divides the proceeds from Rosalie with me."

"You receive half the plantation's profits? Is this a typical arrangement for the manager of a plantation?"

"No. Lord Windmere is an uncommonly generous man. I attempted to refuse this arrangement and he circumvented me to set it up with his banker. As I assume you already have ascertained."

"Thank you. Mr. Hastings, did you know Lady Windmere?"

"Yes, sir. Quite well. Although she resided in London, she had visited Rosalie more than once over the years of their marriage."

"Did you have any personal exchanges with her during this most recent visit?"

"Yes. The morning after she arrived, she inquired after Mr. James Manning."

"Rosalie's overseer? Did she have business with him?"

"I did not ask."

"She gave no indication why she needed to speak with him."

Hastings' austere mien grew discomfited. Rachel knew how little he liked airing such unseemly details.

"Mr. Hastings?"

"The lady had spotted Mr. Manning in the fields. She commented that he looked like a … well, as I recall, her words were 'a brawny, lusty lad.'"

"Did it strike you as unusual that your employer's wife would speak to you in this manner?"

"No, sir. I know my capacity, and I knew the lady."

"Was that the end of your experiences with her?"

"No, sir. She inquired after Miss Camisha Carlyle. She demanded to see the woman's papers verifying her freedom."

"Why?"

"The lady had little respect for those she viewed as subservient. Lord Windmere accorded Miss Carlyle a liberal degree of autonomy that Lady Windmere disliked."

"How did Miss Carlyle come to live at Rosalie?"

Here we go, thought Rachel. Never, no matter how deeply provoked, would Hastings lie under oath.

"She was a companion to Miss Sheppard, who is my guest."

"I'm told you're a relative of Miss Sheppard. Specifically, how are you related?"

His blue eyes met Rachel's for several seconds, and they seemed to glisten.

"Mr. Hastings," Thomas pressed, "please answer the question."

"Rachel is my granddaughter."

A shiver stole over Rachel. Hastings' principled honesty left no room for doubt. But ... how could it be? He must mean it in a general way. Still, it undoubtedly meant he was her ancestor. Thomas went on, giving her no time to dwell on it.

"Were there other exchanges with the lady?"

"I avoided her, sir. Each time I met her, it was an unpleasant episode."

"But would you characterize your personal relationship with the lady as cordial?"

Hastings examined his hands as they lay on the rail. Finally he looked up at Thomas. "I detested her. When she woke up each day, Lucifer rejoiced for the suffering and anguish she wrought on decent people."

"Thank you, Mr. Hastings."

The governor glanced at Randolph. "I've no questions, excellency."

Hastings returned to his seat.

Thomas said, "I call Donovan Stuart, marquis of Dunraven."

Girlish whispers and a giggle or two passed around the room as Donovan Stuart moved forward. He glanced at Grey as he went by, but his gaze was grave. He was sworn in.

"Lord Dunraven, what's your occupation?"

"I'm a lawyer here in Williamsburg."

"What's your relationship to the accused?"

"We once were the best of friends."

"And now?"

"I still have high regard for Grey, but I'm afraid I haven't proven worthy of his."

"What do you mean by that?"

"Twice in the last seven years, I had a liaison with his wife. When they were first married, and during a brief visit she made to Williamsburg four years ago."

Thomas glanced at Grey, but his face was expressionless.

"There's been much conjecture today about the character of Letitia Trelawney. You admit, apparently without qualm, to an adulterous affair with her."

"Affairs are of little enjoyment when qualms are attached," Donovan said with a faint smile.

Rachel saw the slight quirk at Grey's mouth, and she was grateful for the respite Donovan provided.

"And did you continue this affair when she arrived here most recently?"

"No, sir. She indicated an interest, and I declined."

"What do you know of Lady Windmere's arrival here? She hadn't visited in several years, had she?"

"While on a recent trip to Philadelphia, I met an associate from London. He told me then that Letitia had left London in disgrace."

"Disgrace?

"Her careless affairs were the talk of the *ton.*"

A single loud chuckle came from the gallery of justices. The man next to the merry justice cast a withering glance from his colleague to Donovan, and Donovan sobered.

"My apologies," he said, then went on. "She approached me when she arrived because she sought a discreet liaison."

"Did she say why?"

"Yes. She said Grey had no sense of adventure."

"Sense of adventure? Did she make it clear what that meant?"

"Men of my profession don't play at conjecture, sir. She told me plainly that he had no interest in the games she enjoyed."

"Describe, in as much detail as you're comfortable with, the games to which she referred."

Donovan folded his hands behind his back and glanced at the ceiling. "Four years ago, Letitia decorated a chamber at Rosalie that I doubt Grey even knows about. I visited the room several times."

"Why would you conduct such behavior in the home of a man whose wife you were seducing?"

"'Twas the lady's preference. The room held devices she was fond of, that I couldn't readily replicate."

"Devices?"

"Oh, dear." Donovan hesitated, wet his lips, and plunged in. "Well. Whips and things. Handcuffs. Removable shackles. Some of them, I still don't know their purpose. All handcrafted by a French jeweler to suit Lady Windmere's taste—and her delicate frame, such as her wrists."

"Shackles?" Thomas prompted, wanting more detail.

"Heavens, must we?" Even Donovan's sensibilities had their limit.

"Please."

"All right, yes, shackles. Letitia enjoyed—among other things—being bound to the bed while having sex."

A chorus of astonishment captured the room.

"Mr. Trelawney!" the governor interrupted, "the personal peculiarities of Lady Windmere are not an issue we have interest in. There are ladies present."

"I am aware of that, sir. Should you think it necessary to remove them, please do so. A man's life is the issue here, and Lord Dunraven's testimony is key to establishing the true cause of her death."

The governor sighed. "Very well. Should anyone prefer to leave, we heartily encourage it at this time. The testimony contains objectionable material necessary to discern the truth."

Many men rose to escort their wives to the door, promptly returning. Some women refused to leave, atwitter at the prospect of hearing Donovan Stuart describe his lovemaking. One couple began bickering and continued all the way out the door. Rachel saw the half-smile linger at Donovan's lips.

"Did you think this was normal?" Thomas asked Donovan.

"Heavens, no. Letitia was beyond bizarre. In the end, she grew bored with me."

"What do you mean?"

"She asked things of me that even I couldn't provide. She required a sustained level of violence that no man who loves women as I do could satisfy. In addition, she told me of a diary she kept that contained the names of all the men she'd known ... in the biblical sense, sir. She named several who are now in the colony. Most have wives of their own, and she knew she

300

could count on their discretion. As a bachelor, I believe she told me their names to remind me that my name, too, was in that book, and as easily mentioned to others. Even four years ago, she feared exactly the sort of disgrace that she ended up suffering in London."

"Then she broke off your affair back then?"

"No, I did." He smiled. "I was afraid that someone would get hurt, and that it might be me."

"Did Lady Windmere ever ... leave bruises on you?"

"Routinely, sir. Blood was sometimes drawn, though she oftener reserved that for the bondservants. That was another thing I disliked about her. She abused her servants terribly." Sobering, he said, "Virginia gentlemen avoid speaking plainly when it comes to their womenfolk, and I regret the lady's passing. But let me say this. Letitia Trelawney was a prurient, savage woman, and I believe she was killed at the hand of a man who liked the violence too well. I know this. Any number of men in this town—any number of men in this courtroom, for that matter—could have killed the lady. Except her husband."

"Why do you say that?"

Donovan stared silently at Grey for several moments. "I know—more than any man in this room today—that Grey would never commit murder, as has been suggested, in a jealous rage, over an unfaithful wife."

"Why?" Thomas pressed.

"Because, were he so inclined, he would've committed murder years ago. On the contrary, he made the honorable choice." Donovan's gaze returned to Grey, and his expression was sober. "And now, he is blessed with a charming daughter he rightly adores. He has everything to live for. Moreover, Grey visited me just before he left for Richmond."

"Why?"

"His purpose was twofold. He desired to change his will, to provide for the manumission of his bondsmen, on his death. He also made other changes, but they have no bearing on this trial. And he desired to petition for a divorce. I warned Grey that it would take a great deal of time and money."

"And his response was?"

"Let me get it right. He said, 'For seven years I've endured hell. I'll enjoy seven years of looking forward to heaven.' And might I add, sir, with all due respect to the attorney general, that this farcical testimony … well, I can't quite follow the storyline. Is Grey presumed to have killed his wife so he might have someone else, or to keep everyone else from having his wife?"

Laughter skittered through the room. Donovan knew he'd gone beyond the line of questioning, and he gave a placating nod to the governor. "I'm sorry, excellency, but it's important to the truth of this trial. Grey is an intelligent man. Why would he commit such a stupid crime, with all the so-called evidence pointing clumsily in his direction?"

Thomas nodded. "Thank you, Lord Dunraven."

Governor Gooch glanced at Peyton Randolph. "Mr. Randolph?"

"No questions, your excellency."

Thomas said, "I call Miss Rachel Sheppard to the stand."

Rachel took a deep breath and went forward.

"Miss Sheppard, what is your relationship to the accused?"

She looked at Grey. How did one sum up a lifetime of need and but a moment of fulfillment? "I am his friend."

"Are you in love with him?"

Aghast that Thomas would ask such a thing in this context, she reluctantly nodded. "Yes."

A loud hubbub crossed the room.

"Yet you knew he was a married man?"

"I did not know at first. He assumed I did. By the time I knew the truth, I already cared for him."

"Did Grey Trelawney ever say or do anything to lead you to believe he might harm his wife?"

"No. He said he was honor bound to her."

"Honor bound? Would his attention to honor have provoked him to dispatch his wife, freeing him to marry you?"

"No." She was relieved to see at last where he was going. "A man so hesitant to seek a divorce, because of his honor, would never murder a woman. The night he was arrested, he had just asked me to be patient, because a divorce might take years."

She glanced from the gallery of dignified justices to Grey. He stood with his hands behind his back, focused on her.

"In the last few months," she went on, "I've come to understand there's nothing more noble than a man with honor. And," she said, her gaze resting on Manning, "nothing more despicable than a man without."

Thomas asked, "How have you learned these things?"

"From Grey Trelawney."

"Thank you, Miss Sheppard. Mr. Randolph?"

Peyton Randolph rose and approached Rachel, and she felt a sinking in her stomach. She was the only witness he'd chosen to cross-examine.

"Miss Sheppard." He watched her as if she were a skittish cannon. "You speak a great deal of honor. Almost as if it were a foreign commodity in your homeland."

Rachel was silent.

"Exactly where is your homeland?"

"My family comes from Virginia."

He nodded. "How did you arrive in Williamsburg?

"I came to learn of the colonial capital."

"I see. But why Rosalie?"

Now, her superficial truths grew woefully inadequate. "I had heard a lot about the Trelawneys, and I believe I came here to remember a painful part of my past. A past I'd chosen to forget."

"Why would Rosalie serve such a purpose?"

"Because Grey Trelawney lives there. And in him, I saw a gentleness I'd not known since I was a child. In watching Grey's tenderness with his daughter, I remembered the most joyous part of my life. And I learned that although there are painful parts of the past that we cannot change, there is a great deal of goodness and virtue there as well."

She stopped as the realization seeped into her. As Malcolm had promised, she had found what the past—and her past—meant to her.

"And this honor you speak of—what has this to do with Lord Windmere's guilt or innocence?"

She looked at Grey. "I hope that men of honor will see that he never could've killed his wife. And that he will be restored quickly to his daughter."

Randolph bowed his head. "I've no further questions, your excellency."

"Mr. Attorney General, I call Grey Trelawney to the stand."

Chapter Thirty-Seven

Rachel's heart beat rapidly as he was sworn in. "Grey, tell the court where you were on the night of June thirty."

"I was in the countryside between here and Richmond, on my way home."

"What was your business in Richmond?"

"I'd recently learned Miss Sheppard's parents had been murdered, and I was attempting to discover who had done the crime."

Rachel hung on the sound of his soft, quiet voice. How the knowledge pierced her.

"Were you at Rosalie on the night of June thirty?"

"No."

"Did you bind your wife and cast her into the river?"

"No."

"Grey, did you kill Letitia Trelawney?"

"No."

"I've no further questions, your excellency."

Peyton Randolph hesitated a long moment. At last, he rose and walked forward. "Grey, did it anger you to learn just now that your wife had an interest in Lord Dunraven?"

"It was not news. I knew they once were lovers. I assumed they would be again."

"Would you characterize yourself as a jealous man?"

He hesitated only a moment. "As much as the next man."

"If you learned that the woman you loved had been unfaithful, could you find yourself capable of murdering her?"

Grey's gaze settled on Rachel, and his eyes searched hers for a long moment. He shook his head. "No, sir. Never."

"Did you love your wife, Grey?"

Grey looked at the floor, then back at Randolph. "Ours was a marriage arranged by my grandmother, Philippa Harrington. And I had hoped to come to love her."

"Yet you did not?"

"I learned her true nature on our wedding night. I pitied her. And I afforded her all the other comforts and protections a man offers his wife."

Randolph folded his arms across his chest. "When did you leave Richmond?"

"June twenty-nine."

"With whom did you travel?"

"I was alone."

"When did you return to Williamsburg?"

"The first day of July. I had to stop first at Rosalie to find out whether Hastings had need of me. He had only just returned from a social event at Carter Burwell's. I left for Williamsburg in the early afternoon."

"Is there *no one* to testify to where you were in that time?"

"No, sir. Only an itinerant artist I met, and I've no idea how to find him."

Randolph gave a weary sigh, and a lengthy silence passed. "Grey Trelawney, did you kill your wife?"

"No, I did not."

"I've no further questions, your excellency."

Grey was dismissed.

"Your excellency," Thomas said, "we rest our defense."

Randolph stood before the court, preparing to make his closing statement, when a hubbub began in the back of the room. An old man was shoving his way through the crowd.

"Excuse me, your excellency?"

Rachel blinked.

It was Malcolm, standing there before the governor.

The governor glared at Malcolm. "Do you have business with this court, sir?"

"As a matter of fact, I do."

Rachel glanced at Grey, surprised at the delight dawning in his eyes. How could he possibly know Malcolm?

Camisha watched Malcolm with suspicion.

"This is quite out of the ordinary," Governor Gooch said.

"But I've testimony to offer, your honor—er, your grace. Your *excellency*."

"Very well," the governor said with a sigh. "Will someone swear this man in?"

Randolph gestured Malcolm forward, and they clustered around Grey and Thomas, speaking in hushed tones. The room had fallen so still you could hear the rustle of silken shirts in the gallery as the justices leaned forward, attempting to hear what was said.

Presently, Randolph spoke. "Your excellency, I call Malcolm Henderson to the stand."

Malcolm was sworn in.

"Please state your occupation, sir."

A merry smile played over his face. "Well ... I do a little of this, and a little of that."

Rachel anxiously pressed her fingertips against her lips. This was no time for him to go babbling about time-travel.

"Can you be more specific?"

"I suppose you could say I'm a good, old-fashioned Renaissance man."

"I beg your pardon?"

"Renaissance man. In reference to that era, of course."

Randolph's brow wrinkled. "We're not familiar with that term, sir."

"Well, of course you are! We're well out of that period—" He stopped himself.

Craaaap, Rachel thought. He was off the rails already, using words that hadn't come into usage yet.

The attorney was clearly at a loss, and a knot formed in Rachel's stomach. She was beginning to think Grey might've been better off without Malcolm. It was like watching a car wreck in slow motion.

"My apologies, sir," Malcolm put in. "Shall we say I'm a man of leisure, with various interests?"

Randolph seemed at a loss how to question the man, and he gestured with a touch of impatience toward Grey. "Are you acquainted with the defendant?"

"Indeed I am, sir. I met him a few days ago."

"When was that?"

"When I was on my way to Richmond. He told me he was on his way back. And we made camp together."

Malcolm rubbed his chin. He removed his glasses, squinting in concentration as he polished the lenses on his handkerchief. Nodding, he said, "The twenty ... ninth. Yes. The twenty-ninth, that was it."

"You were together on the night of June twenty-nine."

"Yes, sir."

Rachel's heart sank. The date he mentioned left Grey plenty of time to get back to Williamsburg and murder Letitia.

"I see. And the next day ..."

"Well, I finished painting the portraits, of course."

"The portraits?"

"Lord Windmere has a little daughter, you know, and he mentioned her—the daughter, of course—wanting some miniatures for a locket she'd been given. I like to have a model when I paint, you know, but in a pinch I can get by off another likeness, and ..."

Randolph watched him go on, with far more patience than Rachel felt.

"I worked on them as long as the light was good the first night, then began again with first light the second day. It took most of that day, as well. He was anxious to get started back—missed his family, he said—and he left early on July first."

"Lord Windmere was in your company on the night of June thirty?"

"Oh, yes, sir."

"Now. As specifically as you can, please tell me how far you were from Williamsburg."

"Fifteen miles."

Randolph's eyebrows rose. "You say that with some degree of certainty, without hesitation."

"I'm positive."

"How do you know?"

"Oh, I didn't have any idea where we were, to tell the truth. But Lord Windmere knew quite well. He said that in all the years he'd navigated the seven seas, fifteen miles had never seemed such a great distance. As I said, he was eager to get home. But I think he was happy with the miniatures."

"When did you retire that night?"

"Early. Perhaps seven o'clock. We were both eager to get an early start the next day."

"Now. Would it be conceivable that Lord Windmere had time to leave the camp, travel to Williamsburg, commit the murder, and return to camp during the night?"

"No, sir."

"Why?"

"Because I woke in the middle of the night and found him sitting at the fire, staring at the miniatures. Sir, he was there the entire night. He couldn't have killed the lady."

The crowd seemed to give a sigh of relief at the alibi.

"Thank you, Mr. Henderson." He deferred to Thomas, who declined to question him.

Malcolm was dismissed, and he moved into the crowd.

Silence pervaded the chamber as Peyton Randolph stood before the court. He stared at the Bible for a long time.

"Governor Gooch, honored justices. In my studies of law, I've come to rely on the steadfast quality of justice. I've faith in our system of dispensing it. Miss Sheppard's testimony to honor struck a chord in me. Grey Trelawney is a dear friend of mine. The deceased was my distant cousin. Such things are set aside, however, when we discuss the execution of justice. We've learned that no man should be above the law. We punish those who kill bondsmen more swiftly than those who kill a free man. And today I've come to believe that I'm prosecuting the wrong man.

"You've heard the evidence as I have. I remind you that a woman was brutally murdered, and that there are two witnesses who've sworn to God and to the Crown that they saw Grey Trelawney kill his wife. You've heard the testimony of a man who places Grey Trelawney fifteen miles away from the murder site, on the night of the murder. You've heard the testimony of those who've sworn the witnesses for the Crown have committed perjury. I leave it to you to find the truth in your souls."

Randolph returned to his chair, and Governor Gooch nodded. "Mr. Trelawney, do you have any remarks?"

Thomas stepped forward. "Your excellency, honored justices. The sheriff said a remarkable thing today. He said there's never been any love lost between the Trelawney men. The truth is, a great deal has been lost, never to be recovered. This is not the place to try to undo wrongs that began thirty years ago on the other side of a cold, bleak ocean. The time I have been given with my son is but a speck. And yes, too much love has been lost. Had I been the father he deserved, he never would've strayed down a path that's come to this tragic end."

He stopped for a long time before he finally went on. "I ask you to consider why we're here. Honor. The belief that a man whose guilt hasn't been proven must be found innocent. The fact is, not only is Grey Trelawney innocent, he is the victim of the man who did commit this murder. All evidence leads to the truth: that the murderer conspired to condemn Grey, to save his own hide, when a despicable, illicit game went too far.

"Gentlemen, Grey Trelawney is innocent of this crime." His voice fell to an impassioned plea. "If you find him guilty, the murderer of Letitia Trelawney will go free, and you'll be guilty of murdering an innocent man. May God give you wisdom to find Grey not guilty." He returned to his chair.

"Gentlemen of the council," Governor Gooch said, "I give you leave to find your verdict."

Chapter Thirty-Eight

Byrd and the other justices left the room, and Rachel grew fearful. The brief hope roused by Malcolm's alibi wavered; he was an outsider, a stranger, and an eccentric one. His testimony might well be heavily discounted. The longest minutes of Rachel's life began to drag by.

Grey looked over his shoulder at her, and as their eyes met, a smile dawned over his face. Her heart rose up to him, amazed that in what he knew might be the last minutes of his life, his main concern was cheering her.

Her throat ached, and her eyes burned as she thought of how dear he'd become to her. And of everything he'd given her. He'd restored to her the most precious photographs lost within her heart. He'd shown her there were men of conviction, men who could recognize and reject their own human failings. And he'd loved her—with the kind of love she'd never hoped to know.

Only now, with so much between them that they were powerless to overcome, did the truth come to her, finding an equal mixture of hope and fear. She wanted, more than anything, just a chance to love him. To awaken with him each day, to argue with him over minor irritations, to rest complacent with the sound of his voice nearby, the touch of his hand within reach. She wanted to make a life with him—no matter what. How petty all else seemed, when faced with the grim reality of what could happen here today. Unspeakable images flashed through her mind—Byrd reading a guilty verdict, an unemotional Clancy dropping a black hood over Grey's head, a hemp rope around his neck. And although it had been a while since Rachel had prayed, she did so now, fervently.

The chamber door opened, and Rachel looked up.

"Will the defendant please face the council?"

Her heart hammered and her throat was dry as Grey rose.

Governor Gooch spoke. "Mr. President, how does the council find the defendant?"

Byrd stood and faced Grey, and his voice was solemn. "Your excellency, the justices of this court find the defendant, Grey Trelawney, earl of Windmere, not guilty."

Tears of relief flooded Rachel, and she saw Grey and his father embrace for a long, emotional moment. The elder man's arm was bent around Grey's head as he spoke into his son's ear, words that Rachel couldn't guess, but that put an end to their enmity for all time.

Then he turned abruptly, his eyes catching hers, and his smiling gaze was ripe with expectancy as he found his way through a crowd that cheered the verdict. He reached her in seconds, and he crushed her to him in a soundless embrace, revealing his own fear. Never had anyone held her tighter, and she knew he'd thought never to do it again.

"Awww. What a lovely couple," said one of the ladies she'd noticed at the beginning of the trial. "I told ye 'e didn't do it, Myrtle."

"Aw, go on, now. I told *ye* that."

His eyes sparkled with joy, with the appreciation of freedom, as he raised his head. "This is the finest moment of my life."

Camisha arrived, and Rachel turned to her. She saw tears in her eyes as they embraced. "Thank you so much."

"Believe me, I'm as happy as you are."

Grey turned to the woman who had helped save his life. He held out his hand, meeting her gaze with quiet expectation.

Kissing her hand, he held it between his own. "Miss Carlyle, I owe you a debt I can never repay."

Her lips hooked in a crooked smile. "I think that rogue Donovan had more to do with it than I."

Rachel smiled, but Grey's gaze was grave. "I speak of crimes I am undoubtedly guilty of. I pray that—in time—you can forgive me and my kind."

Malcolm stood a few feet away, scrutinizing the exchange.

"Until then, I'll work to undo the injustices I've bred and overcome the institution I've abetted. And I hope I can always count on the friendship you've shown today."

She smiled at Rachel and shook her head, as if marveling. "He *is* something."

Rachel laughed softly, "Grey, I promise you. Camisha's friendship is something you can always count on."

"I hope so. I think perhaps I shall need it, with the plans I have."

"What sort of plans?"

This came from Malcolm, and Grey turned. "Mr. Henderson," he said, shaking his hand. "I cannot thank you enough."

"'Twas only the truth. What plans have you in mind?"

"To do whatever it takes, to make people understand the reality of slavery. Men in their banking houses and drawing rooms don't see it, and have no cause to care. Those who do care have no means or power to make change. I do. And I will."

Malcolm nodded thoughtfully. Then he met Rachel's gaze. "Do you have a few minutes, Miss Sheppard? And Miss Carlyle?"

"Certainly." Rachel was eager to speak with him.

When they were alone, she said, "Malcolm, I remembered it all. It was horrible. I saw my parents murdered."

"Did you see the man who did it?"

"Yes."

Malcolm reached inside his waistcoat. "Did he look like this?"

It was a modern snapshot—of the same man.

"Yes. That's him. Who is it?"

"His name is Jack Sheppard—apparently Max's brother. He's in a sanitarium outside Lynchburg."

A shudder went over Rachel's skin. "How did you find out?"

"We investigated Max, as we told you we would. Did you know he was born in Virginia?"

"No. He never talked about his childhood."

"And we visited Jack. He's rather harmless now—I suspect if one's told often enough that he's insane, he begins to believe it. Especially when he insists on advertising the fact that he's traveled in time."

"What?"

"Jack apparently attended one of your father's classes at William and Mary, although there's no record of him as a student. Your mother was taking classes there, Rachel, and she befriended Jack, who was rather a disturbed person. And he fell in love with her. Unfortunately, he learned a deadly secret your parents shared. And when she refused his attempts at romance, he devised a scheme to win her, by traveling back in time to the eighteenth century."

"What difference would that make?"

"Your mother was born in the eighteenth century. And that's where your father met her."

She stared at him, unable to speak.

"But as he eventually would learn, it made no difference. He thought if he met her before your father did, he could have her. He didn't understand; your father crossed centuries to find his one true love. And no one could stop the hand of fate. In point of fact, if we see someone attempting to, we will stop it."

Excitement bubbled within her. "Then—then Hastings was telling the truth."

"Of a fashion."

"Then I have to talk to him."

"You'll do nothing of the sort."

"Malcolm! He's the only relative I have left."

The old man's eyes were clear with warning. "But you are not the only one he has left."

"Darling? Are you ready?" Grey asked as he joined them.

Startled, she glanced at him.

Malcolm gave a somber smile. "I suspect she is. And I still have a great deal of work to do elsewhere. Miss Sheppard, I expect we'll see each other again."

She nodded, a little numbly.

"Miss Carlyle," Malcolm said, "I'll escort you back to Rosalie. We have more to speak of."

"Thank you."

"Mr. Henderson?" Grey asked.

Malcolm glanced at him.

"We would welcome you at supper tonight."

"Thank you, Grey. I'll try to arrange it."

When they left, Rachel walked with Grey and Thomas, her thoughts occupied by the mystery that was so close to unraveling.

"Grey." It was William Byrd, slowly making his way to them. "Congratulations."

"Thank you, sir."

"Randolph has arrested Manning and Griffin."

"That's good," Rachel said. "But I'm a bit puzzled."

"Oh?"

"You returned that verdict in less than five minutes."

"They had no choice," Thomas said.

Grey groaned. "You didn't seem as sure twenty minutes ago."

Thomas chortled, and Rachel marveled at what a beautiful pair of men they were. "What do you mean, they had no choice?"

Byrd smiled mysteriously. "Even without the alibi your artist provided, the testimony edged too close to their back doorsteps when Dunraven came forth, chattering like a none-too-bright squirrel. At least one of the men sitting in judgment of Grey had—well, shall we say, at one time aided Letitia in her adulterous pursuits?"

Rachel's mouth dropped as she remembered the dignified gentry and landowners who comprised the council.

"I suggested it would be unwise to convict Grey. With the gentleman in question, I suggested it quite strongly."

"You ... blackmailed him with his affair?"

"Blackmail! Heavens, no. 'Tis an ungentlemanly sport, dear. I prefer to think of it as persuasive reasoning."

Rachel grinned. "You, sir, are an unscrupulous judge."

"I'm no judge, Rachel. I'm a simple country squire who found himself having to apply the rule of law to—as Dunraven rightly said—a farcical trial. And whoever killed her should be rewarded for doing a moral service to mankind. And, perhaps, to the matrons of Virginia," he added, his lips quirking. "Now, I must get home. This has been too great an excitement for my old bones." He held his hand out to her. "I remain in your debt, dear. You've reminded me of a folly from which I hope we can turn straightaway. Ours is a land founded on the idea of working hard for prosperity. I don't relish it becoming just another corrupt place where one person works for the wealth of another."

"Sir, I'm afraid it will take more than one changed heart to prevent that."

His coach awaited, and a footman handed the elderly gentleman up into it. Only as she watched the coach make its way down Duke of Gloucester Street did the reality of it strike home. She'd seen firsthand the intricacies of a colonial trial; she'd watched the council William Byrd sat on exact swift justice, a drama that would no longer exist in her time. Except in one small, nearly obscure Virginia town called Williamsburg.

Rachel, Grey, and Thomas walked along the sidewalk, chatting in quiet companionship. When they arrived at the house, a chambermaid met them at the door, and the look on her face alarmed Rachel. "What's wrong?"

"It's Mrs. Trelawney. Her time's come."

Chapter Thirty-Nine

"Where's the doctor?" Rachel asked, as she rushed up the stairs. She stopped and looked down.

Aileen, the maid, gestured nervously. "We've called for him, but he was at the Capitol. So we sent a boy to bring the midwife from Rosalie."

Rachel, Thomas, and Grey arrived in Jennie's room. Emily held one of Jennie's hands and patted her as they slowly paced the length of the room, while Aileen hovered.

"How are you feeling?" Rachel asked.

Jennie nodded unevenly. "'Tis a trifle uncomfortable."

"Emily," said Grey gently, "come with me."

The child clearly felt as if she were deserting Jennie, but Jennie smiled at her. "I'll be fine, poppet. Go on with your papa."

With Grey and Emily gone, Thomas hovered uncertainly. "Let me help you lie down, darling."

Aileen put in, "Begging your pardon, sir, but walking helps the babe come faster."

"What can I do?" Rachel asked.

"Boil some water," Jennie said.

"All right. Then what?"

Jennie laughed nervously. "Make tea with it. I'll leave the doctor to worry about the rest."

Rachel found her way to the breakfast room, where Grey had already involved Emily in making tea. Her gaze settled on him in earnest, for the first time in too long. When he noticed her, subtle pleasure lent his eyes a stormy quality. He gathered her against him. "How I've missed you."

She pressed her cheek to his chest, thinking she'd never take for granted another moment with him. Then he tilted her head, finding her mouth with his. "I love you," he murmured.

"Papa," Emily said plaintively, "the kettle's whistling."

Rachel moved away to settle the silver ball into the teapot, then poured the hot water into it.

"What do you want it to be, Father? A boy or a girl?"

"I want the same thing your grandfather does. A strong and healthy child. I suppose you want a girl."

"Of course."

"She says boys are shaggy things with filthy fingernails," Rachel said as she set saucers and cups on a tray.

Grey glanced at his hands. "Perhaps she's right. At the first opportunity, I'm finding a hot bath with a scrub brush."

A rap on the front door interrupted their chatter, and Grey left to answer it. Rachel heard Dr. McKenzie's soft-spoken voice as Grey led him upstairs, and presently they both returned.

"How is Jennie?" she asked.

"This will be a long labor for her," the doctor said. "It's her first, and I believe she's overdue."

"What can I do?"

"Just try to keep her distracted, and help her rest. The baby may not come until tomorrow. Fetch me at my office when her pains are closer."

Grey walked the doctor to the door, then returned to the kitchen. "I'm going to take Emily home for a while. She'll be in the way here."

"No, Papa. I want to be here when the baby comes."

"We'll come back. You'll see the baby before you know it."

He gave Rachel a lingering kiss, and she lay her palm against his cheek, stroking his face. "Take care."

And he was gone.

It was long after midnight when Jennie's contractions grew as close as five minutes, and Rachel sent for the doctor. Though Jennie had tried to spend the day resting, her rest had been fitful, interrupted by the sporadic contractions. At first, Rachel suspected it might be false labor, but the pains grew inevitably more frequent and intense.

When Thomas went outside for a short walk, Rachel sat on the bed beside Jennie, bathing her forehead with a cool cloth.

Jennie smiled weakly. "Thomas is as helpless as a child," she said quietly. "I hope this babe comes soon. The floor can't take much more of his nerves."

She stroked her hair. "He'll be a splendid father."

"I'm glad he and Grey are reconciled. Grey was suffering so much, for so long, and for so little reason."

"Male ego is no little thing," Rachel said.

"And he had no idea how Thomas was suffering," Jennie went on. "Perhaps he'll see someday that in each act of love for this child, Thomas expresses a bit of the love he wasn't able to give Grey—for all those years."

Her features contorted as a contraction seized her, and Rachel held her hand, silently counting. The duration was longer, yet they still remained just under five minutes apart.

Jennie's damp hair clung to her temple and neck, and her eyes were shadowed with blue-gray circles. And she was weakening; something within her seemed to be giving up the struggle.

Rachel grabbed both her shoulders. "Now you need to brace up and be strong, Jennie! Think how sweet it will be to hold the baby."

"I want to name the child Ambrose, if it's a boy."

"Ambrose?"

"Thomas—Thomas will want to name him Bronson. But…" Jennie smiled. "Ambrose means 'immortal.'"

"It's a beautiful name."

Dr. McKenzie arrived presently with Zina, the midwife, arriving not long after, and Rachel moved away from the bed.

Zina was carrying a large butcher knife; when she caught
Rachel watching her slide it underneath the bed, she nodded
meaningfully. "To cut the pain."

They were big on using knives as pain-relief these days.
Rachel would have felt a lot better had she been sterilizing it
for cutting the baby's cord. After placing the knife, the midwife
moved into the shadows of the room. Rachel was relieved the
doctor was here instead.

The room was still and muggy, and she opened a window.

"Close it. The night air will give the child the fever."

She obeyed reluctantly, remembering they weren't exactly at
Johns Hopkins.

Thomas returned to sit by his wife's bedside, holding her
hand when another strong contraction overtook her. The dark
rhythm went on, with Thomas staunchly refusing to leave his
wife's side, and Jennie desperately gripping his hand and
Rachel's as the severity of the contractions multiplied and grew
closer. The doctor grew increasingly apprehensive as he
examined her, all the while time passing without a live birth.
After yet another hour, the doctor gave Rachel a grim look.
What did it mean?

"Thomas, could I have a word with you?"

Thomas was torn between the doctor and leaving Jennie.
At last he rose, and she heard their voices in the hallway—first
subdued whispers, then more vigorous. "I don't *care* what it
takes! She is everything to me."

Rachel prayed silently, trying to ignore her fear. Jennie's
face was pale and pasty, her lips parched.

"Thomas, you know I'll do all that's within my power. But
she's small, and she's very weak. And this labor has already
gone on too long."

The midwife sat in Jennie's rocker, rocking to and fro while
staring at Jennie grimly. She stopped the rocker and rose, then
approached Jennie, whose eyes were closed as she rested
between contractions.

Abruptly the midwife trembled, her head falling back as she
shrank away from Jennie. She fell against the wall near a

window. "I see death," she whispered, grasping at the curtains, hiding her face in the heavy velvet. "I see a curse. She will die—like her brother—like their uncle…"

"You!" Jennie said, her face sallow, her eyes ringed with shadows that made her eyes seem even larger. "You!"

It took Rachel only a moment to put it together—Zina was the seer Jennie had found at Rosalie.

Rachel rose and leaned across Jennie to block her view of the woman. "Go away!" Rachel told her. "Get out of here."

From the doorway, Aileen said, "Ma'am, she's also a nurse. Perhaps we should keep her—just for a while, in case the new mum needs help."

"Fine. But get her downstairs and out of the way."

"*Thomas!*"

Jennie's sudden scream shocked her, and her small hand gripped Rachel's with startling strength. The creepy midwife had jangled Rachel's nerves.

"Jennie," she said, smoothing her hair away from her face, "it's all right. I'm here. Thomas is here, too."

"Thomas?"

He sat at his wife's side, his large hands swallowing hers. "I'm here, my own heart," he whispered.

Rachel drew away, fear lumping in her throat at the frantic fright on Jennie's face as she looked about. "I can't see you!"

He passed a gentle hand over her forehead, his face taut with worry. He pressed his cheek against hers. "Then feel me, Jennie," he choked. "I won't leave you. Please, dear God, don't leave me."

"Thomas, swear … swear you'll always love him," she whispered.

"You know I shall."

"Not—not like Grey," she gasped. "You can start all over with this babe. Swear it, Thomas. No matter what."

"Jennie," he cried, "I swear it. Darling, please. I cannot bear the thought of this life without you."

Dr. McKenzie touched Rachel's shoulder. "You'll need to wait outside."

Stunned and frightened, she withdrew down to the breakfast room as time dragged on. She looked around the small, cozy room where they had shared so many secrets, where they had laughed and cried, where they had remembered and planned, and where Jennie had proven to be a true friend. Never had she mentioned the rumors Rachel knew she must've heard about her, except in an effort to protect her.

The clock in the outer room chimed four, and she heard the front door open and close. Grey entered, his face alight with curiosity. The sight of him gave her illogical hope; with Grey here, everything would be all right.

"I couldn't sleep," he said. "What's the matter?"

She went into his arms, pressing her face against the clean warmth of him. "She's having a terrible time. I'm so afraid—"

They both heard it, then. A faint but distinctive cry; first tentative, then a lusty bawling. The sounds of life.

"Oh, Grey!" she whispered joyfully. "The baby!"

The child's cry was interrupted by a piercing, agonizing scream, and the sound chilled Rachel's elation. It was Thomas, and he screamed one word.

Jennie.

Grey froze in her arms, and then they both hurried up the stairs with apprehensive dread. He silently pushed open Jennie's door. Dr. McKenzie stood wrapping the wailing child in a small blanket. He saw them, and he shook his head and moved to the cradle Jennie had arranged with things she'd fashioned, things that would welcome her son or daughter into this world.

When he stepped aside, they saw Thomas bent over the bed, holding Jennie in his arms, rocking her back and forth as he wept. "Jennie," he cried, "my darling Jennie."

Tears spilled down Rachel's face as she turned to Grey. Oblivious of her, he stared at his father in miserable pathos.

Jennie was gone.

Chapter Forty

Grey entered the room, but the doctor stopped Rachel.

"Was there ... nothing that could be done?"

"Not by anyone save the Lord. I differ from my colleagues, miss. I believe life is in the blood—and Jennie lost too much of it." He sighed. "The babe needs nourishment. Get the nurse."

"But—there isn't one. Jennie was going to—"

"Unless you would have this child follow his mother to the grave, you'll find a wet nurse. Now. Ask the midwife, she'll know."

"Not in a million years. She's a superstitious loon. I'll not have her near Jennie's baby."

"Ma'am?"

Rachel turned to find Aileen, her face wet and mottled with grief.

"The kitchen wench, Izzie, is weaning her babe."

"Oh, Aileen. Can you find her, please?" She would have taken the old woman in her arms to comfort her, but Aileen ran down the stairs, her shoulders shaking as she wept. Rachel followed her, heartsick as she noticed the table where she and Jennie had first gotten to know each other.

I want to name the child Ambrose. It means immortal.

A discarded cup of tea lay on the sideboard, where Jennie might have set it aside the day before. Aileen's oversight showed her devastation; the old woman had practically raised Jennie.

Presently, Grey entered the kitchen with the small bundle cradled in his arms, gazing at the child. His eyes met hers. "He's dazed by grief. He won't look at the child."

She sat in the rocking chair by the hearth, and he placed the baby in her arms. She was stirred by the lively movement of the child. Light, reddish brown fluff covered his red head. "'Tis a fine, handsome lad," Grey said softly.

She couldn't speak as she cradled him against her breast. She remembered, as if it were yesterday, holding her sister so. His wailing grew distracted as he began rooting for a nipple.

"And an impatient little wretch," Grey added with a smile.

"Can you try to find Aileen?" she asked, awkwardly brushing her finger against the baby's cheek in a vain attempt to distract him from his hunger. "She went for a wet nurse."

He sat motionless, and she cast him an impatient glance, surprised at what she saw. His face was wreathed in adoration. "I can't see you so without imagining you nursing our child." He sighed then, shaking his head dolefully. "And I can't help but imagine my father's agony when he sees you."

"Little Ambrose," she murmured.

"Ambrose?"

"It's the name Jennie chose for him. She ..."

"What?"

"It means immortal. It was as if—as if she knew her own time here was brief."

Izzie arrived and took the child, and Grey climbed the stairs to Jennie's room, where Thomas gazed blankly out the window. He'd tucked the covers about his wife, as if she slept.

"Will you come out, sir? Perhaps see the babe."

"*No.*" The word was a low shudder of rejection.

Grey hesitated, pained at the listlessness of the man. Something else lingered within him, and he sought to say that which he'd never said.

"Leave me, Grey."

His voice was a dull monotone, and Grey closed the door.

Later, he and Rachel napped with the child between them, and when his movements awakened her she called for Izzie. While they waited, she saw his somber gaze on Ambrose.

"He has her eyes. The color of the sky."

"They'll change."

He shook his head. "Not a color that vibrant. Each time my father looks at this child, he shall think of her."

She heard the regret in his voice, saw the hardness of his jaw. "He refuses to touch him. To look at him."

"He's in shock, Grey. Give him time."

"How much time? Thirty years?" He sighed, rolling out of the bed. "I have to go to Rosalie. Emily will be worried—dear God in heaven, how shall I ever tell her?"

"Perhaps we can take Ambrose home with us," she suggested, "until Thomas is better equipped to deal with him."

He brushed his lips against hers, his hand curving around her throat. "Let's ask him."

Izzie entered the room and took Ambrose, and Rachel glanced at the babe as Izzie prepared to nurse him. The commonplace sight stung her.

It should be Jennie. Jennie should be here, nursing her child, watching him draw sustenance from her own body. Why couldn't life occasionally be fair?

Two women arrived from Bruton Parish Church to prepare Jennie's body for burial. Thomas surprised Grey and Rachel by admitting them into her room and returning silently to his own adjoining room.

After the women left, Grey and Rachel approached Thomas. He sat at his window and stared, unseeing, at an open volume. It was the Bible, turned to Psalm 22. What had he found there, on his way to comfort?

"We're going back to Rosalie, sir, for a few hours. But I'll be back later tonight, to stay with you."

"I need no one here."

A moment's silence followed, and Rachel rested her hand on Grey's back. "We'd like to take the baby with us. If that's all right with you. Just until—"

"Take it. What should I do with it here?"

The cold inflection in Thomas's voice disturbed her. She knew he was suffering, but she could almost taste his bitterness.

"Thomas, he's your—"

"Leave me in peace," he choked out. "I want no part of it."

Grey tensed, and she squeezed his arm. "Let's go."

In another quarter-hour, they'd assembled Ambrose's belongings in Grey's coach and were on their way with Izzie to Rosalie. When Ambrose was settled with his nurse into a room, Rachel went straight to Hastings' office. For the past day, she'd thought only of Jennie. Now, she remembered his revelation on the witness stand—and Malcolm's warning. Through the open door, she saw him in a corner, reading. The rays of the afternoon sun slanted across his book, and he raised his head as she entered.

"Why didn't you tell me?"

He closed the book and set it aside. "Ah, well," he said softly. He rose, putting the book in its place on the shelf. Staring thoughtfully at a globe standing nearby, he said, "An unseemly practice, becoming entangled in the life of a young lady whose fate I have no hand in. Of course, your eccentric Mr. Henderson gave me no choice in the matter."

She hesitated. "All my life, I would've given anything for even the smallest story about my family. I cherish the memories I do have. But I'll never see any of them again. You ... you're the only relative I have."

His head jerked up. "And is that to give a man cheer? Responsibility for a headstrong harpy such as yourself?"

She smiled. "Hastings, you old softie."

He touched the globe, one delicate hand coaxing it into a lethargic turn. "Had I told you, you would have asked innumerable questions I cannot answer. Undoubtedly I would ask as well."

"I'll tell you anything you'd like to know."

"An awkward thing, having a glimpse of the future. It's often asked: were one given the chance to know one's fate, what should one choose?" He silently examined the globe. "Rachel, each of us holds dreams, no matter our station in life. Even I. Do not wish for such ill-conceived knowledge. Were we to know our every dream in this world would come true, should we then strive as necessary to achieve those dreams?

"And were we to learn our dreams would come to naught, then what becomes of life? That bitter truth, erasing all hope— the essence from which life springs—would be more than a mere mortal could endure. In either case, the end result that we should desire to know is the better person we become for having striven."

She saw canny wisdom in his eyes. How many fateful decisions would be made in their family over the time between his life and hers? Had he seen the headline in her newspaper and found facing the future of his descendants a forbidding prospect?

"You said that I was your granddaughter. That's obviously impossible. What did you mean?"

"Do not presume to know what is and isn't possible. And I am no more privy to knowledge than you. I know only that …" He stopped and turned away. "I received a letter from my son today that his wife gave birth to a healthy daughter. They named her Cassandra." Cassandra? It was her mother's name. And as she opened her mouth to tell him, she stopped.

But you are not the only relative he has left.

In a moment, she understood Malcolm's warning, and her foolishness—how close she'd come to telling him— immobilized her.

She could never explain it to him, of course. Like his great-granddaughter, her mother Cassandra, too, would travel in time—to the twentieth century, where she would marry Rachel's father.

And where she would be murdered.

But did he already know? Had he read part of the newspaper story? Did he know the fate his granddaughter would suffer … and was he torn now between protecting her safety, and the knowledge that if he kept Cassandra secure in the eighteenth century, neither Rachel nor her sisters would ever be born?

He turned to her. "It is necessary to learn from the past, Rachel. But although the future is held slave to the past, the present—wisely or not so—is the master of both, life itself. My heart has been ... so very cheered to have known you, but the delight I have found in you lies in your unique character. Not by any miniscule drop of blood that may flow in your veins."

His words held a poignant reassurance. They were the words she'd long dreamed of hearing from Max. And it gently distanced them both from the tragedy that bound them together.

The next day passed in a terrible promenade of decorum. They arrived at the Trelawney home for Jennie's funeral, and black bunting adorned the home. Thomas remained in a state of indifference. Rachel knew it was his mind's way of dealing with the unthinkable, but the revulsion he felt for his newborn son frightened her. Would she and Grey raise the baby who was his half-brother?

At last, Jennie was buried in the small, enclosed garden she had loved, and Emily wept pitifully. "But she didn't *want* to live with the angels, Papa! She said I was her very own angel!"

Grey took the sobbing child away, and tears streamed down Rachel's face. Ambrose slept in her arms, blissfully unaware that his mother was forever gone and that he would never know her.

She found purpose in caring for the child Jennie had loved. She knew she was coming to love the small boy as her own, and she welcomed him into her heart.

The morning after Jennie was buried dawned slate-gray. No rain had fallen for weeks—in fact, since she'd first arrived—and they needed it. They ate lunch on the lawn, and Emily played peek-a-boo with Ambrose, hiding her locket behind her back, then flashing it before his eyes. He blinked, his eyes following the shiny silver trinket.

"I'm going to hide the locket so you can't find it, you little angel," Emily whispered in the baby's ear.

Ambrose turned toward her, as if in mild interest. Emily darted into the grove of young oak trees nearby.

They heard the sound of wheels rolling down the drive, and Grey walked to an opening in the hedges. "It's my father." He disappeared around the side of the house.

A few minutes later, the men appeared at the back steps. Rachel smiled uncertainly at Thomas as he looked toward her. He slowly walked down the steps, with Grey just behind him.

"Grandfather!"

Emily's excited trill caught his attention, and she raced from the nearby oak grove toward Thomas. Alarm rose within Rachel; what if the grieving man rejected the little girl who adored him?

Her fears were dashed as a joyful agony crossed his face. He knelt to catch Emily in his arms, crushing her to him in a desperate embrace. "Dear child, how I've missed you."

She nodded, patting his cheek with childish grace. Her face was woebegone. "I miss Jennie."

His face fell. "I miss her, too, darling."

"But I love my little uncle. He smells so sweet. And his fingernails are clean, and so tiny! Come and see, Grandfather!"

"Emily," Grey interrupted, "why don't you fetch your new frock to show your grandfather?"

Her face lit up at the prospect. "Why, I shall!"

With Emily gone, Thomas straightened and stared bleakly at the child in Rachel's arms. After a long moment, he turned toward the river, and he laughed shortly, an unhappy sound. "Every image I've ever had of that babe is wreathed in memories of Jennie. Seeing you so, Rachel, brings each of them to mind.

"Jennie blessed my life with more love than I'd ever known. No woman had a greater talent for love."

Rachel ached at the lost expression on his face as he turned, as his eyes roved over the baby. "She wanted, more than anything, a boy. She wanted to give me the chance—" The muscle in his jaw clenched as he looked at the ground. "She saw Grey and she knew my regret. She saw me yearning to reach out to a boy whose heart had long ago been irreparably damaged at my own hand. She gave me the hope that someday,

I might find the chance to love him again. And until then, she wanted to give me what no human being can give another. A chance to begin again. To be the father I never was with Grey."

Thomas looked at Grey with tears in his eyes. "Grey, the night after you first came to me, after I'd come to accept the truth, I went back over the life you might've had. I imagined holding you in my arms and whispering in your ear the name I gave you. Did you know your mother named you after my father? She gave me an honor I little deserved. Since then, not a day has gone by that I haven't prayed my most earnest prayer for you. I loved you with my whole heart then—and I love you with my whole heart now. I have lived seven years yearning for the sound of the word *Father* on your lips, knowing I never deserved to hear it. All I can ask of you now, my dearest son, is your forgiveness."

Rachel saw the bittersweet longing in Grey's eyes, and something else. Redemption. Thomas reached out one quivering hand, and Grey took it. The men embraced without awkwardness, with nothing between them but thirty years of remorse. And Rachel heard it, quiet but unmistakable. A single word Grey had longed to say to this man since he was old enough to form words.

"Father."

Presently they separated, and Thomas wiped at his eyes. "Now, there's the child of a woman I deeply love. And she knew me too well. She made me swear to love him."

Rachel rose, lifting the child in her arms. He stood beside her, staring at the baby who looked up at him drowsily before letting his eyes close for his nap. She saw the pain spear through him, and his words were a pained whisper. "He has her eyes."

She carefully handed him into Thomas's waiting hands, and his eyes fluttered closed as he placed his cheek against the baby's. "I do love you so, my son."

Rachel's eyes met Grey's, and she saw his happiness.

"Dear God, he's as soft as satin," he whispered. "What have you been calling him?"

"Ambrose. It's what Jennie wanted to name him."

"Papa!" Emily's plaintive cry interrupted them, and she arrived in the gardens. "There's a rip in my pink gown."

Grey patted Emily's shoulder. "Shh."

Thomas brushed a finger against the baby's nose, and the child stirred in his sleep. "Then that shall be a second name."

"Second name?" Grey asked.

"He shall be called Bronson, in honor of Jennie's brother."

"Jennie has a brother named Bronson?"

"She never told you?"

"No."

Thomas frowned. "Bronson died last year, just before his thirtieth birthday."

The air was still and warm, yet Rachel felt a sudden chill in the afternoon. Thunder rumbled faintly in the distance, and before she could speak, the sound of a rider on the dusty drive commanded their attention. Presently, the rider approached the gardens, and he swiftly dismounted. It was Stephen Clancy. "Something most unfortunate has happened. I fear you all may be in danger."

"What is it?" Grey demanded.

"It's James Manning. He's escaped."

Chapter Forty-One

Rachel hurried toward the cabins, with Grey in close pursuit. "Rachel, I tell you he won't come within a mile of Rosalie. He knows it would mean certain death. I've men posted at all—"

"Grey! The whole estate's blanketed by woods. Do you really think he wouldn't find his way here? Camisha humiliated him! He'll be here, if he isn't already."

She turned to the last cabin and knocked urgently on the door.

The door opened, and Malcolm emerged. Camisha stood behind him.

"You've got to come up to the house. Manning's escaped." Only then did Rachel see the traces of tears on her face. "What's wrong?"

She swallowed, and her lips went tight with the effort to contain tears. Her dark, liquid eyes darted to Malcolm, who seemed to understand her grief.

Rachel glanced at Grey, and he nodded and joined Malcolm a few feet away. She moved inside the cabin with Camisha and closed the door.

"Rachel, we're going away."

"Going away?"

Camisha nodded. "To Ashanti's home, in Boston."

Rachel shook her head. "Boston's too far away. We need to stay together." She gave a short, exasperated snort. "This isn't a different country you can just decide to settle in, because you like the people—"

"You think I like the life I know I'll live?"

"Does Malcolm know this?"

Her lips pressed together briefly, and she gave a quick nod. "Yep. He knows."

"What if—what if he can't find you, once you're there, when it's time to go home?"

"A man who can travel in time can't find me in Boston? Please." Camisha smiled. Her voice was soft, and she shook her head. "I'll miss the hell out of you, girl."

"Stop it! Have you forgotten who you are?"

Camisha's eyes glittered with tears. "No. I've remembered. Same way you have."

Rachel grew frustrated at her stubbornness. Damn it, *she* was the one with the common sense; *she* was the one who'd always kept Rachel straight. How could she get through to her? "This *isn't* your life! You're not supposed to be here."

Camisha's hand was gentle as it rested on Rachel's face. "You go on, now. Be with him, while you can."

"If something happens to you—if Manning finds you—"

"Daniel was right, Rachel. God will be with us." She smiled that smile, like a sunburst exploding on her face. After a moment, she went on softly, "Remember that time in our senior year that Max grounded you for stealing his Jack Daniel's?"

Rachel laughed. "Yeah. It was after he yelled at me for going to church with you. He had me seeing the therapist for six months about my closet alcoholism."

"And you'd never touched the stuff in your life."

"The therapist still thinks I was repressing it."

"Remember how Max's aquarium of barracudas died the next week?"

"You didn't."

"Jack and Saltwater, mm-mmm." Her eyes twinkled. "Tell him those fish went out laughing."

A sudden crack of thunder startled them, and Camisha sobered. "Rachel, you take care of yourself."

How could she begrudge Camisha the hope she clung to—that she could find happiness with the man she loved? Then how might she herself still hope? Instead, she thanked God for this woman, and the friendship that had spanned their lives.

"We'll see each other again. Boston isn't far away."

Camisha hugged her hard for another moment, and tears stood in her eyes when she withdrew. "Don't ever forget, Rachel. The past makes us who we are. But we make the future what it is."

Rachel half-smiled and patted her face fondly. "You and your closing arguments. Watch out for Manning, I mean it. He's crazy."

"You don't worry. Ashanti can take care of me."

A gust of wind caught the door as Rachel opened it, and Grey stood there with Ashanti, Daniel, and Hastings.

"Where's Malcolm?"

"He said he had business to attend to."

"Rachel."

She glanced at Hastings.

He hesitated. And then he did a peculiar thing. He walked forward and hugged her. "Take care, my child."

"Are you going with them?"

"I'll see them safely to the bay, then return."

"Then *you* take care." She gave him an impulsive kiss. Her great-grandfather. She hugged him again, holding him close. "I forgot to say, earlier ... Thank you so much, sir. For everything. I'll see you soon."

He held her a moment longer, then released her.

Then Grey did something she had never seen him do. He reached out to shake Hastings' hand. "Thank you, Hastings. I can never repay you—"

The older man put his other hand over Grey's. "Thank *you*, sir. Do take care of her for me."

Thunder crashed through the atmosphere, and she shivered at the temperature drop.

"We'll have to hurry to stay ahead of the storm." This, from Grey. "Finish your goodbyes."

She looked back once and saw Camisha. The wind whipped at her homespun skirts, and Ashanti stood stalwart beside her. She smiled and raised her hand. "Good-bye, Rachel."

"See you soon!" A faint sense of foreboding about the goodbyes niggled at her. But even in the eighteenth century, Boston wasn't far; and Grey had his own ship. Hastings would be back from the Chesapeake Bay by that night. "Please be careful!" she called after them as they started off. Then she dismissed the worry; it was simply the thunder.

The rain started just before they reached Rosalie. "I'm worried about them, Grey. They have so little. If Manning finds them—"

"He won't. The *Swallow* is waiting at the dock, to take them down the James to Norfolk. The ship is a snow, Rachel—she's heavily armed. Ashanti missed his home, so I offered my escort."

"Papa! I'm so glad you're home!" Emily arrived in a flurry. Thomas was close behind.

"Did you see them safely off?"

"Hastings is escorting them. They'll be all right. Let me put Emily to bed, and I'll join you in the drawing room."

Weary from the day's emotion, Rachel changed out of her wet clothes and into a nightgown and robe, then ventured downstairs and joined the men in the drawing room, where Thomas was speaking with a quiet fondness of Jennie.

"She was just a sweet girl from a good family," he murmured, staring into his wine. "I think I quite frightened her. She and her brother were always close, and he didn't trust strangers. Bronson trusted few people at all, to tell the truth. A ... curse had followed his family, if one believes in such things. Jennie didn't even know about it. She was raised by a spinster aunt, and the woman was quite no-nonsense, a woman after my own heart. When I asked the lady for Jennie's hand, she told me about the legend in jest. Of course, I never mentioned it to Jennie. While I don't believe in such nonsense, I do believe that one can bring on such accidents by worrying too much about them. But I admit, the coincidences are rather eerie. For the past two generations, the men have never lived beyond their thirtieth birthday."

"What happened to Jennie's parents?" Grey asked.

Thomas raised his eyebrows. "Died in a carriage accident— and in answer to what you're thinking, yes, it occurred not long before her father's thirtieth birthday."

His words stopped Rachel where she stood in the doorway.

"Hello, darling." Grey rose with his father as she entered. "Is something amiss?"

She shook her head. "No, everything's fine." She sat beside him on a couch as he poured a glass of wine for her. "Go on, Mr. Trelawney."

"From what they say, it goes back to the turn of the century. In 1699, one of the Dandridges killed a man deep in the Virginia countryside. It would've been around where Richmond was settled.

"His widow was a superstitious sort, and she placed a curse upon the Dandridge family. To this day they call it the Miller curse, for the man who was killed. Robert Miller."

Rachel looked at Grey, and she saw the seriousness in his gaze. Still, there was more than even Thomas said. And Grey knew whatever it was.

"Rachel."

She turned her head, listening. Had someone called her name?

Thomas went on speaking. He'd apparently heard nothing.

There it was again. A faint, distinctly distressed call, the sound of her name.

"Did you hear that?"

"Hear what?" Grey asked.

"Surely you heard it. You're sitting right beside me."

"What is it?"

"Maybe Emily's calling me. Let me check on her real quick."

She climbed the stairs. Two candles burned in Emily's room, and her sewing kit lay in the midst of her bed, but the child was gone. Rachel noticed the smell of wood burning. Odd; in the summer heat, the fireplaces were all cold. No one would be burning trash this late.

"Emily," she called. As she walked past her room, she noticed the window was ajar, and rain drenched the rug nearby. She moved toward the window to close it.

"Rachel, help me! I can't find it anywhere!"

Rachel stopped breathing. Emily stood beneath her window in the torrential rain. Cascades of blonde hair hung dripping around her shoulders, and huge blue eyes blinked up at Rachel imploringly. She wrapped her arms around her body, as if to ward off a chill. She wore a pale pink satin dress, covered with a mud-stained white apron. A shiver stole up Rachel's spine.

"Please?"

Exactly as it had been, that first night.

What could it mean?

Exactly as it had been, that is, except tonight, Manning might well be out there. And that knowledge eclipsed her dread over the recurring thunderstorm chase.

"Emily," Rachel whispered, then found her voice. "For God's sake, stay right there. I'll be right down." She hurried down the staircase on trembling legs. "Grey, Emily's out in the storm."

She knew there was no time to lose, and she rushed outside. Emily obediently waited beneath the window, but she darted away as soon as she saw Rachel, waving at her. "Hurry! Papa will be so unhappy if he finds I've slipped out of bed!"

Rachel hurried after her, oblivious to the heavy rain, to the crash of thunder that battered the night sky. The child ran swiftly, calling over her shoulder as she ran. "I left it—beneath a tree this afternoon, you know. Oh, do hurry—"

"Emily, stop!" Rachel shouted, and the sound was lost in the wind and the storm. "Darling, please come back!"

"I'm over here! Hurry, we must find it! Oh, they'll be ruined—"

She disappeared in a thicket of trees, and Rachel's heart pounded madly as she raced into the woods. The wet underbrush ripped at her feet, but she raced on uncertainly, having lost sight of Emily. It was too gruesomely familiar. She heard Grey's shout, and she stopped while he caught up with her.

"Emily's in the woods," Rachel said, grabbing his arm.

"Oh, God." Grey's anguished whisper was nearly lost in the noise of the storm. They shouted her name as they found their way through the trees, but the wind and rain swallowed the sound. Grey was frantic with fear. "If Manning should find her—"

"Grey!" Thomas's shout caught their notice, and they found their way to the clearing. Rachel cried out in astonishment.

Rosalie was engulfed in flames. In the violent tempest of the storm, the fire raged unquenched. The windows of the third floor exploded as the fire rushed through, and flames appeared at the second floor windows as she stared, horrified. Rachel gripped Grey fearfully, and only then, as she remembered smelling woodsmoke, did it occur to her. Emily had saved them all, by rushing out into the storm.

"Dear God," Thomas gasped, cradling the baby against him. "I went up to check on Bronson, and fire was in the next room."

"But ... who would do this?" Grey whispered.

"'Tis clear enough to me," Thomas said. "You had warnings of the man's despicable nature. You trusted the black, and he betrayed you."

Rachel couldn't quite believe it; straight out of the trial where Ashanti's wife had saved Grey's life, he fell back on his own prejudice. "Ashanti didn't do this!" she said. "Camisha wouldn't—"

"Emily!"

Relief flooded Rachel. As easily as she'd disappeared, the child materialized at the edge of the woods not far from the house, perhaps thirty yards away. Grey ran toward his daughter.

"I remember now! I left it next to little Bronson's cradle." Still smiling at Rachel, she scampered toward the house.

Grey's desperate shout echoed over the land, but Emily was focused single-mindedly on her mysterious search as she disappeared into the burning building. Grey followed her inside, and his shout became Rachel's as he was swallowed in the raging furor of the fiery mansion.

"No!!"

Rachel ran to the building, feeling the blistering heat of the fire as she reached the door. As she raised her hand and turned her face from the blinding glare, she caught a glimpse of something at the edge of the woods. A man stood there, dispassionately watching the flames. She had only a fleeting glimpse, but his face was clear in the bright light from the fire.

Manning. His lips were twisted in a cold, cruel smile.

Both Grey and Emily died in the fire that destroyed Rosalie.

The ravenous inferno raged from the upper stories where it had begun, and its roaring fury was deafening. Over the roar, she heard a blessed sound: Emily's voice, wonderfully close. "I've found it!"

Emily's small hand slipped into hers, and Rachel felt the chain of her locket between their palms.

Then she heard Grey, sputtering, coughing. "Emily, darling—"

In that same second, Rachel heard a ponderous groaning, then an ear-splitting crash, and a blinding pressure seemed to shatter within her. And then she heard nothing, and she gave herself up to the blackness of oblivion.

Chapter Forty-Two

Soft, black hands were fluffing her pillows. Her head felt heavy—was she sick? Had Camisha come back to Rosalie to take care of her?

"You coming 'round, honey?"

The voice wasn't Camisha's, and Rachel opened her eyes. And then she struggled to breathe. She lay in a hospital bed. In a very modern hospital.

"*No*," she whispered, her voice weak. "No."

The soothing voice pierced the web of numb confusion and heartache suffocating her. "I'm Denise Jackson, your nurse."

"Where am I?"

"Williamsburg Medical Center." The nurse changed an IV bottle, explaining as she went about her work. "You've been out of it; you took a nasty bump on the head, day before yesterday," she went on, picking up the phone. "Yeah, this is Denise. Rachel Sheppard's awake. Call Doctor Rayburn."

She hung up the phone. "Sorry about that. Anyway, your father found you out around some old mansion off Highway 5. Rosewell, Rosemary ... Looked like you got caught out in some storm."

Rachel remembered in anguish. The horrifying flames that engulfed Rosalie. Emily disappearing inside the house. Grey,

340

whose world revolved around the child, disappearing after her. Their voices echoing through the burning house—and then, the deafening crash. She collapsed against the pillows in wrenching sobs.

"Your father's anxious to see you," Denise said comfortingly, patting her arm. "Don't worry, honey. It'll be all right. I'll get you something to help you sleep."

She heard the door quietly close behind the nurse. Her grief captured her, and she wept as she remembered the man she'd loved, and the child she'd held as dear as her own.

They died in a fire, in the eighteenth century.

But ... she, too, had stood inside Rosalie as it collapsed under the destruction of the fire. Hadn't she?

You took a nasty bump on the head. They found you out at some old mansion ...

She remembered that first night at Lottie's, and how she'd gone into the storm to find Emily. She remembered the blinding pressure in her head as she crossed the threshold of the ruins. What if she ... could it all have been a ...?

No way. It was too vivid to have been the stuff of dreams.

Then she worked out a possible explanation. What if the ruins had been the portal in time? She remembered her first night at Rosalie, wandering in a dream state, and the shivering cold, and Grey warming her in his bed. She would have been found exactly at the old rear entrance to Rosalie, where she had entered the ruins.

So perhaps she went into the rain and the ruins day before yesterday and into the past, then—as far as the present day was concerned—immediately returned in the next moment, like entering or exiting a room.

The nurse returned, and she held out a small paper cup; inside were pills. "Your father's downstairs. He's on his way up."

Rachel dismissed the pills. "I don't want to sleep. And I don't want to see him. Where's Camisha?"

"Who?"

"Camisha Carlyle. A friend who was with me at Rosalie."

"I don't know. Doctor Rayburn is on his way down. He'll be able to answer any questions better than I can."

Fear flooded her as she remembered the last time they'd seen Max. What if he'd done something with Camisha?

The door opened. A slender, older man with thinning hair and an easy smile walked in. "Hello, Rachel," he said, skimming her chart. "I'm Joe Rayburn. Are you feeling any pain?"

"No." At the moment, she was blessedly numb. "Can you tell me what happened to me?"

"I'll tell you what I know. Night before last, when your father got to Rosalie, they discovered you'd gone out into the storm. One of the servants saw you go into the ruins, and your father says a pretty sizable tree limb fell on you."

If she'd been hit by a tree branch, why didn't her head hurt? Instead, it only felt immensely heavy, just as it had when she first went back in time.

"I'm only telling you what I've been told."

"Can you tell me where Camisha Carlyle is?"

He hesitated. "Miss Carlyle is missing."

"Missing?"

"She hasn't been seen since the night she left."

She forced herself to remain silent. "How soon can I leave?"

"Well, I'd like to keep you overnight. I'll speak to your father when he gets here and see what he says."

"Doctor Rayburn, Max Sheppard is a dangerous man. And I *don't* want to see him."

"Rachel, there's no need for you to be anxious. I've been speaking with your therapist, and he tells me—"

"My therapist?"

"Doctor Malone. In Dallas."

"Did he mention I haven't seen him in almost ten years? Did he mention that I never authorized the release of my medical records?"

"No, on both counts. Your father suggested I call Doctor Malone. But why wouldn't he have mentioned that he hasn't been treating you?"

"He does what Max tells him to do. I tell you, he is a powerful man."

The doctor studied her, and she wondered if he was looking for signs of her insanity—or simply assuming it.

"I assure you, I have only one interest, and that's in your recovery."

"Thank you." She raised her hand to shake his, but stopped. Her hands were bandaged.

"You have some minor burns. We believe lightning struck the tree, and you tried to shield yourself as you fell."

No, Rachel thought as the truth dawned. It was no dream. And there had been no tree. Doctor Rayburn left her alone, and she rested against the pillow.

The door opened, and Max walked in. Peculiar, how he seemed genuinely concerned. But that was what had enabled him to live a lie for twenty years. He was good at it.

"I sure am glad to see you." He brushed her forehead with a kiss and squeezed her shoulder.

"Glad to see me?" she repeated contemptuously, shrugging away from him.

He looked injured. "Yes. For a while, we thought you were gone. That was a hell of a tree branch that fell on you."

"There was no tree branch."

"What do you mean?"

"That isn't what happened. The truth is, I went back in time. To the year 1746."

His complacency slid away, and he chuckled uncomfortably, patting her hand blandly. "Well, you're back in Kansas now, Dorothy."

She sought refuge in her memories. Grey's faith, his freely given love, his contentment as he found wholeness in his father's love. His patient love as her memory was restored to her. How could she have dreamed such things?

"Did you react this way when your brother told you he went back in time?" she asked. "Is that why you had him locked away? To keep him from embarrassing the family with a double murder conviction?"

He swore. "Thought you'd had enough time to come to your senses, girl. Looks like I was wrong."

"While I was in the eighteenth century, I remembered everything. I remembered how my parents died. Camisha and I figured out why. Where is she, Dad? What have you done with her?"

"I haven't seen her, Rachel. Believe me when I say that."

"Why should I? It's all truth versus beauty, and no one gives a damn about the truth. You less than anyone." She reached for the nurse's call button. "I'm getting the hell out of here."

"When you've had a head injury, your mind can play some mighty strange tricks on you. Hallucinations aren't the same as memories. You don't want to go back there and make people think you've flipped your lid."

Rachel gazed at him for several seconds. She knew that tone; she'd heard him use it countless times with an intractable associate. It was no more than a thinly veiled threat. "I'm getting out of here," she repeated, "and I'm going to the police."

He grabbed her arm. "Go ahead. And when you've made sure they know you're out of your mind, I'll—"

The door opened.

"Oh, I almost forgot," the doctor began casually. He stopped, his gaze on Max. "Is there a problem?"

Max released Rachel. "No."

"Then Rachel needs to rest."

Max exhaled and left, rattled. It wasn't often that he displayed his true personality in public.

"What's the deal with your father?"

"My *father* never deals with anyone he can't control. And he knows he can't control me anymore. I haven't quite figured out yet whether you're in on it, too."

"The only thing I'm in on is your health and well-being."

"Hm. Then you haven't been corrupted yet."

"Why's he trying to control you?"

"In a nutshell? Because his brother murdered my parents. And I witnessed it. I'd suppressed the memory for 20 years, but now I remember."

Deep lines were etched between Rayburn's brows. "I suppose you know I'm going to have to go to the authorities."

"Don't bother. He's got that covered."

"He hasn't bought off the entire commonwealth of Virginia." He reached into a pocket and dropped something into her palm. "This was in your hand when you were found."

A silver chain poured over her fingers, and she stared at the faintly tarnished locket, turning it over. *As time is, so beats our hearts—tender, immortal, forever.*

She pressed the clasp, and the locket opened. Two portraits were there, now faded with age. Rachel saw her own face, and tears welled within her at the second face. The blonde curls, the winsome smile, and the love in her eyes—as if she were gazing at Rachel, even now—were all perfectly captured.

It was Emily Trelawney—a little girl who'd lived and died in the eighteenth century.

Chapter Forty-Three

"Welcome to Colonial Williamsburg."

The bellman greeted Rachel, and at the front desk, she retrieved another room key from the front desk clerk.

"Did my belongings arrive from Rosalie?" she asked. She hadn't had the nerve to drive out to the place to retrieve her clothing and cell phone and had hired a courier to do so.

Ringing the bell, he said, "Yes, ma'am, they just arrived. I'll have the bell captain take them up for you."

"Thanks," she said, tipping him.

"Oh, Miss Sheppard? There's a Mr. Henderson, waiting in the dining room to see you. And a woman."

Malcolm and Mary van Kirk sat sipping tea, both dressed in period costumes, but Rachel had accepted they were no costume. "Rachel, I'm glad you've returned."

"We were beginning to worry about you," Mary said, smiling.

Their casual civility baffled her. After all she'd been through, they spoke as if she'd been away to take a phone call. As she moved to sit, Malcolm stopped her. "Oh, no, dear. We have to go. You're late for the press conference as it is."

"Press conference? Mr. Henderson, I've been through a lot in the last—what kind of time does that count as? I think you owe me an explanation."

"Well, it can wait. Everything will be explained in time."

"Max Sheppard—"

Mary gave a nonchalant wave. "Oh, heavens. You know we're not afraid of him. Malcolm, do take care of the check."

He fished out a bill, peered at it myopically as if to make sure he'd grabbed the right currency, and tossed it on the table, then hurried after them.

"You don't understand," Rachel pressed. "He's done something with Camisha."

Malcolm glanced at her. "Rachel, you'll understand soon. What matters now is the press conference."

"I don't want to—" she began, stopping at the end of the circular drive. The sunlight was warm already, and the bright morning only heightened her loneliness. Frustrated, she followed. "Listen to me! Malcolm, I can't. I'm giving Kingsley my notice."

"Yes, dear. I know that. But you should still attend."

"But—"

Mary suddenly stopped, as if they had all the time in the world. "Rachel, you must be there. Surely, after all you've learned, you understand that."

They arrived at Tarpley's Store, on a corner of Duke of Gloucester Street, and her gaze moved along the scene before her. Her heart was pounding madly. Only a day had passed. A day and 270 years. So much was different.

But oh, it was all the same. The same dirt roads, the same dusty grass, many of the same cherished landmarks. The courthouse now standing on Market Square was a modern addition—circa 1770—but it was all a part of this beloved place.

"Yes," she whispered. "I understand. But I need to find Camisha."

"The timing is not right," he insisted. "Do you not see?"

Rachel's chest ached. "I see that all those I loved are now dead. Except Camisha. And I have to know that she's all right. That what she found was what she was looking for. She was the reason we went back, wasn't she? I thought she came to be with me—but the whole reason I was here was for her."

"Is that what you think?"

"It's what I'm asking you."

"Did you find nothing, Rachel?" Malcolm asked. "How can you even say that?"

"You said … you said I would learn what the past meant to me. And I did. But along the way…"

"You fell in love," Mary said. "And was that not a blessing in itself?"

"Yet something else happened," Malcolm pressed. "Something that mattered to you even more at one time."

"I remembered my parents—and who killed them."

"Yes. It's one of the reasons you went, as you know."

"But … why couldn't I stay?"

His face held gentleness as he spoke. "Heavens, child. How you've changed. From a woman who scorned the past, to one who loves it. The fact of the matter is, your being in the past was becoming a bit of a problem. Too many people were discovering the truth. Not necessarily about your origins, but truth in their own lives. Had they only been those whose beliefs were in line with the future, it would be of no consequence. A little change is good, but sometimes, cataclysmic change—even for the better—can prevent necessary events. You cannot give divine knowledge to a man with ready ties to social historic occurrences. The responsibility is too great. With the best of intentions, terrible things can occur. Had you remained, it's impossible to tell what might have happened."

"You mean Grey—" she swallowed.

"Between his time and yours, dozens of events shall occur that some would try to undo, with good intentions. Yet these events make us who we are. The Civil War, to cite one tragic example. The destruction of the Third Reich. How might the entire world be changed, had an internationalist like Thomas Jefferson been confronted with the future? To live in the past, my dear, requires a deep respect for it."

"Jennie was to die in childbirth," Mary said. "Emily and Grey will be explained as they first were—that they died at Rosalie. Dear, he was simply too passionate."

Tears stung her eyes. "He had too much of a conscience, you mean."

"If you prefer. But we did warn you about trying to change people in the past."

"And Malcolm told us, after Camisha had been beaten, to disregard that warning."

Mary glared at Malcolm. "You what?"

"I did no such thing!"

The women gaped at him, and his shoulders slumped.

"I meant on a *personal* level. When two souls are meant to find one another—as yours and Grey's were—nothing will stand between them. And nothing ever will."

Rachel was despondent. Nothing—except two and a half centuries.

"Well, here we are."

Noticing the news vans parked near the steps of the Capitol, she felt fainthearted. She who had spent her life before the camera now loathed the prospect of facing those probing lenses. The last time she'd been here, Grey had been at her side, and she was triumphant in the knowledge that the future was theirs.

"I can't—"

Mary took her hand. "You must, child. Remember what he gave up for you, so at least one part of the world—that which he had touched—would be better. Had you never gone back, imagine how much worse the world might be."

She gazed at the peculiar old couple. Malcolm with his ill-fitting glasses, tricorn hat, and old brown waistcoat and trousers. Mary with her silver-white hair, kind, blue eyes, and frilly, cornflower blue gown. "Aren't you coming in with me?"

Malcolm smiled. "You've no longer any need of us, dear. And the fact is, we have work to do. And so do you."

"Work?" she repeated miserably, turning away. For several long seconds, she thought how empty and pointless the rest of her life would be. "Trying to destroy the place that's come to mean everything to me?"

She looked up, only to discover she was alone. Malcolm and Mary were both gone. She hesitated in the archway of the Capitol.

And suddenly, her anxiety over Camisha began to ease. Something deep within her told her she was all right. Rachel knew it beyond doubt.

You must be there for the conference. Surely, after all you've learned, you understand that.

The morning was bright and clear, and she could see the faint silhouette of William & Mary at the other end of Duke of Gloucester Street. The spire of Bruton Parish Church, in the distance, rose heavenward.

In 1926 the rector of that church, Dr. Goodwin, persuaded John D. Rockefeller Jr. to save Williamsburg. If Dr. Goodwin hadn't found a benefactor in Mr. Rockefeller, Williamsburg would've been lost in the mists of time, existing only as a dusty college town with asphalt running over its archeological riches.

Her heart swelled with a passionate, somber awareness. This town was the one bit of Grey Trelawney that was left in her world; she saw him in each elegantly costumed interpreter, heard him in each archaic greeting. In it lived—as nowhere else in the world—the foundation of a freedom that would guide the rest of the world. Since her childhood she'd loved this place, a place to which her father had introduced her when she was too young to appreciate it or even understand it. A place that charged her with such tumultuous emotions that she'd carefully kept the memory of it locked away.

A place, she knew now, she was meant to protect. Not destroy.

Chapter Forty-Four

Rachel blinked away tears and opened the door. Someone was speaking in the room where the House of Burgesses had once met.

"Miss Sheppard?" She didn't know the middle-aged businessman smiling at her. "I'm Walter Stafford. I'm with the foundation. We were concerned to hear of your accident at Rosalie."

She shook his hand, and before she could speak, he went on. "Please, go ahead and join your group at the main table. The gentleman speaking now is John Smith, the president of Colonial Williamsburg. He's fielding questions from the media."

"Thank you."

She'd had no plans to speak here; she certainly wasn't inclined to further Kingsley's cause. She spotted Roger McNamara, the president of Kingsley Entertainment, at the table, and she started toward him to give her resignation without delay.

The man at the podium stopped speaking. "Miss Sheppard?"

"Yes."

"I thought I recognized you from your press package." He had a kind face, and eyes that twinkled when he smiled. "Some of you may be aware that Miss Sheppard, Kingsley's public relations director, had an unfortunate accident at Rosalie plantation."

He touched his chin, then he went on. "Now, Miss Sheppard, I know that in the tidewater area, Kingsley has its share of detractors. But—" He laughed. "I want to make it *clear* that I had nothing to do with your accident."

Soft chuckles went through the crowd at the dad joke. She joined in their laughter and met him halfway to the podium, where he enthusiastically shook her head. "I'm very glad to know you're feeling better."

His sincerity startled her—he treated her as if she were a generous benefactor, rather than the enemy. "Thank you. It's a pleasure to meet you."

He lifted a hand toward the podium, then stepped away. She hesitated, and the crowd quietened as she stepped up to the microphone. "Thank you, Mr. Smith. But I hadn't planned to participate today. I'm sure Mr. McNamara would be happy to answer any questions you have."

"Miss Sheppard," a voice in the crowd said, "I have a question only you can answer."

She glanced toward McNamara, who gave a nod. There was just no getting out of it. "Yes?"

"I understand that only this morning you left Williamsburg Medical Center after claiming to have traveled back in time. To Williamsburg in the year 1746."

McNamara's eyes seemed to say, *What the hell?*

"Yes, I hear you met with Thomas Jefferson and Benjamin Franklin," another reporter said. "Miss Sheppard, does Kingsley overwork their staff to the point of mental exhaustion?"

Chuckles moved through the crowd. The first man rejoined, "My sources say you met Robert E. Lee and Stonewall Jackson. Will Kingsley be so indiscriminate with anachronisms in Americana?"

Her face burned as the crowd tittered, and she understood at last. Since she'd returned to her time, she'd told only one person the truth. And as her gaze roved over the crowd, it settled on that familiar face. There he sat, in the third row, smiling complacently. Max Sheppard. He'd planted the time travel to destroy her credibility. The local media were having a heyday with it, and they refused to get past it.

"Is it all a publicity gimmick?" the reporter pressed. "Did you plant this nonsense to drum up a story about Kingsley's genuine interest in history?"

Her gut instinct—the one Max Sheppard had instilled in her—recognized the escape that reporter had offered her; with another ten words, she could turn this crowd around.

All at once, she was overwhelmed by a memory she couldn't escape, no matter how she tried. It would be with her the rest of her life. The memory of a little girl, waving at her from a window, as she had once waved at her father on the darkest night of his life. A little girl who had stolen into Rachel's heart in a moment and trusted her to help her find something she'd lost, to restore to her a life that was destined to be snuffed out on a stormy night. A little girl who loved flowers and sewing and apple butter—and her father—and who cherished the mother she'd finally been given. And in the end, Rachel had been powerless to save her life.

And the memory of Camisha, fighting for Rachel when the fight nearly cost her her life. Now, Rachel feared what Max might have done to retaliate. Her breath caught on a sob, and she gasped against the pain. Dear God, this was a nightmare. Never had such a heaviness pressed against her heart, as if it were the very hand of God. "I—I'm sorry..." she began.

Tell them the truth.

And promptly join Jack Sheppard in his cell.

"Miss Sheppard." This from a different voice, near the back of the room. A deep, rich voice with the lyrical undertones of old Europe and a little tidewater Virginia. She *should* be locked away, to hear him even now. And then she saw him, moving through the crowd with patient, stubborn progress. Rachel stared, stricken, at the colonial vision that appeared.

It was *Grey*.

It was Grey, watching her with a resolute tenderness, with as tender faith. Swift, disbelieving joy rose up within her, and tears stung her eyes as he walked forward.

You cannot give divine knowledge to a man ... Had you both remained, it's impossible to tell what might have happened.

"*If* such a thing could happen—" Grey said softly, his gaze supporting her when she thought her knees would surely buckle, "and of course we all understand it never could—what do you expect we might learn from that time?"

Dear God, she thought. *If I'm dreaming, let me never wake up.*

Ten feet from her he stopped and waited, a smile of steadfast faith wreathing his face, and he gave a slight nod of encouragement. As she wiped her eyes, her gaze flickered away from his and fell on the press badge of a woman in the front row. *Washington Post*, it said.

Sudden awareness swept her; never again would she have such an opportunity. When she spoke, her voice trembled.

"The man who taught me everything I know about PR work has a favorite saying that few of you are aware of. The world is all truth versus beauty, he says, and no one cares about the truth. We buy the beauty."

A few chuckles crossed the room. She caught the eye of a man in the second row beside an old woman, and she remembered him as the stern-frock-coated minister-type who'd greeted her that first day with a protest sign. And that distrustful minister became her audience.

"That has been my creed," she went on. "It is indeed a lovely thought, that families would visit a Kingsley park and receive an understanding of American history between the roller coaster and the laser light show. Fireworks present dramatic entertainment; a Boston Tea Party ride makes for rollicking fun.

"But how *does* one glamorize a slave auction? Has the ride yet been invented that can explain a bunch of ragtag farmers fighting for freedom against the greatest military strength in the world? Amid our bells and whistles, how do we depict the silent drum of a fallen drummer boy?"

She glanced from McNamara, whose face had paled in disbelief, to the minister; the old man's blue eyes were lit with suspicion. *Just another trick*, he seemed to think. He was a tough nut to crack.

"The colonial era has been called the age of enlightenment and the age of reason. Yet American slavery was born in that period. Three hundred years later, are we any wiser than the ancestors we condemn? Men are still driven by greed; others, still enslaved by poverty. John D. Rockefeller had a creed for Colonial Williamsburg. *That the future might learn from the past.* I hope my former colleagues will do that."

The room was hushed with expectancy.

"To answer the question of the first reporter: Yes, I traveled back in time. If you would take my hand now, you, too, can walk out that door and into the past. We can learn of a time when brave men and women from foreign shores formed a new country. Some came to find adventure—or the freedom to worship as they chose. Some were forced to come against their will, and found a harsh existence. But they all played a vital role in the drama of what would become our great country."

The memory of Camisha staring wistfully at the Wythe house that first day returned to her, and a pang went through her. *That doesn't make my ancestors any less important a part of it than those fine families.*

She swallowed hard. "None of these accomplishments must be forgotten. Our nation's history is a many-colored quilt—some threads are brighter, some darker, but all are a part of who we are. Such a complex tale cannot be told except in the context of the time. To propose that anyone could find entertaining those most tragic, noble elements of that drama is the epitome of presumption."

Even the *Washington Post* reporter was agog; she'd stopped scribbling soundbites, and Rachel hoped she had the recorder running. But not everyone in the crowd approved of her speech, and she noticed Max rise and leave suddenly. She forced herself to refocus her thoughts, and went on, looking back at the old minister.

"In only one place in the world, time-travel isn't an impossibility. It's a promise. In Colonial Williamsburg, you walk the streets George Washington walked—not only as the first commander-in-chief, but as a boy visiting the capital, dreaming of going to sea. You can sleep in a room where Thomas Jefferson slept when he studied law here. You can sit in this chamber, where the last royal governor of Virginia ruled, where the King's whim was law, and where Patrick Henry denounced that law as tyranny.

"Bring a young boy here and let him be inspired with vision, as Washington was. Bring the boy's sister, and she will learn firsthand that she has opportunities that girls in colonial days didn't. Bring children here, and their imagination and their love for country comes to life. Put them on a roller coaster, ladies and gentlemen, and that imagination is put on hiatus."

The minister's face had softened; clearly he knew he was responsible for her change of heart.

"Before coming here, I had no more interest in history than a boy on his way to a theme park. In this historic village, the great drama of our heritage still lives. That," she said, her voice falling to a whisper, "is a *miracle.*"

The woman who sat beside the minister dabbed at her eyes, and Rachel understood at last the depth of their love for this place.

Roger McNamara, however, was no longer watching her. He was staring at the floor, lost in thought, and her heart leapt with hope. Either he was reconsidering, or he was contemplating suing her.

"I bear no ill will toward my former colleagues. Before I came here, I was driven by the same motivation that drives them. But today I ask each of them where their true interest lies. Is it in educating the minds of tomorrow? The legacy of Americana is not a legacy of love; it is not a legacy of vision. It is a legacy of greed."

"Ladies and gentlemen, we have learned history's painful lesson of what happens when greed and gain are more important than conscience and consequence in the lives of our children.

"Today I ask Kingsley to set aside the beauty and examine the truth. The best that can come of this project is offending the many Kingsley patrons who recognize the worth of our nation's history, in all its flawed glory. The worst that can come is the destruction of that history. History is presented best by those who have dedicated their lives to it. And I urge each of you to fight anyone who would dare threaten that dedication. Thank you."

The room was quiet for only a moment before a thunderclap of applause rang out through the crowd. And the first to stand was the stern old man in a frock coat. The crowd came to its feet, the preservationists who had come to denounce Kingsley and the journalists whose hands shot eagerly into the air. But Rachel noticed none of them.

Grey arrived at the lectern, and a faint smile quirked the corners of his lips. But in his eyes, she saw his elation. He reached for her hand, and the room fell silent as she placed her hand in his, then stepped down from the podium. He watched her with silent pride. Too courtly a colonial gentleman to do otherwise, he reined in his gut instinct, which was to place a resounding kiss on her deliriously smiling mouth.

He smiled as he hastily led her out of the room and into a hallway, where he pulled her into his arms. Her fingers slid over his face in wonder, absorbing the warmth of him, the reality of him. Tears streamed down her cheeks as she held him, as he slowly lowered his mouth to hers.

"Miss Sheppard, can you explain—"

"Does this mean you'll—"

Grey raised his head impatiently. "I humbly beg your pardon, kind sir, but can you not see a gentleman busy kissing a lady?"

With that, he returned to the business at hand.

Chapter Forty-Five

As Rachel and Grey turned to leave the Capitol, she heard a voice. "Miss Sheppard—"

"Did I not say—" Grey stopped abruptly. "Oh. Mr. Smith."

"I had no idea you knew Miss Sheppard," he said, smiling. "But it seems obvious you do."

She smiled. "Mr. Smith. I'd like to help you fight Kingsley, should they be foolish enough to proceed. I'm rather certain I'll have some time on my hands."

"As a matter of fact, I'm looking for a Marketing Director, so if you're interested in that, call my office and make an appointment. In the meantime, I have the pleasure of telling you that Roger McNamara has just announced their decision to withdraw plans for the project."

Rachel laughed. "Really?"

"The press is in a lather. The *Post* plans to run excerpts of your speech online. It simply held too much truth for Kingsley's comfort. Surely they've been considering just such a move for some time. This story was just enough to push them over the edge."

Later, walking down Duke of Gloucester Street, Grey pulled her close to him, and she smiled. They stopped near the home where his father had once lived. "But how did it all happen?" she asked.

"Malcolm told me that night at Rosalie what was to happen—that I could live out the rest of my life with you, but only if I turned my back on my old life."

"You *knew*? Why didn't you tell me?"

"There wasn't time. He told me just before the fire. Of course, at the time I didn't know that the fire would explain my disappearance. I was terrified. When we entered the house, I could see nothing, and the smoke was suffocating. And then, a thunderous crash. And I don't remember anything until we awakened in Lottie Chesterfield's home. She recognized your name, and said you were to appear at a conference of some sort the next day. Apparently, we arrived here the same morning you did, and Mrs. Chesterfield had a servant bring us to Clara's. Malcolm was waiting for us there, and he told me you were to arrive soon, but that I couldn't see you until after the storm."

"Grey, the first night I was at Rosalie, I saw Emily—just as I saw her the night Rosalie burned. I thought she was a ghost ... but she couldn't have been, could she?"

"She's very much alive. I believe the bond between you and Emily was just too strong. It was that kinship that conjured her spirit, leading you back in time to me, just as she would lead me forward in time to find you."

"But early that morning at Clara's, it was really her."

"It's her, indeed. She thinks we're on a fabulous journey. And I suspect we are."

She smiled. "What do you think about this time?"

"Oh, I have a job! A *job*," he said, perhaps a bit proudly. "And do you know what I'm doing?"

"What?"

"Telling people about my life." At her surprise, he nodded. "When the woman conducting the interview said, 'Tell me about the kind of work you've done in the past,' I, well, thought she meant the *past*. At any rate, when I told her, she thought I was play-acting. And a curious look came over her as

I described my life. She had tears in her eyes by the time I told her about Camisha, and she told me I was hired."

"Oh, Grey. Camisha's missing."

"Missing?"

"Yes—she was with me at Rosalie, and then we both went back in time, and I think when she came back ... Max might have done something terrible to her. She knows his brother murdered my parents."

"We'll find her. Don't worry."

"Rachel!" A voice called down from the window above.

Emily—dressed in a pink satin gown and white apron, artlessly blowing a kiss at Rachel.

Her breath caught on a joyful cry. "Oh, Emily!"

She darted away from the window, and Rachel raised her eyes to Grey. A few moments later, Emily raced through the door, and she stumbled to meet her, catching the lively girl in her arms. "Oh, Rachel! I missed you so."

"I missed you, too. And I have something that belongs to you."

"Truly?"

She reached inside her collar and pulled the silver chain over her head. Emily gasped. "Oh, my locket! How wonderful!"

Rachel kissed her forehead, then straightened, reaching for Grey. "I never knew one person could be so happy."

He held her gently. "Let's go inside."

Clara Trelawney, perhaps in her 70s, had merry brown eyes, round wire-rimmed glasses, and snowy-white hair worn up, with a complexion like soft rising dough. Her cheeks held a merry flush. "I've just made tea."

Emily served, and for a few minutes they chatted about inconsequentials as they sipped their tea.

Clara leaned forward and touched the child's shoulders. "Emily, why don't you run and play with the doll collection in the bedroom for just a few minutes?"

As soon as she was gone, Clara said, "Rachel, I have some difficult news for you. I didn't want the child to hear."

Her cup clattered against her saucer. "What's wrong? Is it Camisha?"

"Well, I received a call from a Doctor Rayburn just before you arrived. It seems your father went to the Williamsburg Inn and made quite a scene, looking for a friend of yours."

"That's Camisha!"

"Yes. At any rate, when they told him they had no knowledge of her whereabouts, he grew quite violent. It took three police officers to subdue him. He's under psychiatric observation at the hospital now, and he will be until they can do an evaluation on him. Or make sense of his wild accusations—which could take a dreadfully long time, I'm afraid. Rachel, he's quite taken leave of his senses."

She stared into her teacup. If he honestly didn't know what happened to Camisha ... Then who did?

"Papa! Rachel! Quick, come see!"

Emily's cry interrupted her gloom, and they all rose, walking through to the back of the house. Outside the sitting room where Rachel and Jennie had once shared so much, they saw the garden still colorful with a riot of blossoming flowers.

But Emily's gaze was fastened on a portrait that hung near the door. She glanced over her shoulder at them, then pointed at the portrait. "Look!"

It was a portrait of four men in a tavern, mugs cluttering their table.

"Yes, that's Thomas Jefferson," Rachel said. "And that's Patrick Henry."

"That's the Apollo Room at the Raleigh," Clara said.

But how did Emily know who Thomas Jefferson was?

It was the same portrait she and Camisha had seen at the tavern when they first arrived, so long ago. They'd taken a selfie with the portrait. What had changed to have put the portrait here rather than the Raleigh, where the interpreter had claimed Thomas Jefferson had given it as a gift?

Rachel grabbed her camera out of her pocket and pulled up the photo. Camisha smiled brightly on one side of the photo, and she missed her all over again.

But it was different now. All the men in the selfie portrait were white. Rachel looked closer at the portrait on the wall.

"Look!" Emily insisted. "It's Cammie's husband. Mr. Adams."

The man leaned close to another man his own age, as if whispering a joke; they were the only two without wigs. The other man, a blond, smiled broadly. Rachel saw the uncanny likeness between Ashanti and this man.

"But it couldn't be. Ashanti would've been close to sixty. This portrait was done around ... oh, I forget when. The interpreter called it the prelude to independence."

"Then it was between May and July of 1776," said Clara.

Rachel looked again at the photograph on her phone. The smiling blond man was the same. The young black man was not.

Clara said, "The young African-American man was a friend of ... well, a friend of your brother's, Grey. And the fourth man at the table, the blond, is Bronson himself."

All four seemed well into a keg of ale. The whole portrait painted entirely too merry an image of Jefferson to have ever earned its way into the history books.

"Rachel," Grey said with a grim quiet, "look at the woman, there in the background. The servant woman. Do you see her?"

"Oh, no." Rachel cried out, stricken.

A white dust cap covered the woman's head, and her face was wreathed in a serene smile as she watched the men at the table. Despite her age, she held a timeless beauty, and Rachel's throat ached with the sudden heaviness of sorrow. No simple servant woman would watch this young man with such fondness. She was his mother. And she was Rachel's dearest friend.

The past makes us who we are, Rachel. But we make the future what it is.

"Did you know her?" Clara asked.

To live in the past requires a deep respect for it.

Tears spilled from Rachel's eyes.

TENDER

"Excuse us, Clara," Grey said quietly.

When Clara ushered Emily out, Grey took Rachel in his arms. He stroked her hair silently, absorbing her grief.

"She stayed there," Rachel said. "Camisha stayed there, to try to make things better. That's—that's why she was so upset that last time I saw her. She knew we'd never see each other again."

"Would you have expected anything different from her?"

She shook her head. "No. She stayed with the man she loved."

"And I suspect Adams was originally destined to influence history—hence their remaining in that time."

"But I'll never...I'll never see her again."

He held her close until, at last, she said, "We need to go visit Helen. Camisha's mother."

"Yes. I'd very much like to know her. To thank her."

She touched the portrait, then impulsively lifted it off the wall, staring in wonder at Camisha. What had those dark eyes seen over the course of her life?

As she replaced the portrait on the wall, her fingers brushed against something on the back. She turned it over.

A leather portfolio was attached to the frame. Painted in large, neat lettering, was a series of numbers: *18.1.3.8.5.12.*

Rachel. It was her name, written in the childhood alphabet code. She had so many memories of this woman—but the summer they'd been separated, forced to hide their friendship, was among the dearest.

Her hands were shaking as she carefully removed the leather from the back of the frame.

"What are you doing?" Grey asked.

A flap was tucked into the portfolio on the side that had been facing the frame, and she carefully opened it, looking inside. Two letters had been tucked inside the leather pouch. One was labeled "Mom." The other, "Rachel." She withdrew her letter.

On the outside of the old envelope, faded with age, her name was written—in Camisha's handwriting.

"Oh, Grey." Her fingertips trembled over the old paper. "It looks like the letter is folded to make its own envelope. Will you ...? I'm afraid I'll tear it."

Anne Meredith

He unfolded the letter and gave it to her, and her heart beat hard as she left the house for the sanctuary of the gardens. Although Camisha had protected it well within the leather pouch, the paper was ancient and fragile, and the wax seal crumbled with her faintest touch. She unfolded and began reading aloud. The letter was dated April of 1776—nearly thirty years after they'd last seen each other.

"My dearest Rachel,

"I miss you more than you could ever guess. In my old life the word sister meant many things—but in every sense that mattered, you were my only sister, and I will always mourn losing you.

"Since I know you're probably pretty steamed, I have to say Malcolm wouldn't let me tell you what was happening, that last day we were together. If I did, he said, you'd refuse to leave me, and you would never get back to the twenty-first century. And matters at Rosalie were such that Grey couldn't stay in the eighteenth. You would've been destroyed, had you lost his love. I know that. It had to be this way, and I hope you'll understand.

"Ashanti and I have four children, two boys and two girls. My firstborn, I named Rashall, after you. He's courageous and more than a bit reckless, and when we visited Williamsburg once—he was only ten—he met Grey's brother. The boys became fast friends, despite their differences and Thomas's overprotectiveness. Tell Grey that what Thomas neglected with him, he's more than made up for in Bronson's life.

"Would you believe that Rashall's a privateer? I'm proud to say that he and Bronson are the terror of every respectable British ship in the northeast. Rumors of legitimate privateering, legalized piracy, for all practical purposes—abound, and I know it's inevitable. War looms on the horizon.

"Beyond this, I fear I must remain vague. Yes, I have seen a great deal in my life, which continues to be the sort of adventure I dreamed about as a child. But the adventures of a child's imagination don't include the heartbreak and I've seen my share of that as well. When one reads about the Boston Massacre in a history book, it is merely a tedious number to remember for a test. When one has known a child slain there, it is real, it is your life. I am put in the unpleasant position of knowing tragedies will

364

occur before they do—and my memory of American history is unfortunately excellent. So as the first shots of the American revolution were fired at Lexington and Concord, what was I supposed to do? Did I warn my husband to avoid Lexington? Did the urge live within me to tell the housewives of Concord to hug their boys hard when they left in the morning with nothing to protect themselves except a brave heart? Of course not. They do as mothers always will, and boys die fighting rich men's wars as ever they will. I can only trust that God will watch over my boys, and give me courage to match theirs.

"The land—so unspoiled! Each time I miss a convenience of my old life, I walk for a mile or two and see an earth that by your time will no longer exist. For that, my dear Rachel, you have my pity.

"My mother will be worried about me, so I ask you to visit her right away. I have attached a letter for her, but please be sure she's prepared to read it before you give it to her. Perhaps together you and Grey can explain it to her. Please give her the portrait, and let her know how happy I am. I believe she'll be happy for me.

"Rachel, I have been in correspondence with many at Rosalie including Godfrey Hastings, who began recording the lives of those men and women and children who were freed by the fire that destroyed Rosalie. As time passed, he recorded more details and eventually he passed the book on to Daniel for posterity. When Hastings came back to Rosalie that night and found the destruction, he was forced to take shelter in the overseer's house—no doubt after fumigating the place. I believe that you will be able to find this book, perhaps with the help of your sisters. And when you do, I am sure Grey will be comforted to know that his actions were not without good effect. Ruth, Daniel, little Dan, Sukey—these people and all their friends, at least, in the end, they had a chance at a life of freedom, a life lived according to their own dreams and desires.

"I wanted to find a way to tell you that I will always love you, and will ever hold our time together as the dearest time in my life. I find a bit of grim irony in the fact that I believe, despite all odds, this letter will ultimately reach you. But in the logical progression of time, you cannot find me, and that saddens me deeply.

"Then again, have our lives ever been exactly logical since we first met old Malcolm and Mary? Is plain old life in the twenty-first century, for that matter, very logical? (Though I have to admit, there are days I miss

the telephone very much, as well as central heating and definitely plumbing.) Perhaps we shall meet again. Perhaps ... well, life is uncertain, Rachel. I have been blessed for nearly sixty years. I was blessed to know your love for the first half of that. If things don't work out for us to see one another in this life, I hope for that day when we're all back together in Glory (Rev 21:4). All my love to you, my dearest friend.
"Camisha."

Rachel hastily dabbed her cheeks, and when she looked up, Grey was watching her with a quiet tenderness. "Revelation 21:4," she mused. "Happen to have a Bible handy?"

"'And God shall wipe away all tears from their eyes; and there shall be no more death, neither sorrow, nor crying, neither shall there be any more pain: for the former things are passed away.' That verse is near the very end. My mother taught it to me for comfort."

She remembered Ruth preparing Camisha for her wedding, dressing her with a cherished family heirloom—a simple scarf headdress her mother happened to have been wearing when she was taken from her home and sent thousands of miles away, to a strange land.

My mama wore this in her hair when she was taken from the motherland. She say it stands for the day we all be back together with our loved ones in Glory, when He wipe every tear from our eyes, and there be no more mourning, no more crying, no more pain.

"Camisha was happy. She found exactly what she was looking for."

He nodded, joining her on the ornamental iron loveseat, idly stroking her hair. "And you, darling?"

"I found much more. I'm so glad she was clever and thoughtful enough to find a way to let me know." She raised her gaze to his. "But I'm so sorry about your father, Grey. You'd just made your peace with him."

"Exactly."

"What do you mean?"

She moved away enough to watch him; it was simple to see the sadness of the loss was still fresh with him. So much bitterness and foolishness, so much forgiveness and reconciliation—all lost.

He spoke quietly. "It was the only bit of unfinished business keeping us at Rosalie. I would have loved to have known him longer, known him better, but these are the consequences of life's choices. Just as I would love to have carried out my plans to heal the lives of people I left injured with my deeds. But it's 'the tender leaves of hope' that matter—not the killing frost. In Bronson, Jennie left him hope. In my escape from Rosalie—my presumed death—all of the men and women and children were granted the hope of freedom they should never have been denied to begin with. Staging my death was the only way to grant their release sooner than later. Had I never known you and Camisha, I would've in fact died in the fire, and the men and women I held would have been transferred to my father. Fortunately, due to Hastings' shrewd management of the estate, they would have been given an inheritance and the freedom to stay on as paid employees. And for that, a richness of grace of which I am undeserving, I am ever grateful."

"What do you think about this book she mentions?"

A smile came to his lips. "Can't you guess? I think we need to find it. If only it weren't so difficult to locate people."

She laughed and reached for her cell phone. "My sweet, naïve darling. Let me introduce you to a world of information and cat videos." Then, looking up at the perplexity in his beloved eighteenth century innocence, she put the device away. "Next time I'll tell you."

His eyes warmed on her. "Next time?"

"This time, I fear I'm distracted."

And she inhaled the sweetness of the day before them, with the ever familiar scents of home.

Home.

With life's promise ahead, her dear memories of her family restored to her. With the man she loved in her arms. With the sudden laughter of their daughter as she skipped out the door to the gardens to greet them.

She laughed as Emily ran to them, and she took her onto her lap. "Aunt Clara has apple butter to go with our dinner," Emily said with solemn excitement.

Rachel kissed Emily's temple, thankful for the happiness that filled her heart. She felt Grey's hand at the nape of her neck, lightly stroking. "Apple butter and pretty ladies," he said, smiling. "Yes, my darling. We are blessed indeed."

NOTE FROM THE AUTHOR

Those familiar with the historic figure of William Byrd II of Westover will point out that—along with being one of the most genteel, witty, and accomplished men in history—he in fact passed away in 1744. Please don't let his presence in this book set in 1746 alarm you. While the author fights anachronisms, it was impossible to exclude one of the greatest wits of the colonial tidewater from this story about that time and place. It is her belief that he would've enjoyed sticking around to play a round or two of *I Come from the Twenty-First Century*.

Anne Meredith is a native Texan and the author of *Love's Timeless Hope*, *Love Across Time*, and *Tender (The Trelawneys of Williamsburg, Book One)*. Contact her via Twitter @_AnneMeredith or on Goodreads. Reviews of this book are always welcome on Amazon.com and Goodreads.

For more information:
www.amazon.com/author/annemeredith

LOOK FOR THE HIGH-SEAS ADVENTURES OF BRONSON TRELAWNEY AND RASHALL ADAMS IN IMMORTAL (THE TRELAWNEYS OF WILLIAMSBURG, BOOK TWO) DUE OUT IN LATE 2016